SEARCHING FOR CARYN

Eagle Point Search & Rescue, Book 4

SUSAN STOKER

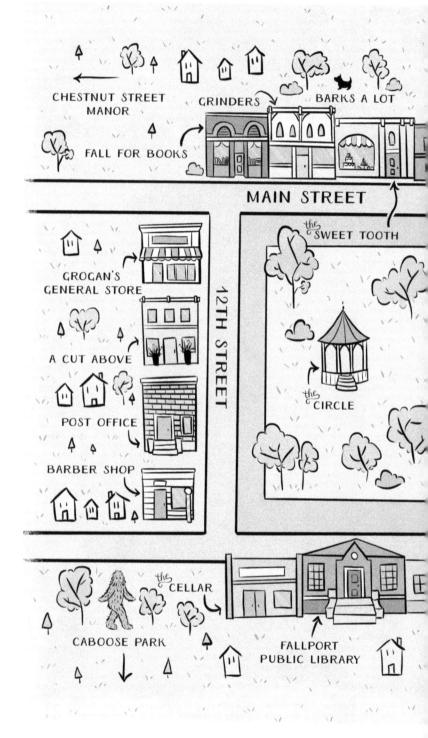

CHAPTER ONE

Caryn Buckner quietly cracked opened her grandfather's bedroom door for what seemed like the sixtieth time since they'd gotten home yesterday. She couldn't stop checking on him. When she'd heard he'd been hurt, *stabbed*, she'd immediately put in a leave of absence and started the drive down to Roanoke from New York City.

Her fire chief had told her if she left, her job might not be there for her when she got back, but Caryn didn't care. Her one and only remaining family member was more important than her job.

Once upon a time, she'd had hopes that her fellow firefighters and their wives might be her new family, but those hopes were dashed fairly soon after starting the job at her first fire station. It wasn't that the men weren't nice, they were, but there were too many politics in the fire service and too many people who didn't think she could do the work simply because she was a woman.

It was bullshit in this day and age, but the good ol' boy network was still as robust in New York City as it was anywhere else.

Which was why Caryn didn't care if the chief hired someone to take her place. She was tired of the city. Soul-deep tired. At first it had been exciting and new. She loved the diversity and all the ethnic restaurants, the way the city never slept, and all the different cultures coexisting together. It was so different from Fallport, Virginia, where she'd spent summers with her grandfather.

But eventually the grind had worn her down. The comments behind her back, the snickers to her face, the way people didn't think she could carry a hose, put in IVs, or do *anything* as well as her male counterparts. She'd slowly begun to crave the simpler, slower small-town life.

The only person who'd ever supported her one hundred percent was her grandfather. Her mom had never understood her or had much time for nurturing a daughter. She sent her off to Fallport every summer to stay with her grandfather, and those were the best times in Caryn's life. When she could be exactly who she was—a tomboy who loved to get dirty and wandering around in the woods behind her granddad's house.

When she could be free for three months out of every year.

Most people would think Fallport was boring as hell. A backwater Virginia town in the foothills of the Appalachian Mountains that time had almost forgotten. And they wouldn't be wrong. But at forty-one, Caryn had discovered it was exactly the kind of place she wanted to live in. Where everyone knew everyone else's name, and where your neighbors noticed—and cared—if you came home five hours after your shift was supposed to be over, too exhausted to cook for yourself.

Shaking her head, Caryn realized she'd been standing in her grandfather's doorway for way too long. Art was sleeping soundly.

The stab wound had been too close for comfort. He'd said he jerked away at the last second, which had probably saved his life. If he hadn't, the blade almost certainly would've sunk into his heart. Or at least his lungs. As it was, it missed both and instead tore up some muscle and skin. He'd bled a lot, and that was just as bad. At ninety-one, he was fairly fragile, even if he didn't want to admit it.

Reassured that Art was fine for the moment, she closed his door and walked through his small house. She was an early riser, always had been. And she wasn't used to sitting around. So she took an hour or two for herself in the mornings before her grandfather woke up. Caryn spent the time getting to know Fallport again. Sometimes she went for a run. Or she did sit-ups, push-ups, and other cardiovascular workouts in the park. There wasn't a proper gym in Fallport. Or a building tall enough to make climbing the stairs worth her while. Keeping in shape was mandatory in her job, but there were still days when she felt every second of her forty-one years. On those days, she simply went for a walk in the woods to clear her mind.

Making sure the door was locked, Caryn headed for her Hyundai Sonata. It wasn't a fancy car, as it was an older model, but it got her to where she needed to go. In New York, she took public transportation almost everywhere, but now she was very glad she hadn't sold her car, since she'd needed a way to get to Virginia to look after her grandfather.

As usual this early in the morning, she didn't pass anyone on her way to Rock Creek Trail. It wasn't the most difficult trail around Fallport, but it had enough gains in altitude to give her a good workout.

When she arrived at the trailhead, Caryn wrinkled her nose. There was another vehicle already parked there, a black Jeep Wrangler.

And the only person she knew who had a car like that was the one man she definitely didn't want to run into this morning. Drew Koopman. The man made her uncomfortable for some reason. Maybe because he didn't seem to care for her too much...which stung more than she cared to admit.

It was crazy, Caryn had spent her whole life trying to fit in. First with her largely absent mother, then as an outsider to Fallport, followed by each firefighting job she'd taken. Her whole life, she'd felt as if she had to prove herself. She wasn't feminine enough, strong enough, or the right gender to be a firefighter. So she'd worked twice as hard as her co-workers to prove that she could do just as good a job as everyone else, if not better.

But deep down, she suspected she'd never measure up in most people's eyes. She'd always be lacking. And she wished she could blow off everyone else's opinions. Wished she could be content with who she was. But a lifetime of always trying to gain approval, and failing, was tough to overcome.

So the last thing she needed was to run into a man whose opinion shouldn't matter...but somehow did.

Caryn considered leaving to find another trail to hike this morning. But with a shake of her head, she pressed her lips together and straightened her spine. No, she was here, and she had just as much right to hike this trail as Drew. Besides, she might not even see him. And if she did, he'd probably just nod at her like he did most times when their paths crossed and go on his merry way. Which was fine with her. Perfect, actually.

Done giving herself a pep talk, Caryn climbed out of her car and slipped her keys into the hidden pocket in the waist of her bike shorts. She slid her cell into the side pocket and did some stretches before setting out on the trail. She knew as well as anyone that her cell phone likely wouldn't work on the trail, but she felt better having it with her. And if she ran across anything she wanted to take a picture of, she'd be able to.

Caryn was alone with her thoughts and the wilderness for around two miles. It wasn't until she got to the top of a steep incline and rounded a corner when she finally ran into the man she was dreading seeing.

Drew was sitting on a rock, staring pensively into the forest.

She stopped in her tracks and studied the man. He hadn't noticed her approaching, which was surprising. As a former police officer, she'd found him to be especially aware of his surroundings at all times. He was watchful almost to the point of paranoid...which wasn't all that different from a lot of officers she knew. Her ex had been that way too.

Caryn had done her best to stay away from Drew simply because she was surrounded by men just like him every day. Assessing. Suspicious. Alpha. She figured he'd be no different from the macho, judgmental assholes she'd gotten to know over the years. But her grandfather had a different opinion, as did the residents of Fallport.

And seeing him now, lost in thought, a furrow in his brow and looking as if he had the weight of the world on his shoulders, she was surprised to feel a jolt of...commiseration.

She knew he was forty-five, but she never would've guessed by looking at him. He didn't have any streaks of gray in his hair, few lines on his face, and he was as fit as any of the twenty-somethings she worked with in the fire service. He had a closely trimmed beard and mustache, and he currently twirled a stick between his hands as he stared off into the woods.

The sudden realization of how attractive the man was hit Caryn hard. She wasn't the type of woman to care overly much about someone's looks. She was more concerned about the kind of person they were. And from everything she'd learned about Drew—at least from the perspective of the locals—he was hardworking, kind, selfless, and was always the first person to volunteer to help someone in need.

But they hadn't gotten off on the right foot. When they'd first met at the hospital in Roanoke, after she'd arrived to be with her grandfather, they'd butted heads—hard. She'd been stressed because Art was in quite a bit of pain, and she'd taken it out on Drew when he'd innocently stopped in to see her grandfather.

It hadn't helped when Art told her Drew used to be a cop. It was wrong of her to assume things about him based on his previous occupation, but considering her experience...she hadn't been able to stop herself.

When she'd seen him again in Sunny Side Up, the diner in Fallport, her chance to clear the air between them was dashed when a patron started choking...and Drew tried to muscle her out of the way when she'd attempted to help. Once again, her past had dictated her response, and she'd been a bitch to him —after she'd helped the distressed man recover, of course.

Caryn wasn't proud of the way she'd acted. Not at all. But there was something about Drew that had her defenses up. Maybe the cop thing just reminded her too much of her ex, but that wasn't fair. From everything she'd heard about Drew, he was nothing like Jonah.

Refusing to think about her disaster of a marriage, Caryn shifted on her feet and must've made some sort of noise, because Drew's head snapped her way and their eyes met.

For a moment, Caryn was frozen. The awareness in his light brown, almost amber eyes and the way his hand immediately went to his hip, as if reaching for a sidearm, made her stand stock still so as not to be seen as a threat.

But Drew wasn't wearing a firearm, and the intenseness in his gaze bled out when he realized who she was.

"Morning," he said quietly.

Caryn responded the way she did anytime she felt out of sorts or uneasy. She lifted her chin and said a bit too defensively, "You don't own this trail."

One of Drew's brows lifted in response as he said, "I know I don't."

Caryn took a deep breath. *Shit*, she was being a bitch—again—and she hated herself for it. "I'm sorry," she said immediately. "That was rude."

Drew acknowledged her apology with a small nod. "It's a beautiful morning for a hike."

"It is," she agreed. She stood where she was, feeling awkward. Should she continue on past him, or just forget hiking any farther and go back to her car?

Drew made the decision for her. "I'm not going to bite, you know."

"I know," she replied a little too quickly.

Drew sighed and turned away from her.

The second his too-knowing eyes weren't pinned on her, Caryn felt as if she could take a full breath once again. This man really got under her skin, and she had no idea why. He made her feel defensive, as if she somehow wasn't good enough to share his same airspace. Which was stupid. He hadn't done or said anything to warrant that kind of reaction. It was just her insecurities getting the best of her. And Caryn needed to work on that. She forced herself to take a couple of steps closer.

"You okay?" she blurted.

He turned her way again and tilted his head in question.

"I just...you're just sitting there. Did you roll your ankle or something?"

"No, I'm good. Just enjoying the silence of the morning," he said.

Caryn immediately felt guilty. "And I'm disturbing you. Sorry. I'll continue on my way."

"You want to sit with me for a moment?" Drew asked.

Caryn was genuinely shocked by the invitation. "Why?"

A small chuckle escaped his lips. "Am I really *that* bad? I mean, I know you don't seem to like me for some reason, but I promise I'm harmless. I just thought maybe you could use a break for a second. To stop and enjoy your surroundings. This is very different from New York, for sure."

Caryn's knee-jerk reaction was to be pissed. *She* didn't like *him*? It was definitely the other way around. Then she took a deep breath. She hadn't heard any condescension or irritation in his tone. He was just being polite.

She really should keep on walking. Leave him to whatever was going on in his head. But before she knew what she was doing, she'd walked over and sat on a rock to his left.

Drew had a small smile on his face, and Caryn wanted to ask what he was thinking, but was too afraid that he might be laughing at her. Shaking her head a little, she frowned, hating that she cared so much about what others thought of her. She'd been trying to break that habit her entire life...without much luck.

"Lots of thoughts going through your head," Drew observed. "This isn't the kind of place for thinking too hard. Close your eyes and just be, Caryn."

Surprisingly, she did as he suggested. With every day she spent in Fallport, Caryn felt herself relaxing more and more. She'd been going nonstop for years, trying to prove herself, trying to be the best she could be, better than those around her. It felt good to take a moment and not have to think about anything.

Drew didn't speak, and with her eyes closed, Caryn could

smell the dirt under her feet, hear birds chirping, and practically taste the humidity in the air. It had rained the night before and she could smell the dampness in the mountains. Her short blonde hair was probably plastered to her head from the exertion of climbing the hill to get to this spot, but for the first time in ages, she wasn't thinking about how she looked, or what Drew might think of her. She let the peacefulness of the quiet moment sink into her soul.

This was what she needed this morning.

"How's Art feeling?" Drew asked after several minutes had passed.

Instead of being upset that he'd broken the peaceful stillness, Caryn was pleased he cared enough to ask.

"He's good," she said, opening her eyes and turning toward Drew. He had on a pair of cut-off cargo pants and a plain red T-shirt. His hair was mussed and kind of sticking up on his head. He was leaning over with his elbows resting on his knees, his head turned her way. "Feeling a little cooped up. I think he's also feeling his own mortality a bit more than he's comfortable with. Yes, he's ninety-one, but deep down, I think he felt as if he had lots of time left. Currently, he needs a little help when he walks...and he hates it. He never felt his age until that attack happened."

"Understandable," Drew said with a small nod. "Hell, I've never met a ninety-one-year-old as spry as him. He's proud of you, you know."

Caryn blinked in surprise at the change of topic. But didn't get a chance to say anything as Drew continued.

"Talks about you to anyone and everyone. Just the week before his attack, he cornered me at the post office and told me all about the fire you fought on the twenty-fourth floor of some apartment building. Described in detail how you carried a woman down every single flight of stairs, then went back up to get her sister. Impressive."

Caryn couldn't stop the flush of pride that swam through her. That day had been hell. The smoke had been so thick on their floor, and the two women were handicapped and couldn't make it down on their own. While her fellow firefighters had been battling the fire on the floor above where the sisters lived, she'd been sent to make sure everyone had evacuated. There hadn't been anyone else to help the women, so she'd simply done what needed to be done. She'd mentioned it in passing to Art one night, when they'd talked on the phone, and he'd been impressed as well.

"Although, I'm guessing the part where he said flames were licking at your feet the whole way and how you ran through a wall of fire might've been a slight exaggeration."

Caryn burst out laughing. "You'd be right," she said with a smile. "There was a lot of smoke in the stairwell, but once we got below the twentieth floor that dissipated. No walls of flames anywhere."

"He's lucky to have you," Drew said seriously a moment later.

"Wrong. I'm lucky to have *him*," Caryn countered immediately.

They were silent for a few more minutes before Caryn screwed up the courage to ask, "I heard you were a police officer."

Drew nodded.

She waited for him to elaborate. To tell her all about his accolades and how much he loved what he did...but Drew didn't say another word.

Caryn frowned as she struggled to come up with another topic of conversation. She wasn't good in social situations, and this just proved it. She sucked at small talk. She'd honestly thought Drew would jump at the chance to talk about what he did, but instead the mention of his previous career seemed to make him uncomfortable, which hadn't been her intention at all.

"You wanna keep going?" Drew asked, motioning down the trail.

Caryn blinked in surprise. "With you?"

Drew's lips twitched. "Yeah, with me. I wasn't hinting that I've had enough of your company, if that's what you thought."

Feeling guilty—because that was *exactly* what she thought he'd meant—Caryn did her best to keep from blushing. "Well...I just... You don't even like me."

"I like you," Drew said without hesitation, sounding sincere.

Caryn was at a loss for words. She'd literally done nothing to make this man like her. The opposite, in fact. The few times they'd talked, she'd been downright rude.

"If you'd rather not, I understand. Just because I like *you* doesn't mean you have to return the sentiment."

Feeling uncomfortable and out of her element, Caryn blurted, "You think you can keep up with me?"

Drew chuckled. "Probably not, but I can at least try."

Wow. Most men would never in a million years admit that a woman could outperform them. Yet, Drew didn't seem the least bit perturbed at the fact she might be in better shape than he was.

Impulsively, Caryn nodded. "Okay."

It wasn't exactly an enthusiastic yes, but Drew didn't seem to notice.

"Great." He stood. "You want to take the lead or let me?"

Caryn stood, once again surprised at his question. In her experience, men didn't ask if she wanted to go first. They just took the lead without hesitation. She gestured to the trail. "Be my guest."

"If I'm going too slow for you, let me know."

"I won't lie, I came out for some exercise, but I'm not

trying to set a world record or anything," she told him with a small grin.

He returned it. "Good thing. I'm a bit out of shape."

Caryn seriously doubted that. "Right."

He gave her one last look, then turned and headed down the trail.

Taking a deep breath, and hoping she wasn't making a mistake, Caryn followed.

CHAPTER TWO

Drew wondered what in the hell he was doing. He'd impulsively asked if Caryn wanted to hike with him, but he honestly hadn't expected her to say yes. He'd actually been irritated when she'd first shown up, interrupting his peaceful morning with what he just *knew* would be more of her predictable brusqueness. And her opening line seemed to prove it.

But...as she sat next to him with her eyes closed, soaking in the peacefulness of their surroundings, he'd seen more than he'd noticed before.

The stress lines around her eyes. The dark circles, as if she hadn't been sleeping well. The way her shoulders were hunched, as if the weight of the world was on her shoulders.

None of it had sat well with him. No, they hadn't exactly gotten along since they'd met. But she hadn't truly done anything bad enough to make him dislike her. And she needed the healing the forest could provide more than anyone he'd met in a very long time.

When he'd first come to Fallport, he'd spent a lot of time walking the trails. Trying to find some equilibrium. Trying to find himself again. There were still days when he needed the stillness of the forest to ground him, like this morning.

He'd had a dream last night—more like a flashback—and it had unsettled him. A large protest...and he'd been on duty. He actually agreed with the issue the protestors were bringing to light, but that hadn't mattered to the trouble-makers in the group. They saw all law enforcement as the enemy. He'd seen so much ugliness that night, it still haunted him to this day.

He'd fled to the forest as soon as the sun began lightening the sky. He'd been trying to block out the images from the past when Caryn made a noise, startling him. For a second, he was back there in that protest-turned-riot. Someone was rushing forward, intending to do him harm. He'd reached for his weapon, only to find it wasn't there.

He immediately realized where he was, and that Caryn was no threat. Still...all these years later, Drew hated that his first response was to go for his weapon.

He resisted the urge to check on the woman behind him. He could hear her right on his heels. She was more than capable of holding her own out here. Probably more so than him. She was also clearly in shape. Her muscles proved that. And the fact she wasn't even breathing hard.

Seeing her in the form-fitting shorts that outlined her muscular thighs was *definitely* not a turnoff. It was all Drew could do to keep from ogling her when she sat beside him. She wore a tank top that showed off her toned biceps too.

Yes, she was definitely a woman who could hold her own physically. But somehow he knew that mentally, she wasn't quite as confident.

He took a quick glance over his shoulder. Her blonde hair framed her face, a few damp tendrils sticking to her cheeks, and even with the sheen of sweat making her glisten, Drew was drawn to her. He knew from talking to Art that Caryn was forty-one, but when she wasn't looking so stressed, she could totally pass for someone in her early thirties or even late twenties. They were the same height, and it was nice to be able to look her in the eyes when they were standing.

He had nothing against petite females...like Rocky's girlfriend, Bristol, who wasn't even five feet tall. But he'd always been attracted to taller women.

As they walked, the silence between them lengthened. Drew knew he should talk to her, but he couldn't think of anything to say and didn't want to risk pissing her off. Feeling bad that he was a horrible conversationalist, he turned his head and said, "Sorry, I'm not very good at small talk."

To his surprise, she chuckled. "That's okay. I'm not either."

He grinned a little at that. For just a second, a flash of them sitting across from each other eating dinner came to his mind, both concentrating on their meals and not talking. For some reason, he suspected it wouldn't feel weird. Just comfortable.

Another few minutes went by before Drew said, "At risk of irritating you, which isn't my goal, not at all, I'm just curious...how much longer before you have to go back to New York?"

She sighed, and he was relieved she didn't sound pissed at him for asking. "I'm not sure."

Drew looked back at her. "You have that much leave saved up?" He winced as soon as the words were out of his mouth. "Sorry, don't answer that."

"Actually, I do...but the longer I'm here, the more reluctant I am to go back."

Drew stopped in the middle of the trail and turned to her.

Caryn shrugged self-consciously. "Crazy, huh?"

He was surprised she'd opened up to him like that, but he couldn't help but be pleased. It probably wasn't because she wanted to share with *him*, specifically, so much as prompted by the time and place. It was his experience that the forest had a way of breaking down barriers. He couldn't count the number of times people he'd found in the woods told him all sorts of personal information as they were being escorted back to civilization.

"Not really," he finally replied. "Fallport has a way of sucking people in."

She smiled at that. "Some days I can't wait to get out of here and get back to my life in the city, and other days...most days...I can't imagine ever going back."

"What would you do if you don't go back?" Drew asked.

Caryn tilted her head as she stared at him. "What? You aren't going to tell me there are no jobs here? That working for an NYC fire department should be a dream come true?"

"Why would I? It's only a dream come true if that's what you truly want. Every job has its ups and downs, pros and cons, and I haven't walked in your shoes, so it would be arrogant and stupid of me to assume anything about what you like and don't like."

"I...thank you. It's just...I love being a firefighter. Love helping people. But I hate the politics that come with the job. Hate having to prove myself day in and day out to the people who should trust me implicitly. You have no idea what it's like to constantly be told to work the hoses. Or to make sure a building is evacuated instead of being able to take lead at a scene. I'm just as good as the others in my firehouse, but because of my gender, I'm seen as not as capable."

"You're right, I don't know about that second part, but I definitely understand wanting to help people but hating the politics of a job. And while I haven't seen you in action, I've heard enough stories from Art about your abilities to think that the people you work with must be idiots."

They were standing in the middle of the trail, and Drew

studied the woman in front of him. "If you could do anything in the world, *anything*, what would it be?" he asked.

"Stay here in Fallport. Look after my grandfather. I know he probably doesn't have a ton of time left, and he's the one person in my life who's always supported me. One hundred percent. He's always been there for me. I'd like to be there for *him* now. Of course, after he gets back on his feet, we'd probably drive each other crazy. And I'd get bored out of my mind. It's a stupid idea and—"

"Don't do that," Drew interrupted.

"Do what?" Caryn asked.

"Don't belittle what you want. I'm sure you and Art drive each other crazy even when you *aren't* together. And we all get bored, no matter if we're living in a small town or the most exciting city in the world."

"True," she said quietly.

"Do you want to continue to be a firefighter?" he asked. Drew knew he was pushing, but he couldn't seem to stop.

"I don't know."

"Fallport has a full-time fire department," he said. "What's stopping you from seeing if you could get hired here?"

"Paul Downs."

"Oh yeah, that guy. I've dealt with him a couple of times."

"Yeah. He's the captain, and he hates me. He's always hated me. Every summer, no matter my age, he did what he could to make my life a living hell. He'd tease me, bully me, make me feel like an outsider."

"Is that it? The only thing that's keeping you from moving to Fallport full time?"

Caryn's lips pressed together and she glared at him. Responding a little aggressively in her frustration. "Why would I want to move to a town that's probably just as discriminatory as New York? Or even more so? And I'm an outsider. That's a big deal in small towns like Fallport."

17

"You aren't wrong," Drew said patiently. He couldn't tell if she really believed what she was saying or was just feeling defensive. "But they also have huge hearts. How many people have stopped by Art's house to look in on him? How many have brought him casseroles? Or offered to clean and do his laundry? How many have welcomed you back without hesitation?"

Caryn sighed. "Okay, you have a point."

"All I'm saying is that life is short. Spending it doing a job you dislike isn't worth it."

"Is that what you did? Quit because you didn't like being a cop anymore?"

Drew didn't want to get into that, but her question was only fair. "Pretty much."

"And now you're an accountant."

"Yup."

"Are you seriously satisfied sitting in an office crunching numbers, rather than experiencing the adrenaline rush that comes with being a police officer?" she asked.

Drew didn't hear any antagonism in her question. "Yes," he answered without hesitation. "Working with the Eagle Point Search and Rescue team satisfies the need within me to help others. Gives me that adrenaline rush every now and then."

He couldn't read the look in Caryn's eyes. "So...what if I wanted to join the SAR team?"

Drew blinked in surprise. He hadn't expected that.

Caryn didn't give him a chance to get his wits together. "Right. That's what I thought. It's okay for you to be on the team, but a woman? No way. And it's the same no matter where I go. I know Paul would react similarly if I wanted to join the FFD. The good ol' boy network is still going strong everywhere. Thanks for the hike, but I think I'll be heading back. I want to stop by the diner and get Art some breakfast. Later."

Before Drew could protest, Caryn had turned on a heel to head back the way they'd come. Back to the trailhead and the parking lot.

Drew stared at her retreating back until he could no longer see her, then sighed. He hadn't meant to piss her off. She'd just surprised him.

It was true he and the rest of his teammates on the search and rescue team were close, but that didn't mean they wouldn't welcome another qualified member. Caryn's gender had nothing to do with it. In fact, she'd be a huge asset. With her firefighting experience, she'd have an advantage when they were called out to help with wildfires. And she was a paramedic, so she'd be another resource in medical situations. She was in great shape, wasn't afraid of hard work, and it was apparent she had the same drive he and the rest of the team did when it came to helping others.

Drew sighed once more. He'd fucked up. He'd made Caryn think he was just like the judgmental assholes she worked with back in the city. And he hated that.

Not wanting her to think he was stalking her, Drew walked back toward the parking area slowly. He'd give her some time...but they weren't done talking about this. He'd go home, shower, then pop over to Art's house to check on him —and maybe finish the conversation he'd started with Caryn.

If she wanted to move to Fallport, she shouldn't let anyone stop her. Not Paul Downs. Not him. No one. He meant what he'd said, life was too short. And she obviously wasn't happy with her job in New York. She'd be much more appreciated here. Yes, life was slower in a small town, but she knew that. She'd spent plenty of summers in town. And it might be a slower pace of life, but it was just as enriching, maybe more so than the city. She could hike whenever she wanted, the locals were genuinely kind for the most part...

Drew had a feeling Caryn would fit in better than she thought.

* * *

An hour and a half later, Drew was at his rental home. He'd showered, eaten breakfast, and was preparing to head over to Art's place to check on the older man and talk to Caryn. To apologize. To explain that she'd taken him by surprise, and he was nothing like the morons who thought she couldn't do her job as well as any man could. But then his phone rang.

Tensing, because lately it seemed as if phone calls brought more bad news than good, he answered. "Koopman."

"Hey, Drew, it's Ethan. We've got a missing person."

Shit. So much for being able to apologize to Caryn. "Where? Details?"

"Falling Water Trail."

Double shit. "How far out?"

"Far," Ethan said. "We got a call from the hiker's son. Said his dad, who's around sixty-five but in good shape, was going out on a solo multiday hike on the Appalachian Trail. He was supposed to be at their rendezvous point this morning, but there's been no word from him."

"How long's he been out hiking?" Drew wasn't going to even think about how not-smart it was for the man to go hiking by himself. Hell, he couldn't really talk, as he'd been out in the woods plenty of times by himself. Including that very morning. Although, he wasn't on a multi-day hike and he was twenty years younger than the missing man.

"He left two days ago. Was supposed to meet his son this morning to resupply, and then continue on for another two days."

"And there's no possibility he's just running late?" Drew asked.

"Not according to the son. He said he talked to him yesterday and they confirmed the time and place for meeting this morning."

"All right. We meeting at the trailhead?"

"Yup."

"Who's in?"

"Me, you, Brock, and Tal. The others are on standby to relieve us if necessary."

Drew mentally nodded. He knew Bristol's leg was still healing from her ordeal and Rocky wasn't ready to leave her by herself. Not after what she'd been through. Raid's blood-hound had also just had minor surgery to remove a fatty cyst the day before and wasn't trail-ready yet. And Tony had strep throat, which meant Zeke wanted to help his woman, Elsie— Tony's mom—keep a close eye on him to make sure he didn't get worse. Hopefully, they wouldn't have to bother any of them.

"Sounds good. I'll meet you there as soon as I can."

"Don't forget your satellite phone," Ethan reminded him.

"As if I'd forget our newest toy," Drew said with a roll of his eyes.

"Right, just making sure. See you soon."

Drew hung up and considered giving Art a call, but dismissed it. Although the thought of not being able to clear the air with Caryn didn't sit well with him. There was no telling how long they'd be gone, considering they didn't know how far out the missing man could be. Maybe they'd luck out and he'd be found close to the trailhead. If he was supposed to meet up with his kid, it was possible he could've run into trouble close to the end of this leg of his trip. But it was equally as likely something had happened yesterday, right after he last contacted his son.

Swearing under his breath, Drew headed for his bedroom to change into hiking gear. When he was ready, he grabbed his pack and left the house. As he climbed into his Jeep, he thought about that morning. About how comfortable he'd felt hiking with Caryn. She hadn't filled the air with needless chatter, and knowing she was behind him was...reassuring. There weren't many people he trusted to have his back.

Drew had no idea what it was about Caryn that made him feel that way, especially considering their constant friction. Maybe it was simply because she was a first responder like he used to be. Firefighters and cops sometimes had an adversarial relationship, but Drew had never felt that way. He was thankful for the job firemen and women did, and he was certainly glad he didn't have to run into burning buildings.

Praying that they'd be able to find the missing man sooner rather than later, and he could apologize to Caryn before any bad feelings could solidify, Drew forced his attention toward the job ahead. Being distracted could get him or his teammates hurt faster than anything. He had to concentrate on the task at hand for now. But when all was said and done, he was more than ready to grovel if he had to the next time he saw Caryn.

He had a feeling she'd be worth a little groveling...even if he didn't completely understand why.

CHAPTER THREE

Caryn was in a bad mood. She thought that maybe, just *maybe*, Drew would be different from most of the men she'd worked with in her life. Thought he would be supportive of her interest in the search and rescue team. Instead, he talked a good game, but when push came to shove he was just as sexist as the other men she'd known.

Sighing, she let her head fall back on the headrest behind her. She'd arrived back at her grandfather's house but hadn't yet left her car. Closing her eyes, she scowled.

She wasn't being fair. She knew it. And yet the hurt still lingered.

Now that she'd stopped and thought about what happened, Drew hadn't actually *said* anything to illicit the kind of reaction she'd had. He hadn't scoffed at her. Hadn't blown her off. Hadn't actually said one damn word. She hadn't *given* him a chance to say anything. She'd assumed his silence meant he didn't want her on his team.

She'd walked away without letting him speak, solely to protect herself from hearing something she didn't want to hear. Any reasons why a woman joining the team wouldn't work.

It wasn't necessarily the job she craved, so much as the camaraderie she sensed Drew and the others had. All her life, she'd been on the peripheral of that kind of connection. Starting in school and continuing into adulthood. None of the fire stations she'd worked at had wanted a female in their ranks. She suspected most went along with it because they had no choice, and because having her on the roster fulfilled some sort of affirmative action checklist.

"I'm such an idiot," she mumbled, opening her eyes and staring ahead blankly. "I should've listened to whatever he had to say."

She really needed to work on her knee-jerk reactions and her habit of assuming the worst. Yes, she was trying to protect herself, but she'd been extremely rude. If Drew was keeping track of the number of times she'd bitten his head off, Caryn had to admit even *she* wouldn't give her another chance.

She'd actually been enjoying the hike until that moment. Drew had a calming presence about him. And while she could tell he was hyper alert, he wasn't paranoid about it, despite her previous opinion to the contrary.

Sighing deeply, Caryn knew she'd made a colossal error. She really *wanted* to know what Drew's thoughts were on her possibly joining his team. Not that she was seriously thinking about staying in Fallport...was she?

With a self-deprecating chuckle, she shook her head. She *was*. She wanted to stay. Here with Art. In the small town where she practically grew up. She had such great memories of summers here, Paul Downs aside. The people were generally friendly and she loved the quirkiness of the place.

Besides, hadn't her chief back in New York practically told her that he wouldn't hold her job? He'd been looking for a reason to hire someone new, and she'd presented him with the perfect opportunity.

But if she was going to move to Fallport, she needed to have some way of earning a living. As far as she knew, the Eagle Point Search and Rescue team members were volunteers. She *could* inquire at the FFD. Even though she and Paul Downs didn't get along, working with someone who didn't approve of her wasn't something new. But did she want to continue to be a firefighter? That was the question.

She was a paramedic. She could look into getting a job with the Fallport Rescue Squad. Or perhaps join the county's hotshot crew, the men and women who went into the forests to fight wildland fires.

Then there was that *other* gig she did on the side...

Shaking her head, Caryn dismissed the idea. She truly didn't think it was a viable way to make money. Not enough to be able to live on. She just did it for fun.

Abruptly, Caryn pushed open her car door. She needed to get out of her head. Go inside and check on Art. Bring him the food she'd picked up on her way home. At some point, she was going to have to see Drew again...and apologize. She'd been incredibly impolite yet again, and she never should've left him the way she did. She was forty-one years old. It was past time she stopped letting her emotions overrule her good sense.

Grabbing the bag of food, Caryn headed inside. Art would cheer her up. He always had something funny to say, some story about his friends or the residents of Fallport that could make her smile and forget her worries for a while.

* * *

A few hours later, Silas and Otto were at the house visiting her grandfather and bringing him up to speed on the gossip he was missing while at home recuperating, instead of sitting outside the post office—the trio's daily routine for years. She was sitting quietly in the corner of the living room with a book, only half listening, when her attention was jerked back to the present from Otto saying something about a missing person. According to her grandpa's friend, the Eagle Point Search and Rescue team had headed out a few hours ago on a rescue mission.

"Apparently an older fella was hiking by himself, wanting to traverse the entire state, and he didn't make the rendezvous point he'd arranged with his son. So the team was sent out to see if they could find him," Otto informed them.

"I could totally do that," Silas said confidently.

"Do what? Hike the state of Virginia?" Art asked, clearly skeptical.

"What, you don't think I could do it?" Silas asked.

In response, both Art and Otto burst out laughing.

Caryn did her best to keep her lips from curling upward.

"I could!" Silas insisted. "I'm not *that* old and decrepit yet!"

"Silas, you bitch about having to walk across the square," Otto retorted.

"And your bones creak when you sit down," Art threw in.

"Yeah, well, I'm not saying I'd be skipping and jumping, but I could do it," Silas said a little grumpily.

"You'd be eighty before you finished," Art told the sixty-nine-year-old with a shake of his head. "Besides, why would you *want* to? You'd have to eat granola and freeze-dried stuff, carry it all on your back, sleep on the ground, and the coffee would be crap."

"True," Silas mumbled.

"Besides, you'd miss out on all the gossip around here," Otto said.

Caryn thought the way the three men interacted was

kind of sweet. Yes, they made fun of each other, and were very competitive, but nothing was done or said maliciously. They were snarky, then turned around and made sure they were all on good terms by teasing. Like they'd just done with Silas. Poking fun at him for thinking he could do a long backwoods hike, then giving him an "out" by telling him all the things he'd miss if he left. There might be a decade between each of them in age, but they truly were the best of friends.

"Anyway, I heard only four of the SAR team went out on the search," Otto said. "Assuming because Elsie's boy is sick, and Bristol is still recuperating. It'll be a while before Rocky feels comfortable leaving her, I'm sure."

"Raid and Duke didn't go?" Art asked.

Silas shrugged. "Guess not."

Caryn had so many questions, but she kept them to herself out of habit. Looking too eager had never served her well in the past. Her fellow firefighters would often use it against her or roll their eyes at all the questions. Her job had been to follow along and do what she was told. Not ask questions.

Still, she couldn't tamp down her curiosity about how the SAR team went about finding someone who was lost. What kind of signs they looked for in the woods, what the protocol was when they actually found someone. She assumed if the person was fully ambulatory, they escorted them out. But what if they were injured? Did they carry them? Call in a helicopter? There were so many things she wanted to know.

She tuned the three men out once again when they began to argue about the score of their chess matches. Though it was great to see Art with more color in his cheeks and the strength to sit in the living room and visit with his friends for as long as he had today. There had been moments right after the attack when Caryn seriously thought she would lose him.

But luckily, Art was a tough, stubborn old coot, and he was healing remarkably well.

She was also extremely grateful that Doc Snow, the local doctor, was willing to come by every day to check on his patient.

Her thoughts drifted back to that morning, like they had frequently over the last few hours. The more she replayed what she'd done, the more embarrassed she became. She'd literally stomped off like a toddler having a temper tantrum. She'd obviously surprised Drew with her suggestion of working on the search and rescue team, and instead of giving him a chance to digest the idea, she'd assumed his silence meant he didn't approve.

She needed to apologize. He might not want to hear it, might not want anything to do with a woman who had such knee-jerk reactions, but she needed to apologize all the same. She *liked* Drew...which was somewhat surprising. After her divorce, and after working alongside some really bad policemen, she hadn't thought she would voluntarily spend time around one ever again.

Caryn knew that wasn't fair. There were some excellent police officers in New York and around the world. Being in law enforcement wasn't anything she'd personally want to do, but she had a high level of respect for the shit they went through on a daily basis. Despite that, living with her ex had taught her that most cops were genuinely suspicious.

Jonah, in particular, was constantly on watch, waiting for shit to go down at any possible moment. It was exhausting. That and, as it turned out, he wasn't actually a very nice person. He'd give her grief when she was late getting home from a shift, even though he was often late himself. He'd bitch about the apartment being a mess or her "laziness" when she didn't make dinner—despite never lifting a finger to cook or clean himself. He accused her of being careless with her—and his—safety.

They'd grown apart quickly, their marriage lasting just two years before they'd both called it quits.

She could see that same...*awareness*, for lack of a better word, in Drew, but he didn't seem to be overly jumpy or judgmental. Maybe that was because it had been some time since he'd been in uniform. Or maybe he just had a better personality. Either way, despite being on alert, Drew didn't seem much like Jonah.

Her cell phone ringing in the other room snapped her out of her thoughts, and she got up to go answer it. The three men didn't even seem to notice her leaving, which might've been a blow to her ego if Caryn wasn't so thankful that Silas and Otto were keeping her grandfather so entertained.

"Hello?" she said as she answered. She hadn't recognized the phone number.

"Caryn? It's Drew."

Caryn blinked in confusion at hearing Drew's deep voice in her ear. "How'd you get my number?" she asked.

Drew chuckled, and the sound sent electric currents shooting down her spine. God, had he always had such a sexy voice? Maybe it was just a phone thing.

"It's Fallport."

Caryn supposed that was all the answer she needed. Still, she was surprised he was calling her after her abrupt departure that morning. "What's up?"

"I was wondering if you could come out to Falling Water Trail and give us a hand."

Now she was struck speechless. But that didn't matter, since Drew continued.

"You might've heard that we were called out on a search? We found the man we were looking for, but he's not in great shape.

He got disoriented trying to find his way back to the trail, then dehydrated and dizzy, and he's pretty out of it at the moment. He also sustained a small injury, so we're having to walk him out on a stretcher, and we could use some help. Zeke, Raiden, and Rocky are on standby, but they all have personal reasons to stay in town, if possible. I'd rather not bother them if I don't have to."

When she still didn't say anything, Drew went on. Maybe trying to convince her.

"The hiker fell and hurt his knee. We think it's a patellar dislocation, and he can't put any weight on it. If you can't, or if you need to stay with Art, I understand. I just thought, after you expressed an interest this morning, you might be willing to help out."

Caryn finally found her voice. "Yes! Of course. I can leave in a couple of minutes. How far out are you?"

"Right now, we've got about ten more miles to go. The man wasn't far from where Falling Water Trail meets up with the AT. If you come out here, given the drive to the trailhead, you can probably meet us around the five-mile mark. We can normally handle one hiker on our own, but...this guy isn't light. Having an extra pair of hands would be welcome."

Anticipation, excitement, and gratification swam through Caryn. She was also relieved Drew gave no sign of being pissed over her childish behavior from earlier. "I'm sorry about this morning," she blurted.

"Nothing to be sorry about," he said calmly. "See you soon?"

"Yes. I'll be there as quick as I can."

"Thanks. Be safe. Don't get yourself hurt trying to get here."

When was the last time someone had told her to be careful? She couldn't remember. "I won't."

"Later."

"Bye."

Caryn hung up and stood in the middle of Art's kitchen for a split second, before spinning around and heading for the small guest room she'd been using during her stay. She changed into cargo pants, hiking shoes, and a tank top before returning to her grandfather.

"I need to head out for a while. Will you guys stay with Art?" she asked Otto and Silas.

"Of course," they both said.

At the same time, Art asked, "Where are you going?"

"Drew called and asked if I'd go out and help with the extraction of the missing hiker." She could see the immediate interest in the older men's eyes. She knew if she gave them a chance, they'd pump her for as much information as possible to fill their gossip-loving hearts. "I said yes, but I just want to make sure someone stays here with you."

"We'll stay," Otto told her.

"On one condition," Silas added. "That you give us all the deets when you get back."

"Who says *deets*?" Otto asked.

"I'm fine," Art grumbled. "I don't need a babysitter."

"I know you don't," Caryn reassured him as she walked to the side of his recliner and kissed his forehead. "But the last time I left for just an hour, I came back to find you sitting here with a few stitches torn out because you decided you wanted to go for a walk around the house by yourself."

"I was hungry," Art protested.

"Which is why I want your friends to stay. Is it really that much of a hardship? You could get out your chessboard and try to even the scores a bit."

Art sat up straighter at that suggestion. "You mean get further ahead than I am now."

"Sure, that's what I mean," Caryn soothed, then turned to his friends. "Thanks, guys. I appreciate it."

"Not a hardship," Silas promised.

Otto winked at her. "Can't wait to hear all the details when you get back," he said.

Caryn couldn't help but smile. "Right. I need to go. I'll call if it gets too late."

"Not on your cell, you won't," Silas told her. "Regular cell phones don't work out there. But the guys have fancy new satellite phones that Bristol bought for the team, so you can use one of theirs."

"Of course," Caryn said. "Leaving now."

"Have fun stormin' the castle!" Art called out as she left the room.

Caryn grinned at his *Princess Bride* reference. She was obsessed with the movie when she was young, and her grandfather never complained about having to watch it every other evening when she was there several summers in a row.

She got into her car and quickly headed for Falling Water Trail.

CHAPTER FOUR

When Caryn arrived at the Falling Water trailhead, she was a little surprised to find the only person there was Simon Hill, Fallport's Chief of Police.

"Hey, Caryn," he said when she got out of her car.

"Hi. Where is everyone?"

"What do you mean?"

She frowned in confusion. "Well, when I was little, I remember searches being a big deal. Everyone showed up to help. Where's the fire department? The volunteers?"

Simon shrugged. "The FD doesn't show up for searches. There was a long meeting about responsibilities when the Eagle Point Search and Rescue team was formed, and I guess it was decided that the FD would stay in their lane...you know, fires and medical calls—and the team would cover searches."

"Well, that's stupid," Caryn muttered. She'd never heard anything so ridiculous. When someone's life was at stake, it didn't matter what someone's official responsibilities were. You helped out. Period. "What about volunteers?"

"The mayor decided it wasn't safe for those who weren't

trained to be tromping around the woods and possibly getting lost themselves," Simon said with a shrug.

Irritation rose within Caryn once more. She was a training officer back in her department in New York, and everyone was expected to learn as much as possible about every single aspect of being a first responder. They also frequently met with junior firefighters from local high schools to teach them what it took to do the job. The thought that no one was helping Drew and his team was hard to believe.

She wanted to ask more questions about why in the world things had changed so much in Fallport, and why the Eagle Point Search and Rescue members were clearly on their own, but she needed to get on the trail and meet up with the guys and the victim. "You heard anything from them?" she asked Simon, motioning to the trail with her head.

"Ethan called not too long ago. Said they were making progress, but it was slow going since they had to keep stopping for breaks."

Caryn nodded. The worst thing that could happen on a rescue like this was one of the team getting hurt. If they couldn't carry the victim out, they were all stuck.

"Glad you were called. You done this before?" Simon asked.

Caryn could read the skepticism in his tone, and she felt a familiar tickle of irritation. "You asking because I'm female?" she asked, a little harsher than she intended.

But the police chief didn't take offense. "Not at all. Because I'm guessing you don't have to endure too many five-mile hikes with a victim on a stretcher, in the middle of the woods, over rough terrain," Simon said.

Caryn couldn't help but chuckle. "What, you don't think Central Park is just like this?" she joked. "And you're right. But then again, I've carried unconscious victims down twenty-plus flights of stairs, then walked back up those same twenty flights to continue fighting a fire."

"Point made," Simon said easily. "Go on then, I'm standing by to meet the ambulance. I'll see you when you're out."

She nodded at him, then turned to the trailhead. She set out at a fast pace, wanting to meet up with Drew and the others as soon as she could. It felt good to be needed, and to stretch her legs for the second time in one day. She'd been a little too lazy since she'd been in town. Caryn made a silent vow to remedy that as soon as possible. Even though she and Paul didn't have the best relationship, maybe she'd stop by the Fallport Fire Department and see if she could work out with the other firefighters.

Caryn estimated she'd hiked around six or so miles when she heard voices ahead of her on the trail. Her heart started beating faster because she knew she'd finally caught up with the SAR team and their victim. She refused to admit, even to herself, that she was a little anxious—and excited—to see Drew again.

She rounded a corner and found the group resting in the shade of one of the trees alongside the trail.

"Hey!" she said as she approached.

Four sets of eyes turned her way, and she couldn't help but lose her step at the intensity of all those eyeballs on her.

"Relief is here!" Tal quipped.

She smiled. She'd heard all about the men on the team from Art, who delighted in telling her as much gossip as he could remember about them all. Tal was from the United Kingdom, which wasn't hard to tell since he had a British accent. He was a barber in town, and even now he looked extremely well-kept, despite being in the middle of the forest on a rescue mission.

Brock was only a few inches taller than her. He had short

brown hair and a friendly look in his dark eyes. "Good to see you, Caryn," he said in a rumbly voice.

Ethan was the de facto leader of the group. She knew he was madly in love with his fiancée, Lilly, for whom Art said Ethan was a total softie. But he still had a hard look about him. Caryn definitely wouldn't want to be on his bad side. He was a former Navy SEAL, and she could totally see him doing the job. He nodded at her respectfully, letting her know he was thankful she was there, before running a hand through his mussed black hair.

Caryn didn't see any doubt or hints of animosity on any of the men's faces, which she appreciated. She'd dealt with so much doubt in regard to her abilities, it was second nature to feel the need to prove herself before anyone even said a word. But not with these men. All she saw was respect and genuine relief that she was there to help.

Finally, her gaze swung to Drew. She felt all sorts of conflicting emotions around him. For some reason, he made her wary. Of what, she had no idea. He also made her feel flustered. And defensive. And hot and bothered.

It was that last one that put her so off-kilter. When was the last time she'd been so attracted to someone? Years. At least. The man's focused gaze seemed to cut through any bravado she had. As if he could read her mind, somehow knew how uncomfortable she felt around people most of the time. She hid it well, but she had a feeling she wasn't fooling him.

"Thanks for coming," Drew told her.

"Of course. What's the plan?" she asked, trying to keep her thoughts toward the task at hand...evacuating the injured man.

"If you can grab my spot here at Mr. Pierce's feet, we can get started again," Ethan said. "We can switch out every five minutes or so. We've been walking for fifteen minutes and resting for ten, so having the extra pair of hands means we won't have to take as many breaks and can get back to the trailhead faster."

Caryn nodded, but instead of immediately walking to where Ethan was standing by the injured man's feet, she veered toward the head of the stretcher. She knelt down in the dirt and smiled at the older man.

"Hi," she said softly. "I'm Caryn. What's your name?"

"Gunner. Gunner Pierce," the man said in a tremulous voice.

"That's an unusual name," Caryn said, as if they were meeting each other at a social function rather than in the forest in the middle of an evacuation.

"It's Scandinavian. My grandparents were immigrants."

"Awesome. It's unique. My name's mostly used to make fun of middle-class white women who act privileged... although it's spelled differently, so I guess that's something."

The man chuckled. "Nothing wrong with your name. From where I'm standing...er...lying, you look like you're the opposite of a person who'd act in the manner a 'Karen' would act."

"Thanks. I am. Though that whole thing is ridiculous...I hate how society has used a name to make fun of people. It's stupid. Anyway...before we get going again, can you tell me how you're feeling? What's hurting? And is there anything we can do to help make this easier on you?"

Caryn could feel the team's attention on her, but there was no way she could move on without at least talking to Gunner. It was her experience that forging some sort of connection with whomever she was helping went a long way toward making her job, and the experience for the victim, a lot smoother.

"I wrenched my knee pretty good," Gunner said. "I'm so sorry I can't walk myself out. I got lost and was stupidly wandering around, trying to get my bearings, when I stumbled and fell."

"Don't be sorry. This kind of thing happens, and that's what Drew, Ethan, Tal, and Brock are here for. Heck, you probably made their day...got them out into nature so they could take a little walk."

This time, she heard chuckles from the others, as well as from Gunner.

"And now that we've got an extra set of hands, we'll have you reunited with your son before you know it. Good job on making sure he knew where you were supposed to be, and when. Otherwise you might've been out here for a lot longer than you were."

"Are you single?" Gunner asked.

She heard one of the others make what sounded like a protest in the back of his throat, but she didn't take her eyes off Gunner. "I'm flattered, but you might be a little old for me."

Gunner's smile widened. "Not for me, young lady. For my son. He's single, and I already like you."

"I like you too," Caryn said. "You're not whining and complaining, and I have a feeling you're gonna keep me smiling all the way back to the trailhead." She ignored the mention of his son. She'd been hit on so many times while on the job, she was pretty good at deflecting someone's interest by now. "You ready to get out of here?" she asked.

Gunner nodded.

"Great. If something changes with how you're feeling, you need to let us know immediately. If your pain increases or there's too much pressure on any part of your body. We can stop, check you out, shift you in this litter so you're more comfortable. Okay?"

"Okay," he agreed. "I can't say this is the most comfortable bed I've ever been in, but it's a hell of a lot better than lying on the ground, wondering if I'll make it out of here."

"Absolutely. I'm gonna be right here by your head. And I tend to talk a lot. If you want to take a nap or something, that's cool. Otherwise, you're obligated to laugh at my corny jokes and pretend that I'm the most fascinating person you've ever met in your life."

Gunner laughed again. "I'm thinking that wouldn't be much of a stretch."

Caryn stood and winked down at the older man. "Actually, it would. I'm very boring."

"Right," Gunner said skeptically.

Caryn turned to apologize to Ethan for not taking position at the man's feet, as he'd directed—but she was momentarily struck speechless by the intense regard of four intimidating men.

"What?" she finally asked, uncomfortable being the center of attention.

Ethan merely shook his head.

"Unbelievable," Brock muttered.

"*Impressive*," Tal added.

Caryn wasn't sure what they were talking about. She turned to Drew. He stepped closer and lifted a hand, as if he was going to touch her face, but dropped it before he made contact.

"Thank you," he said after a moment.

She wasn't sure what he was thanking her for, but Caryn nodded anyway.

"You guys ready to get on the road?" Brock asked.

Everyone agreed and took up positions around the litter.

"On the count of three...one, two, *three*."

Caryn, Drew, Tal, and Brock stood with the litter at the same time. Ethan walked ahead of the group, making sure the path was clear.

As they walked, Caryn divided her time between studying Gunner's face and monitoring his condition, and watching where she was walking. Even one of them taking a tumble could be disastrous for poor Gunner. He was at their mercy, and she took his safety extremely seriously.

As they walked, she learned that he used to run marathons in his younger days, until a decade ago. He'd stopped doing those when he hurt his knee in his last race and had taken up hiking as an alternative form of exercise. His wife passed away five years ago, and even though his son wasn't all that thrilled with his solo adventures, he put up with them because his father so obviously enjoyed his time on the trails.

"Does that mean you're going to think twice about hiking by yourself after this?" Caryn asked him.

"No way," Gunner said. "But I *am* going to get myself one of those satellite phones you guys have."

"They come in handy," Drew said from in front of Caryn. They were carrying the man feet first as they headed through the forest. "Although we didn't always have them. Made the job a bit tougher for sure."

That comment led to Tal telling Gunner—and Caryn, since she hadn't heard the full story yet—about how their teammate Rocky had met Bristol, and the subsequent gift of satellite phones courtesy of the grateful woman.

Conversation waned a bit after that, but Caryn jumped right in to keep Gunner's mind occupied on something other than his current predicament and the pain from his injury. "So...you see Bigfoot while you were out here?" she asked him.

He chuckled. "Nope. Not this time."

"This time?" she asked.

The group paused briefly on the trail so Ethan could

switch places with Drew. They immediately started walking once more.

"Yeah. I can't prove it, but when I was hiking in Alaska a few summers ago, I swear I saw one in the distance. He stopped about a hundred yards down the trail, stared at me. I stared at him. And then he disappeared into the trees."

"Maybe it was a moose," Brock suggested.

Gunner snorted. "I know the difference between a moose and a Bigfoot," he said.

"So you believe then," Caryn said.

"Obviously," the man said with a bit of sass.

She was glad to hear it. There was a little color coming back into his cheeks now, and he seemed more alert than when she'd first come upon the group.

"I'm guessing you don't?" Gunner asked Brock.

"Nope," Brock said without a moment of hesitation.

"It's a load of bollocks," Tal piped up.

"I have to agree," Ethan added.

Caryn couldn't help but look at Drew, who was now in front of them, making sure the way was clear.

He glanced back at Gunner and shrugged. "I haven't seen any Bigfoots. Bigfeet? And I've been in the woods a lot."

"That's a non-answer if I've ever heard of one," Gunner said. "What about you, Caryn?"

"I don't *not* believe," she said with a shrug. "And I do think there are countless species that are living their lives quite happily without us knowing they exist, especially in the oceans. Mother Nature is constantly evolving, so I'm guessing there are new hybrids being born every day that scientists have no idea are out there. Heck, there are entire groups of people living in the Amazon rainforest that haven't had any contact with modern society. So why can't there be large humanoid creatures lurking about too?"

"Very diplomatic," Gunner said.

"Thanks," Caryn said with a smile.

The trip back to the parking area went by surprisingly quickly. Caryn switched out with the others a couple of times, but kept up a steady stream of conversation with Gunner. The guys joined in here and there, but they seemed content to let her take the lead when it came to communicating with their patient.

Ethan was once again in the lead when they approached the trailhead.

"We're here!" Caryn told Gunner excitedly. Her hand hurt from where she'd been gripping the litter, but she refused to show even one iota of discomfort. She'd had a lot of practice hiding any pain she felt, simply so no one could use it against her at a later date. And that had definitely happened. Once.

It was when she was a rookie, and after an especially grueling five-alarm fire. They'd fought it throughout the night, and she'd felt limp as a wet noddle by the time they were done. She'd made a comment about how tired she was when they were on the way back to the fire station—and the others in the truck immediately began to mock her. Calling her weak, telling her she needed to toughen up if she thought she could make it in the fire service with the big dogs.

It didn't matter that she'd heard them bitching just as much earlier about how sore they were and how the fire had kicked their asses. She'd learned her lesson. She had to be twice as tough as the men in order to get half the respect. It was infuriating, but she'd learned to live with it.

Not only that, but the last thing a patient wanted to see, or hear, was someone who was responsible for their life complaining about being tired or sore. They needed to have the utmost confidence in her ability to get them through whatever crisis they were going through safely. So she'd bury her aches and pains until she was by herself.

"Your son is going to meet you at the clinic," Ethan told

Gunner. "He wanted to be here, but when I spoke to our police chief earlier and reassured him that you were doing well, he said he'd have your son go to Doc Snow's office and start the paperwork."

"Thanks," Gunner said.

When the group stepped into the clearing of the parking area, there was an ambulance waiting for them. They walked straight for the doors at the back, which opened as they approached. They got Gunner transferred to the gurney without any fanfare.

Before he was wheeled into the back of the ambulance, Gunner reached out and grabbed Caryn's hand.

"Thank you," the older man said.

"Just doing my job," she answered. Words she'd said more times than she could count in the past when someone thanked her.

But Gunner shook his head. "I was really shaken up. I was feeling sorry for myself and wondering what the hell I was doing. I'm too old to be wandering around the wilderness by myself."

"That's not true," Caryn protested. "If you were hunched over with a bad hip and using a walker, I might agree. But you're obviously in great shape, and you know your limits. You aren't running the trails, you're taking them at a reasonable pace. Anyone could've gotten turned around and taken a spill. I expect you'll be back up on your feet in no time."

Gunner smiled. "I agree. I was going to say, I was feeling sorry for myself, lost in my head, then you showed up and made me laugh, and pulled my head out of my ass. So thank you."

"You're welcome," Caryn said softly. "Now...as I've told my ninety-one-year-old grandfather too many times in the past few weeks—take it easy. Your body won't bounce back as fast as it used to when you were twenty years younger. You'll get back to your regular routine in time, but not if you push yourself too hard."

"Yes, ma'am," Gunner told her.

Caryn felt a hand on her arm, and she turned to see Drew standing by her side. Ethan, Tal, and Brock were a few feet behind him. "They need to get going," he said gently.

"Right," Caryn said, turning back to Gunner. When Drew's hand fell from her arm, she swore she could still feel her skin tingling where he'd touched her. "Take care of yourself," she told Gunner. "And be sure to thank your son for calling for help so quickly."

"Oh, don't worry, I will. He's a worrier, but in this case, I'm grateful. He really is single, so the offer still stands to introduce you if you want," Gunner told her with a grin.

"You're incorrigible," she said with a small shake of her head. "Get well soon."

"I will, thanks to you and your team."

"Oh, they aren't my..."

But the paramedics were already closing the doors, so she didn't have time to explain that she was in Fallport temporarily. That she wasn't part of the search and rescue team, but instead just helping out.

She stepped back and watched as the ambulance pulled out of the parking lot. Simon walked over and shook everyone's hands, including hers, and thanked them once more.

Then it was only her and the other four men in the parking lot.

She felt a little awkward around them now, even though they hadn't given her a single reason to feel that way. Before she could speak, Ethan beat her to it.

"You were amazing," he said.

Caryn blinked and shrugged. "I was just helping. You guys did all the hard work by finding Gunner in the first place and getting him as far down the trail as you did."

"Do you always do that?" Tal asked.

"Do what?" Caryn asked, genuinely confused.

"Deflect a compliment."

Caryn hadn't even realized she'd done it, but now that he'd brought it to her attention, that was exactly what she did. At all times. And she knew why...because of the toxic environment she worked in.

She loved what she did—fighting fires, helping people in a medical emergency, even saving the occasional cat from a telephone pole—but navigating the minefield of politics and trying to stay off anyone's radar at the station was exhausting. Staying off the radar meant downplaying any praise. Insisting she was a small part of a larger group effort.

It was whacked, but the truth was, if one of her male co-workers got wind that she was in line for a commendation, or even if she was just praised too much, there was every chance they'd accuse her of trying to sleep her way to a promotion. It was complete bullshit, but it happened to women in nearly every field. Even more so in jobs traditionally considered "men's work."

Doing her best to stay in the background, to come across as average, was a survival method. But realizing just how far she'd sunk to keep the status quo, to keep the attention off herself, made Caryn suddenly feel ashamed.

"You were incredible with Gunner," Ethan said firmly. "Zeke's our go-to guy when it comes to chatting up our patients. The rest of us aren't so great at small talk. And it's obvious you have a talent for getting people to relax around you. I could literally see the old man getting calmer the more he talked. I'd bet everything I have that his blood pressure probably dropped a ton between the time you came up on us and when he got into the ambulance."

The compliment made Caryn feel good. The urge to deflect his praise was still there, but she swallowed it down.

"Thank you," she said instead. "I actually like talking to people. Connecting with them. If I can help them feel less scared, I feel as if I've done my job."

"Well, you definitely have a special touch. But I do have one question."

Caryn's stomach clenched as she braced for whatever it was Ethan wanted to ask her. "Yeah?"

"Do you really believe in Bigfoot?"

She was so relieved, she snort-laughed. When she had herself under control, she said, "Hey, if Gunner said he saw Bigfoot, who am I to contradict him?"

The four men were all smiling at her...and it was such a rare experience to be surrounded by support rather than disdain, or men who felt as if they had to compete with her, it was almost surreal.

"Caryn is playing with the idea of staying in Fallport, and she expressed an interest in joining Eagle Point Search and Rescue," Drew said nonchalantly.

She turned to him, shocked and not all that happy he'd blabbed to the others about her off-the-cuff remark about staying in the small town.

Before she could go off on the man, Brock spoke up.

"Yes."

One word, that was all he said. But she felt it all the way to her toes.

"*Hell* yes," Tal agreed. "You were incredible out there today...and you're a hell of a lot prettier than we are."

"We can always use qualified personnel on the team," Ethan said a little less exuberantly, but no less heartfelt.

"I don't know anything about searching," Caryn felt the need to say.

Ethan shrugged. "We can teach you. And since we never go into the woods by ourselves—well, almost never; Rocky was the exception, and he learned his lesson—an extra pair of eyes when searching for someone is certainly appreciated."

"Um...thanks. But I haven't decided if I'm moving here yet," she said honestly.

"You should," Brock said. "Art's missed you something fierce. He brags about you to anyone who will listen. He'd be over the moon if you stayed."

"Over the moon? Who says that?" Tal asked.

"I just did, apparently," Brock said without sounding perturbed.

Caryn couldn't help but laugh at that. "I know he'd love to have me here, but I need to find a way to make a living."

"I heard there's a position open at the fire department," Ethan said.

"There is?" Caryn asked.

"Really?" Drew said at the same time.

"From what I understand, yes. They're having a hard time finding qualified applicants. Apparently Fallport is too far off the beaten path for most people, and the pay isn't exactly on par with the big cities," Ethan said.

Caryn figured he was warning her as much as he was making a general comment. She shrugged. "The cost of living here is way less than in a big city too," she said.

"True," he answered with a nod.

"You gonna apply?" Brock pushed.

Caryn couldn't help but smile at him. "I don't know. Paul and I don't exactly get along."

Tal snorted. "He's a prat."

"A what?" Caryn asked, confused.

"A twit. A knob head. A tosser. An arsemonger."

The other guys burst out laughing.

"Translation...he's an asshole," Brock said, still chuckling.

Caryn agreed, but didn't think it would be polite to say so.

"I don't know him too well, but we didn't get along when we were younger and I visited during the summers."

"And he's likely carried his idiotic prejudices into adulthood, you mean," Brock summarized.

"Pretty much."

"Well, he might be an ass, but he *is* the captain at the fire department and probably has a lot of say in who gets hired," Ethan said.

Caryn glanced at Drew. He'd been fairly quiet so far, but somehow she wasn't surprised to see his gaze locked on her.

"He'd be an idiot not to hire you," he said with conviction.

Caryn found herself blushing. Somehow their rocky start had morphed into him doing his best to convince her to move to Fallport. She wasn't sure what to do with that.

"Anyway, if you were serious about joining our team, we can sit down and talk more about it later. I can go over what it entails, how the training works, and how often we get called out...things like that," Ethan said.

"Thanks."

"Or Drew can," he said with a wink. "Say hi to Art for us, will you?"

Caryn refused to look in Drew's direction, feeling shy all of a sudden. And she wasn't exactly a shy person. "I will."

"Thanks again for the assistance. You were a big help," Brock told her.

"Ditto," Tal said with a smile.

Moments later, it was only her and Drew left in the parking lot.

"You hungry?"

Surprised, Caryn looked down at her wrist. It was almost dinnertime. "Um, yeah. But I should get back and check on Art."

"I thought maybe we could stop by On the Rocks. Zeke's home with Tony, but Elsie's working and I wanted to introduce you guys. We could pick something up for Art while we're there. It's not Sandra's cooking from the diner, but it's definitely good."

"Why?"

"Why is it good? Because Zeke hired a great cook. He's—"

"No, why would you want to introduce me to Elsie?"

Drew frowned. "Why wouldn't I? She's amazing. And she's married to Zeke. And Zeke is on the SAR team."

Caryn's brow furrowed. "I still don't understand."

"We're a family," Drew explained quietly. "Close. When Zeke got together with Elsie, that closeness extended to her and her son. Same with Lilly and Bristol. Being part of SAR means spending time with the team *and* their significant others. We're a protective bunch, and if something happens to any of us, or those we love, we won't hesitate to do whatever we need to in order to be there for them."

Caryn could only stare at him. He was describing what once upon a time she thought she'd have when she took her first firefighting job. She envisioned hanging out at her brothers' houses, being friendly with their families, and being close even when off duty. But that hadn't happened, at any of the stations.

At this point, she didn't expect to be included in the kind of close-knit group Drew and his friends obviously had. Still, she yearned for it.

Even though she had a feeling it wasn't smart, and she should protect her heart better, she found herself saying, "Sounds good."

Drew stared as if he could see the turmoil going on inside her. But he simply said, "Great. I'll meet you there then."

Caryn nodded, and as he turned to head to his Jeep Wrangler, she blurted, "Why'd you call me?"

Without having to ask what she meant, Drew turned back

to her and said, "Because I knew you'd say yes. And that you could do the job." Then he nodded at her hand, the one that had cramped from holding the heavy litter, and said, "We'll get you some ice for that when we get to the bar. You okay to drive?"

Shocked that he'd noticed her favoring her hand, and even more surprised that he'd bring it up, she simply nodded.

"Okay. And for the record...the first time I carried a litter through the woods, my hand cramped so badly I literally couldn't use it for a full twenty-four hours. See you in a bit." And with that, he turned and walked toward his car.

Reflexively, Caryn curled her hand into a fist, feeling the sore muscles in her palm and fingers protest. But amazingly, she felt lighter than she had in a long time.

She pulled out her car keys and climbed into the driver's seat.

Today had been a good day. A confusing one...one that left her off balance at times...but good all the same. She just hoped having dinner with Drew and meeting Elsie would end it on the same high note.

CHAPTER FIVE

Drew took a deep breath as he drove. He'd taken a lot of risks today, and so far they'd all seemed to work out. He didn't think his teammates would mind if he called Caryn for assistance, and they hadn't. And she'd been incredible.

None of them had connected too well with Mr. Pierce. He'd been grumpy and in pain and it had taken all their cajoling to get him to agree to be carried out of the forest in the first place. The hike back had been mostly silent, and therefore awkward...until Caryn had arrived.

She'd somehow tamed the older man within minutes, changing his attitude entirely. By the time they'd arrived back at the parking area, he'd been laughing and so much more at ease despite his ordeal.

Seeing Caryn work had been eye-opening. He'd had a feeling she was good at her job, but he hadn't realized exactly *how* good. He regretted blurting to his friends that she was thinking about staying in Fallport. He hadn't asked if that was confidential or not, but it was too late once he'd let the cat out of the bag, so to speak.

His friends had been incredibly supportive, which he

knew they would be. After seeing her with Mr. Pierce, and the way she jumped in to do her part in carrying the litter with no complaints, even though they could see how much her hand hurt, there was no doubt they all knew she'd be an asset to the group.

But she was right, since the SAR team was voluntary, she needed to find a way to make a living. As far as Drew knew, she wasn't a secret millionaire, but then again, he didn't really know her much at all.

She'd mentioned that she and Paul Downs didn't get along, and he wasn't surprised. Tal's response wasn't out of place. The man *was* an ass. But surely he wouldn't pass up the chance to have a professional such as Caryn join the ranks of the Fallport Fire Department. Time would tell.

The invitation for Caryn to join him at On the Rocks had been impulsive, but he didn't regret it, not at all. Normally after a job he'd go home and decompress, but for some reason, he wanted to prolong his time with Caryn. Wanted to get to know her better. She came across as curt and short-tempered, but her eyes swam with emotion she tried hard to hide. And he could tell she was uncomfortable with compliments, which was a shame.

But, he reminded himself, friends was all they could ever be, no matter how much she intrigued him. He wasn't a good bet for a relationship. He was moody and standoffish. Also, she'd already been married to a cop and from what he'd heard, she wasn't chomping at the bit to get into a relationship with one again.

Shaking his head, Drew pulled into the parking area behind On the Rocks. Why was he even thinking about a relationship? The only relationship he was going to have with the pretty firefighter was professional.

Even as he had the thought, Drew knew he was kidding

himself. He was interested. *Too* interested. For a split second, he considered bailing on dinner at the bar, but he dismissed that idea just as quickly. He wasn't that kind of guy. Besides, he really did want to introduce Caryn to Elsie. She was hungry for deeper connections with people, anyone could see that. The longing in her expressive blue eyes was easy to see when he'd talked about being a family with his teammates and their loved ones.

Before he knew it, Drew was standing in front of the bar on the square, watching Caryn turn the corner from the back lot. She hadn't been too far behind on the way over. He couldn't help but admire what he saw as she approached. Her short blonde hair fit her face and her non-fussy personality. She walked with a confident stride and the tank top she wore highlighted her muscular arms.

It was safe to say that she was definitely his type.

Putting that thought to the back of his mind, he smiled as she approached and reached for the door handle. "You been here before?" he asked as he pulled the door open.

"Yeah, but it's been a while. Drinking isn't really my thing," she said.

It took everything within Drew not to put his hand on the small of her back as he followed her into the bar. He wasn't usually a touchy-feely person, but with Caryn, the urge felt natural.

Hank Blackburn was behind the bar, and he gave Drew a chin lift in greeting as they entered. Valerie McGee, one of On the Rocks' regular waitresses, called out a greeting as well. But Drew's gaze was drawn to the woman walking toward them. Elsie.

Her brown curly hair was in disarray around her face and she looked a little frazzled. "Hi!" she said as she approached. "I take it you found him?"

Drew wasn't surprised she knew where they'd been. Even

though Zeke hadn't been on the search, and wasn't there now, he obviously kept his wife in the loop.

"Hey. Yeah, we found him and he's with Doc Snow now."

"Cool. You must be Caryn. I've heard so much about you," Elsie said, the smile on her face never dimming as she turned to the woman at Drew's side.

"That's me. And I'm not surprised you've heard about me."

Elsie chuckled. "One thing Fallport is good at is gossip. Not that I gossiped about you, but it's hard to not listen. And Art talks about you all the time...he brags on you. I mean, who wouldn't? Especially when it's his granddaughter who's hanging at the end of a rope sixteen floors above the ground rescuing a woman hanging outside her window."

Caryn's eyes widened. "You heard about that?" she asked.

"Who didn't? I swear, Art told that story to anyone who happened to come to the post office for an entire week."

"You're trained in rope rescue?" Drew couldn't help but ask.

Caryn shrugged. "Yeah."

"I didn't know that."

"You didn't ask," she said with a small satisfied smile.

Drew couldn't help but return the grin. She was right. He hadn't. He had a feeling there was a lot this woman could do that she didn't talk about. She wasn't a bragger. She did her job and probably didn't think she was doing anything out of the ordinary. "The team could use someone who has rope rescue skills in their repertoire," he said.

"Wait, are you thinking about joining the SAR team?" Elsie asked, her eyes going wide.

"Thinking about it. I mean, I have other decisions to make before that one...namely if I'm even going to move here full time."

"That would be awesome!" Elsie said. "Seriously! I know

Zeke's been working really hard lately, between the bar and helping me with Tony, and it feels as if there have been more callouts for the team recently, and that's not going to change anytime soon with the Bigfoot show about to air. Having you here with your skills would be so great."

Caryn looked surprised at Elsie's quick and heartfelt acceptance of her desire to possibly join the search and rescue team.

"Um...thanks."

"I'm not an outdoorsy person myself...just ask Zeke. Well, when you see him, since he's not here tonight. I did hike out to the Eagle Point watchtower, but I think that topped me off for at least a year. I mean, him decking out the tower so we could sleep up there and not on the ground in a tent was awesome, but the ten-mile hike to get there...not so much. And I know we were walking really slow too. Oh, and don't get me started on having to walk down all those stairs to pee. Anyway, I think you'd be a huge help to the guys."

Drew could see that Caryn was a little overwhelmed with Elsie's info dump, so he gently said, "Think we could get a seat? It was kind of a long afternoon."

"Oh! Yes! I'm so sorry. I'm standing here chatting and you're probably hungry and thirsty." Elsie gestured for them to follow her and kept talking as she led them to a table. "What can I get you to drink? Drew, do you want a beer?"

"Not today. I think a strawberry lemonade."

He felt Caryn staring at him, and he turned to see the look of surprise on her face.

"What? A guy can't order a lemonade?"

"It's not that," she protested. Then she shrugged sheepishly. "Okay, it *is* that."

Drew didn't take offense. It took a lot to offend him. He had extremely thick skin. He chuckled. "You haven't tasted On the Rocks' strawberry lemonade."

She tilted her head in agreement then turned to Elsie once they were standing next to a table. "I guess I'm having the strawberry lemonade too."

Elsie beamed. "Good choice. I'll be right back with a pitcher and menus. I know you guys are probably super thirsty."

"Thanks, Else," Drew said.

"No problem." Then she spun around and was headed to the bar.

As they sat, Caryn said, "She seems nice."

"She is," Drew said without hesitation.

"Art told me what happened to her and her son. She seems to be doing okay."

Drew wasn't surprised. She probably knew more about the citizens of Fallport than anyone. Living with one of the kings of gossip would have that effect.

"She is, but that doesn't mean she doesn't have low moments. She's kicking herself for trusting her ex. Has times when she thinks she's the world's worst mother and hates that she gave him a second chance at being a father after he hadn't shown any interest in Tony for most of his life."

"I get that. Hindsight being twenty-twenty and all that. It's not the same thing at all, but I've felt that way after gnarly calls that haven't gone well," Caryn said after getting settled in the seat across from Drew.

"Like what?" he asked, then winced. "Sorry, you don't have to answer that."

"No, it's fine. For instance, there was this huge pile-up on the interstate once. It was foggy and one person rear-ended another, and that set off a chain effect. There must've been thirty-five cars and trucks involved. We started attempting to triage, finding people who were trapped in their vehicles and figuring out who needed to be extracted first. There was a woman in one car who was talking to the first responders at her door, and she was pinned in her car. Since she was awake and lucid, the decision was made to wait on extracting her. I had a gut feeling we shouldn't, but I couldn't exactly contradict the captain in charge of the scene..." Her voice faded.

Drew couldn't help but reach out for her hand. He curled his fingers around hers and squeezed lightly. "What happened?"

"She died. Bled out. Her femoral artery had been punctured and since her seats were black, no one noticed the bleeding when they did the initial assessment. She didn't complain about her pain level, didn't demand to be extricated...I don't even know if she knew how serious her injury was. She simply told the rescuers to help someone else who needed it more than her. I still think about that day and what I could've done differently."

"Mine was a 9-1-1 call," Drew said softly, feeling compelled to tell her one of his own biggest failures. "The dispatcher thought it was a kid on the other end of the line, but couldn't be sure. All she said was she needed help. I was sent to investigate. When I got to the house, the lawn was immaculate... flowers along the sides, the grass mowed. It was in a relatively nice area.

"I knocked on the door and a woman answered. She was well-dressed, had her hair done, makeup on. I said we'd received a 9-1-1 call from the address, and she looked completely shocked. She said it was just her and her five-year-old daughter there at the time and everything was fine. As was protocol, I insisted on seeing her daughter. She readily agreed and brought the little girl to the front door. She was incredibly shy and wouldn't meet my eyes, but she looked healthy enough. Had on jeans and a cute pink floral top. Her blonde hair was neatly brushed, and both mom and daughter seemed okay. I thanked them and said my farewells."

It was Caryn's turn to squeeze his fingers now.

"The next day when I got to work, I found out that little girl had been murdered by her mother. I guess she was being abused for quite a while, but her bruises were all hidden under her clothes. Calling 9-1-1 was the last straw for the mom, and after I left, she took her daughter upstairs, ran a bath, then drowned the little girl. I should've asked more questions. Talked to the child one-on-one. Something. *Anything*."

"It wasn't your fault," Caryn said softly.

"I'm sure you tell yourself the same thing about that woman in the car accident," Drew said with a slight shrug.

They shared a long commiserative look. They might have been in different professions, but obviously they had some things in common.

"Here's the lemonade!"

Elsie's happy, perky tone jolted Drew back to the present. He let go of Caryn's hand as Elsie put the pitcher and two full glasses on the table.

"And menus, although I'm guessing you don't need one, Drew," she said.

He shook his head. On the Rocks had good food, but not nearly the huge selection Sandra had over at Sunny Side Up. He'd memorized the menu a long time ago.

"What's good here?" Caryn asked.

"Everything," Elsie said confidently. "But I'd recommend the cheeseburger. I know that seems boring, but it's not. I don't know how Max does it, but he flavors the meat with something before he cooks it on the griddle. It's super juicy but not underdone. Oh, and our special sauce is the icing on the cake, so to speak."

Caryn smiled. "How can I pass that up?" she asked. "I'll take it."

"With all the fixin's?"

"Of course."

"Great. And for you, Drew?" Elsie asked.

"I'll have the same."

"No tomatoes, right?"

"Right."

"Awesome. I'll get that in and be back soon."

"Thanks," Drew told her. Elsie remembering everyone's preferences made her an excellent waitress, along with her positive attitude. She was definitely a favorite at On the Rocks, and not just because she was married to the owner.

"Go on and try the lemonade," Drew said after Elsie had left.

In response, Caryn leaned forward and wrapped her lips around the straw in her glass. The second the sugary-sweet concoction hit her taste buds, her eyes widened.

Drew chuckled as he took a long swallow of his own drink.

"Holy crap!" Caryn exclaimed when she sat back.

"Right? Told you."

"That is *amazing*. Just the right combination of tart and sweet."

"It goes down extremely smooth for sure," Drew agreed.

"I'm gonna need a gallon of that to go. I think it's my new obsession."

Drew couldn't help smiling. He'd had the same reaction as Caryn the first time he'd tried the drink. He hadn't even wanted it, but Elsie had egged him on and he'd given in so he wouldn't look like a jerk. And of course, he'd been hooked from the first swallow.

"You know, Art's told me so much about Fallport, the businesses, who's dating who, and all the gossip he can remember, so I kind of thought nothing about the town could surprise me...but I'm realizing there's more to it than I thought."

"Like amazing strawberry lemonade?" Drew asked.

"Uh-huh. Like that. And you."

"Me?"

"Yes. Art's mentioned you a few times over the last few years, but I pretty much dismissed anything he had to say about Fallport's single men. Especially an ex-cop. I never in a million years thought that I'd actually like you."

A startled bark of laughter burst out of Drew's mouth.

Caryn blushed. "Shoot, that sounded a lot worse out loud than it did in my head. Sorry."

"No need to apologize. Since we're being honest, I kind of felt the same way every time Art went on and on about *you*. I figured there was no possible way you were as amazing as he constantly said you were."

"I'm thinking our preconceived ideas about each other didn't help get us off on the right foot when we met in the hospital in Roanoke, did it?" she asked.

"Nope. But I can admit that I was wrong. You're pretty amazing, Caryn."

"I am. And that's high praise coming from a cop," she quipped.

Drew raised a brow and tilted his head at her.

She grinned. "I'm guessing you're waiting for me to say the same thing about you, huh?"

"Well, you know. My ego might never recover if you don't. I might fall into a deep depression and never leave my house. My clients will all get pissy because I'm ignoring their accounts, and the IRS will come calling because I screw up their taxes. I'll get run out of town, be homeless, and have to scrounge change from soda machines to eat."

"Oh Lord, such dramatics. Okay, fine. You aren't so bad yourself."

Drew couldn't remember being more entertained by a woman in a long time. Caryn was not only damn good at her job, she was funny, down to earth, and he found his respect for her growing by leaps and bounds.

Not interested in a relationship, he reminded himself.

"Not so bad. You're brutal, woman," he said after a moment.

"I'm harmless," she countered.

"Right. For the record...I like brutal. Like I said earlier, I'm a hard man to offend."

"Comes with the territory of being a former police officer, right?" she asked.

"Pretty much. I've been called every name under the sun, been accused of many things, but I was a good cop. Stand up. Went out of my way to help people any way I could. I know what I am and what I'm not, so what someone else thinks about me doesn't mean shit."

"I wish I felt the same," Caryn said quietly. "I care *too* much."

Drew hated that for her, but didn't think this was the time or place to get into a deep conversation about her psyche and the way she saw herself, especially considering they'd just started getting to know each other.

"Well, I think you're A-plus," he told her. "And I appreciate you helping us out today. I knew you were pissed at me after you left this morning, but I hoped you might help anyway."

"I was pissed about nothing," Caryn said. "You didn't do or say anything. I overreacted and didn't even give you time to respond to my abrupt and out-of-the-blue declaration about joining the search and rescue team. I was too worried about what you *might* say, so I didn't give you a chance to say anything at all. I should be the one apologizing."

"I'm thinking when you constantly have to monitor what you say and do to avoid any scrutiny, you get used to protecting yourself from any kind of potential backlash. You have nothing to apologize for."

"Thanks, but I still think I do. I'm trying to recognize my faults and get better with them."

"Protecting yourself is not a fault," Drew said firmly.

"Even so."

"Right, well...again, thank you for coming out today. You really were great with Mr. Pierce."

"He was scared. And upset with himself. He just needed to relax."

"I agree. And you did that, not us. How's your hand?" It was an abrupt change of topic, but Caryn didn't seem to mind or notice.

"It's okay. I didn't realize how hard it was to carry a litter like that."

"Okay, meaning you aren't going to be able to move it in a few hours, or okay in that it's sore, but a few painkillers will take care of it and you'll be good to go in the morning?" Drew asked.

She grinned. "The latter."

"Right. If you don't want to ice it now, I definitely recommend ice tonight. That really helps."

"Already planned on it."

"Good."

Drew studied Caryn across the table. They shared a lot of the same experiences. She was easygoing. She obviously cared deeply for her grandfather; her dropping everything to come to Fallport proved that. She wasn't afraid to admit she had some shortcomings, and she was humble.

In short...he liked her. And he had a feeling the more time he spent with her, the more he'd *want* to spend.

"Holy crap," Caryn breathed as she watched Elsie walk toward them. "Those plates are bigger than our heads."

Drew smiled. She wasn't wrong. Zeke and his staff didn't

scrimp on the size of meals served at On the Rocks. Elsie put the plates down on their table.

"Here we are. Two cheeseburgers, yours with all the fixin's. Drew, yours without tomatoes. Curly fries and a side of green beans, because I figured it couldn't hurt to get some greens in you along with the carbs and protein. I'll bring you a refill on the pitcher when you're ready. And dessert tonight is German chocolate cake, so save room!"

Then Elsie spun around to head back to the bar to get them more lemonade.

"Seriously, this is a lot of food."

"You saying you aren't hungry after that hike today?" Drew asked.

"Starving. But still," she protested.

In response, Drew picked up his burger and took a large bite. He grinned at her while he chewed. After he swallowed he said, "You won't care about how much you're eating once you start. It's that good."

Caryn followed his lead and took a bite of her own cheeseburger. Her eyes got big in her face as she chewed, and Drew couldn't help but love that her reaction to the burger was the same as when she'd tasted the lemonade.

"All right, I'm thinking I've been remiss in not eating here before now," she said after swallowing. "I stupidly figured the food would be simple bar stuff. I stand corrected."

Drew chuckled. "I'm guessing Zeke's heard that a lot."

They ate their food as they chatted about nothing in particular. Caryn asked about some of the locals she knew from her time spending summers here. Drew shared how it took a while before the townspeople accepted him and the rest of the Eagle Point Search and Rescue team when they'd first arrived five years ago, but now most people treated them as if they'd lived there forever.

They'd both already finished their meals when the door to

the bar opened once more. People had been coming and going ever since they'd sat down, but this time when Drew glanced up to see who'd entered, he saw Lilly. She was with Davis Woolford, a homeless veteran who'd made Fallport his home.

They walked up to the bar, where Elsie talked with Davis. After a short conversation, Lilly patted the man on the back and he took a seat. Then, as if she already knew he and Caryn were there, she made a beeline for their table.

Drew couldn't help being a little disappointed. He was enjoying his time alone with Caryn. Well...alone wasn't really the word, but talking to her one-on-one.

But he liked Lilly. And maybe she'd be able to help him learn more about the woman sitting across from him.

CHAPTER SIX

"Hi!" a woman said happily as she approached, pulling out the chair next to Drew before sitting.

"Have a seat, Lilly," he said dryly.

Caryn smothered the chuckle that threatened to escape. Drew might pretend to be annoyed that the woman had invited herself to sit with them, but it was obvious he wasn't truly upset.

Lilly ignored him, smiling at Caryn.

She hadn't talked to Ethan about anything personal on the trail. They'd all been busy getting Gunner out of the woods safely. But when the others mentioned his fiancée briefly, she could hear from his tone that he was madly in love with her. It had been a good while since she'd been around guys who weren't afraid to show they were completely devoted to their women. The firefighters at her station liked to be seen as macho, and it wasn't considered manly to openly admit how much they loved their wives or girlfriends.

Which was stupid, in her opinion. So the fact that Ethan had no problem affectionately talking about Lilly made her want to meet the woman.

"Oooh, strawberry lemonade!" she said with enthusiasm.

Just as she did, Elsie appeared with a clean glass, a straw, and a full pitcher of the delicious drink.

"You're a lifesaver," Lilly told her happily.

"I aim to please," Elsie said.

"How's Tony?"

"He's on the mend. I think Zeke was more freaked out than either of us. It's the first time he's been sick since we've been together, and he's being a little overprotective," Elsie said.

"That's sweet," Lilly told her.

"It is. Anyway, enjoy the drink and if you want anything to eat, just let me know."

"I will. Thanks."

After Elsie walked away, Drew asked, "How are *you* doing, Lilly? Any more word on wedding plans?"

"I'm good," she said with a shrug. "Rocky's working hard to get the barn on the land he bought for Bristol up to snuff in time for our ceremony. I don't care where we get married, honestly. As long as I get to be Ethan's wife, I'm good. But…I didn't come to talk about me. I wanted to meet Caryn, and tell her how impressed Ethan was with her today and how excited he is that she's gonna join the team."

Caryn was surprised at the comment. "I'm happy to meet you too, but I think Ethan has the wrong idea. I haven't actually made the decision to move to Fallport yet."

Lilly looked crestfallen. "Well, shoot." Then she perked up. "But that 'yet' means we can still convince you."

Caryn laughed. "I guess so."

"Right, so…Art's your grandfather, so you probably know all the good and bad about the town. Bad first—Whip Johansen," Lilly said, leaning forward in her seat.

Drew looked amused as he sat back, seemingly content to let Lilly do the talking.

"The guy who owns the pool hall?" Caryn asked.

"That's him. He's a jerk. He's the only business on the square who doesn't put up Christmas lights, doesn't participate in the Halloween trick-or-treat thing with the kids, and he didn't close for the Fourth of July parade. Not to mention, he's lax about security at his place. As long as people are paying for alcohol, pretty much anything goes. Simon and his deputies have had to go over there way too many times late at night to break up fights and stuff.

"Then there's the mayor. He's *kind of* a jerk. I mean, I wouldn't want to be a politician, no way, and I don't envy him his job, but yeah, it'd be nice if he went to bat a little more for our guys. Bristol donated the satellite phones to make their jobs easier and safer because he was still hemming and hawing about the cost and the budget."

"That was nice of her," Caryn said.

"Yeah, it was. After Rocky rescued her, and he didn't have a way of calling for help and had to carry her for six miles to get her out of the woods, she saw firsthand the necessity to have a way to communicate with others while on the trails."

"Like you did today," Caryn said, glancing at Drew.

"Yup. Have to admit it was nice to be able to get a call out when we were that deep in the forest," he said.

"That's cool," Caryn said.

"It is," Lilly agreed.

"Paul Downs...another bad," Drew interjected.

"Who?" Lilly asked with a frown.

"The captain of the fire department," Caryn answered for him. "If I'm going to move here, I'm going to need a job. And I wouldn't mind joining the FD, but Paul hates my guts, so I'm guessing he's not going to want to hire me."

"Well, that's stupid," Lilly said. "I mean, I don't know him, but why would he not like you?"

"I honestly don't know. I haven't done anything to him.

And it's been a long time since we were kids...which is when we first met."

"Right, well, whatever. If you don't get that job, you'll find something else," Lilly said breezily. "I didn't know what I was going to do when I moved here either, and I found something I love."

"She's the resident photographer and videographer in town," Drew explained to Caryn.

"And I'm way busier than I thought I'd be. I'm constantly meeting people to talk about new projects, their wants and needs and budgets. Ethan is encouraging me to raise my rates, but I feel bad doing that. Hey, I could use an assistant..." she said, smiling slyly, her voice trailing off.

Caryn smiled apologetically. "I'm not sure I'm cut out to do that. I don't have a creative bone in my body."

"That's okay," Lilly said. "I'm sure you'll find something. What do you like to do in your spare time?"

Caryn chuckled. "Read. Although I'm not sure that'll pay the bills."

"Maybe not, but you could do something related to that."

Caryn immediately thought about Thomas Robertson.

A very successful thriller author, he was known around the world, and his books were translated into over two dozen languages. Every time a new book came out, he was at the top of the bestseller lists for weeks. She'd met him about ten years ago when he was in New York. A fire broke out in the bookstore where he was doing a signing, and she'd been tasked with getting him and his dozens of fans to safety.

He'd made a comment about putting the incident in a book and had given her his business card, asking if he could contact her if he had questions about the fire service. She'd said yes...and they'd shared quite a few phone calls afterward, talking about her job. He'd asked a million questions so he could make his firefighter character authentic.

To her shock, when he'd finished writing the book, he'd asked if he could send it to her for any suggestions she might have. Of course she'd said yes—and felt *awful* when she'd found countless factual errors, and even a plot hole or two in the story.

But Thomas had been extremely grateful. He'd explained that so many beta readers swore his work was amazing and flawless when it wasn't, either because they were fans or because they were reluctant to upset him.

That had led to him asking her to read his subsequent books, and now she was his official beta reader. She'd kind of stumbled onto the job, but she loved doing it. Thomas had insisted on paying her for her work, and the money was welcome, but since he wasn't the fastest writer, the few thousand bucks it brought in a year was more like bonus money rather than a real paycheck.

He'd told her many times over the years that if she wanted to be a beta reader full time, he had several author friends who would jump at the chance to get her to critique their manuscripts before they went to their publishers. She'd always said no...but now that Lilly had brought up the possibility of turning her hobby into a job, she couldn't help but wonder if taking Thomas up on his offer might be the opportunity she was looking for.

"I see the wheels turning," Lilly said with a big smile.

Caryn shrugged. She wasn't ready to even entertain the idea yet. She was a firefighter. Not a publishing professional. She wasn't sure she could turn her back on her training and what she'd spent most of her life doing.

"Anyway, so...we talked about the bad, but there's so many good people in Fallport. Davis Woolford, for one. He's an amazing human being and the locals have really stepped up to try to take care of him. The town is actually building him a tiny house behind the diner. Sandra agreed, and she'll help keep an eye on him."

"That's awesome," Caryn said, completely meaning it.

"It is. And Finley makes the most amazing cinnamon rolls at her bakery here on the square. It's called Sweet Tooth, which is totally appropriate. And since you said you liked to read, there's both the library and the used bookstore. And of course the diner. And if you get bored, you can go bowling, or hang out at Caboose Park. And Doc Snow is wonderful. Oh, and we don't have a regular movie theater, but we do have the Starry Skies Drive-in, which is fun. Ethan took me the other night. They have mostly second-run movies, but nobody seems to mind. The schools are some of the top in the state, according to test scores and all that. But what I like most is that even though Fallport is small, it's diverse."

Caryn couldn't help but chuckle.

"What?" Lilly asked.

"Did you even take a breath while reciting all that?" she asked.

Lilly blushed a little. "No, but seriously, I didn't know what I was missing until I came here. Although you aren't really a newcomer, so you probably already knew all that stuff anyway."

"I did, but it's interesting to hear another perspective on the place," Caryn reassured her. "And you'd make a great Fallport ambassador. It's obvious you love it here."

"I really do. But it's not because of the bowling alley or bookstore. It's because of the people. Most everybody is generous and would do anything in their power to lend a hand to someone who needs it."

"I've seen that with my grandfather," Caryn said.

"Oh yeah. How full is his freezer with food people have dropped off?"

"Overflowing," Caryn said with a small laugh. And that

wasn't an exaggeration. They had way more food than they could eat—and just like that, Caryn felt guilty that she was eating out tonight.

"Don't feel bad," Drew said, interrupting her thoughts.

Lilly turned to look at him with a frown on her face. "Feel bad about what?" she asked.

"Caryn's thinking about that overflowing freezer, and now she's regretting eating here tonight instead of having some of the food people have brought over."

How he knew that was what she was thinking, Caryn had no idea.

Drew shrugged as if he really could read her mind, and said, "I'd be thinking the same thing, so I figured that's what put that look of consternation on your face."

"I really should probably get home. I left Otto and Silas with Art when you called, and they've either started World War III over a game of chess, or those two have sprung him out of the house against Doc Snow's recommendations and they're causing havoc across town as we speak."

Drew and Lilly laughed.

"Well, if you get bored, which I doubt will happen because you seem like the kind of woman who keeps herself busy, give me a call and I'll go with you to the library or bookstore. I can introduce you to Khloe. She works with Raiden in the library. On the outside, she's a little prickly, but she's actually really nice. And Raid's bloodhound loves her to death, much to his owner's chagrin. And I don't know the owner of the bookstore, but I probably need to remedy that. Oh, and Bristol's gonna be upset that both me and Elsie have met you but she hasn't, so we should probably plan an outing with all of us at some point. How long are you staying in town?"

There was that question again. Caryn shrugged. "I don't know really. I'm waiting for Art to get a little more mobile and self-sufficient. I'm kind of relying on Doc Snow to let me know when he thinks he'll be okay on his own. But at his age, I'm worried that might be never."

"Art's strong," Drew said firmly.

"I know, but he's also ninety-one," Caryn added. "I mean, how many ninety-one-year-olds do you know who still live on their own without even some drop-in care?"

"Well, I met a sixty-something-year-old man today who still hikes the AT by himself," Drew countered.

Caryn couldn't help but smile. "Right. Touché."

"I'm sure Art would be tickled to death if you moved to Fallport. But like you and Lilly were just discussing, even if you don't, he'll be okay. There will be plenty of people who are willing to check on him. And I can guarantee, after what happened, the townspeople will be more aware of their friends and neighbors and if they haven't heard from them or seen them in twelve hours or so, they'll be checking in."

Drew was right, Caryn knew he was, but that didn't stop the feeling that time was running out for her and her grandfather. He wouldn't live forever, and she wanted to spend as much time with him as she could. He'd been the one person in her entire life who'd never wavered in his love for her. No matter what she did, what job she took, he was always there, cheering her on.

Refusing to think about her mother—not now, when she was feeling fairly mellow from a full belly and after her first successful search and rescue mission—she nodded at Drew. "And I appreciate that."

"Get my number from Drew," Lilly said. "And Bristol and Elsie's too. You want to meet at Sweet Tooth in the morning for breakfast? I can introduce you to Finley and you can see what I mean about her cinnamon rolls being to die for."

"Does everything around here revolve around food?" Caryn couldn't help but ask.

"Pretty much."

"Yes."

Lilly and Drew answered at the same time, and they all laughed.

"It's how small towns work."

"I'm gonna be as big as a house if I don't start working out more regularly," Caryn complained, eyeing the empty plate in front of her. She couldn't even begin to think about how many calories she'd just consumed. Even without the German chocolate cake both she and Drew had declined when Elsie asked if they were ready for dessert.

"You run?" Drew asked.

Caryn nodded. "Yeah."

"I try to work out every morning, including running a few times a week, at least when I'm not neck-deep in tax season. If you wanted to join me, I wouldn't mind."

Did she want to do that? She was already more attracted to Drew than she'd like. Then again, maybe sweating her ass off in front of him would be a good thing. He'd realize quickly that she wasn't like most women. Didn't wear makeup, couldn't care less about designer clothes. Hell, most of the time she didn't even carry a purse. And spending more time with the man would surely highlight some of his flaws, as well.

She found herself nodding before she could second-guess the decision.

"Great. I could meet you outside Art's house. Six too early?"

"That's fine. I'm usually up by five-thirty or so."

"Every morning?" Lilly asked.

"Almost."

"Well, that's crazy. So is getting up to work out," she said with a smile. "Or working out in general."

"As if lugging around those heavy cameras and bags isn't

exercise," Drew said with a roll of his eyes. "How much did that camera weigh when you were on the show?"

"Whatever," Lilly said with a laugh, not answering his question. "Anyway, it was great to meet you, Caryn, and I was serious about getting together. So...cinnamon rolls tomorrow?"

"Sure. After my run?"

"Absolutely. How's ten sound? I know that's a little late, but you can go for your run and get your grandfather settled before we meet."

Caryn appreciated her thinking about Art. "Sounds perfect."

"Great. Thanks for the lemonade, Drew. See ya later." With that, Lilly stood.

"If Ethan or Rocky need help with anything at Rocky's new place, let me know. I'm not the best at constructing stuff, but I can help carry and hold shit up like a champ."

"I'll let them know." Lilly waved at them both and went over to where Davis was sitting at the bar, eating a hamburger. She said something to him before hugging Elsie and heading for the door.

"You guys really *do* seem pretty close," Caryn said, a little embarrassed at the longing in her voice.

"We are," Drew said. "They're good men and women, and I'm proud to call them friends."

As well he should be. Caryn wondered how much different her life—and her occupation—might have been if she'd had a support system like Drew and his friends did. But it was no use wishing to change the past. It was what it was.

"You ready to go?" Drew asked.

Looking at her watch, Caryn mentally winced and nodded. "Yeah."

"Art's fine," Drew said, once again reading her mind. "If

something happened, Otto or Silas would call one of the guys, or Simon, and they'd get in touch with you."

"I know. I just feel bad. I came here to be with Art, help him recover, and it feels as if I've spent more time doing my own thing."

"He'd never hold that against you," Drew said. "He's so happy you're here. And...he probably doesn't *want* you hovering over him. He'd want you to be out and about, getting to know Fallport again. Especially if he knew you were considering moving here. Have you told him?"

"Are you crazy?" Caryn asked as they walked toward the door. Drew had paid for their meal just before Lilly joined them, and even though she'd tried to pay her half, he'd waved her offer away. She'd obviously been in the city too long, because the last two dates she'd attempted, the guys had expected her to pay her own way. "No way would I tell Art that I was thinking about moving here if I wasn't sure. He'd get his hopes up and if I decided against it, he'd be crushed."

"You're probably right. But I'm guessing he's gonna find out sooner or later. You know how fast word travels around here."

"Shoot, you're right." Caryn sighed as Drew held the door to the bar open. "I'll talk to him. I just don't want him to be disappointed."

"I don't think he could ever be disappointed in you," Drew said. "So...six tomorrow for running. How far do you usually go?"

Caryn was glad for the topic change. His compliments made her feel too good. "It's been a couple weeks since I've run, so maybe I should start out moderately. Six miles okay?"

Drew grinned. "Six miles is moderate for you?"

"Well, yeah," she said with a shrug.

"Right. Then sure, six miles is great. See you in the morning. If you need anything, just call."

"Um...I don't have your number," she told him.

"Shit. Sorry. I forgot." He reached into his front pocket and pulled out his cell.

Caryn got her own phone out of her pocket and they exchanged numbers. Then he proceeded to give her numbers for Bristol, Lilly, and Elsie, along with those of his team members.

"Okay, I think that's enough for now," she teased. "I mean, I can get the numbers of the rest of the residents of Fallport tomorrow."

He chuckled. "Just making sure you have the most important ones first," he quipped. Then he looked her in the eyes and said, "You did great today, Caryn. You were just what we needed. Thank you."

"You're welcome," she said softly, trying hard not to immediately blow off his compliment and accept it graciously.

They walked together to the parking lot behind On the Rocks, and he stood beside his car until she got into her Sonata and pulled out of the lot. Art's house wasn't far from the town square, and she watched in her rearview mirror as Drew turned the opposite way she did when he left.

Being around Drew was...unsettling. Mostly because she felt a pull toward him she didn't fully understand and hadn't felt with anyone else before. She'd spent her life building a pretty high wall to protect herself. Starting at a very young age...otherwise, she wouldn't have been able to function. Her mother was a terrible parent, and it was amazing Caryn was as functional as she was.

She knew she had her grandfather to thank for that. And the town of Fallport. Here, she'd been able to just be a kid. Carefree. The things she'd experienced and learned here had carried her throughout her life.

The move to Fallport should be a no-brainer. Her grandfather wasn't getting any younger, and she wanted to spend as much time with him as possible. She wasn't happy with her job in New York and didn't particularly like living in the city any longer. And the more she got to know Drew and his friends, the more she yearned to be included in their inner circle.

Which was part of the problem. What if she moved here and things didn't work out?

She wanted to be positive about the thought of making a change, of a potential move, but her fears still gave her pause.

Taking a deep breath, Caryn made a conscious effort to push any negative thoughts aside. If she did move here, Fallport would be a new start for her. A much-needed one.

Making a decision to let the chips fall where they may, including whatever connection she and Drew seemed to have, Caryn felt lighter when she pulled into the driveway of her grandfather's house. Being here felt right, and she just needed to go with the flow...for once in her life.

She was looking forward to running tomorrow. And since she was being honest with herself, much of that excitement was because of who she was running *with*. She could also practically taste the cinnamon roll she would have afterward. Lilly had been extremely friendly, as had Elsie.

Yeah...being here in Fallport was good. Caryn was cautiously excited to see what her future held.

CHAPTER SEVEN

Drew knocked on Art's front door at five fifty-eight the next morning. He was looking forward to this run more than he'd anticipated. He'd spent some time the night before trying to analyze exactly what it was about Caryn that drew him in, and after way too long pondering—and not figuring it out—he decided to just go with it for now.

She was an intriguing mix of vulnerable and tough. She was smart, hardworking, and sweet all at the same time. She gave as good as she got and didn't let anyone run roughshod over her. But he could still see her need to be accepted and liked. And he suspected it didn't just extend to her firefighter co-workers.

The door opened—and it was all Drew could do not to make a fool of himself by letting his jaw hit the ground when he saw Caryn. She wore a pair of biking shorts that clung to her sleek thighs, similar to what she'd worn while hiking. The tank top was just as tight. She wasn't skinny, but neither was she fat. She was...solid. And Drew liked every inch that he could see.

Then she turned to lock the door behind her—and Drew

almost swallowed his tongue when he got a look at her gorgeous ass.

Caryn Buckner was sexy as hell. It took everything in him not to step closer to her and put a hand on those luscious full globes.

She turned around and immediately caught him in the act of checking her out. In return, her own gaze ran up and down his body, but Drew was pretty sure his shorts and ratty old T-shirt with the sleeves cut off weren't nearly as impressive as *her* outfit.

"A little early for the googly eyes, isn't it?" she asked as she unzipped a hidden pocket in the waistband of her shorts at the small of her back and stashed the key to the house.

"Can't help it...you're definitely in shape," Drew said.

To his surprise, Caryn smiled. "Thank you. It feels as if I have to work twice as hard as everyone else at the station to keep up. I swear it was easy to keep the weight off and run through the training exercises...until I turned forty. It was as if my body flicked a switch and was like, 'nope, done.'"

Drew grinned. "I know the feeling. Although since I moved here when I was forty, I didn't have to worry about qualifying or keeping up with the younger officers."

"Not to mention no more chasing bad guys," Caryn said with a smile.

"That too. You need to stretch before we start?" he asked.

"Nope. I'm ready. I got up a bit early to make sure I was good to go when you got here."

"Great. I thought we'd stick to the town this morning. Run around the square, to Caboose Park, maybe down to the high school...if that's okay."

"That's fine."

"Another time we can run west on Main Street out toward the trails. It's a little more sparse out that way though."

Caryn nodded. "I wouldn't mind staying closer to Art for

now. Just in case." She had her phone strapped to her upper arm in a plastic holder that fastened around her bicep with Velcro.

"If I'm going too slow or fast, let me know," Drew told her as they started off at an easy jog.

"You gonna lose your mind if I say you're too slow?" she asked.

"Nope," Drew said immediately. "I know I'm not the fastest runner, but I've got great stamina."

As soon as the words were out of his mouth, he realized how sexual they sounded. He hadn't meant them that way, but...hell, it was true about his running speed *and* his lovemaking.

Caryn smirked as they settled into a comfortable pace. "I'm trying to decide if I should let that go or not," she admitted.

"Feel free to give me shit about anything. I can take it."

"It's been my experience that stamina is probably the most important asset. Running hot and fast is all well and good, but sometimes it's more satisfying to prolong things."

Drew couldn't stop the sharp bark of laughter from escaping. When he had himself under control, he said, "I agree. And for the record, I haven't had any complaints about my performance in the past."

Caryn was still grinning as they neared the square. "Are we still talking about running?" she teased.

"I don't know, are we?" Drew shot back.

The woman simply shook her head. They jogged in silence for a while before she said, "You really aren't at all what I expected."

"What did you expect?" he asked.

Caryn shrugged. "A hard-ass. Someone who was a stickler for rules. No sense of humor."

"If you'd met me right after I quit with the state police,

that's what you would've gotten," Drew told her honestly. "But in the last five years, I've tried really hard to put that person behind me. To embrace small-town life. To enjoy the slower pace. I'm not sure I've been completely successful, but I've learned that it's okay to break the rules now and then. But trust me...I'm still really not all that funny."

She chuckled. "Right."

"I'm serious."

"I know you think you aren't, but, Drew, you've made me laugh more in the last few days than I have in a very long time."

"Why is that?" Drew asked, honestly wanting to know. "From where I'm standing, and from what I hear from your grandfather, you're amazingly good at what you do. You're down-to-earth, hard-working, and so far, you've been a great workout partner."

"It's been what, ten minutes?" she asked with a small laugh.

"True. I take back that last thing...I'll let you know how I feel when we're done," Drew joked.

They jogged for another few minutes before Caryn finally said, "I'm not like this, usually."

"Like what?" Drew asked.

"Nice."

He blinked in surprise. "I don't believe you. I mean, you've had your moments, but there were extenuating circumstances."

She chuckled, but it wasn't a very humorous sound. "You're being generous. In my defense, back in New York, I'm constantly on guard. If I say the wrong thing at work, it can actually hurt my career. People are always ready to get on me about something. Am I too liberal? Too conservative? Did I do something wrong on a scene? Did I complain on a job? Did I endanger one of my fellow firefighters? Move too slow, too fast...? Honestly, it's exhausting. I don't have the luxury of relaxing."

"That sucks," Drew said.

"Yeah," Caryn agreed. "I feel awful admitting this, but I was relieved I had an excuse to take a leave of absence. And that makes me the worst granddaughter in the world...happy Art got hurt so I could take a break from my job."

"I think it makes you human," Drew countered.

A full minute passed before she asked, "You aren't going to comment? Tell me I should quit because I'm too good to be treated like that?"

Drew shook his head. "I don't have to. You already know it."

He heard her sigh.

"Besides, I get it. I was right there with you. It's extremely hard to be in law enforcement these days, even more difficult now than five years ago when I quit. But even back then, it was a daily grind for me. Everything I did was scrutinized. My body-camera videos were analyzed to death. Anything I said or did was fodder for a reprimand or to be picked apart. Don't get me wrong, I think some level of oversight is absolutely necessary. Too many officers get away with horrific discriminatory actions way too often, but for those of us who were truly doing our best to do our jobs well, to keep people safe...it's hard. I don't think I laughed for at least a year after I moved to Fallport. So...I get it."

"Do you regret quitting?" Caryn asked.

Drew didn't know how the conversation had gotten so heavy, but he wasn't sorry. If he'd had someone to talk to in those last years as an officer, he might've been able to stick with it longer, or he might've been able to quit with a lighter heart. "One hundred percent no," he told her. "The first few months, I wondered what I'd done, sure. I worried about money, about what others would think of me, wondered if I was letting anyone down...but now that I'm five years out, I can say it was the best thing I ever did for myself. Many people wouldn't think being an accountant is very interesting, but I like it."

"And like you said before, you have the search and rescue team to fulfill your desire to help others."

"Exactly," Drew said with a nod.

Once again, silence fell over them for several long minutes, the only sounds their feet hitting the pavement and birds chirping in the trees.

"Sometimes I wish someone would just tell me to quit. It would make the decision easier for me," Caryn said.

Without hesitation, Drew looked at her and said, "Quit. Move to Fallport and spend what time your grandfather has left with him."

Caryn chuckled. "Right. It's not that easy."

"Of course it's not. There are a million details you'll have to work out. But you did say you wanted someone to basically give you permission to quit. So I did."

She looked at him then, and Drew couldn't help but once again realize how pretty Caryn was. Not in the conventional sense, he supposed. But right this moment, with her cheeks flushed, sweat glistening on her forehead and chest, her blonde hair curling over the fabric band wrapped around her head...she was definitely turning him on.

"Thanks," she said after a moment.

The conversation for the rest of their run was much less heavy. Drew told her how slammed he was with tax work for the first four months of the year, but after that, he had an easy schedule. He regaled her with some stories of their more memorable search and rescues. She talked about the older woman who lived next door in her apartment complex back in New York and how she was literally a crazy cat lady. They discussed the merits of different flavors of coffee and what the best flavor ice cream was.

By the time they neared her street at the end of the run, Drew felt as if he knew her much better...and hopefully she felt the same about him. "I'm sorry about anything I might've said or done when we first met, that ticked you off," he blurted.

She looked over at him in surprise. "What?"

"You were stressed, had just heard what happened to Art, and I could have been nicer."

She shook her head. "It's already forgotten. I wasn't exactly little miss sunshine myself."

That was another thing Drew liked about her; she didn't hold grudges.

"You want to work out again tomorrow?"

"Yes." Her answer came without hesitation.

"Great. Same time?"

"This works for me if it works for you."

"It does." Drew's mind was working overtime with ideas on what else they could do for their workouts. Running was good, but it could get boring. "How about taking a hike with me tomorrow? I can start showing you the main trails we're usually called out on and explain some of the things we look for when we're on the hunt for someone."

Her blue eyes lit up with excitement. "Yes! I'd love that."

"Great. I think we can skip the Fallport Creek Trail. It's easy and only about a mile long, one way. So maybe the Barker Mill Trail tomorrow. It's three miles one way, and every so often we get unprepared hikers out there who over-estimate their abilities and get hurt. We can work our way up to the Rock Creek and Eagle Rock trails."

"Sounds good. But I'm assuming people generally get lost when they're off trail, right?" she asked. They'd arrived back at Art's street and were walking while cooling down.

"Correct. But they usually start off on one trail or another. It's rare when people disappear into the woods far from any marked trail. When that does happen, though, we use the same tracking principles we do when we're on an established path."

"Makes sense. How many people have you guys found?"

Drew shrugged. "I'm not sure. I think Ethan keeps track, more for the mayor and city council, to prove that the money they spend on us is worth it, and to use as leverage when we need something...like the satellite phones."

"Which Bristol bought for you."

"Yup. She didn't want to wait around for them to *maybe* get approved in the city budget."

"I like her already."

"She's highly likable," Drew said with a smile.

Caryn tilted her head. "You really consider them friends, don't you?"

"Who?"

"Your friends' girlfriends."

"Lilly, Elsie, and Bristol? Absolutely. Why are you so surprised?"

"It's just that in my experience, guys mostly tolerate the wives and girlfriends of their friends."

"Well, that's not how it is here. They're just as important to me as Ethan, Zeke, and Rocky. Mostly because their women make them happy. More content. It's easy to see."

Caryn nodded. "I should get in. Check on Art."

"Right. Thanks for running with me today and not complaining that I was holding you back the whole time."

"Thanks for inviting me. And I'd be an idiot to run at my regular speed the first time out in a couple weeks."

Drew chuckled. She'd totally been holding back but was too nice to say so. "See you around."

"Later."

It was actually difficult for Drew to turn away and head for his car. He loved this area. It was small and close to the square, Art's older house surrounded by others very similar. It was a cozy neighborhood. Quiet. Perfect for Art...and a great place for his granddaughter to find herself again.

* * *

It was an hour before Caryn got into the shower, after helping her grandfather through his morning routine. She helped him to the bathroom, made his coffee, and got the morning paper from the porch, which he liked to read while sipping his morning brew. While he was doing that, she prepared a bowl of oatmeal and chopped up some fruit. She dropped off both and then headed to the bathroom to get ready for the day.

While she stood under the hot spray, she thought about that morning. Drew was so completely different from any cops she'd ever known. She felt guilty for having such judgmental thoughts about him when they'd first met. He hadn't hesitated to apologize for his own behavior when, in reality, they were both at fault, letting their preconceived ideas of who the other was guide them, instead of getting to know each other properly.

Their circumstances weren't terribly different...it sounded as if he was just as burned out five years ago as she was now. Although his reasons for wanting out of his job were different.

Caryn so desperately wanted to be accepted in her field, to be included in the fraternity and share in the companionship the rest of her fellow firefighters had. But ever since she'd stepped inside her first station, she'd been excluded. Made to feel inferior, almost like a burden. She'd put up with it for years, and she'd practically drained herself trying to become smarter, faster, stronger...and like she'd admitted this morning, she was exhausted.

Pushing the depressing thoughts aside, she switched back to Drew Koopman instead. She wasn't sure why he was being so friendly, but she couldn't deny she liked it. Somehow, a person she thought she'd never connect with in a million years had become someone she looked forward to seeing and talking to. He understood her. Had dealt with similar types of life-or-death situations. The way he could read her mind was definitely uncanny.

And...she couldn't deny she was attracted to him.

He was an intoxicating mix of rugged and tough mixed with a little bit of nerd. She liked that. A lot. Probably because that was how she felt herself. She loved to read. Devoured her favorite authors' new romance books as soon as they came out. But she could also lift a fully grown man and carry him out of a burning building without too much effort. She knew all there was to know about the science of fire, and yet still got a rush from sitting in a firetruck racing down the street with its sirens blazing.

And Drew definitely took care of himself. Yes, she was a faster runner, but he was no slouch when it came to his physique. For a second when they'd gotten back to her place, she had a daydream of stripping his shirt off and licking straight up the center of his chest. It was shocking how intense the urge was, actually.

But they were friends. New friends, at that. And she still hadn't made the decision to move here. The last thing she wanted to do was start a relationship, then leave town.

As she rinsed the conditioner out of her hair, she had the quick thought that she didn't need a full-blown, committed relationship. She could simply have casual sex with the man and go back to her life in New York City without any issues.

But she'd never had a fling in her life. It wasn't how she

was wired. She fell hard and fast—much as her mom always had—and she'd always avoided getting physically involved with a man until she was sure they had more in common than just lust. It hadn't always been easy. Caryn longed to have a partner. She'd thought she had one in Jonah, but she quickly found out that wasn't the case.

Sighing as she turned off the water, Caryn decided not to think so hard about what was going on with her and Drew. Whatever happened with the man...happened. And she'd either stay or go back to New York. She wouldn't spend her time and energy worrying.

The day went by quickly. Caryn met Lilly at The Sweet Tooth and got a cinnamon roll bigger than her head. It was just as delicious as Lilly had claimed. She got to meet Finley and immediately liked the shy, curvy baker. And she learned the Bristol everyone was eager for her to meet was actually Bristol Wingham, the incredible stained-glass window artist. She'd seen one of her creations in a church in New York and was blown away by how the intricate scene seemed to jump right off the glass. She could admit to being a bit intimidated about eventually meeting her.

When she'd said as much to Lilly, the other woman had shrugged off her apprehension. "Bristol's totally lovely. So down-to-earth. You'll get along great, I just know it!"

Then she proceeded to tell her all about the glass she was designing for one of the panes at Sunny Side Up. A forest scene with a man wearing an Eagle Point Search and Rescue jacket, walking along a path. It was her way of paying tribute to her fiancé and his friends for all they did.

Shortly after, Lilly had to leave for a client meeting, and Caryn stayed a bit longer. Finley, who'd overheard their conversation, came over after Lilly was gone and told Caryn that Bristol was also planning on putting a Bigfoot in the stained glass, peeking out from behind a tree. It sounded like a fun idea, though Finley further explained that Lilly had conflicting feelings about the whole Bigfoot craze, considering what happened on the paranormal show she'd been part of.

Caryn understood where Lilly was coming from, even if she'd had nothing to do with the death of one of the actors on the show...or the lengths her ex-producer had apparently gone to in order to manipulate the episode's footage.

After promising to come back to the bakery soon, and adding Finley's name to her contacts list in her cell phone, Caryn wandered over to the used bookstore, Fall For Books, just a couple doors down from the bakery. She spent way more time than she'd planned to poring over the books and talking about authors with the owner.

Yanelis Sanchez was in her fifties, had married the love of her life when she was eighteen, and lost him just a decade later. She'd raised their two children by herself and moved to Fallport not too long ago. She bought the used bookstore from the previous owner and spent her days happily surrounded by the things that brought her the most joy —books.

Neli, as she liked to be called, was thrilled to talk to another bibliophile, and somehow Caryn found herself telling the woman all about her relationship with Thomas Robertson. She left the bookstore with a bag full of books and the sense that she'd made another friend.

It was kind of crazy how easy it was to connect with people in Fallport. Caryn had never felt as welcomed or at home as she did there. She thought back to that morning, when she'd verbalized the wish for someone to simply tell her what to do. And how Drew hadn't hesitated to give her permission to quit and move.

She wished it was that easy.

But then again...wasn't it?

Making a snap decision, Caryn quickly walked the short distance to Art's house. She checked on her grandfather and was happy to see he was holding court with the ladies who usually hung out at the beauty shop, gossiping. Dorothea, Cora, Ruth, and Clara were all there. Clara was warming up one of the casseroles someone had brought over and the others were engaged in a lively discussion about the latest city council meeting minutes.

Caryn made sure her grandfather was good and didn't need anything, and when he promised he was just fine, she let him know she'd be back again in about an hour or so. He waved her off, and Caryn headed out to her car with a clear conscience.

She headed for the Fallport Fire Department. If she was going to seriously think about moving here, she needed to know if the rumor that they were looking for a full-time fire-fighter was true. She also wanted to check out the atmosphere...see if they were receptive to hiring a woman.

Caryn knew she was damn good at her job, but that didn't mean a thing if she was walking into another good ol' boys atmosphere. She'd had enough of that to last her a lifetime. If that was how the FFD operated as well, she'd have to pass.

She parked behind the building and at first glance, was impressed. The exterior was pristine, and through the bay windows she could just see a brush truck, fire engine, and a heavy rescue vehicle parked inside.

She knocked on a door to the left of the bays. When no one answered, she pushed it open and said, "Hello?"

Silence greeted her, and Caryn was just deciding to leave and come back another time when a man walked by and saw her in the doorway.

"Can I help you?" he asked.

Caryn pushed the door open the rest of the way and stepped inside. To her relief, the man wasn't Paul. She knew she'd have to talk to him sooner or later, but was glad that time wasn't right this second.

"Hi. I'm Caryn Buckner," she started.

"Right," the man said. "You're Art's granddaughter. The firefighter from New York. We've heard a lot about you. Sorry about what happened to Art. That totally sucks."

"Thanks. And yeah, it does, but he's doing really well."

"Glad to hear it. I'm Oscar," the man said, holding out his hand.

Caryn shook it, not surprised when he gripped her fingers a little tighter than necessary. She refused to back down or show even one iota of discomfort. She clasped his hand just as tight before he nodded at her.

"What brings you in?"

"Thought I'd stop by and say hello," she said lamely.

Oscar chuckled. "And I'm guessing you heard about the job opening."

Caryn shrugged and didn't deny it. "That might've crossed my mind."

"Well, you're obviously qualified," Oscar said. "If the rumors are true."

"They're true. I've got my state quals in New York, but I also took the national test, so I can work anywhere. I realize I'd need to be certified in Virginia, but I don't think that'll be an issue. I'm also a paramedic, and again, have passed the national test."

"Impressive," Oscar said.

Caryn couldn't hear any sarcasm or derision in his tone, so she just nodded.

"You want a tour of the place?"

"Sure."

Oscar was a good host...but the more Caryn saw, the more worried she got. In every firehouse she'd worked at, the crews kept them extremely clean. Rookies were responsible for doing the dishes, mopping the floors, and generally keeping the place sparkling. Everyone who lived there during their twenty-four or forty-eight hour shifts kept their bunks made and their stuff off the floor and out of the way.

But this place was a mess. It reminded her more of a frat house than a fire station. There were heaps of dirty dishes in the sink and a pot of leftover spaghetti sat on the stovetop. Empty bottles of soda dotted the tables around the couches and chairs in the TV room, and a huge stain was hard to miss in the middle of the carpet.

She was even more appalled at the state of the turnout gear and boots in the garage. They were filthy. Mud on the boots, the jackets hung haphazardly. They looked like they'd been thrown up in haste. She had no idea how anyone was able to find their own jacket in the jumbled mess.

But seeing the trucks themselves almost made her want to cry. She'd spent many, many hours washing and drying the firetrucks at her station back in New York. It had been her experience that firefighters found satisfaction in a clean and shiny truck. It not only showed pride in what they did, but it was a good activity to kill time between calls. And of course, every time a truck was parked in front of the station, inevitably children were drawn to it. Washing the trucks was a great way to get to know the locals and to make some kid's day.

But the FFD trucks were covered in mud and dirt. The chrome was dull in the bright lights of the bay. Not only that, but the hoses on top looked to be shoddily stacked, instead of meticulously folded or wound on spools. Hose lines like that could be a disaster at a fire. They needed to be pulled off the truck easily and quickly. If they got tangled it could mean the difference between life and death for a trapped victim, or the complete loss of a structure.

She wanted to ask what the hell was going on, but it

wasn't her place. Not at all. Some of her dismay must've shown on her face though, because Oscar said a little guiltily, "We're trying to talk the council into funding a new truck. These are old. And we just had a grass fire the other day."

The other day? Caryn wanted to roll her eyes and tell him a few hours were more than enough to clean the damn trucks and take care of their bunker gear, but she kept her face as blank as she could. "Where is everyone?" she asked.

Again, in her experience, the fire stations were always buzzing with activity. People watching TV, cooking, playing a video game, working out, or cleaning. But she hadn't seen a single soul during their tour. And this was a full-time station. The firefighters were paid to be ready at a moment's notice during their shifts.

"Oh, I think they're in their bunks taking naps," Oscar said.

Once again, Caryn felt her eyes widen. It was literally the middle of the day. And it didn't sound as if the crew had been up late into the night, fighting a fire. They should definitely be up and doing *something*.

Aware she was being extremely judgmental, Caryn tried to rationalize what she was seeing and hearing...but nothing she could personally think of would justify the firefighters all sleeping at the same time.

"I appreciate you taking the time to show me around," she told Oscar as they walked back outside. She hadn't seen a workout room in the fire station, which was highly unusual. It was imperative the crew stayed in shape. Fighting fires was hard work. She prided herself on doing everything she could to be as fit as possible, both to make her job easier, and so she could help anyone, medically or in a fire situation, when needed.

"No prob," Oscar told her. "If you're truly interested in

the job, you should stop by and talk to Paul. He's in charge of the search committee."

Caryn already knew that was probably the case. It didn't exactly thrill her, but it had been quite a few years since she'd seen her childhood nemesis. Maybe he'd changed.

She almost snorted, but managed to hold it back.

"I might just do that."

Oscar nodded at her, shook her hand once more, and headed back into the station.

Caryn sat in her car for a long moment, staring at the firehouse. It was closed up tightly, uninviting to anyone who might want to stop by with their kids to see the trucks, or just a local hoping to pop in and tour the place. She realized for the first time that while there might be a lot of things she didn't like about her station back in New York, there were also some things she loved...starting with the immense pride every firefighter took in the place.

Starting her car, she pulled away from the FFD and headed back to Art's house. She had some more thinking to do before she made a decision about her future. For now, she just wanted to spend some time with her grandfather. She was gone more than she should've been the last couple days. He was healing remarkably well, but that didn't mean he was back to one hundred percent. Doc Snow would be stopping by later this afternoon, and she wanted to be there to hear what he said about Art's recovery.

Even with the disappointment over seeing the condition of Fallport's fire department, Caryn's enthusiasm for the town hadn't dimmed. She was still eager to learn more about the place she called home in the summers when she was a child.

CHAPTER EIGHT

A week and a half later, Caryn waited at her grandfather's living room window, looking for Drew's Jeep to pull down the street. They'd fallen into a routine of working out every morning, and it was the highlight of her day. She wasn't sure if that was because of the workouts themselves, which were invigorating, or because she got to hang out with Drew.

He'd taken her for hikes on all the major trails in the area, and she understood a lot better how difficult it could be to find someone who was lost. There were thousands and thousands of acres and only having a general idea of where someone might be wasn't enough to actually find them. Drew had taught her how to look for disturbances in the dirt and foliage, to study the leaves of the bushes they passed, and how important it was not to panic if she found herself turned around and lost in the woods.

Maybe most importantly, she was taught to *listen*. They spent a lot of time simply standing in the middle of the forest and listening to the sounds around them.

Drew pointed out how the absence of sound from the animals could be just as telling as when they made a lot of noise. He'd even tested her the other day by heading down the trail and hiding, ordering her to find him. She'd walked by the place he'd gone off trail twice before finally seeing the subtle signs that someone had stepped into the mud on the side of the path. She'd been embarrassed that it had taken her an hour to find him, but Drew praised her and said he was impressed.

He admitted that the first time he had to look for Ethan, he'd actually failed completely and Ethan had come out of hiding after two and a half hours, complaining he was hungry and wasn't going to sit out there all night. Caryn didn't know if he'd been fibbing or not, but she couldn't deny the story went a long way toward making her feel better.

Today, Drew said he had a surprise for her, and she couldn't wait to see what he'd planned for their workout. Instead of making him knock on the door when he arrived, Caryn slipped out and met him on the front lawn.

"Excited much?" he teased.

"Hey, you were the one who talked this morning up. If it sucks, I'm gonna be disappointed."

"Ouch," Drew said, putting a hand over his heart.

He looked just as good this morning as he did every time they met up to work out. He had on a pair of black shorts—his go-to—but he was wearing a tank top instead of his normal T-shirt. Caryn could just see some black hair peeking out from the collar of the tank, and her fingers itched to pull the material up and see if he was covered in hair or just had a smattering.

She mentally smacked a hand on her forehead. It didn't matter how much chest hair the man had. Not at all.

Except with every day she spent with him, her attraction was growing. She liked Drew. As a person. A friend. A man. She was *drawn* to him, really. It was getting harder and harder not to let her interest show. The last thing she wanted was to ruin a good friendship. But she couldn't deny she badly wanted to taste his full lips and see if he kissed as well as he did just about everything else.

"Well, I think you'll like what I have planned, but if you don't, that's okay too," he said...in an almost too-casual tone.

Caryn realized he was nervous, and it endeared him to her even more.

She made a mental note to pretend to love whatever it was he'd planned this morning, even if she hated it. Which was just another sign of how much she liked this man. Never in her past had she lied about something so trivial, simply to please someone. She usually said exactly what was on her mind and didn't beat around the bush. She supposed that came from working with men who were often rough around the edges and did the same thing. But the last thing she wanted was to make Drew feel bad if he'd gone to a lot of effort to set up whatever workout they were going to do today.

Instead of heading out on a run, he gestured to his Jeep. "We need to drive today."

This wasn't the first time they'd driven to their workout. When they'd walked the trails, they'd had to drive to the trail-heads. So Caryn simply nodded and climbed into the passenger side.

"It's not far, but I'm thinking we'll both be too tired and sore to run back here when we're done."

Caryn raised an eyebrow at him. "I'm intrigued."

Drew simply smiled as he started the engine.

She was intrigued by just about *everything* involving this man. His Jeep was immaculate. Not one fast food wrapper or piece of trash to be seen, which was unusual these days. While she wasn't a slob, her own car had all sorts of crap in it. And her room at Art's house wasn't exactly tidy. But Drew was very neat and organized. He claimed it was the math geek in him.

The drive wasn't long, and when they pulled in front of the car shop where Brock worked, she turned to Drew with a confused look on her face. The place had an actual name, Old Town Auto, but most of the residents simply called it "The Shop."

Drew told her that Brock had found his calling while tinkering with cars after getting out of Customs and Border Protection.

"Please tell me we aren't here to try to get me a job," Caryn said.

It had kind of become a running joke between them, after hearing her thoughts on the state of the FFD, for Drew to offer suggestions for various jobs she could try outside of firefighting. From beautician, to high school English teacher, to highway maintenance...his suggestions were more about making her laugh than serious recommendations.

"Nope. And before you ask, yes, Brock knows I'm here. I have a key, so I'm not breaking in. Come on, you'll see in a minute."

More curious than ever now, Caryn followed Drew to the gate in the massive fence that was behind the property. When he unlocked the wooden gate and swung it open, Caryn stared in surprise. She had no idea this was here.

She stepped into what could only be called a junkyard.

"Brock and the others haul off unwanted cars for people and bring them here. Then they use whatever parts they can to fix the vehicles brought in. It helps keep the costs down for customers. And I think the guys simply love tinkering with the old cars as well," Drew explained.

The space was impressive. There were junkers lined up as far as she could see. Trucks, foreign models, cars that had obviously been in accidents, with various sides smashed in.

"Um...I know nothing about cars," Caryn told him. "So if our workout involves me trying to find parts, I'm not going to be of any use."

Drew chuckled. "Nope. I came last night to set things up." He led them to a wide space between two rows of cars—and Caryn could only gape at the setup.

"We'll start here with the tire," Drew said, pointing at a very large tire lying in the dirt. "The goal is to lift and flip it, end over end, to the end of the row. Then race back here while putting your feet between the rungs of the ladders on the ground, hopefully without falling. Then come over here," he pointed to two particular cars up on blocks, "and crawl under them. Then do ten push-ups and ten sit-ups. Real ones—not on your knees or crunches. Then a shuttle run...from here to there, to here, to there, to here, to there."

He pointed at spray-painted lines in the dirt progressively farther and farther apart, marking their course.

"Then to finish, you'll put me over your shoulder, carry me over there, put me down, drag me to that next row of cars, pick me up again, then run back to where we started. I couldn't find a practice dummy to use, and since we're the same height, we could take turns being the carrier and the carry-ee."

Caryn stared at him in stunned disbelief.

"What? Stupid idea?" he asked. "If you don't want to do the last part—or hell, any of it—we can just go for a run instead."

"No!" Caryn shouted a little too loudly. She shook her head and said a little more calmly. "This is *amazing*. It's incredible, Drew."

"I went online and looked at some of the things firefighters do to work out, and I thought about the tasks you perform, then I did my best to come up with activities that might simulate them. I was out of luck with the stairs. Fallport doesn't exactly have a high rise building we can use. The closest thing is the stadium at the high school, and I figured we'd save that for another day."

"Seriously, Drew, this is... I'm not sure anyone's *ever* gone to as much trouble for me as you have."

"You're worth it," he said quietly.

They shared a long, intimate look. Caryn wasn't sure what to do. Hug him? Kiss him? She really wanted to do the latter. Or both.

But he broke the moment by saying with a grin, "I'm expecting you to kick my ass at this. And if you don't, I'm gonna let everyone know that you've gone soft."

Her competitive nature kicked in, and Caryn grinned back. "Not a chance in hell of you beating me, doughnut man."

He laughed.

It was hard to believe she was standing there, with a cop—even a former one—and he didn't seem the least bit worried that she might beat him at an obstacle course.

"You want to go through it once so you can get a feel for everything?" he asked.

"I'm good if you are. It seems straightforward enough."

"Right. Then there's only one thing left to do."

"What's that?"

"Rock, paper, scissors to see who goes first. Winner gets first crack at it."

Caryn grinned and held out a fist.

"One, two, *three*!" Drew said, and on three, they each held out their choice.

Caryn won with paper over his rock.

Drew nodded at her in acquiescence. "Let's see what you can do."

She was more than ready. Caryn found that she was actually giddy with excitement. Not so much for the working out, but the fact that Drew had gone to such trouble to do something like this for her. He didn't have to. They could've kept going for runs or hiking the trails, but this was a *challenge*. And the fact that he'd gone online and done research to find a workout that would be relevant to her job...it made her feel a little warm and gooey inside.

Obviously, she wasn't like most women, who were touched by flowers and jewelry. This was so much better.

She took a deep breath and stepped up to the huge tire on the ground.

"Ready? Set, *go!*" Drew said.

Caryn crouched, grabbed one end of the tire and stood, making sure to put the pressure on her legs and not her back. She grunted as she felt the full weight of the tire. It was extremely heavy. Her arms strained as she lifted, then shoved it over. It hit the ground and a puff of dust rose up all around it. She immediately squatted and reached for it again. She did it over and over until she reached the end of the row.

She spun and raced back to where she'd started, carefully and quickly placing one foot inside each of the rungs of the ladders. Then she made a beeline for the cars and threw herself to the dirt, crawling under the vehicles.

As she did the ten push-ups and sit-ups, she heard Drew cheering her on. He was telling her how amazing she was doing, reminding her what the next task was. Caryn realized she was smiling as she ran toward the starting line for the shuttle run. When was the last time she truly had fun like this? She honestly couldn't remember.

When it came down to the last obstacle, she found Drew lying on the ground. She was supposed to pick him up and carry him, then place him back on the ground, drag him for about twenty feet, then pick him up once more. She hesitated momentarily.

"You got this, Caryn. Do it."

"I don't want to drop you," she blurted.

"You won't. Come on, pretend I'm a victim and you have to get me out of the line of fire—literally."

Taking a deep breath, Caryn crouched and grabbed one of his hands. She hauled him over her shoulder just as she'd done with training dummies more times than she could count. But this felt way different. Mostly because this was a real live human being...but also because it was *Drew*.

She'd been hanging out with him just about every day lately, and even though she was more and more attracted to the man, she hadn't actually touched him. Except for accidental brushes of their hands or shoulders as they worked out. Having him draped over her shoulder like this felt... extremely intimate.

"Good job!" he told her as she walked to the next part of the obstacle course. He was doing his best to be dead weight against her, and Caryn knew it couldn't be comfortable having her shoulder in his stomach, but he didn't complain.

"Impressive. Now, set me down and drag me over to that blue car," he ordered.

"I know where I'm going," she retorted, but she wasn't irritated with him, not in the least. Having his support, and knowing he was impressed with her, was heady. She leaned over and set him down as gently as she could, then grabbed his wrists and began to drag him through the dirt.

Looking down, she saw him smiling up at her. Dust was being kicked up by her feet as she shuffled backward but he didn't seem to care. He'd also set up this course perfectly... enough to make her out of breath by this point, but not too exhausted that she couldn't finish.

"Right, one more lift. You're almost there," he encouraged.

Taking another deep breath, and feeling her heart beating hard in her chest, Caryn once more hefted Drew over her shoulder. It was a good thing he wasn't any taller or heavier, because she wasn't sure she'd be able to do this if he was.

There was no way he could know, but this was the biggest thing most of her fellow firefighters questioned about her skills. The ability to carry them out of a burning building or dangerous situation if one arose. She'd done her best in training exercises to prove that she could, but the distrust remained.

She staggered under Drew's weight, but managed to cross the final line he'd drawn in the dirt on the ground. After she'd deposited him on his back, she stayed bent over, her hands on her thighs, breathing hard.

"Not too shabby," Drew told her as he sat up and looked at the watch on his wrist. "But I bet I can beat you."

That made Caryn's eyebrow fly up. "No way in hell."

He laughed as he got up from the dirt.

As they stood there staring at each other, Caryn had the strongest urge to throw herself at him, grab the hair at the back of his head, pull his lips down to hers and kiss the hell out of him. She actually took a step forward before stopping herself.

Her heart was beating hard and she curled her fingers into fists to keep from acting on her urges. They stared at each other for a long moment before she took a final deep breath and broke eye contact.

"For the record?" Drew said softly. "You're incredible." Then he backed away and turned to the tire lying in the dirt. He lifted it as if it weighed next to nothing and rolled it across the lot, back to the starting position. It fell to the ground with a thud and he clapped his hands together to remove the dirt. "Ready to time me?" he asked.

Shaking her head slightly to get herself back in the game, she nodded and reached for the watch on her wrist. "Ready to watch you get smoked," she sassed.

The grin on Drew's face was boyish and oh so tempting. He braced his legs shoulder width apart and looked at her expectantly.

"What?" she asked.

"You need to do the countdown for me to start."

"Right, yeah, sorry. Ready, set, *go!*" she said.

Watching Drew was like watching an Olympic athlete perform. He claimed all the time that he was old and out of shape, but there was no way the man in front of her was out of shape by *anyone's* definition.

When he bent over, Caryn's gaze went to his ass. She wasn't exactly ashamed, any red-blooded woman would take the opportunity to check him out. Before she knew it, he was running back to where she was standing, his feet flying in and out of the spaces of the ladder without hesitation. He was under the cars in seconds and she hurried to get to the place where she needed to be for him to carry her.

His push-ups made his biceps bulge, and Caryn licked her suddenly dry lips. The shuttle run was completed without any fanfare—and then he was there standing over her, grinning. He flung her over his shoulder without any difficulty whatsoever, and she stared at his ass again as he practically jogged to where he needed to place her on the ground. He did so with much more control than she'd done with him, and she swore when he grabbed her wrists, his thumbs caressed her sensitive skin before he started the drag. Then she was once again over his shoulder and he was crossing the finish line.

Caryn barely remembered to hit the stopwatch on her wrist.

"So?" he asked when he'd placed her on her feet once more. "Who won?"

Feeling extremely off-kilter, the desire to throw herself at him still pressing down on her, Caryn scowled at the time on her watch. "I'm thinking you had some practice at this."

He grinned. "Nope. I made Brock run through it to make sure everything worked the way I wanted. Although, I'm guessing the fireman's carry is a little unfair, since I outweigh you. Maybe next time I can carry some weights to try to even the scales a little more. Want to do it again?"

"Yes!" Caryn said without hesitation. Even with the uncomfortable and kind of scary feelings coursing through her veins about Drew, she was having a good time. Her muscles would definitely protest the extreme workout tomorrow, but right this second, she didn't care.

"Bring it on!" she told him with a grin.

How many times they each ran through the course, Caryn wasn't sure. At one point, Drew suggested maybe instead of carrying each other at the end, they could pick up a large tire and carry that instead, but Caryn protested. It wasn't exactly comfortable being thrown over someone's shoulder, but it was authentic to what firefighters might have to do in an emergency situation. And she liked having Drew draped over her shoulder, just as much as she enjoyed being slung over his.

By the time they decided they'd had enough for one morning, they were both drenched in sweat and had definitely put their bodies through an intense workout.

As they sat in the shade and sipped the water they'd brought, Caryn turned to Drew. "That was so fun. Thank you."

"It was. And you're welcome."

The silence between them was comfortable, and Caryn felt better than she had in a long time. She never felt this...*satisfied* after a workout back in New York. Everything always felt like a competition. As if she was being judged. It was never about having fun and simply enjoying pushing her body to its limits. With Drew this morning, she'd felt her competitive streak come out, but she wasn't afraid of not performing up to some arbitrary standard he might have.

"Have you talked to Paul about the open position?" Drew asked after a moment.

Caryn sighed. "No. I stopped by the fire station like I told you, but I haven't been by since."

"What's holding you back?" he asked.

Caryn stared out at the cars around her. "I'm not sure." That wasn't exactly true. She couldn't shake the unease she felt when she'd gotten a look at the station.

"The job won't be around forever," Drew said quietly.

She knew that. And because she did, she didn't get irritated with the man next to her. "I know." She'd been mulling over moving to Fallport for a while now, and she needed to quit being wishy-washy and make a decision once and for all. Her chief back in New York was demanding a response as to when, or if, she was coming back. Even though he'd threatened that she might not have a job when she came back, it was obvious that for whatever reason, he didn't really want to fire her outright. And Art was doing remarkably well. He was at a point where he could pretty much be on his own again. Just the day before, he'd gone back to his spot outside the post office for half the day.

It was time for her to quit screwing around and make a choice.

Making a decision, she turned to Drew. "I'll talk to him this week."

Drew smiled. "So? What does that mean?"

Feeling overwhelmed, she huffed. "You still wanna know when I'm leaving?" she joked, referring to when he'd asked her that very question in Sunny Side Up, after she'd done the Heimlich maneuver on the choking man.

Instead of getting defensive, Drew simply said, "Yes."

Licking her lips, Caryn whispered, "I think I want to stay."

"Good. Because there are lots of people who want that too."

Then he lifted a hand slowly. He brushed the backs of his fingers against her cheek, and Caryn felt herself leaning toward him.

His lips twitched before he adjusted his hand. He put a tiny bit of pressure under her chin, tilting her head up. Caryn saw his head lowering, and her eyes closed almost involuntarily as her heart beat out of control in her chest.

His lips brushed against hers once, as if testing her reaction. When she didn't pull away or tell him to stop, his hand slid around to her nape, holding her still for him, and his lips touched hers once more.

This time he didn't kiss her tentatively. His tongue came out and traced the seam of her lips and Caryn immediately opened for him, eagerly welcoming him in. The feel of his facial hair against her skin was sensual and erotic, and a small whimper escaped her throat.

She felt his fingers tighten on her neck, but his hold wasn't uncomfortable in the least. Their tongues dueled, giving and taking, and Caryn appreciated him not dominating the kiss.

Pins and needles seemed to be prickling all over her body. One of her hands tentatively reached out and landed on his thigh, and this time it was Drew who moaned in his throat. Knowing that she affected him as much as he did her was a heady feeling.

How long they sat there making out, touching only at their lips, her neck, and his leg, Caryn didn't know. She felt energized, as if she could run through his obstacle course another ten times and not be out of breath by the end.

She'd never felt like this with someone before—and it was that thought that had her ending the kiss. As soon as he felt her pulling back, Drew lifted his head, but he didn't let go of her neck. He stared down at her for a long moment, his brown gaze boring into her.

She wanted to ask him what he was thinking, but was also scared to death to know.

Then he inhaled deeply through his nose and said, "Old man Grogan is throwing a watch party at Caboose Park for the Bigfoot episode of that paranormal investigations show Friday night. Will you go with me?"

Caryn had heard all about the watch party. Lilly had no intention of going. She'd said more than once that she wanted nothing to do with the show, and even though she'd met the love of her life as a result of everything that had happened, she still felt sick just thinking about anyone making a profit over someone's death.

Elsie and her son Tony were going, though, as was Bristol. And of course, if they were going, so were their men. Caryn assumed Brock, Tal, and Raiden would also be there...as would most of the town of Fallport. Everyone was extremely curious as to how the town would be portrayed, and if the show would actually cause an influx of tourists coming here to check out the trails to see if they could catch their own glimpse of Bigfoot.

She'd obviously been lost in thought for too long, because Drew's hand left her nape and he began to pull back.

Without thinking, she grabbed his wrist and squeezed his knee. "I'd love to," she said quickly.

"The whole town is gonna be there," he said, and it felt kind of like he was warning her.

"I figured," she said.

"I want this to be a date," he went on. "I'm not willing to pretend we're just friends."

Ah, there was the reason for the warning. Caryn brought his hand back up to her face. He palmed her cheek as she spoke. "Good. Because I'm not either. My life is completely up in the air. I have no idea if I'll have a job when I move here, but I do know that the more time I spend with you, the more I want to. I'm not the best catch, Drew. I've got a lot of baggage. I've never really had a relationship that's worked out, and that scares me because the last thing I want to do is mess this up."

"You won't. *We* won't," he said without hesitation.

"I'm not so sure about that."

"I'm willing to try. Are you?"

"Yes." She didn't have to think about her answer.

"Good. So we'll go to this watch party. I'll bring chairs and a blanket. Maybe even some snacks. We'll hold hands, I'll kiss you now and then to make sure everyone knows you're off the market, and we can go from there."

Caryn couldn't help but laugh. "Marking your territory?" she teased.

"Abso-fucking-lutely. I'm not an idiot," Drew told her. "Even if you don't think so, you *are* one hell of a catch, and I've seen how the men in this town have been circling you."

Caryn tolled her eyes. "They have not."

"You just go right on thinkin' that, sweetheart."

He was completely crazy. No one was knocking down her door to take her out. She knew that, but if Drew didn't, she wasn't going to correct him.

"I'm gonna do my best to make this work," Drew said seriously, "but I've got my own faults. January to April is my busiest time of the year. I work almost nonstop. I'm not all that trusting—comes with my former profession—and pretty much don't have any friends except the guys on the team and their women. I've—"

Caryn reached up and covered his lips with her hand. "You aren't perfect, got it. I'm not either. It's all good."

She felt him smiling under her hand before she lifted it.

"I don't know what it is about you that's gotten under my skin. It hasn't happened before," he mused.

Caryn nodded. "Same with me."

"So we'll just play it by ear, yeah?"

"Sounds good."

"What are your plans for the day?" he asked.

"Art wants to go to the post office again today, but first he has an appointment with Doc Snow. I want to get official approval before he goes back to his normal routine. He might think he's in his twenties and can bounce back with no consequences, but he's not."

"Although, getting back to his routine can't be a bad thing," Drew mused.

"It's not, but I don't want him overdoing it," Caryn said. He'd moved his hand from her cheek to rest on the side of her neck once more. His thumb was gently caressing the sensitive skin and goose bumps had broken out on her arms as a result. This man was lethal without even trying.

"I agree. You think he'd want to come with us to the watch party?" Drew asked.

"You wouldn't mind?"

"Not at all. I mean, you and your grandfather are kind of a package deal. And I like the old guy. But, for the record, if he comes with us, that doesn't mean I'm not going to be holding your hand or kissing you. He gonna be all right with that?"

Caryn chuckled. Why wasn't she surprised Drew wasn't going to back off his alpha-man tendencies just because they were accompanied by her grandfather? "He's gonna be perfectly all right with that," she told him honestly. "He respects you, and because we've been hanging out a lot lately, he's begun to drop some not-so-subtle hints about us hooking up."

Drew chuckled. "Knew I liked him," he said. Then he tugged her closer and lowered his head once more. This time, their kiss was short and sweet. "I need to get you home so you can make sure Art's ready for the doc. Can I call you later?"

"I'd like that," Caryn said somewhat shyly.

"Great."

As they stood, Drew helping her up with a hand under an elbow, she asked, "What do *you* have planned for the day?"

"I need to start looking into setting up an investment account for Bristol. We met the other day to talk about her comfort level with how conservative she wanted to be, and I want to dive into her last few years of taxes to see where and if I can save her some money. I need to review some of my other clients' info as well."

"So a fun-filled day for you," Caryn teased.

But Drew didn't crack even the smallest smile. "I love working with numbers. They can't let me down like humans do so often."

"I wasn't making fun of you," Caryn said. "There's nothing wrong with what you do."

Drew shrugged. "It's not very exciting."

"I bet it is for the people who save thousands of dollars on their taxes because of you, or for those whose investment portfolios double."

He did smile at that. "True."

"You be you, Drew. Screw what everyone else thinks."

"I just worry about what *you* think," he admitted.

"Well, don't. So far I haven't learned anything about you that makes me want to run the other way."

"I hope it stays that way. Come on, I'll take you back to Art's house."

They walked hand in hand toward his car.

"Don't we need to clean things up around here?" she asked as he opened the passenger-side door for her.

"Naw. Brock's cool with leaving it. There isn't much to pick up anyway, just the ladder and maybe move the tire."

The drive back to her grandfather's house went way too quickly and before she was ready, it was time for her to get out. Caryn stared at Drew for a heartbeat before mentally shrugging. She leaned toward him, taking the initiative in their kiss this time. He immediately leaned into her, and the kiss they shared was just as intense as their first one.

He ran his hand over her short hair and smiled. "Say hi to Art for me."

"I will. Thanks again for this morning. I had a lot of fun."

"Me too," he said. "I'll talk to you later."

Caryn nodded and reached for the door handle. She wasn't surprised when Drew didn't immediately back out of the driveway, instead waiting until she'd opened the front door and turned to wave at him. He might think he wasn't trusting enough, but for a girl who'd lived most of her life in the big city, taking care of herself, having him be protective of her felt good.

Before she went to check on Art, Caryn leaned against the closed door and smiled, thinking about her morning. Apparently, she and Drew were now dating.

Her grin widened. She was more than all right with that. Her future was still up in the air, but having made the decision to stay, and to see where things with her and Drew could go, it felt as if a huge weight had been lifted from her shoulders. She felt excited about her future for the first time in ages.

The smile was still on her face as she pushed off from the door and headed down the hall to check on Art.

CHAPTER NINE

Drew didn't mean to kiss Caryn. But he literally hadn't been able to stop himself. Thank goodness she'd returned that first kiss and hadn't pulled away in shock and anger.

Since then, the last few days had been good. Comfortable.

Nothing between them seemed different, except now they touched each other a lot more. And the kisses they shared were definitely a bonus. They still met up each morning to work out and their conversations seemed more intimate, now that they were officially dating.

Dating. Lord, it had been way too long since Drew had attempted to get close to someone. Since he'd *wanted* to get close to someone. But Caryn had drawn him in with no effort on her part. He liked just about everything about her. Her compassion toward her grandfather, her competitiveness, her drive to be the best firefighter she could be.

Tonight, he was taking her to the watch party for the Bigfoot episode of the paranormal series that had filmed here. He had to admit that he was curious about the show. And regardless of his feelings about the existence of Bigfoot

—and the fact a possible influx of people coming to town to search for the legendary creature meant he'd be spending more time searching for those who got lost—he was still glad for all the businesses in town that would benefit from the tourists.

Caryn had told him Art was tickled pink that they were dating, and he'd enthusiastically agreed to come to the watch party. Apparently, Doc Snow had given him the okay to do whatever he felt up to, but if he was fatigued or in any pain, he was to contact him immediately.

Drew jogged up to Art's door and raised his hand to knock, but it opened before he could make contact with the wood. Caryn stood there with a huge smile on her face.

"Hi!" she said.

He'd seen her that morning but for some reason, it felt as if that was ages ago. "Hi," he answered. To his amusement and joy, Caryn threw herself at him and he caught her with a laugh. She hugged him tightly, and he loved how they fit against each other. Since they were the same height, all their best parts lined up perfectly.

She kissed him quickly on the lips then stepped back. She grabbed his hand and towed him into the house. "We're super excited about this. I mean, I know people have mixed feelings about the show, but it's still cool to see our town on TV."

Drew's eyes wandered down Caryn's body as she pulled him into the small living area of Art's house. She had on a pair of jeans and a navy blue NYFD T-shirt she'd tucked into the waistband of her pants. On her feet were a pair of sneakers. She looked comfortable and down-to-earth, and it was all Drew could do not to grab her and tackle her to the couch.

"Good to see you," Art said, pulling Drew's attention away from Caryn.

"You too. Hear you're doing really well. That's good news."

"It is," Art agreed. "Appreciate the invite to come with you guys tonight. And for the record...Otto and Silas are going too, and they're going to save me a seat with them." The old man winked. "Wouldn't want to be a third wheel."

"Oh, we wouldn't think that," Caryn said, but Drew simply nodded at Art in thanks. They shared a smile.

It took a bit of time for Caryn to pack up the small cooler she insisted on bringing. Drew told her he'd take care of all the snacks, but she wanted to contribute so he didn't complain.

They were in his Jeep, on the way to the park, when Caryn said, "We match."

"What?" Drew asked.

"Our clothes. Jeans, sneakers, blue T-shirts." She was grinning as she said it.

Looking down, Drew realized she was right. They hadn't planned it, but indeed they were wearing T-shirts that were almost the exact same shade of navy blue. His was one of the many Eagle Point Search and Rescue shirts in his drawer. "So they do," he said with a grin.

"You aren't embarrassed, are you?"

"Nope," Drew said. "Anytime you want to wear matching shirts, I'm all for it."

"Really?" Caryn asked skeptically. "I can't count the number of times the guys back in New York made fun of the tourists who did that."

"Well, I'm not them," Drew said firmly. "If it makes you happy, I'm good."

"I'll keep that in mind," Caryn told him.

Drew reached over and took her hand in his as Art spoke up from the back seat. "Remember that one Fourth of July parade when you were around ten and you insisted that we both needed red, white, and blue outfits? We looked ridiculous," he scoffed.

But Caryn didn't take offense. She laughed. "We were awesome," she countered. "And you didn't complain back then," she told him.

"Yeah, well, you were excited that we matched each other and that we were dressed the part for the holiday," Art said.

"Didn't we get our picture in the paper because we looked so cute?" Caryn asked.

"Yeah. I've still got it somewhere."

Caryn turned so she could look at her grandfather. "You do? That was like thirty years ago."

"So?" he asked. "I've got lots of memories like that one squirreled away."

"I'd love to see them. You know, if you wanted to show me," Caryn said tentatively.

Drew squeezed her hand. He could hear the emotion in her voice.

"Of course. We need to do that before you head back to New York," Art told her.

Looking over at her in surprise, Drew couldn't believe she hadn't told her grandfather she was staying. Caryn looked uncomfortable for a moment before she took a deep breath.

"About that. I'm pretty sure I've decided to stay in Fallport. That is...if it's okay."

The last part came out sounding quite a bit unsure. Drew had no doubt that it would be more than okay with Art.

Just as he thought, Art immediately put her mind at ease.

"Yes!" he whooped enthusiastically as he pumped his fist in the air.

Caryn chuckled. "I guess that's all right with you."

"Child, if I could've gotten you to move here right after you graduated from college, I would've. But I knew you had to go out and sow your wild oats. See the world. Realize that everything you might be looking for in life is right here in Fallport."

Drew turned and met Caryn's gaze. They had a small moment in that split second of complete understanding before he had to turn his attention back to the road.

"When you're right, you're right," Caryn said. "But there's still a lot that I have to figure out. Where to live. Get a job. You know, the big things."

"Pshaw," Art said. "You can stay with me as long as you need to. I know you'll want your own place sooner or later, but in the meantime, you aren't going to be homeless. And the town would be stupid not to hire you at the fire station. That is...if you still want to be a firefighter."

"Why wouldn't I?" Caryn asked, then immediately followed that question up with another. "And what would I do if not that? It's not like I've got some secret skill in my back pocket that I can pull out."

"You can do anything you damn well put your mind to," Art said fiercely.

Drew loved how supportive her grandfather was.

"You're smart as hell, always have your nose in a book, which is a good thing if you ask me...you haven't polluted your mind with all that mindless drivel that's on television these days. Whatever it is you decide to do, you'll kick ass at it."

"Thanks, Granddad," Caryn said quietly.

Drew squeezed her hand once more, before reaching for the steering wheel to parallel park. The parking lot at Caboose Park was full, as he expected, and there were cars lined up all along Main Street. But he'd lucked out and found a place his Jeep could fit.

As Caryn helped her grandfather out of the car, Drew opened the back hatch and took out their chairs, the bag of snacks he'd packed, the blanket, and the cooler Caryn had packed. Caryn took the blanket and wrapped her arm around Art's while Drew followed with the rest of their things.

They found Otto and Silas fairly quickly and got Art set up with them. Caryn gave them a million instructions about calling her if Art got tired. It wasn't until her grandfather interrupted, insisting he wasn't an invalid and shooing her away, that she relented.

When Drew finally got to put his arm around her waist, he felt himself relaxing.

"You think he's going to be okay?" Caryn asked as they headed over to the members of his team, whom he'd spotted earlier.

"He'll be fine. Almost the entire town is here and everyone will keep an eye on him," Drew reassured her.

Grogan had set up a giant screen in the middle of the large field near the old red caboose. There were speakers set up strategically around the field as well, so no matter where someone was sitting they'd be able to hear the show. He saw a few vendor tables off to the side offering T-shirts and other Bigfoot paraphernalia. He couldn't help but chuckle under his breath. The owner of the general store wasn't going to let any chance to make money slip away.

Two kids ran up to them and handed both he and Caryn a small, squishy Bigfoot figurine. It was made out of the same material as stress balls. On the back were the words, "Grogan's General Store, Fallport, VA."

"A gift from old man Grogan!" one of the boys said before they both darted off to give away more of the small gifts.

"This is awesome," Caryn said with a huge grin on her face.

It was all Drew could do not to roll his eyes, but he had to admit the quirky gift was kind of funny.

"Hey, guys! Good to see you made it!" Elsie said.

"Look! Did you get one?" Tony asked, holding up his own Bigfoot squishy to show them.

Caryn raised her own and smiled. "We did."

"Cool!"

"I see Art is already holding court," Bristol said from her chair. Rocky had set her up in a comfortable-looking lawn chair and her leg was propped on a small cooler they'd obviously brought as well. Her leg had been re-broken after an obsessed fan had kidnapped and gone all *Misery* on her. But from what Rocky said, it was healing well and she was already up and about with her knee walker.

"He's happy to be back in the swing of things," Caryn reassured her.

"I'm so relieved he's okay," Bristol said sincerely.

When Caryn had met the woman just last week, it had been extremely emotional. Bristol kept apologizing for the attack—her stalker fan was the man who'd stabbed Art in his own home—and Caryn had been overwhelmed by the other woman's support and earnestness. Caryn had told Drew later that her worries about meeting the famous artist had been unfounded. That she was as sweet as everyone had told her she'd be.

"He's great," Caryn reassured her. "Doc Snow gave him an almost clean bill of health, just told him to give himself another month or so before he's off and signing up for Fallport's Autumn 5k."

Drew got to work spreading out the blanket and setting up their chairs while Caryn greeted the others. He was thrilled with how well she got along with everyone. That was important to him, but not as important as it was to Caryn. He knew she craved a deeper connection with people.

He sat back and let the conversations roll over him as he enjoyed a feeling of contentment. This was what he'd wanted when he quit law enforcement. The ability to come to an event like this and just relax. Not have to worry about anyone resenting his presence. He had good friends, a new girlfriend he was eager to get to know better, and a support system that was just as strong, if not stronger than anything he'd had as an officer.

After greeting Duke by giving the bloodhound pets that he didn't even open his eyes to acknowledge, saying hello to Raiden, Tal, Brock, and the others, Caryn came to sit next to him.

"This is great," she said with a smile.

"Yeah," Drew agreed.

"I'm sorry Lilly and Ethan aren't here, but I understand why."

"I'm calling them when the show's over to give them a rundown. In the meantime, they're actually over at Rocky's house working on the barn."

"You think it's going to be ready by Halloween for their wedding?" Caryn asked. "It's not that far away."

"Even if it's not perfect, they won't care," Drew told her. "They just want to be married."

"That's sweet."

Drew shrugged noncommittally, but he couldn't help envying his friend a little. "What about you?" he asked her. "You have an ideal wedding that you've dreamed about your entire life?"

Caryn chuckled. "Nope. I mean, don't get me wrong, I've always wanted to find someone to spend my life with, but after my first disastrous marriage, I'm not that eager to jump into another one."

"What was your first wedding like?" Bristol asked, obviously having overheard their conversation.

Caryn turned to her. "Neither of us had a lot of time to plan anything, with our crazy shifts. So we just decided to go to the justice of the peace one day when we were both off." She shrugged. "It wasn't anything special. I probably should've realized marrying him was a bad idea when I didn't really care about the wedding itself," she said with a shrug.

"I'm not sure it's the wedding ceremony that makes or breaks a marriage," Rocky said as he reached for Bristol's hand. "It doesn't matter if it's done at the courthouse, or if it's a huge ceremony with thousands of guests...it's whether or not the two people involved are ready and willing to pledge to do whatever it takes, together, to make the relationship work long term."

Drew nodded. He agreed with his friend one hundred percent. And he could tell that Caryn did too.

Bristol looked at her fiancé and said, "Is that your way of saying you don't want to wait until December?"

"Not at all," Rocky said easily. "I'd marry you today, but I'd also be happy if it never happened. You're it for me, period, and no ceremony or lack thereof would change that. I'm perfectly willing to wait until December because I know this is important to you. As long as I know you love me and that you're safe and happy, I'm content."

"Awwwww," Elsie said quietly.

"Show off," Zeke told Rocky with a roll of his eyes.

That made everyone laugh.

"Well, I do want a wedding on our fabulous property, because I want to share how amazing you are with everyone," Bristol said firmly.

Rocky picked up her hand and kissed the back of it. "Then that's what you'll get."

"What about you?" Caryn asked Drew quietly when everyone else had started talking again. "What kind of wedding have you thought about having?"

"Honestly? A quiet one. I don't like being in the spotlight, and it seems like kind of a waste to spend all that money on a huge ceremony."

Caryn chuckled. "Spoken like a true accountant."

Drew could feel his cheeks heating, but he shrugged. "Can't help it. I mean, I want my woman to feel like a princess on her special day, but I'd rather not invite half the world. I'd like it to be more of an intimate exchange of vows. Something that's just between the two of us."

"That sounds nice," Caryn said.

They stared at each other for a long moment. Drew wasn't sure what was passing between them, but he liked it. Even though they were in a public park with hundreds of people milling around, it felt as if they were the only two people in the world at that moment.

"Hey, Buckner, I hear you're interested in the open fire-fighter position."

The words were like a bucket of cold water being thrown on them, and Drew turned to see Paul Downs standing in front of him and Caryn. Also with him were some of the other Fallport firefighters—Lou, Dennis, and George.

"Hi, Paul. Yeah, it's an option I'm considering," Caryn said diplomatically.

"We thought you might want to come sit with us. Get to know the crew a little and ask whatever questions you might have about the position and stuff," Paul said.

Drew tensed, but he didn't speak up. He knew this was actually a good thing. Caryn needed to break the ice and talk with Paul at some point, since he was the captain of the station, and him coming over and offering an olive branch, so to speak, was surprising but good.

"Oh, but—"

"We've had a couple of applicants and we need to make a decision," Paul interrupted. "I mean, if you don't want the job, that's fine, but since the mayor asked me to consider you, I figured we should get on with it."

Drew wasn't exactly surprised that word had gotten out

about Caryn staying. Even if she'd just decided herself, it was obvious others in town wanted her to stick around as well.

She looked over at the FFD tent the station had set up. They had bottles of water they were giving out to the locals and several more firefighters were standing around. Drew could sense the conflict within Caryn. She enjoyed being with him and his friends, but she yearned for comradery with her fellow firefighters as well.

"Go," Drew told her.

"But...I'm here with you," she protested.

"I'm not going anywhere," he encouraged.

She gave him a long look. "Are you sure?" she asked.

They had no privacy, not with Paul and his buddies standing there, as well as his own friends listening in, so Drew couldn't really say all the things that he wanted. He simply nodded and said, "Of course."

"Okay. I won't be long."

"It's fine. I'll be right here."

Caryn gave him a shy smile, then stood. She introduced herself to the other men and they each shook her hand in turn. When she walked away, she was already deep in conversation with Lou.

Drew watched her with a sense of pride...and a tiny bit of regret. He hated to share her, but this was what she wanted. To get to know the firefighters and hopefully make a good first impression. Not that he thought that would be a problem. Caryn was extremely capable in what she did.

"Did some guy just come over and steal your girl while you were on a date?" Tal quipped.

"Shut up," Drew said gruffly, glaring at his friend.

"That kind of wasn't cool," Bristol said quietly.

"It's fine," Drew told everyone, not liking the idea that they disapproved of Caryn's decision. He could've told Paul to fuck off. He could've told Caryn that he wanted her to stay with him and his friends. But given what she'd told him about her visit to the station, the Fallport Fire Department *needed* her. He'd be selfish if he insisted she stay by his side when socializing with the firefighters could make or break her chances at the job.

He was genuinely happy for her. Paul's timing could've been better, but Drew wasn't going to deny Caryn this opportunity.

"She's been trying to figure out a way to talk to Paul, so this is a good thing. I guess they haven't gotten along in the past, so for him to come over here and invite her over...it's a promising sign. Especially since she's made the decision to stay."

"She has?"

"Good for her!"

"Do you think I can get a ride on one of the firetrucks?"

That last question came from Tony.

Drew smiled at him. "I'm sure that could be arranged."

"Yay!"

For the next fifteen minutes, Drew kept an eye on Caryn as she talked and laughed with the men at the FFD tent. Everyone seemed to be getting along, which was a relief. Drew had looked forward to this date for days, but he wasn't going to hold her back in any way, and she wasn't the kind of woman who would take kindly to being told who she could and couldn't talk to.

"You all right?" Raiden asked as he took the seat Caryn had vacated.

"Of course. Why wouldn't I be?" Drew said a little too defensively.

"Because your girlfriend abandoned you to hang out with young, buff firefighters?" Raid asked with a completely straight face.

Drew rolled his eyes. "If she gets the job, she'll be hanging out with them all the time," he told his friend.

"True. I didn't like the look in Paul's eyes though."

Drew hadn't taken his gaze off Caryn when Raid sat down, but now he turned to his friend. "What do you mean? What look?"

"Calculating. I used to see the same look all the time when I'd board boats to search for drugs. The bad guys always thought they could outsmart us. And when they figured out they couldn't, they'd get this look in their eyes right before they did something stupid or rash."

"Like?" Drew asked.

"Like pull out a weapon. Or jump overboard."

"Really? Where did they think they were going to go or hide?"

"No clue. But I'm telling you...I saw the same look in Paul's eyes."

Drew sighed. "I appreciate the heads-up. But I can't and won't get in Caryn's way. She just decided to move here, she needs that job. And...she's not naïve. She knows she isn't Paul's favorite person. She needs this chance to show him that they can work together professionally, no matter what their history might be."

"She's certainly more than qualified for the job, but the last thing she needs is to jump out of the frying pan and into the fire," Raiden said.

Drew agreed, but he was in a precarious position. He and Caryn had just started dating, and while they had a fairly deep connection—or at least, *he* thought so—he wasn't sure they were at a point where he could caution her against the only job she felt qualified for. "She's a smart woman," he told Raid. "If Paul's up to something, she'll know."

Raid nodded. "I hope so."

Drew appreciated the fact that his friend didn't argue with him.

With a chin lift, Raid stood and went back over to his chair. Duke hadn't moved from his spot in the grass while Raid was gone. The dog took his naps extremely seriously, and even all the commotion of a park full of people didn't seem to faze him.

As the time approached for the show to start, anticipation filled the air. Everyone might complain about the ridiculousness of the show, but behind closed doors, most of the townspeople were secretly excited about the notoriety it would bring to their little corner of Virginia.

When the opening credits of the show started, the crowd grew quiet. Drew couldn't help but look over at Caryn once more. She was talking to Oscar and a few other men Drew didn't know. A pang of possessiveness rose within him, but he did his best to tamp it down. Caryn was a grown-ass woman, and she was allowed to talk to anyone she wanted.

Turning his attention to the screen, Drew did his best to pay attention. Even though Lilly and Ethan hadn't wanted to come, he knew they were still curious about how the producers had decided to portray the events they'd lived through. Drew hoped for their sake there would be no mention of what Lilly had endured.

* * *

Caryn wasn't sure what to think of the Fallport fire crew. On the surface, everyone was being friendly and positive and saying all the right things, but she couldn't help feeling like something was...off. Since she couldn't put her finger on it, and the men were welcoming enough, she put the feeling out of her mind.

She'd never been made to feel like an equal among a group

of firefighters. Everyone in the service swore that women and men were treated exactly the same, but that wasn't the case, at least not in her experience. Maybe it was different in rural areas like this. She wouldn't have thought so, but this evening was making her want to believe it.

She'd met a bunch of the men. Not only Paul's close friends—Lou, Dennis, and George—but Oscar greeted her with a smile, and she met Nico, Treyvon, Frank, Darnell, Steve, and a few others whose names she couldn't remember right this second. Everyone was interested in hearing her experiences as a firefighter in New York City, and she shared a few stories about some of the more harrowing things she'd endured. In return, they'd told her about some of the more ridiculous calls they'd been on in Fallport.

All in all, mingling with Fallport's firefighters was going surprisingly well. But Caryn couldn't help but look over to where Drew was sitting. Her chair sat vacant between him and the others, and she thought back to what he'd said earlier...about wanting a quiet wedding and not wanting to be in the spotlight. Seeing him sitting a little ways apart from his friends made her heart hurt. She wanted to be over there with him.

She also hated herself a little bit at the moment. She was supposed to be with Drew and his friends. *Wanted* to be with them. But instead, here she was, spending her date with the FFD.

She'd never felt so torn. She was experiencing something she'd wanted throughout her entire professional life—to be part of a team. To fit in. And she couldn't enjoy it because she wanted to be with Drew. But she literally couldn't be in two places at one time.

"So, what do you think of our little crew?" Paul asked, jerking her thoughts back to the present.

Caryn turned to the man who'd done his best to make her

visits to Fallport hell when she'd been a child. Even when she'd visited as an adult, he'd sneered whenever he saw her and generally treated her like shit. The fact that he'd invited her to come talk to everyone tonight seemed very out of character. And while she was happy to have the opportunity to meet the other firefighters, she was still wary of his motives.

"They're all very nice," she told him.

Paul snorted. "Nice. Yup. That's us. So...you're really staying here? Why in the world would you want to leave a nice cushy job in New York for this backwater town?"

Instead of answering him, Caryn shot back, "Why are *you* here? If you hate Fallport so much, why haven't you moved away, found a job in a big city somewhere?"

He stared at her for so long, Caryn resisted the urge to shift uncomfortably where she stood. Then he smiled. "Touché. So, you think you might be interested in the job?"

Caryn nodded. She might not like this man much, but she *did* need a job.

"Cool. If you go online to Fallport's website, you can click on the Fire Department logo and apply through there," he told her.

"Will do."

"I don't know how long it'll take to process the applications, but you'll still have to go through the interviews and stuff," Paul warned her.

"I understand."

"Things are done differently here than in New York."

Caryn frowned and wondered exactly what he was trying to say. "I realize that."

"I hope you do." Then his eyes wandered to something behind her, and Caryn turned to see that Lou and Dennis had approached.

"Hey, you want to hang out with us sometime? Get to know the crew better?" Dennis asked.

Caryn was taken off guard by the invite. "Um...sure." The answer was almost automatic. She wasn't sure what they meant by "hang out," but the last thing she wanted was to piss anyone off right now.

"Cool. We usually go to The Cellar on Friday nights, maybe you could meet up with us there."

Caryn wasn't so sure about that. She'd heard all about the pool hall and how rowdy it was. The owner didn't give a shit what people did in his bar as long as nothing was damaged. Art had told her all about the huge fight that broke out in the place just the other night, and how all the owner, Whip, seemed concerned about was who was going to pay for the broken pool cues. He didn't even care that one of his patrons had gotten seriously injured after someone pulled out a knife in the middle of the fistfight.

"What?" Dennis asked when she hesitated. "You scared to go there?"

Caryn's spine stiffened. How many times had fellow fire-fighters accused her of being scared or intimidated? Too many. As if just because of her gender, surely she must be more timid than her male counterparts. "Not at all," she said with as much confidence as she could muster.

"Great. We'll see you there then. We'll be in touch when we're meeting up again. It'll be fun," Lou said. Then he nodded at her and Paul, and he and Dennis headed to the other side of the tent.

Caryn swallowed hard and reminded herself that this was what she wanted. She wanted to belong to a tight-knit group of firefighters, and if she had to pretend to have a good time socializing at a bar, so be it. It wouldn't be the first time she did something she didn't really want to do in the name of getting along with her co-workers. And any kind of good impression she could make would be a positive thing when it came to getting this job.

Harry Grogan got on the loudspeaker then and thanked everyone for coming. Caryn was about to head back to Drew and the others when George said, "We saved you a seat."

She looked from the empty chair at the end of the row of firefighters, then over to the search and rescue guys. "I should go back," she said as she gestured over to where Drew was sitting.

"What, you'd rather hang out with the nerd?" Paul asked.

Caryn frowned. The answer was, *yes*, she would totally rather hang out with Drew than these guys. But Paul didn't give her a chance to say anything.

"I guess we can't blame her for wanting to get some dick instead of hanging with us, huh?" he said, making all his friends chuckle. Caryn ground her teeth together as the guys told lewd jokes or tried to outdo each other with stories of their sex lives.

On the one hand, she really wanted to solidify her place with the other firefighters. She wanted this job so she could stay in Fallport. And oddly, the fact that they weren't curbing their ribald language or policing their words in front of a woman made her feel more like part of the team than anything else they'd said tonight.

But the longer she stood there listening to these men, her possible future co-workers, demean the women they'd slept with, the more she realized maybe this wasn't the kind of solidarity she'd been looking for all these years.

The show started, and the guys immediately started making fun of every little thing on the screen. While Caryn might not believe in Bigfoot, she definitely didn't like the way these men, who were supposed to be serving the town, ridiculed every local who appeared on the show. Just minutes in, she felt extremely uncomfortable. It was still hard to shake the need to belong, to be included amongst her peers, but she desperately wanted to be anywhere but here.

Her eyes strayed over to Drew once more. At some point, Tony had sat on his lap and had his back against Drew's chest, his head on his shoulder. They watched the show together, and every now and then, Caryn could see Drew saying something to the little boy. Tony would nod his head or laugh, but his attention never strayed from the screen.

That was it. She was done.

"It was great meeting all of you," she said, then without waiting for a response, stood and headed back to Drew.

The episode was almost halfway through, and Caryn mentally kicked herself for not leaving the firefighters sooner. She sat in her chair next to Drew and gave him a small apologetic smile.

"You okay?" he asked.

And once more, Caryn felt regret for leaving this man for one second. He should be pissed at her. Should be resentful. But instead, he was checking on her and making sure she was all right after visiting with men he knew she wasn't so sure about.

"Yeah," she said softly. There was so much more she wanted to say, but the show was still playing and she didn't want to miss any more of it than she already had. And she didn't want to distract Tony, who was completely absorbed in what he was watching.

To her surprise, Drew's free hand reached out and gripped her fingers.

Caryn closed her eyes for a moment. She didn't deserve this man—and she vowed to do better by him. Yes, she wanted the job at the fire station so she could stay, but she didn't want to sacrifice whatever it was she and Drew were forming in the process.

The show ended on a cliffhanger, which Caryn thought

was brilliant. A great way to keep the audience interested and to make sure they came back the next week to watch. By the end of the episode, the "researcher" was still missing and his fellow stars assumed the worst, that Bigfoot had carried him away.

Drew turned to her and asked, "What'd you think?"

Caryn stared at him for a moment before saying, "It wasn't bad. I guess I expected something...different, after hearing about what happened from Lilly."

"Yeah," Drew agreed.

"It was great!" Tony said, hopping off Drew's lap. "I mean, we all know what happens, that Bigfoot didn't really steal that guy away, but they really made it seem like it. I can't wait to see the rest of the show next week!" Then he waggled two of the Bigfoot squishies in front of him as if they were fighting with each other.

"Tony! Please come help us pack up," Elsie said. "You can play with your Bigfoot toys in the car on the way home."

The boy turned without another word and went to help his mom.

Drew started to clean up their area and pack up the stuff they'd brought.

Caryn stood there a little awkwardly. She wanted to be accepted by Drew's friends, and she had a feeling she'd blown it big time by choosing to leave them all behind in favor of hanging out with the firefighters.

"It's okay, you know. We understand," said someone behind her.

She turned to see Raiden, with Duke sitting at his side. The bloodhound was drooling, as he usually seemed to be when he wasn't asleep, but Raid didn't even seem to notice.

"Understand what?" she asked.

"That you need to get to know the men you might be working with. You need to trust them, just as they need to learn to trust you. In emergency situations, there's no time for pettiness or doubt."

Caryn stared at him.

"If you're going to work with them, you need to do what you can to get along."

If anything, his understanding and words of encouragement made her feel even worse than she already did. She'd come to the watch party with Drew, then abandoned him and his friends the second Paul beckoned. She should've gone over there, met everyone, then immediately come back here before the show started. She shouldn't have let her desire to fit in sway her from what she truly wanted to do.

"Right," she said after a moment.

"No one's gonna get upset with you for doing what you have to do in order to make a new life here," Raid said.

"I'm sorry I didn't get to spend more time with you guys," Caryn told him.

Raid shrugged. "No one's keeping score," he assured her. "I'm sure we'll have plenty of opportunities to hang out." With that, he briefly scratched behind Duke's ears, then turned to pick up his chair.

"You ready to get Art?"

Caryn jerked in surprise. She turned and saw Drew standing next to her with their chairs under one arm, the blanket thrown over his shoulder, and the cooler in his other hand. He'd managed to pack everything while she was talking with his friend. She reached for the cooler. "Let me carry that."

"I've got it," Drew told her, and Caryn winced.

"I'm sorry," she whispered.

"Nothing to be sorry for."

But Caryn knew he was wrong. She'd been an idiot, and she had no idea how to fix what she'd done. Yes, she'd come back to watch the rest of the show with him, but she regretted leaving his side in the first place.

She walked next to Drew as they headed toward where Art was sitting with Silas and Otto. Her grandfather talked nonstop all the way back to Drew's Jeep. He recounted just about every part of the show, sometimes in disgust and other times with excitement. No matter how much he might've not wanted to enjoy the paranormal program, it seemed as if he did anyway.

Drew got the chairs and stuff stashed in the back of the Jeep and made sure Art was comfortable before climbing behind the wheel. As soon as he started the engine, his phone rang. He answered it through the Bluetooth in the vehicle.

"Hey, it's Ethan. So? How was it?"

"Not bad, actually. You're on speaker, and I've got Caryn and Art with me, by the way."

"Hey, guys," Ethan said.

Both Caryn and Art said their hellos to Drew's friend.

"So? Give me the skinny so I can share it with Lilly."

"Well, for one, the cinematography was excellent. Tell Lilly she's a hell of a videographer."

"I'm sure you had no idea which shots were hers," Ethan said with a chuckle.

"Okay, that's partly true, but I do remember some of the stuff she specifically filmed, like at the town hall meeting that first day, so I'm not completely talking out of my ass here," Drew said with a small laugh.

"Right. What else?"

Caryn listened as Drew gave his friend a synopsis of the show and what it covered. Then he said, "We weren't in this one, as they cut it right as everyone realized Trent was missing...and presumably carried off by Bigfoot. But overall, it was actually well done. The stuff the crew was doing in the woods to try to entice Bigfoot to show his face was all bullshit, but entertaining."

"So we can definitely expect an influx of people," Ethan said.

"Oh yeah," Drew said.

"Where do you think they're going to go with the story line next week? Do you think they're going to share all the details about Joey being the culprit and killing his friend?"

"No idea...but I'm guessing probably not. Anyone could look up the details on the Internet if they want, but most people are lazy and will wait to see what happens on the show next week. I'm guessing the producers will probably string out the missing-person aspect and the Bigfoot connection. Then there will probably be a small note at the end or something, dedicating the season to Trent, and that'll be that."

"Cynical much?" Ethan said with a chuckle.

"Tell me you don't think the same thing," Drew countered.

"Okay, you're right. Anything in the show that'll bother Lilly if she watches it?" Ethan asked.

Caryn's respect for the man rose at hearing that. He clearly didn't give a shit about the show, but he did worry about its effect on his fiancée.

A longing hit her...so strong it made her belly clench. Had anyone worried about her like that? Ever? She didn't think so. She knew Art loved her, but a family member's love was different from that of a partner, of course.

"No," Drew said. "I mean, it might bring back some unpleasant memories of what she went through, but it's all about the team of so-called investigators in the field trying to find Bigfoot."

"Okay, thanks, man. I recorded the show so we could watch it later, but wasn't sure if we should."

"You want me to come over and watch it with you guys?" Drew asked.

And once again, Caryn was reminded of what a good guy the man next to her was.

"I think we're good. Knowing you think it'll be okay is good enough for me. Sorry we didn't come tonight."

"Don't apologize. We understand. Everyone would've totally been watching Lilly for her reaction, which would've made her, and you, uncomfortable. It's all good."

"Yeah, that's a big reason why we didn't come."

"Old man Grogan's got some pretty cool Bigfoot shit though," Drew said. "Shirts, hats, the whole shebang. And I think Elsie picked up an extra Bigfoot stress ball thing for you guys tonight."

"Tell me you're kidding," Ethan groaned.

"Nope."

"Well, we knew he was planning on capitalizing on the show airing. But seriously? Stress balls?"

"They're kind of cute," Caryn blurted.

Ethan chuckled. "Right. Sure they are. Anyway, I'll let you go. See you soon."

"Later," Drew told his friend.

Caryn and Art both added their goodbyes and Drew clicked off the connection. A minute later, he pulled up in front of Art's house. He got out to help Art out of the back seat, but Caryn couldn't make herself exit the vehicle.

"I'll just go on in. Take your time," Art said with a sly smile as he walked slowly toward the front door of his house.

"Can we talk?" Caryn asked softly, turning in her seat to look at Drew.

He studied her for a long moment, then nodded as he returned to the driver's seat and closed his door.

Biting her lip, Caryn took a deep breath. She knew she needed to have this conversation, but she wasn't sure where to start. Her stomach was in knots and she felt like shit about how the night had gone. She'd been so excited to spend time with Drew, and she felt like she'd ruined things between them.

As she opened her mouth to apologize, Drew reached over and slid his hand around the back of her neck.

And just like that, tears sprang to Caryn's eyes. Why was he being so nice? He should be pissed at her. She'd left him to go hang out with a bunch of other men. If their roles had been reversed, she wouldn't be so forgiving.

Knowing she needed to say something, she raised her gaze and looked at him.

CHAPTER TEN

Drew's feelings were all over the place, but when it was obvious Caryn was struggling to talk to him, he couldn't help but reach out for her. He wrapped his hand around her nape and caressed the sensitive skin there with his thumb.

He hated to see the anxiety and regret in her tear-filled eyes as she looked at him.

"I'm sorry," she croaked.

But Drew shook his head. He'd gone through a gamut of emotions in the last couple of hours, but he genuinely understood why Caryn had left to go talk to the firefighters. He'd hoped to have a fun first date, but he should've known *any* kind of date when half of Fallport was along for the ride was wishful thinking.

"As I said earlier, you have nothing to apologize for."

"Drew, I left you to hang out with stupid Paul and his friends."

"I would've been upset if you *hadn't* gone," Drew told her.

Caryn gave him a skeptical look.

"Look, I get it. You need to make a connection with those guys if you want the job. You told me that you and Paul haven't gotten along in the past, and the fact that he came over to see if you wanted to join them was a good thing. I'm not mad, Caryn. Promise."

"The whole time I was talking to them, I wished I was sitting with you," she said softly.

"It's okay," he said.

But Caryn shook her head. It was obvious she was struggling with the decision she'd made. "All my life, I've been the odd man out. I didn't have the cool clothes because my mom wouldn't buy them for me. I didn't make friends easily because I was the 'weird' tomboy kid. In college, things got a little better, and when I got my first firefighter job, I was on top of the world. I had visions of being best friends with my fellow first responders. But that didn't happen. I was on the outside once again, simply because of my gender. It didn't matter that I worked twice as hard as everyone else or that I could do everything they could, I was still treated with derision.

"I changed stations, hoping it would get better, but it didn't. With every move to a different firehall, I had hopes that maybe I'd find my place. But time after time, I was shunned. Sometimes directly, and other times more subtly, but I felt it. All I want is to be accepted for who I am. For what I can do. My skills. Because I'm a damn good firefighter, Drew. Tonight, I just...I was right back there in that hopeful stage. Wanting to be accepted and be a part of something special, but not really holding my breath that it would happen.

"But...even though most of those guys aren't really people I'd choose to hang out with, they seemed to accept me. It was a heady feeling, and I was happy with how open they were."

"That's good," Drew said.

"It is, but at the same time, I was upset that I wasn't with you."

"Look at me, Caryn," Drew ordered. He waited until she'd raised her gaze to meet his. He pulled her a little closer to him as he spoke. "You're amazing. I haven't seen you at a fire, but it's obvious you love what you do. And I've worked out with you and seen firsthand that you can more than hold your own. You've been picking up the things I've been teaching you about search and rescue faster than I did when I was learning. I hope things work out with the firefighting gig, and I'm glad that Paul seems to have finally gotten the stick out of his ass when it comes to you, but...I need you to truly hear what I'm about to say."

She nodded.

"No matter what happens between us, no matter what you decide to do for a job here in Fallport, I accept you *exactly* as you are. As does Ethan. And the rest of the team. Elsie, Lilly, and Bristol too. We're all misfits in our own right, and you're one of us. You don't have to prove anything to belong, you already do. Understand?"

In response, Caryn closed her eyes and he heard her breath hitch.

He gave her time to get her emotions under control before he pulled her forward and kissed her on the forehead. "I missed being by your side all night, but at no time did I *ever* resent you for doing what you needed to do in order to further your career."

Her eyes opened and she took a deep breath. "You're too good to be true," she whispered.

"Nope. Just a man who knows a good thing when she appears in front of him," he said with a small shrug. "I wouldn't feel right if I didn't say one thing though...but I don't want you to get mad."

Caryn blinked away the tears that had been swimming in her eyes. "I think if you didn't get mad that I ditched you on our first date, and have been very understanding about it, I can listen to what you have to say without losing my cool."

"I don't trust Paul," Drew blurted. Caryn frowned, and he went on quickly. "I don't know him, not really. Our paths haven't crossed all that much, but with everything you've told me about your history with the man, I'm having a hard time understanding why he'd suddenly be so eager to be buddy-buddy with you."

"I'm a good firefighter," Caryn said.

"I know you are. And you'd be a hell of an addition to the FFD for sure. But I can't help but be suspicious of his motives." He held his breath as he waited for Caryn's reaction to his mistrust of the man.

To his relief, she nodded. "I thought the same thing. I mean, I was relieved I didn't have to deal with his asshole side tonight, but it *does* seem like an abrupt one-eighty in terms of his feelings toward me."

"All I'm asking is that you stay on your toes. I know you want to be accepted by them, but be on the lookout for any shenanigans," Drew told her.

"You think he's setting me up for something?" Caryn asked.

"I have no idea, but it'd be worth it to be cautious."

"I agree. And I will be."

"Good."

"Drew, do you think we can...have a redo on our first date? Even though I was the one who messed it up, I wouldn't mind a do-over. Maybe without my grandfather tagging along," Caryn said.

"And half of Fallport?" Drew asked with a smile, relieved she hadn't gotten upset with him for not trusting Paul's seemingly abrupt turnaround in his attitude.

"Yeah, that too."

"You have anything in mind? Something you haven't done yet and want to?"

"Maybe we could stay in and watch a movie or something at your place? That way there won't be a chance of anyone or anything interrupting us."

"Except a call out for a search," Drew said dryly.

Caryn chuckled. "Right, except for that."

"I'd love that," he told her.

"I don't even know where you live," Caryn said.

Drew shrugged. "It's not a secret. I rent a small house on the other side of the square. It's nothing fancy."

"I'm sure it's fine."

Drew smiled at her, distracted from their conversation by the way she licked her lips.

"Drew?"

"Yeah?"

"Are you going to kiss me or what?"

He smiled and, without another word, lowered his head. How long they made out in his Jeep, he didn't know, but by the time he pulled back, he knew he was already a goner for this woman. Tonight had been tough, for both of them, but he liked that they'd been able to talk it out. That she hadn't hesitated in wanting to clear the air. And a little part of him deep inside was relieved she regretted spending a lot of the night trying to suck up to the firefighters. He didn't blame her, and he understood, but still...he'd missed her.

"You still want to work out in the morning?" she asked when she had her breath back.

"Absolutely. You aren't slacking off on me, are you?"

She rolled her eyes. "As if."

"You want to run, do the obstacle course again, or head out into the woods?"

"Hike," she said without hesitation.

Drew couldn't help but feel satisfied with that answer. He

enjoyed the time they spent together walking the trails around Fallport. She was like a sponge, soaking in every bit of knowledge he shared about search and rescue, and he loved simply being around her.

When neither of them made a move to separate, Drew's hand still curled around the back of her neck and hers on his thigh, he smiled.

"I guess I should probably get going. I'm sure Art's neighbors are keeping track of how long we sit here and make out."

"Don't care," Drew told her with a shrug.

"You know what? Neither do I," Caryn told him. "Which is a huge step for me because usually I'm obsessed with what others think about me."

"You shouldn't be. Others not liking you is a reflection on *them*, not you," Drew told her. "You're smart, considerate, hardworking, and a million other adjectives. Not everyone in this world is going to like you, and it's okay to be all right with that. The only people who matter are your loved ones. Be proud of who you are, what you've overcome, and what you've accomplished."

She tilted her head. "It's not quite that easy."

"Of course it's not. I think humans are wired to want to belong. To be liked. But I've found that it's literally impossible to be friends with everyone. Some will dislike you because of the color of your hair or skin, your weight, your gender, the way you speak, or a hundred other stupid reasons."

"Like the kind of uniform you wear?" she asked silently.

"Exactly. People hated me on sight simply because they saw my badge and nothing else. No matter how much I wanted to help them, they couldn't see past their own judgements and my occupation. I get it though, there are some incredibly shitty cops out there, and every one of their bad actions reflect on each and every one of us who swear to protect and serve. But just because someone didn't like me, didn't mean I shouldn't do my job. And it's the same in every profession. Believe it or not, there have been people we've been sent into the forest to find and rescue who've hated us on sight."

"That doesn't make any sense," Caryn said with a frown.

"I know. But it doesn't matter, we'll do what we can to make sure they're comfortable, not hurt, and get them back to their loved ones. So...screw anyone who doesn't like you for who you are, Caryn. They're the ones missing out, not you."

"I like thinking about it like that," she admitted.

"Good."

"I'll try. But it's never been easy for me to dismiss others' thoughts so easily."

Drew hated that for her. "I'm assuming from what you've said, and not said, that you didn't have a good childhood. Do you keep in touch with your mother?"

"No," she said shortly.

"Right. And since Art never talks about his daughter, I'm assuming there's no love lost there either?"

Caryn took a deep breath. "I'm not ready to talk about her, but yeah, she wasn't a good mom or daughter."

"Okay, but I'm here if you ever *do* want to talk about it."

"Thanks. Do you have a family?"

"Well, I wasn't produced in a secret government lab in a vat of goo," he joked, wanting to ease the tension.

She laughed, as he'd intended.

"My parents weren't great," he admitted. "They didn't have much time for me when I was growing up, but they provided me with the basics. I moved out right after graduating from high school. Went to community college and got my criminal justice degree and finished up my undergraduate while working full time at a dry cleaners. I was accepted into the Virginia State Police Academy and the rest is history. Both my parents died not too long ago, my dad from a heart attack and my mom from issues having to do with her being an alcoholic for most of her life. I wish we'd had a better relationship, but it is what it is."

Caryn stroked his arm. "I'm sorry."

"We were practically strangers when they died, which I regret, but they never were very receptive to having any kind of real relationship the few times I'd reached out. Again, it's their loss."

"It really is. Because you're pretty wonderful."

For that, she got another kiss. Drew did his best to not to let things go too far this time. There was nothing he wanted more than to pull her against him and show her how much she was beginning to mean to him. He was falling hard and fast but was willing to take things at her pace until she was just as sure she wanted to be in a relationship.

"Six o'clock okay for tomorrow?" he asked.

"Perfect. I should probably go in and make sure my grandfather's all settled."

"He's probably snoring by now," Drew said. "He had an exciting evening."

"He loved holding court and talking to everyone who stopped by to see him," Caryn agreed.

"He's one of the staples of this town for sure," Drew said. Then he forced himself to drop his hand from her nape, already missing the feel of her soft skin against his rough palm.

"Thanks for being understanding about tonight. It won't happen again," she said.

"What won't?" he asked.

"Me ditching you to hang out with someone else."

"We've talked about this. You didn't ditch me," he insisted.

"I did, but I appreciate you being so nice about it," she said with a shrug.

Drew couldn't stop himself from leaning in for one more kiss. "Okay," he told her when he pulled back. He exited the Jeep and walked around to her side. Caryn was already standing next to her door when he arrived. He pulled her into a long and heartfelt hug, feeling content when she returned it just as fiercely.

"Go on," he said, his voice coming out a little gruffly. "Get inside before I *really* give your neighbors something to talk about."

She giggled, as he'd wanted her to. "Thanks for tonight. And for being so awesome. See you in the morning."

Drew waited until she'd opened the door to the house and waved at him before climbing back into the driver's seat of his Jeep. As he drove to his small house, he thought about the evening. It hadn't gone like he'd expected, but in the end, he felt as if he and Caryn had somehow still managed to become closer.

Relationships were never without their bumps and curves in the road. He was just relieved they'd been able to talk things out. He truly understood her desire to be included in the firefighters' inner circle. He just hoped they wouldn't use Caryn's eagerness to be liked and accepted against her.

* * *

Paul Downs sat on the back deck of his parents' house with Lou, Dennis, and George as they polished off a case of beer.

"That show was such bullshit," Dennis said in disgust.

"Completely. And it's gonna be a pain in our ass because it'll bring idiots to town that we'll have to deal with," George agreed.

"Right? More calls for heart attacks that are just gas.

People dialing 9-1-1 about a fire in the woods that's just smoke from someone's campfire. We aren't gonna be able to get a good night's sleep without being interrupted by a call."

"Maybe we can use it to squeeze more money out of the city council," Lou mused. "We could use a better TV and more comfortable chairs in the station. What do you think, Paul?"

"I think you're right. Maybe we can upgrade the appliances too, even convince them we need a full-time cook."

The men all chuckled and agreed.

"What was up with that chick tonight?" Lou asked after taking a swig of his beer.

Paul grimaced. "Caryn Buckner. She's been a pain in the ass for as long as I can remember."

"How long's that?" George asked.

"Since we were kids. She spent summers here because her mom was a deadbeat or something. I don't know and I don't care. But she thought her shit didn't stink back then, same as she does now. She looked down on the local kids and thought she was smarter than everyone. But I'm gonna get the last laugh," Paul said with a smile.

"Yeah?" Lou asked. "Whatcha got in mind?"

"Bitch thinks she's a hotshot city firefighter, and she wants the open position at the FFD. That shit ain't happening as long as *I'm* captain. I don't care how good she looks on paper. No chick is gonna come in and start trying to change shit in my station. Besides, I'm not risking my life by having her on the squad. There's no way she'd be able to drag my ass out of a burning building. Fucking girls shouldn't be allowed to be firefighters. They can't hack it."

The other men all agreed noisily with their friend.

"But you told her how to apply," George said. "Encouraged her to do so, in fact."

"I did," Paul said with a smirk. "But that doesn't mean I have to choose her. I'd never hire her to join us."

"What if the council insists on it? You know, to diversify or some bullshit?" Lou asked.

Paul scowled. "I'll quit before I work with that bitch," he said fiercely. "Anyway, I have a plan. She's obviously gagging to be part of our crew, but before that happens...we need to make her prove she's got what it takes to be on the FFD."

Grins formed on the other men's faces.

"I already talked to Dennis about this before tonight. He set the ball rolling for her first initiation," Paul said.

"Our weekly pool game at The Cellar," George said, obviously recalling the conversation earlier that evening.

"Yup," Dennis said with a smirk.

"You think she'll show?" Lou asked. "You know how people around here hate that place."

"She'll show," Dennis said. "She wants this job, and she knows the only way to get it is to kiss our asses."

"Maybe she'll kiss something else," George said, grabbing his dick.

Everyone laughed.

"Wouldn't mind sticking my cock down her throat," Dennis added. "But I'm guessing she's too uptight for that shit. At least at first."

"You think she slept her way through her career?" Lou asked.

"I'm sure she has. No way any chick could've gotten the kinds of jobs she has without screwing the captains and lieutenants above her," Paul said. "But I ain't touching that pussy. I just want to put her in her place. Make sure she knows despite what she thinks, she's not one of us—and never will be. I'll let her think she has a shot, but in the end, no matter how much she sucks up, she's not gonna get the job."

"Cheers to that," Lou said, holding up his beer can.

The others followed and clanked their cans together.

"We've got a week to think of something good to do for her first initiation," Paul said. "If she doesn't get a clue, we'll come up with something else. Until she figures out she'll never be a member of the FFD."

"Fucking women. Ruining everything," Dennis spat, then let out a huge belch.

"Listen to this," Lou said with a smile, lifting one ass cheek off the plastic chair and farting long and loud.

"Gross, man," George said, laughing as he waved a hand in front of his nose.

"We don't need no woman coming in and ruining what we've built," Lou finished.

"Damn straight," Paul said. "Especially not Caryn fucking Buckner."

"Yeah, fuck her," Dennis said.

"Ha. Buckner, fuck her...Fuckner," Lou said, cackling hysterically at his own joke.

Paul took another swig of his beer, satisfied that his friends had so quickly agreed with his decision. How easily they were steered toward rejecting Caryn. The truth was, he couldn't even remember why he didn't like her. Had no idea what she'd done all those years ago to earn his ire. But it didn't matter. He didn't want a female on *his* firefighting squad, and he'd do whatever it took to make sure that didn't happen.

CHAPTER ELEVEN

"Hey, girl, it's Lilly. How are you?"

Caryn smiled when she heard the other woman's voice on the line. It was three days since the paranormal show had aired, and she'd sent a text to Lilly wanting to make sure she was okay. Instead of texting back, the other woman had immediately called.

"I'm good," Caryn told her.

"Glad to hear it. You up for a girls' night?" Lilly asked without beating around the bush.

Surprised, Caryn could only blurt, "What?"

"A girls' night. I asked Bristol and Elsie, and they're in. Bristol suggested inviting Khloe too, and I thought Finley might want to come. So now we've got a whole thing planned and I was hoping you'd join us."

Caryn wasn't so sure. While she'd met the other women— other than Khloe, who she knew worked in the library with Raiden—that was about it. She didn't know them well at all. Didn't want to feel like the outsider. "Um...when?"

"Tonight!" Lilly said happily. "Everyone's gonna meet at Bristol's place around six. Don't worry about eating before you come, we're ordering pizza and wings and other bad-for-you food from the diner. And I'm sure if she comes, Finley will bring some treats from her bakery. Trust me, even day-old cookies and pastries are to die for if Finley made them. Please say you'll come!"

Caryn couldn't stop the smile that formed. "It sounds like fun." And surprisingly, it did.

"Yay!" Lilly exclaimed, and it was all Caryn could do not to burst out laughing. "We're gonna have wine and beer, and I think the fixin's for some mixed drinks too. And Rocky already said he'd drive anyone home who needed it, so no one has to drink and drive. But don't worry, he won't be here during our girl time. He and Ethan will hang out back at our house."

"Can I bring anything?" Caryn asked, tentatively getting excited about hanging out with Lilly and the other women.

"Nope, I think it's all covered."

But there was no way Caryn was going to show up empty-handed. She wanted to contribute to the fun. She had just the thing in mind, but decided to make it a surprise.

"Oh, but...I feel as if I need to warn you," Lilly said.

Caryn tensed. "About what?"

"We're all gonna want to know all about you and the hot accountant. And for the record, you guys make an adorable couple."

Caryn could feel her cheeks heat. This was Fallport, of course people were talking about her and Drew, but it still felt a little weird. Especially compared to the city, where you were pretty much invisible to everyone and no one cared what you did in your time off or who you were dating. "I'm not sure there's much to tell yet," she told Lilly honestly.

"Doesn't matter. We're gonna beg you for details anyway," Lilly said easily. "If you want a ride, just give me a yell and I can pick you up before I head out to Bristol's. Or I'm sure

Drew would drop you off as well. Will Art be all right if you get home late?"

It was nice to hear Lilly thinking about her grandfather. He was lucky to be so well liked in the small town. "Yeah, he's doing a lot better. Practically back to his old self. Ornery as hell."

Lilly chuckled. Then she said in a serious tone, "He's lucky to have you."

"No," Caryn countered, "*I'm* the lucky one." She'd told Drew the same thing, and she meant it.

"Of course. Now, before I get too verklempt here, I'm excited to hang with you tonight. See you around six."

"I'm looking forward to it. Thanks for inviting me," Caryn told her.

They said their goodbyes and Caryn stood in the middle of the living room, staring into space for a long moment. She was interrupted by Art.

"Whatcha just standing there for?" he asked in his usual blunt way.

Jerking in surprise, Caryn smiled and turned to her grandfather. "Just thinking," she said.

"Well, think your way over to the table and sit your tush down while I fix us some lunch."

Caryn rolled her eyes. As if she was going to sit on her ass while her grandfather waited on her. He knew as well as she did that wasn't going to happen. "What are you in the mood for?"

"Thought I'd make up some fried egg sandwiches," he told her.

"Sounds good. What can I do?" Caryn asked. She had to keep reminding herself that Art wasn't an invalid. And before she'd arrived, he'd been more than capable of looking after himself. She didn't want to stifle that, but she *did* want to help.

"You can grab the cheese and start slicing. And don't be stingy either. Last time I could barely taste the cheese because you sliced the pieces so thin."

Caryn knew her grandfather was just giving her shit. She simply smiled and said, "Yes, sir."

He grinned at her and they walked together toward the kitchen. Caryn knew after he ate, he'd head over to the square to sit with his friends in their usual spot outside the post office. "I'm not going to be home for dinner tonight," she told Art. "Maybe you can go over to Sunny Side Up and grab something."

"Where ya goin'?" Art asked.

"Lilly called and invited me to a girls' night," Caryn said.

Art froze, the frying pan in midair as he turned to stare at her. "Really?"

"Yeah. Why?"

The older man shrugged and put the pan on the stove. "She's good people," he said. "Knew it from the moment I met her. Even though she was working on that stupid show, she wasn't like the others. I could see it a mile away. Assuming Elsie and Bristol will be there too?" he asked.

"I think so," Caryn told him. "And she mentioned something about Finley and Khloe coming, as well."

Art turned to her again—and Caryn could see a tear in his eye. She stared at him in alarm. "Granddad? Are you all right? Come on, let's get you to a seat."

He waved her off and shook his head. "I'm fine," he said gruffly. "It's just...in all the times you've visited, I haven't seen you connect to many people."

Caryn pressed her lips together. He wasn't wrong. She'd been too much of an outsider when she was young, and as an adult, she hadn't spent enough time in the small town to really make any connections. "I also got invited to hang out with guys from the Fallport Fire Department this weekend."

Art frowned at that. "With that Paul Downs character and his friends?"

After Caryn nodded, her grandfather asked, "Hang out where? I'm not sure it's appropriate for you to be spending time with a bunch of men."

"Grandpa, I'm forty-one years old," Caryn said in exasperation. "I can take care of myself. I'm not going to an orgy or to smoke pot or anything."

"Still. I don't like him or his friends."

"If I'm hired, I'll be spending a lot of time with them," Caryn told her grandfather softly. She respected his opinion. He'd lived here in Fallport almost his entire life, and Lord knew he heard everything about everyone. His not liking Paul made her uneasy, but if she stayed, if she got the job at the FFD, she'd be seeing a lot more of the man and his friends.

Art harumphed and turned back to the stove.

Caryn pressed her lips together in frustration—mostly because she agreed with her grandfather. After years of animosity, she didn't fully trust Paul's abrupt change of heart at the watch party. Even Drew had cautioned her against him. But what was she supposed to do? She needed to befriend him and the other guys if she wanted even a chance at the job.

"I know you will," her grandfather said. He sighed and turned his head to meet her eyes. "I just worry about you."

Caryn was almost overwhelmed with love for this man. "I know. And I hope you know that I worry about you too."

"I think I got that when you came down here the second you heard I was hurt. And while I might be ninety-one years old, I can take care of myself," he said, echoing her words from a moment ago.

Caryn burst out laughing. "Right. So...how about you take care of yourself and your favorite granddaughter by getting on with making us some sandwiches."

He shot her a grin and turned back to the stove. "Yes, ma'am."

Later that afternoon, Caryn was alone, doing some housework, when her phone rang again. She looked at the screen and saw it was Drew calling. Even seeing his name had the ability to make doing laundry and cleaning the floors seem not so bad.

"Hi!" she said when she answered.

"Hey, yourself," he responded. "You sound happy."

"Just glad to hear from you."

His voice deepened as he said, "I feel the same when I hear your voice. I heard through the grapevine that you're going over to Bristol's house tonight with the others."

"Yeah. Lilly called me earlier. Why? Something I should know?"

"No, not at all. They're all great. I was just calling to see if you needed a ride over there, and if you wanted me to pick you up when you were ready to head home."

"Do you mind? I don't want to interrupt you or anything."

"I wouldn't have offered if I minded. And seeing you is never an interruption."

Butterflies swarmed in her belly.

"Too cheesy?" Drew asked when she didn't respond.

"No. I just...I guess I'm not used to hearing things like that."

"Which is a shame," Drew said. "What time do you want me to swing by?"

He was such a mixture of mushy and matter-of-fact. Caryn couldn't say she hated it. "I guess things are starting around six or so," she told him.

"I can be there around ten till, if that's okay. It doesn't take long to get to Bristol and Rocky's place."

"That sounds good. Thank you."

"It's not a hardship, Caryn," he said, and she could practically hear the smile in his voice.

"I don't know how long I'll be," she warned him. "But Lilly said that Rocky could drive us home if we needed it."

"I'll be there, just give me a call," Drew said.

"Even if it's late?" she asked.

"Hon, I used to work the late shift. I'm still kind of a night owl. It's fine. Besides, if you think I'm gonna miss out on seeing my girl tipsy or drunk, you're insane."

Caryn laughed. "I'm not much of a drinker, so it's not going to take much."

"I bet you're adorable. Anyway, I'll see you in a few hours. You're going to have a great time."

"I hope so."

"You will."

The confidence in Drew's tone made Caryn relax a bit. She hadn't exactly been worried about tonight, but maybe nervous was a better word. These women were important to Drew. She wanted them to like her.

After she hung up the phone, she found herself standing in the middle of the room, once more staring into space. Thinking of Drew calling her "my girl."

She shook her head and grabbed the mop handle. She needed to stop her silly daydreaming and get her chores done so she could get ready for tonight.

* * *

Drew showed up at her door right at five-fifty, but they didn't leave until a little past six. When she'd opened the door, he'd taken one look and gently pushed her inside, closed the door, and proceeded to kiss the living daylights out of her.

He brushed his thumb over her lips when he finally pulled back, smiling.

"What was that for?" she'd asked.

"Because it's been too long since I've seen you," he'd responded.

Of course, they'd seen each other that morning for their workout, but Caryn hadn't rolled her eyes or told him he was ridiculous. She'd simply basked in the glowy feeling he'd given her.

He'd kissed her once more—a lighter, less-intense kiss—when he'd dropped her off and told her to have fun. Of course she was late, and since the girls were all sitting out on the wraparound porch sipping wine, they'd all pounced on her the second he'd left.

She'd gotten through the initial grilling about her and Drew's relationship and now they were all sitting inside on the couches, relaxing after having stuffed their faces with the food Finley had picked up from the diner.

"I'm stuffed," Elsie complained.

"Ugh, me too," Bristol agreed.

"But are you too stuffed for another glass of wine?" Lilly asked with a smile.

"No way!"

"Never!"

The two women answered at the same time.

Caryn figured this was a good time to bring out the surprise she'd brought. The girls had seen the bag in her hands when she arrived, but hadn't asked about it since they were too focused on firing off questions about her and Drew.

"I brought something for you guys to try," Caryn said as she got up. She was already feeling mellow from the glass and a half of wine she'd had with dinner, but she couldn't wait to share what she'd brought with the girls.

Caryn was surprised the mysterious Khloe hadn't come tonight, but from the little Bristol and the others had told her, Caryn wanted to get to know her better. Apparently, she had some deep dark secrets that made her standoffish—at least, the others suspected as much. Of course, that just made them want to bring her into the fold even more. And because there was obviously some kind of angsty tension between her and Raiden, their curiosity was even higher.

Caryn pulled the bottle out of the bag and held it up as she dramatically said, "Tah-dah!"

"Ooooh, I'm guessing that's alcohol," Lilly said.

"You'd guess right," Caryn told her and the others. "It's apple pie moonshine. Hometown stuff too, straight from the source."

She saw the confusion on everyone's faces. Caryn's arm dropped to her side, still holding the bottle. "*What*? You guys haven't tried Clyde's special moonshine?"

"Clyde?" Finley asked.

"He's the grumpy old guy who lives on the outskirts of Fallport. I swear I thought he was going to pull out a shotgun when we got too close to his property—and one of his stills in the forest, when we were filming in the spring," Lilly said.

"Oh, I've heard about him," Bristol said.

"He's not really all that grumpy," Caryn told them.

"He's not? Could'a fooled me," Lilly said. "He definitely wasn't happy with us. There was actually a short time when everyone thought he'd killed Trent, because his tent and other camping stuff was found in a dumpster on Clyde's property."

"That's because he found it abandoned in the middle of the woods," Caryn said, defending the man. "Wouldn't you be pissed if you found that kind of crap littering your property?"

"Of course," Lilly conceded.

"Besides, he didn't even know Trent was missing at that point," Caryn said. "Otherwise, he would've called Simon himself to tell him about what he found. He thought he was doing a good deed by cleaning up the trail. Instead, he almost got thrown in jail. Well, not really, but he was grilled pretty hard by the cops."

"You sound as if you know him well," Bristol said.

Caryn took a deep breath. She was overreacting, and she knew it. "I just...I know what it's like to be an outcast. It's not fun. And Clyde doesn't deserve the animosity he gets from the people in this town."

"But isn't making moonshine illegal?" Finley asked.

Since Caryn didn't hear any censure in her tone, she relaxed. "Mostly, yeah, but Clyde actually has a permit, and he sells his stuff to stores around Virginia and the south."

Four pairs of eyes widened.

"He does?" Elsie asked.

"Uh-huh. And I know for a fact that he donates a lot of what he earns to charity. Mostly animal rescue groups, because he's not a big fan of people, not that I can blame him. I guess he's a hermit for a reason...and I hate that the locals can't get over his grumpiness long enough to see the good man underneath."

"How in the world do you know so much about him?" Lilly asked, leaning forward.

Caryn realized she was still standing in front of the other women, as if preaching or something. She spun and headed to the kitchen to grab some cups as she answered Lilly's question.

"I met him one summer when I was here. I was playing by myself in the woods and got a little turned around. I came upon him at one of his rundown cabins in the woods—he's got a few. More like shacks, really. He scared me at first, but then I started talking to him and found out he was actually kind of nice. He showed me his still, explained how it worked, gave me a lecture on being by myself in the woods and how dangerous that was, and made sure I got back on the right trail to go back to Art's house."

"How old is Clyde, anyway?" Finley asked.

"I have no clue," Caryn said as she came back into the living area with the cups. "Old. Anyway...you guys have to try this."

She put the cups down on the coffee table, opened the bottle, and began to pour shots of the moonshine.

"I'm not sure. I don't really like stuff that's too strong," Elsie said.

"And I'm guessing moonshine doesn't taste all that great," Bristol added.

Lilly and Finley looked just as skeptical.

"Trust me," Caryn said.

"So says the badass firefighter who goes into a burning building when everyone else is running out of it," Lilly muttered, but gamely reached for one of the cups.

Everyone else did the same and smelled the concoction in their cups with suspicion.

"Hey, this smells kind of good," Bristol said with a raised eyebrow.

"It does," Finley agreed. "Like cinnamon. And I think nutmeg too."

"Leave it to the baker to sniff out the sweet ingredients," Elsie said with a laugh.

"I don't know what's in it," Caryn admitted. "But it tastes exactly like apple pie, so those guesses are probably correct. It's got a strong kick though, so I don't recommend drinking more than a shot or two. I guess the longer it sits around, the more the alcohol ferments or something? I have no idea how it works, but when I got this batch from Clyde, he told me it had been 'brewing' for a while."

"Right, so let's do this," Bristol said.

"A toast," Lilly said with a nod as she got up on her knees and scooted closer to the others.

Everyone held out their cups.

"To new friends. To small towns. To us!" Lilly said.

"I'll toast to that!"

"To us!"

"Amen!"

Everyone clinked their plastic cups together and downed their shot of the moonshine.

There was some coughing, but as Caryn looked around, she saw all her new friends had smiles on their faces.

"That's *good*!" Bristol exclaimed.

"You're right, it tasted exactly like apple pie!" Elsie agreed.

"I'm thinking I need another taste to make sure I like it," Finley added.

Everyone chuckled and held out their cups to Caryn.

She poured another shot for everyone and watched with pleasure as they all swallowed their second shot as easily as they had their first.

"Wooo, that stuff is going straight to my head," Lilly said with a silly grin.

"Told you it was strong," Caryn said as she screwed the top back on the bottle. She didn't mind contributing to their good time, but the last thing she wanted was to get everyone shit-faced. That just wasn't cool.

"Okay, you're officially our liquor dealer," Lilly told Caryn.

The others agreed.

After a while, the talk turned to the guys on the search and rescue team.

"I heard you and Drew didn't get along when you first met," Elsie said.

Caryn didn't take offense. "We didn't," she agreed with a shrug. "I wasn't at my best. I was so worried about my grandfather, and I have issues with his former profession, and...I guess we both let our preconceived ideas about the other get in the way of being polite."

"You didn't like that he was a cop?" Bristol asked.

"To be honest, no."

"I thought cops and firefighters got along. Brotherhood, sisterhood, whatever, and all that," Finley said.

"I mean, we work together a lot, but that doesn't mean we always click. From my experience in the city, the officers think we're a reckless bunch of assholes...not wanting to wait for them to clear a scene before going in to help someone. And in turn, firefighters get irritated with the way police officers sometimes get overzealous when subduing people, and with all their rules and regulations.

"But I do get the latter," Caryn quickly added. "I mean, we have very different jobs. Generally, people aren't trying to hide illegal stuff from us, and they're pretty glad to see us when we show up. That isn't always the case with cops." Not wanting to bring the vibe of the night down, Caryn said, "There is one thing I've learned from police officers though."

"What?" all four women asked at once.

Caryn held up a foot and pointed to her shoe. "Always carry a handcuff key."

The others all leaned in to see a small metal key woven into the laces of her shoe.

"Oh my gosh, Ethan totally carries one in his wallet!" Lilly said.

"And I think Zeke carries one too," Elsie said.

Bristol grinned and nodded. "Rocky slips one into his pocket every single morning."

"Wow, are there that many people being handcuffed against their will around here or what?" Finley asked, her brows drawn down in confusion.

"I'm sure there aren't," Caryn said to reassure her. "But as the guys no doubt learned from their time in the service, it pays to be prepared, just in case. And with that said, I also spent some time sewing little pockets in the back of all my pants, to slip one in there too. That was after a crazy guy set fire to a high-rise building then waited for help to arrive. He bashed the first firefighter on the scene over the head, handcuffed him to a pipe in a utility closet and left him there to suffocate from the smoke. To this day, no one knows why he did it, but the firefighter was lucky. One of the man's neighbors was watching through his peephole and saw the whole thing. He called 9-1-1 and told the dispatchers, then told the police officers who were first on scene. The cops pulled out their handy-dandy handcuff keys and got him out of there before any damage was done."

The women all gaped as she finished the story.

"Why your pants though?" Finley asked.

"Well, the one on my shoe is all well and good, but if my hands are cuffed behind me, I wouldn't be able to reach it very easily. Especially if I was attached to anything. But I could definitely reach the small pocket in the waistband of my pants," Caryn said with a shrug.

"That's so smart," Lilly said.

"Impressive," Bristol agreed. "But sometimes you can't reach either of those places."

The room fell quiet as everyone struggled with what to say to their friend, who was obviously thinking of the time she was held captive not too long ago.

Finley was sitting next to Bristol on the couch, and she wrapped an arm around her shoulders and leaned into her.

"That's true," Lilly agreed. "And sometimes you're not cuffed at all, so having a key wouldn't help."

Caryn felt horrible that what had started as a lighthearted comment managed to evolve and make these two women fall back into such awful memories from their recent pasts. "I think the important thing is to not give up when shit happens," she said quietly. "Whether that's using a hidden handcuff key, fighting with our fists and feet, or simply using our brains to do what we can to stay alive until help gets to us."

"Totally agree," Bristol said. "When I hurt myself in the woods, I had no idea if anyone was looking for me but I didn't give up. I was prepared to drag myself to the trailhead if I had to."

"And I ran into the woods knowing even if I got lost, Zeke would find me, I just had to stay away from my ex long enough for him to give up coming after me," Elsie agreed.

"I knew I couldn't hold onto that rope forever, but there was no way I was going to just give up and let Joey win," Lilly said softly.

"I'm the worst in stressful situations," Finley said. "I can't even handle when customers yell at me. I fold like a house of cards. I'm doomed."

"No, you aren't," Elsie said firmly. "I thought the same thing about myself, but when push comes to shove, you reach deep down and find the strength to persevere."

"Man, we're kind of morose, aren't we?" Lilly said, taking a deep breath.

"I'm sorry, I didn't mean to be a downer," Caryn said.

"You aren't! And I'm thinking we all need to sew little pockets into our clothes so we can be prepared too," she said, sounding determined.

"And we'll need to order handcuff keys in bulk!" Bristol said with a smile.

"I'm already on it," Finley murmured, pulling out her phone.

Caryn smiled. She genuinely liked these women. They were down to earth, funny, and strong as hell.

"I've never even held a pair of handcuffs," Elsie mused.

Caryn couldn't help it, she giggled. Which set off everyone else.

"I'm thinking Zeke could probably help you with that little problem," Lilly said.

"Right? He'd show you exactly what can be done with them," Bristol agreed.

Caryn wasn't going to touch this conversation with a ten-foot pole—but of course she was dragged into it anyway.

"Has Drew gotten out his handcuffs and practiced some of his old moves on you yet, Caryn?" Lilly asked.

Knowing she was blushing, but not able to do anything about it, Caryn smiled. "We haven't been dating all that long."

"Ah, so you're going slow. I can see that about Drew," Lilly said.

"The chemistry between you two is pretty hot," Elsie said. "And I think it's sweet that he brought you over and is going to pick you up."

Caryn couldn't deny that she liked that too. "It's just that...relationships haven't worked out for me in the past, and I've been kinda reluctant to dive into this one...especially considering I don't have a job or anything yet."

"But you *are* staying?" Finley asked.

"Yeah, I'm staying," Caryn admitted. Until that moment, she'd only been half committed to the idea, despite already telling her grandfather. Sitting here now, surrounded by these women who had accepted her without hesitation, she realized how badly she wanted to stay in Fallport. Job or no job, she wanted to see where things could go with Drew, be here for her grandfather, and develop the kind of friendships she'd always dreamed about.

"Cool!" Bristol cheered.

"Are you going to apply for the firefighter position?" Elsie asked.

"I'm guessing yes, if the way you were chumming it up with the guys at the watch party is any indication," Bristol said with a grin.

"What? What guys? What'd I miss?" Lilly asked.

Caryn was embarrassed all over again. And somehow the alcohol in her veins and the ease she felt with these women had her blurting out how horrible she felt for ditching Drew.

"He was okay," Bristol said gently. "I glanced at him every now and again, and he barely took his eyes off you. Even when Tony climbed into his lap, he kept watch over you, making sure you were all right. I'm sure at the first sign of you being uncomfortable, or any of those guys making a move, he would've been over there staking his claim."

"Still," Caryn said. "I went with him, and ditched him to spend time with a bunch of other guys. It's not like I even wanted to hang out with them."

"But you *do* want that job," Elsie said. "And being a team player is part of that, I would assume, especially for a fire-fighter."

"It is," Caryn agreed.

"Our guys are possessive and protective, but they aren't assholes," Lilly said. "Drew isn't going to go all stalker crazy on you if you talk to another guy. But even more so than the others, he'll keep his eye on you, make sure you're okay. It's kind of been engrained in him with his former job."

"I know. And I don't mind that. I just hate that at the time, I thought it was more important to schmooze with Paul Downs and his friends before the show started than hang out with you guys and Drew."

"I don't think you thought it was more important," Elsie said diplomatically. "It's what you needed to do at that moment to ensure your professional future. If you don't have a job, it would make it harder to move here, wouldn't it?"

"Of course."

"Then, there you go," Elsie said with a shrug. "I, more than most people, know how important it is to make your own way. No matter how things go with you and Drew, you want to be able to support yourself. And if you need to take an hour and hang out with the people who might be your future co-workers, get to know them, let them get to know you, I think that's more than okay."

"You guys are being very understanding. I was rude, and I know it."

"Eh, whatever," Elsie said. "Sometimes you have to be rude to do what's best for yourself."

She wasn't wrong. Caryn felt her tense muscles loosening. "You guys are pretty amazing," she blurted.

"Or course we are," Lilly said with a smug smile.

"No, I mean...I just... Shoot," Caryn said.

It was Elsie who leaned over and put a comforting hand on Caryn's leg. "We get it. I was so busy working my ass off to provide for Tony and myself that I didn't have the time or energy to make true friends. But I've learned that having someone to lean on, to bitch with, to laugh with, is more important than making an extra buck."

"Same," Lilly said. "I came to Fallport thinking I was just going to be here for a couple weeks, but the town sucked me in and changed my life completely."

"The fact that Sandra, someone who just met me, was worried when I didn't show up at the diner to say goodbye to her after my visit, *literally* saved my life," Bristol said. "I kept to myself back in Kingsport, sure that I was just an introvert who was fine not having friends, but I was lying to myself. Not about being an introvert. I still am. But having you guys as friends was one of the things that kept me going when I was kidnapped. I knew you were out there looking for me."

"And I'm super shy, but I'm trying to be better because of you ladies," Finley added.

"Shit, now I'm crying," Caryn said with a small laugh as she wiped away tears from her cheeks.

"No crying!" Lilly exclaimed. "We're badass bitches who can handle anything life throws at us!"

Everyone laughed at that.

"And who need to pee," Elsie added as she stood. "I'll be back."

Giggles rang out anew at that, and Caryn relaxed back against the couch once more.

"Finley...can we talk about Brock?" Bristol asked a little hesitantly.

"No," she said with a shake of her head.

"But he likes you!" Bristol said.

Finley snorted. "No, he doesn't."

"He *does*," Bristol insisted. "If you'd give him the tiniest sign that you might be receptive, I think you'd find him just as attentive as our guys."

"That's not going to happen," Finley said. "And I appreciate you trying, but there's no way a man like Brock Mabrey would ever look twice at someone like me."

"Someone who bakes like a dream and is always so nice to everyone who comes into her shop?" Elsie asked. "I've seen you give Davis free food more than once."

"I'm fat," Finley said without an ounce of discomfort in her tone. "I've always been overweight, and I always will be. I like food too much to starve myself, and going on a diet without carbs and sugar? Not possible for me. But I'm okay with who I am. I'm actually more comfortable in my own skin now than I have been in a very long time. But Brock... Brock is muscular and athletic. Hell, all of the guys on the SAR team are. I wouldn't be able to keep up with him. I don't mind hiking and walking, but I'd never be able to go at his pace.

"I see the side glances people give me. I hear their backhanded compliments. 'Your face is so pretty.' As if I don't understand that they're saying my face might be pretty, but the rest of me isn't. I'm not willing to subject someone like Brock to that crap. Or to someone like me."

"That's bullshit," Lilly said, surprising everyone with the venom in her tone. "Brock doesn't care if you carry some extra weight. He's not that kind of guy."

Finley sighed and studied the cup she was holding. "I know he's not," she said quietly.

"Then why don't you go after what you want?" Bristol asked.

"What are we talking about?" Elsie asked as she returned from the restroom.

"Finley wanting Brock but being too shy to go after him," Caryn summed up.

"You guys wouldn't understand," Finley said a little desperately.

"Then explain it to us," Lilly ordered. "Because we've been watching you guys tiptoe around each other. He stares at you constantly, practically begging for a sign that you want to talk to him, and when you don't, he leaves—and then *you* watch *him* go with sad puppy dog eyes. It kills me."

"He deserves better than me," Finley whispered.

"He deserves a woman who will love him with everything she has," Lilly countered. "Someone who will make him his favorite desserts, laugh with him, support him when he comes home tired and hungry from a search. Who will surprise him with lunch at the auto shop, who isn't afraid to hold his oil-stained hand—and who will stand up for him when people give him shit for having a job they look down on."

"Someone's given him shit about being a mechanic?" Finley asked, sitting up straighter. "Why? That's stupid! I mean, are they gonna fix their own cars when they break down? Probably not. Who said something? I'll ban them from the bakery!"

Everyone burst out laughing.

"What? What's so funny?" Finley asked in a huff.

"You are. And you're exactly who Brock needs." Bristol gave Finley a gentle smile. "But I can see that I've made you uncomfortable, and that wasn't really my intention. The last thing I want to say is...don't wait too long. Brock's a good man and a fantastic catch. If you aren't careful, someone else will step in and you'll lose your chance."

Finley was silent, lost in thought, and Caryn really hoped she was able to dig deep and find the courage to see if things could work out between her and Brock. He seemed like a fun kind of guy, and he'd let Drew make that obstacle course on the land behind his shop. She could totally see him and Finley together...if she got over her shyness around him.

"I'm thinking I need another shot of that apple pie stuff," Bristol told Caryn.

She grinned and grabbed the bottle, which was sitting by her hip. "Cups up, girls!" she exclaimed.

By the time everyone was ready to go, it was a little past midnight. Way late for Caryn, but she couldn't deny she'd loved every minute hanging out with the other women. They were funny, madly in love with their men...and at present, more than a little tipsy.

They'd talked more about their guys, the search and rescue team in general and their recent searches, made up stories about all the bad guys they must've faced in their time in the military, discussed their favorite TV shows and movies, laughed, burped, and even farted a time or two. All in all, Caryn couldn't remember the last time she'd had this much fun, or when she'd felt so comfortable with a group of women.

Lilly and Elsie called their guys, deciding against having Rocky take them home. It was obvious they were eager to have some alone time with their men, just as Caryn was.

Bristol had invited Finley to spend the night, and she'd headed off to a guest room shortly before the men arrived.

By the time Drew knocked on the door, she and Bristol were the only ones left. Rocky was cleaning up the kitchen without so much as a word of complaint, which impressed Caryn.

Bristol was a little wobbly on the knee scooter as she escorted Caryn to the door, but Rocky rushed over to stand behind her, keeping her steady. She hugged Caryn tightly before opening the door for Drew.

"She's here and ready for you!" she declared dramatically as she greeted him.

He chuckled and shook his head. "I see that."

"The apple pie she brought over was deficious...no, wait, demichios...shoot. Really yummy," Bristol said triumphantly.

The warm look Drew shot her way made Caryn's legs feel like jelly. "Didn't know you baked, hon."

"I don't," she blurted. "It's moonshine. Clyde gave it to me."

Drew looked surprised for a moment, then nodded. "Ah, that explains you swaying on your feet and Bristol's less-than-stellar pronunciation."

Bristol smiled. "Yup."

Rocky wrapped an arm around her waist. "Time for bed, I think," he said.

"Oooooh, yes please," Bristol said, looking up at her fiancé with a sparkle in her eye.

Caryn looked away from the naked longing in her new friend's face, chuckling. "Make sure she drinks a huge glass of water before she goes to sleep," she warned Rocky.

"Way ahead of you, but I appreciate you looking out for her," he said.

Caryn shrugged. "It's what friends do."

And with that, Bristol threw herself at Caryn again, and it was all she could do to catch the diminutive woman.

"Easy," Drew said, stepping up and putting a hand on Caryn's back, giving her the support she needed not to fall back a few steps.

"Come on, time to get you upstairs," Rocky said as he turned Bristol and picked her up.

"Thanks for having us over," Caryn told her.

Bristol snuggled into Rocky. "We need to do it again."

"Yes!" Caryn said happily, stumbling as she took a step toward the door. But again, Drew was there to hold her steady.

"Thanks," Drew said, giving Rocky a chin lift.

"You got her?" Rocky asked.

"Of course."

Of course. As if he needn't have asked. Happiness filled Caryn. Drew wrapped an arm around her waist and helped her to walk out of the house. He got her situated in the passenger seat of his Jeep, and she watched as he strode around to the driver's side. He climbed in and turned to smile at her. "Have fun?" he asked.

"Oh yeah."

"Good." Then he started the engine and headed for her grandfather's house. The drive was way too short. Just when Caryn's eyes had closed and she was about to fall asleep, they were there.

"Hang on a sec," Drew said when he pulled into the driveway behind her vehicle. He jogged around to her side and helped her out, keeping his arm around her waist as he led her to the door. He unlocked it with her key and walked her through the house as if he belonged there, escorting her all the way to her room and sitting her on the side of the bed. "Get changed," he ordered. "I'll be right back with some water and aspirin for you."

"I'm okay," she told him.

"And you'll be better with some water to dilute that moonshine. Didn't know you knew Clyde," he added.

"You mad about that?" she couldn't help but ask.

Drew frowned. "Why would I be? Clyde's good people. Change, Caryn," he ordered. "If I come back and you're half naked, I'm not sure what I'll do."

She smiled up at him, happy that he seemed to like Clyde. In her opinion, the poor man got a bad rap. "I'm not sure that's incentive for me to change," she said honestly.

The flare of heat in his eyes made her thighs clench together. A bolt of lust shot through her. She wanted this man. He was one of the good guys, she'd bet everything she owned on it.

"The first time we make love, it isn't going to be when your grandfather is down the hall, probably listening at his door to what we're saying. *Or* when you're drunk. When we do go there, we're both gonna be completely sobor and one hundred percent sure of what we want."

"What do you want?" Caryn whispered.

"A partner," he said without hesitation. "And I have a feeling you'd be the best partner I've ever had. Get busy," he said gruffly, before running the backs of his fingers over her flushed cheek and walking out of the room.

He couldn't have said anything that meant more to her. She'd always wanted a true partner but hadn't found one. And knowing Drew had probably had plenty of partners over the years—both in his career and otherwise—and he still thought she could be the perfect one for him... Yeah, she was a goner.

Standing, Caryn whipped her shirt over her head and dropped it on the floor, not caring where it landed. It took a few tries to unhook her bra, but she finally managed and dropped it as well. She grabbed the tank top she usually slept in and pulled it over her head. Then she shoved off her jeans and panties. She almost fell donning the boy shorts she wore to bed, but recovered at the last second. She crawled under the sheet and blanket, sitting against the headboard, just as a light knock sounded on her door.

"You good?" Drew asked from the other side.

"Yeah."

He pushed open the door, holding a large glass of water. He sat on the edge of her bed and handed it to her. Knowing he wasn't going to let her off the hook, Caryn took it—and the aspirin he held out—and drank as much as she could.

"Thank you," Drew said softly as he took the glass from her and put it on the nightstand next to her bed. Then he leaned over her as she lowered herself to the mattress. He stared at her for a long moment before running a hand over her hair. "I love your hair like this," he said softly.

Caryn smiled. "Thanks. I like yours too. And your facial hair. It suits you."

"We suit each other," he said matter-of-factly. "I'm guessing we're skipping our workout tomorrow?"

Caryn wrinkled her nose and looked over at the ancient clock radio on the nightstand. "Um...maybe we can do it later?"

"Sure thing. Nine? Ten?"

Caryn nodded.

A chuckle escaped Drew's lips. "Right. I'll come over and if you don't feel like it, we can skip a day."

"I need to apply for the firefighter position tomorrow. And go to the store. And I have a book I need to get working on." She hardly knew what she was saying. She was comfortable, and loved having Drew hovering over her with his woodsy scent in her nostrils.

"Get working on?"

"Uh-huh," Caryn said, her eyes closing. "Thomas Robertson's newest. I'm his beta reader."

"Really?"

Her eyes opened at the surprise in Drew's tone. "Yup. I read all his stuff before it goes to the editor. To make sure he hasn't screwed anything up."

"You're full of surprises," Drew said with a smile. "He's one of my favorite authors, and you're telling me you have a hand in what he writes?"

"Kinda. Sorta. Not really," she said with a shrug.

"No wonder I like you. Sleep, Caryn. I'm glad you had a good time tonight. And...you're pretty damn cute when you're tipsy."

"Thanks," she said, her eyes closing once more.

She heard his chuckle reverberate through her once more, felt his warm lips on hers, but was too tired to do more than moan contentedly under him.

He kissed her forehead, then the mattress moved as he stood. "Good night, sweetheart."

"Night." She was asleep before the door closed behind him.

CHAPTER TWELVE

Drew couldn't stop smiling as he remembered how adorable Caryn was the night before. She'd called when the ladies finished up at Bristol's, and he was out his door before she'd finished talking. He'd been waiting to hear from her all night, anxious to know if the evening went well. But it was more than obvious when he saw how tight she and Bristol were that it had gone better than even *he* thought it would.

He'd wanted nothing more than to take her up on the invitation he'd seen in her eyes as they stood in her bedroom. But last night wasn't the place or time. It was coming though. And he couldn't wait.

It was a shock hearing that she beta read for Thomas Robertson. The man was a genius with words, and knowing Caryn had a role in his publishing process was astounding. The woman impressed him more and more every day.

He knocked on Art's door at ten o'clock on the dot and nodded at the older man when he answered.

"Hi, Art. How're you feeling today?"

"Good, good. I think the question is, though, how is *Caryn* feeling today?"

Drew chuckled. "A little rough around the edges?" he asked as Art gestured for him to come inside.

"You could say that. I told her not to bring Clyde's moonshine, but she didn't listen to me," Art said with a snort. "Serves her right. That stuff is potent."

"But good, I hear," Drew said.

"Very good. The man's a genius. Standoffish, grumpy, and wary of anyone who steps anywhere near his land, but very good at what he does."

Drew nodded in agreement, but his attention was on Caryn. She was sitting at Art's small kitchen table, a glass of orange juice and a cup of coffee in front of her, as well as a plate with a single piece of dry toast. He grinned.

"Not a word, Drew," she growled without lifting her eyes.

His grin widened, but he did as requested and didn't say anything as he pulled out the chair next to her and sat. "Morning," he said quietly.

"I'm never drinking again," she said softly, finally looking up.

"So says everyone in the history of the world who's been hungover after a night of drinking."

"I'm just not good at it," she complained.

"That's not a bad thing," Drew said, reaching for her hand. He ran his thumb over the back gently. "You sure were cute last night though."

Caryn rolled her eyes. "Right. Cute. Just what every woman wants to hear."

Glancing into the living room, Drew saw that Art wasn't even trying to pretend he wasn't listening. Any comment Drew might want to make about how hard it was to leave her in her bed, alone, would have to wait. "So...Thomas Robertson?" he asked instead.

"I vaguely remember telling you about him," she said, taking a sip of her coffee.

Art walked slowly into the kitchen as he said, "Caryn's his right-hand man. Or woman. He sends his manuscripts right after he finishes writing them—apparently he's a terrible speller. Anyway, she reads it and tells him where it works and where it doesn't. In *Diver Down*, his latest bestseller, you know, the one that's going to be made into a movie? She told me that at first the hero figured out the identity of the bad guy in the very beginning of the book, but at her suggestion, Thomas nixed that and changed practically the entire plot so he didn't realize who the guy was until right before that huge firefight at the end."

Drew hadn't read the book in question yet, but it was on his list. "Yeah?" he asked. "How'd you get into something like that?"

Caryn shrugged and told him a story about a fire in the bookstore where he was doing a signing, and how he'd asked if he could pick her brain because he was writing a book with a firefighter. "Things just kind of progressed from there. I like reading, and his stuff is very good. Even though it's not romance."

Drew grinned at that, then asked, "Is it a paying gig?" It was probably a rude question, but he didn't think Caryn would mind.

"Yeah. He sends me about five grand for every book I beta for him. It's too much, but he refuses to listen to me when I tell him to stop sending me so much," Caryn said.

"He's asked if she'd be willing to do the same for some of his friends, who are super jealous he has my Caryn all to himself, but she keeps telling him she doesn't have the time."

Drew raised a brow. "You're telling me you get five thousand bucks for reading a book and writing a few notes about it—and could be getting the same amount from other authors, but you've turned them down?"

"It's more than writing a few notes," Caryn protested. "What are we doing today for our workout?"

She obviously wanted to change the subject, but the more Drew thought about it, the more he wondered why she wasn't jumping on the chance to earn money doing what she loved... reading. Of course, she enjoyed being a firefighter too, but it wouldn't be a bad fallback job for her. "You up for hiking the Barker Mill Trail this morning?"

She sighed in relief. "Yes."

The Barker Mill Trail wasn't too strenuous. He figured it would be good for her to get out and get her blood moving, but the obstacle course would probably be too much in her hungover condition. And even jogging would hurt her head. The last thing Drew wanted to do was cause her pain.

Caryn picked up her coffee and took a large swallow, then pushed up from the table and said, "I'm ready to go."

Within twenty minutes, they were on the trail and Drew was explaining some of the most common reactions of people who got lost in the woods. "I think most people are taught to stay put when they get lost, but many times their first reaction is to run. Their adrenaline spikes and they're certain they can find their way back home or to the trail. But before they know it, they've gotten themselves even more lost and farther away from their last-known location.

"People today are too reliant on technology as well. They think all it'll take is making a phone call and they'll be rescued. There are so many places along the Appalachian Trail where there's no cell service at all. Even GPS technology can fail. I wish everyone who went hiking was trained on how to use a simple compass. If they took a bearing when they started the hike, they'd be able to find their way back. Do you know how to use a compass?" Drew asked.

"Yes."

In response, Drew pulled out his compass and handed it

to her. He then took a left and stepped off the trail. Caryn followed.

Twenty minutes later, after walking in circles and doing his best to turn her around, he said, "Okay, get us back to the trail. Or the parking lot. Get us unlost."

He was impressed when she simply nodded and looked down at the compass in her hand. They were back on the trail in ten minutes.

Drew grinned at her.

"You didn't think I could do it, did you?"

"I wasn't sure," he said with a shrug.

"Granddaddy taught me everything he knew about the woods when I was little. His lessons stuck."

"Like what? What else did he teach you?"

"If I get lost, stay put, like you said. I know how to start a fire with gunpowder from a bullet, with a battery, a magnifying glass, and using sap from a balsam tree as lighter fluid. He said if staying put doesn't work, if no one comes, to find a source of water and follow it downstream. A brook becomes a stream, which becomes a lake or river. Eventually it will lead to roads, a camp, or people."

"You're already way more knowledgeable than a lot of SAR personnel," Drew told her. "I talked to Ethan, and the next time we get a call out, we'd like for you to come along...if you're serious about joining the team."

Caryn stopped in her tracks in the middle of the trail and gaped at him. "Seriously?"

"Yes."

He loved the smile that crept across her face. "Awesome!"

"Yeah. You'll need to stay paired up with one of us for quite a while, for safety and so we can train you."

"No problem. Thank you so much."

"No, thank *you*. We can use all the trained help we can get."

They continued walking, and after a moment, Drew said, "I've been wondering about this—and you don't have to tell me if you don't want to—but can you tell me why you spent summers here with Art?"

For a while, he wasn't sure she was going to answer. Just when he was about to apologize for prying, she spoke.

"I told you that my mom wasn't a good person. I wasn't exaggerating. She fell hard and fast for every man she ever met. I can't even remember all the names of the guys she dated throughout my childhood and teens. I think she was married around ten times—honestly, I lost count. Sometimes it was literally just for months. And every time, it was the same routine. She'd spend all her time and energy on them until they pissed her off, then she'd rant and rave and tell me how terrible men were. Which wasn't true. Some of the men were actually super nice. But when she broke up with them, that was it. I never saw them again. And while they were together, I was completely ignored by her.

"She sent me to her dad in the summers because she hated having me *underfoot*, as she called it. She wanted to be alone with her men and not have to worry about all the responsibilities that come with raising a kid. When I was with her, I did my best to stay under her radar. The last thing I wanted was her attention, to be honest. While she could be saccharine sweet at times, especially in front of guys, she could also be incredibly abusive. Not physically, but emotionally. Summers were my escape from her. I could be myself here. Free.

"And I don't mean free from rules. Art ran a tight ship. I couldn't run around all hours of the day. I had chores, and was expected to be polite and not be a troublemaker. I did everything Art asked because I actually *liked* the rules. They made me feel loved, like he cared...and I definitely didn't feel loved when I was with my mom. I wanted to move to Fallport full time, but Mom wouldn't give up total control. She didn't like me, but she liked using me to gain sympathy for herself."

"That sounds completely fucked-up," Drew said when she paused.

Caryn laughed, but it wasn't a humorous sound. "It was," she agreed. "But Art was my savior. He made me believe that I was loveable. That my mom was sick, damaged, whacked... whatever you want to call it. He was completely appalled by what his daughter was doing to her only child."

"How'd you get out?" Drew asked.

"I graduated high school," Caryn said without emotion.

"So you *didn't* get out," Drew said in a tight voice.

"Don't feel sorry for me," she told him. "I'm not the only kid who had a rough childhood. It's what you make of your life after the hard times that matters, not the hard times themselves."

"Very true. You're incredible, Caryn."

She took a deep breath. "Most of the time, I feel as if I'm barely keeping my head above water," she admitted softly.

Drew put a finger under her chin and brought her head up so she had to look at him. "I know it feels that way, but it's not true. You've done a hell of a job with your life. You could've taken a different road, become bitter, started taking drugs, turned to a life of crime, or done exactly what your mom did...go from guy to guy, desperately looking for love... but you didn't."

She reached up and wrapped her fingers around his wrist and held on tightly. Then surprised him by putting her other arm around him and stepping closer. She hugged him tightly, and Drew held her as they stood in the middle of the trail in the woods. They spoke without saying a word. It was one of the most intimate moments he'd ever shared with a woman.

He'd seen people in some of the worst circumstances of their lives. Car wrecks, domestic abuse situations, after being shot or stabbed, some high as a kite and out of their mind on drugs. He'd had to comfort kids whose parents were screaming at the top of their lungs at each other, and had held the hands of other children who were scared to death because of situations adults had put them in.

But nothing touched him as much as the woman in his arms, turning to him for comfort. Knowing a little bit of the hell Caryn went through as a child made him respect and admire her even more.

She got herself under control quickly and pulled back. But not out of his embrace. "I'd do anything for Art. He's the father figure I never had growing up. Without him, I'd probably be in any one of those situations you mentioned. He kept me on the straight and narrow and made me believe that I was worthy and loveable."

"Where's your mom now?" Drew asked in a low voice.

She tilted her head as she stared at him. "Why? Are you gonna go and fuck her up?"

Drew couldn't help the snort that left him. "What? No." He might not beat her up, but he could make sure she understood that she was never to contact Caryn again. That she didn't exist in Caryn's world anymore. And if she *did* feel the urge to look up her daughter, she'd regret it.

Caryn stared at him for a long beat before she sighed. "To put your mind at ease, and to save you time so you don't have to track her down, she's dead. One of the men she hooked up with apparently got tired of her stupid shit and shot her."

Drew didn't like the woman, even though he hadn't ever met her, but he still felt an immediate stab of sorrow for Caryn. "I'm sorry."

"I'm not. What's the saying? You reap what you sow?"

"I'm sorry *she* missed out on such a wonderful daughter," Drew said quietly.

She smiled at that. "Thanks."

"Not blowing smoke up your ass, Caryn. I'm being serious."

"I know you are. How'd *you* get to be so amazing?" she asked.

"I'm nobody special," he said with a shake of his head.

She rolled her eyes. "Right. Can we talk about last night?"

"What about it?"

"I practically told you I wanted you...and you still didn't make a move on me."

"I told you, sweetheart," Drew replied. "That when we make love, I don't want to worry about Art overhearing us. When you scream my name, I want to enjoy it."

She grinned. "Are you that confident in your abilities?"

"Yes." And he was. It had been a while since he'd been with a woman, but he hadn't had any complaints in the past. One of his favorite things ever was making a woman lose all her inhibitions. There was nothing better than making his partner feel sexy and confident. Than watching her orgasm and knowing that *he'd* done that.

Her smile faded as she studied him. "You could break me, Drew," she said after a moment.

"Never," he vowed.

She swallowed hard. "I'm scared."

"Of me?" he asked, dismayed.

"Of finally finding what I've wanted my entire life, only to realize it's a mirage. That having a true partner...someone I can share everything with, and who does the same with me... isn't actually possible."

Drew snaked his hand from her waist up to her nape and held her tightly as he said, "I went through twenty-two partners in my time as an officer."

She blinked. "Twenty-two?"

"Yes."

"Why?"

He sighed and dropped his hand. "Maybe I was a shitty person to work with."

"Right—*no*. Why?"

He loved that she was so quick to defend him.

"Honestly? I'm not sure. Several factors, probably. The stress of the job. Because I didn't put up with screwups and was extremely blunt with my opinions about people's actions. I wasn't afraid to stand up for myself, and for the citizens I worked for. I worked extremely hard, didn't spend an extra twenty minutes at dinner when there were calls that needed answering. I didn't talk much while on shift, preferred to stay quiet and observe what was going on around me. I wasn't easy to work with, I know that. And I didn't click with a single one of my partners. So...I have the same fears about partners that you do."

She stared at him for a second, then smiled. "We're a pair, aren't we?"

He returned her grin. "Maybe that's why we fit so well. And for the record...leaving without touching you last night was the hardest thing I've ever done. But I knew if I started something, I wouldn't stop. I'd have you under me, naked, my cock buried in your pussy before either of us knew what we were doing. But I'd never disrespect you by taking you without your full and unaltered consent. And never where your grandfather could overhear."

Caryn shivered. "He's not here now," she said.

Drew stared at her intently.

She gave him a wicked grin. "I'm not saying I want to get naked with you right here and right now, because...dirt and bugs. But a kiss wouldn't be unwelcome."

Without another word, Drew crushed her lips with his. He didn't give her time to change her mind, didn't think about what he was doing. He only knew if he didn't taste this woman right this second, he was going to explode into a million pieces.

They made out in the middle of the trail for what seemed like forever. It took everything within Drew to pull back. He licked his lips and tasted her flavored ChapStick.

"Please tell me I'm gonna get to see you naked soon," she said.

He should've known his Caryn wouldn't be shy.

"You are," he said, keeping his answer short and to the point.

"Good. Now...since kissing you turns me on, and being turned on in the woods when we can't do anything about it kind of sucks, how about you teach me more about finding lost people and then you can take me back to Art's place and we can have a late breakfast? I'm suddenly starving."

"No more hangover?" Drew asked.

"Nope. Not even a twinge of a headache. Your kisses are a miracle cure."

He chuckled. "I'm thinking the fresh air, exercise, and your metabolism are to thank for that, not me."

"Whatever," she said with a shrug. "So, do you find most people close to where they were last seen or miles away?"

Happy to talk about his experiences and what to look for when on a search, Drew turned them back toward the trailhead and the parking area. His heart stuttered a bit when she reached out and took his hand. He curled his fingers around hers and kept talking.

This felt right.

They felt right.

He'd do whatever it took to nurture and protect the flame that sparked between them.

CHAPTER THIRTEEN

It was Friday night, and Caryn was nervous. She hadn't told Drew or any of her new female friends about her plans for tonight. She knew that was probably a sign she shouldn't go, but she couldn't give up the idea of joining the crew. And if meeting with Paul and his friends at The Cellar would help her chances of getting the job at the FFD, she'd do it.

She didn't plan on staying long. She'd just go, say hey to Paul and anyone else who showed up, then leave.

Things with Drew were going so well, it was almost scary. She liked him. A lot. Enough to tell him about her mother, which she never did. She couldn't think of anyone who she'd opened up to about her childhood and her mom. Not even her ex. But Drew didn't judge, and she couldn't help but like how pissed he'd gotten on her behalf. If the woman wasn't dead, Caryn was pretty sure Drew would've used his connections to track her down. She had no idea what he would've done when he found her, but her mom probably wouldn't have enjoyed meeting him.

It was ten in the evening, and Caryn had already talked to Drew. They planned on taking tomorrow off from working out and meeting at Sunny Side Up for breakfast. Then he had a meeting with Bristol about the investments he wanted her to consider. Caryn had agreed to go with him to Rocky and Bristol's house and keep her company after the meeting, while all the guys worked on the barn. They wanted to get everything done well before the Halloween wedding that Ethan and Lilly were planning, which was less than two months away.

She'd dressed for comfort in a pair of jeans, her favorite sneakers, and instead of a T-shirt, she'd actually put on a black blouse. It had a V-neck and tapered in at the sides. There was a bit of lace at the neckline and around the short capped sleeves. She'd always felt pretty in the shirt and figured she needed the extra boost of self-esteem to make it through the night.

Her grandfather had gone to bed about half an hour ago, so Caryn snuck through the house as quietly as she could so she didn't tip him off that she was leaving. It wasn't that she didn't want him to know where she was going, but more that she knew he wouldn't approve. He'd made it very clear what he thought about Paul Downs and his friends...and none of it was good.

Caryn silently closed the door behind her and made her way to her car. Even though the square wasn't far from Art's house, she'd been too conditioned by the dangers of living in New York City to feel comfortable walking around late at night. As her chief always said, "Nothing good happens after two a.m." He wasn't wrong. That was usually when they were called out on the more horrific calls. Overdoses, car wrecks caused by drunk drivers, rapes...

It didn't take long for Caryn to park behind the pool hall on the square. It took her longer to give herself a pep talk before getting out of the car and walking into the dim build-

ing. She saw Paul, Dennis, Lou, George, and Oscar immediately.

She plastered a smile on her face and walked over to
where they were gathered around a pool table, greeting the
crew...and hoping for the best.

Less than an hour later, Caryn was completely miserable.

She'd agreed to play a game of pool, and had done her best to
ignore the inappropriate comments from both the men she was
supposed to be getting to know, as well as other patrons in the
bar. No one stood up for her or told other men to fuck off and
leave her alone. They just laughed when one drunk after another
commented on her ass anytime she bent over to take a shot at the
pool table. She would've defended herself, but she instinctively
knew she'd be made fun of for not being able to take a "joke."

She'd also managed to get herself roped into matching the
guys shot for shot.

Lou had brought a tray of shot glasses over to their table,
and when she'd declined, Paul began to egg her on. Outright
insinuating that if she couldn't handle a few shots with her
crew, there was no chance in hell he'd trust her to have their
backs while on duty. The two things had nothing to do with
each other, but she'd gathered her resolve. Told herself she
could do a shot or two, then leave.

But that hadn't happened. She'd found herself doing one,
then two, then four. The alcohol was making her unsteady on
her feet. Every time she tried to refuse another shot, one of
the guys would start in on her...

She couldn't hang with the "big boys."

She wasn't as tough as they'd thought.

She was whining like a girl.

She should've told them to fuck off. Should've rolled her
eyes and told them that alcohol tolerance had nothing to do
with being a damn good firefighter.

But she didn't. She did what she'd always done...kowtowed in her pathetic attempt to fit in. Ignored her common sense and let herself be ridiculed into capitulating. She hated this side of her. Hated that she wanted to be liked, wanted desperately to be part of the group.

It wasn't until she'd done her fifth shot that she learned this had all been one big setup. Some kind of initiation.

Dennis threw his arm around her shoulders and said, "You've lasted longer than we thought a chick would. You might just work out after all."

And that little bit of backhanded praise was all it took for her stubbornness to kick in. In her increasingly hazy mind, *she was doing it*. She was impressing them.

So she took another shot. And another.

By her seventh shot, she could barely stay on her feet, but everyone was smiling and laughing, so she did her best to continue with the game of pool she was playing. Except she could no longer hit the ball. After missing three times, Oscar took the pool cue out of her hand with a scowl.

When he stalked away to put the stick back in the holder on the wall, Paul approached. "Don't mind him. He's just pissed you're getting along so well with the rest of us," he told her.

Caryn frowned. She'd thought Oscar was a nice guy. She had no idea why he was suddenly looking so angry.

Paul wrapped an arm around her shoulders. "You're not so bad, Buckner."

His praise made her feel good...but also uneasy. She wasn't sure why. In fact, she wasn't sure what she was doing in general at the moment.

Dennis placed another shot in her hand. "One more," he insisted.

Caryn shook her head. She'd had more than enough. But Dennis insisted, and when Paul, Lou, Dennis, and George all knocked back the shots in their hands, she automatically did the same.

She didn't see Oscar glare at his fellow firefighters and stomp away from the pool table at the back of the bar.

A short while later, she had no idea what time it was, just that at some point, one of the guys had steered her to a chair. She watched them play pool while leaning her head against the wall. Why everyone was ignoring her now when they'd been all buddy-buddy earlier, she didn't know, but since the room was spinning, she couldn't be bothered to care.

Finally, when she was half asleep, Paul suddenly loomed over her. He rolled his eyes. "Figures a chick can't hold her liquor," he mocked.

Caryn wanted to protest. Tell him that *no one* would be able to handle as many shots as she'd done. But clearly the other guys had, and they seemed just fine.

"Come on, we'll take you home," he told her. "You shouldn't be driving like this."

Relieved that the night was over, Caryn merely nodded. She stood and immediately stumbled. No one bothered to help her, and she fell on her ass. Lou, Dennis, George, and Paul all laughed uproariously as she stared at them blearily from her spot on the floor.

"Not sure that kind of footwork will get you the job," George joked.

"My grandmother is steadier on her feet," Dennis added.

"How the hell do you think you can carry the SCBA and all the gear we need when you can't even stand up after a shot or two?" Lou said.

Paul just looked down at her, the satisfaction at her position easy to read in his eyes.

He was making fun of her. They all were.

Humiliation swam through Caryn. She wasn't sure what was going on. Why the hell weren't they all just as drunk as she was? She knew she was a lightweight, but maybe she really *couldn't* hang with these guys. Desolation filled her.

Paul stared at her for another second before he reached down and grabbed her biceps, hauling her upright. "You need me to carry you?" he asked.

Caryn quickly shook her head. The last thing she wanted was the embarrassment of having to be carried out of The Cellar. Especially by one of the men she was trying, and failing, to impress.

"I can walk," she said. Mentally adding a maybe to that statement.

She did manage to walk, but only because Paul kept a firm hand on her arm. She stumbled her way to the door, oblivious to the concerned or disapproving looks of the patrons who were still in the bar, watching her leave.

Dennis jogged ahead of them, going to get his car.

"Maybe he shouldn't be drivin' either," she said, slurring her words.

"He's a man. He can handle his liquor," Paul told her.

The dig hit its mark. How fast someone metabolized alcohol had nothing to do with the kind of firefighter they were, but Caryn was still deeply embarrassed.

She stayed silent as the other men around her joked and laughed at her expense. She didn't care anymore. She just wanted to go home and fall into bed.

Dennis pulled up to the curb in front of The Cellar, and Paul not so gently shoved her into the back seat and climbed in behind her. Lou was on her other side, and George got into the front.

As they drove away, Caryn kept her eyes shut. The world was spinning and she seriously didn't feel good.

She must've fallen asleep or passed out or something, because she had no recollection of the drive when she was roughly shaken awake.

"We're here. Get out," Paul said gruffly.

Thankful that soon she'd be horizontal, Caryn scooted across the seat and stepped out of the vehicle, her knees almost buckling. But when she looked up, she realized that she wasn't in front of Art's house.

She was in some gravel parking lot, surrounded by trees.

Caryn stiffened, her consciousness finally sparking. She was alone with four men, drunk off her ass, with no idea where she was—and no way of protecting herself.

Lou and George took both her arms and forced her to walk between them toward the darkness of the nearby tree line.

"Word is that you've been hanging with those pansy-ass search and rescue guys. You want to volunteer? We don't give a shit. But no FFD member is going to associate with those fake fuckers. SAR doesn't even compare to what we do. If you wanna be associated with them, there's no way you'll ever be one of us," Paul informed her.

Caryn blinked in confusion. How could he not think search and rescue was as important as being a firefighter? It wasn't a matter of being harder or easier. The skill set to find someone lost in the woods was completely different from entering a burning building or using the jaws of life to extract a victim from a wrecked car.

"She's not getting it," Dennis said with a laugh.

"Right. Let me make it clear then," Paul said. "No bitch will *ever* be on the FFD if I have anything to say about it. You can't do half of what we can. I wouldn't trust you with my life. No fuckin' way."

"But, I thought—" Caryn stammered, trying to make sense of his words.

"You thought wrong," Paul said harshly, interrupting her.

Then Lou and George shoved her forward, and she stumbled hard, falling onto her hands and knees in the dirt.

"You wanna play in the forest? Here you go."

She turned to stare at the four men in drunken confusion.

"You're at Eagle Rock Trail. You want to spend your time in the woods and be Bigfoot's bitch, have at it."

Glancing over her shoulder, Caryn glanced into the darkness. She could just make out the trail in front of her from the light of the thankfully almost full moon in the sky.

Paul walked toward her and kicked her foot. "Go!" he ordered.

Caryn still didn't move. Surely they wouldn't actually leave her here? The trailhead for Eagle Rock was miles from Fallport. And they all knew she was hammered. They'd made damn sure of it!

"Go on, git!" Lou said as he grabbed a rock from the ground and threw it in her direction.

He missed. Caryn didn't stick around to see what else the men might throw at her.

She stumbled down the dark path, using the trees to stay upright and listening to the laughter of the men behind her. For a second, she thought they'd come after her, do more than just hurl insults and rocks. But soon she heard their voices fade away and the sound of Dennis spinning his tires on the gravel in the parking area as they left.

Breathing hard, Caryn blinked, trying to get her eyes to adjust to the darkness. The night had been a disaster. And it was obvious now that Paul telling her to apply for the vacant position had been a farce. His laughter and scornful words echoed in her head.

Walking slowly, still using the trees alongside the path for balance, Caryn made her way back to the trailhead.

She both hoped and dreaded Dennis came back for her. Maybe they *were* just fucking with her. Only making her think they were going to leave her alone in the woods. But after a minute or two with no sign of them returning, Caryn realized they really *had* driven her miles from town, drunk off her ass, and abandoned her.

Assholes. They were like a bunch of fucking teenagers, not grown-ass men.

She walked over to a large log not too far from the trailhead and sat down heavily, almost falling backward. When she had her balance, she pulled out her phone. Squinting, trying to get her eyes to work properly, she hesitated, wondering who to call.

Her grandfather? No, it was way too late to bother him.

Drew? Hell no—she didn't want to admit how stupid she'd been.

Lilly? Maybe. But then again, she'd tell her fiancé, and he'd probably tell Drew.

Finley?

Yeah, she was probably getting up soon anyway to go to Sweet Tooth and start baking.

Caryn managed to click on her name and brought the phone up to her ear. But nothing happened. Frowning down at the screen, she saw she had no bars.

Sighing heavily and leaning forward, Caryn put her forehead on her knees.

She was screwed.

Served her right. For trusting those assholes. For caving under peer pressure like a stupid kid. For not going back to New York. Why had she decided to stay in this crappy town anyway? She should've known the firefighters' feelings about women in their ranks would be even more outdated and discriminatory than those of city crews, which bad enough.

Feeling utterly depressed, and knowing there was nothing to do but tough it out until the morning and either hope someone showed up for an early hike, or she'd sobered enough to walk back toward Fallport until she had cell reception, Caryn closed her eyes.

The world was still spinning, and she felt seconds from throwing up. No one had even suggested a glass of water while she was being plied with all those shots. But it was completely her fault. She could've said no. *Should've* said no. Should've cut herself off, or not drank at all, or chased each drink with water.

Her desire to fit in, to be accepted, had fucked her over yet again. She was over forty years old...and a lifetime of being rejected still hadn't made her any wiser.

When whould she learn?

Vowing that this time, she'd honestly and truly learn from this colossal mistake, she let a tear escape from her closed eye. Then another. Until she was crying as she sat alone, drunk, in the dark, and feeling lower than she'd ever felt in her entire life.

* * *

Oscar frowned as his fellow firefighters practically carried Caryn Buckner out of The Cellar. He'd thought Paul's idea had been a little bit of harmless fun, but when they hadn't stopped at one or two shots, had continued to ply the woman with way too much liquor, Oscar was done.

It was supposed to be an initiation prank. She'd be doing shots of straight vodka, while everyone else had water in their glasses. She'd get hammered, maybe a little sloppy, and they'd all laugh about it afterward. But instead, Paul seemed to relish the way she got more and more drunk... and then he got mean. Insulting her. Humiliating her. Declaring her inability to handle the alcohol he'd practically forced her to ingest was somehow related to her firefighting ability.

It was all bullshit, and Oscar was ashamed of his captain and fellow firefighters...and even more ashamed of himself.

He'd overheard Dennis and Lou talking about Paul's idea to take her out to the Eagle Rock Trail and leave her. He should've spoken up. Should've told them their hazing was ridiculous and had gone way too far. That they weren't stupid college kids anymore.

The Cellar wasn't known as the safest establishment in town. The people who frequented the place were mostly rough-and-tumble men who did what they wanted, when they wanted, and didn't worry about the consequences. But generally they weren't down with hurting women. Which was the only reason Oscar had come. He had a sister. And a mother. And a niece. The thought of someone doing to any of them what Paul and his friends were doing to Caryn, made him physically sick. It wasn't right.

He didn't stop them when he should've. But he could do something about it now.

His shoulders slumped as he thought about his options. He could go out to the trail and help Caryn himself, but that would make him a target of Paul and his asshole posse. He hated himself for not being willing to make his life more complicated, but he needed his job. He was the sole bread-winner of his family.

He could call Art, but the old man had just recovered from a knife attack. And Oscar had no idea if he was even steady enough to drive.

Then he remembered someone else...someone who wouldn't hesitate to help Caryn.

He pulled out his phone. It took a few calls to find the number of the man he wanted to reach, but he knew enough people in Fallport that it wasn't too difficult.

"'Lo?" a sleepy voice said on the other end of the line.

Looking at his watch, Oscar saw it was after one-thirty in

the morning. He winced but pressed on with what he needed to do. "Drew Koopman? My name's Oscar. I'm with the FFD."

"I know who you are," Drew said, sounding more awake. "What's wrong? Do you need Eagle Point's help with a search?"

Oscar figured that was what Drew would think after a call this late...or rather, early. "No. I'm calling because Caryn needs you."

"What? What's wrong? What happened?"

He was definitely awake now.

Oscar told him briefly about what had gone down tonight. How he'd thought they were going to be playing a harmless prank on Caryn. A kind of initiation. How he had no idea what Paul ultimately had in mind.

"That fucker!" Drew barked. "Where's he taking her?"

"As far as I know, to the Eagle Rock Trail."

"Christ, that's way out of town," Drew said. "There's no way she'll be able to walk back, not if she's as drunk as you say. And there's no cell reception."

"I know. Which is why I'm calling you."

"If one hair on her head is hurt, I'm fucking killing him—and *your* ass is done for right along with him," Drew threatened in a menacing tone. "You were part of this. Why didn't you stop them?"

"It was four against one," Oscar argued lamely, but inside, he felt like shit. He should've said something. Should've stood up for Caryn, who hadn't done anything wrong. She'd just wanted to get to know them, to be part of their team. A team Oscar was deeply ashamed of now.

"That's bullshit and you know it!" Drew fumed. "You know how many times I've heard cops say the same thing? It's no goddamn excuse! I swear to God, if they've hurt her, you'll fucking regret it."

"I already do," Oscar said quietly. He opened his mouth to say something else, but Drew had already hung up.

Sighing, he turned to leave. He had a lot of thinking to do. Drew was right, he should've said something. Done whatever was necessary to stop them.

"Hey, man," the bartender said before Oscar got two steps from the barstool where he'd been sitting.

Looking back, he raised a brow in question.

"I hope that was her man you called."

"It was."

"Good. I was gonna call the police before I overheard you talkin'."

Oscar nodded at him then walked out. The Cellar had a bad reputation, and much of it was warranted...but the bartender had proven that it wasn't *all* bad.

CHAPTER FOURTEEN

Drew's heart was beating a million miles an hour. He was driving way too fast, but it still wasn't fast enough. He needed to get to Caryn. Make sure Paul and his asshole friends hadn't decided that leaving her in the woods wasn't good enough. She was a beautiful woman, and if anyone had touched her, they'd fucking pay.

He turned into the parking area for the trailhead and panicked for a moment when he didn't see anyone. But then his headlights caught on something off to the side, close to the tree line.

Caryn.

He slammed his Jeep into park, left the keys in the ignition, and flew out the door. He was in front of her in seconds. He went to his knees, alarmed when she didn't look up at his approach.

"Caryn? Are you all right?"

When she finally looked at him, his heart nearly broke. The tough woman who gave him shit when they worked out and who teased him without thinking twice was...broken.

He'd been furious on the drive out here. Mad at Paul. At

his friends. And at Caryn herself. What the fuck was she thinking? Going to The Cellar was bad enough, but he knew instinctively that she hadn't told anyone where she was going. Then she'd gotten drunk and left with four men.

So many things could've gone wrong. He was beyond furious.

But seeing her now, his anger leeched away so fast it left him shaking. All he felt was concern.

"I threw up," she said weakly.

"That's okay. It's probably the best thing you can do right now," he said quietly, putting his hands on her knees.

"I'm sorry," she said sadly, her lips dropping into a sad frown.

"Are you okay, sweetheart?" he asked again.

"Drunk..." she said.

"Yeah, I see that."

"I thought they wanted to be friends. I'm so stupid," she said with a shake of her head, tears falling down her cheeks.

Now wasn't the time to rehash what she'd done, or why. Drew needed to get her home. He cupped her cheek tenderly. "Can you stand?" he asked.

She shrugged.

"Let's try, huh?" he cajoled. Getting to his feet in front of her, Drew reached down and wrapped his hands around her biceps, squeezing lightly to lift her.

She jerked away from him with a hiss so suddenly, she almost fell off the log she was sitting on. "Ow!" she exclaimed, rubbing her arm.

Frowning, Drew said, "You're hurt?"

"Sore. From where they held me."

Anger threatened to cripple him. A red haze nearly overwhelmed his good sense. He was going to kill Paul Downs and his fucking friends.

When Caryn made no move to stand, he reached down

and carefully wrapped his arms around her waist instead and hauled her up slowly. She straightened, but as soon as she was steady on her feet, she collapsed against his chest. Her hands clutched the material of his T-shirt at his waist almost desperately, and she buried her face into the crook of his neck.

"I'm so tired," she whispered into his skin.

He could smell the alcohol on her breath, the tremors shaking her entire body from the cooler night air. "I know you are. I'm gonna get you home so you can sleep."

"Tired of tryin' to make people like me. Why don't they like me, Drew? What's wrong with me?"

Drew's heart broke for her when she began crying again. He wrapped an arm around her waist, anchoring her to him as he turned them toward his Jeep. He would feel a lot better once they were out of the middle of nowhere and no one could sneak up on them. He had no idea if Paul and his crew of assholes had stuck around somewhere.

"Lots of people like you, sweetheart. Me, my whole team, Lilly, Bristol, Elsie, Finley...Otto, Silas, Sandra. Hell, I even heard Dorothea and her cronies talking about you the other day. All good stuff too."

She was silent as he shuffled them carefully across the gravel parking area. He opened the passenger side of his Jeep and turned Caryn so she was facing him. "Do you need to puke again?"

She shook her head, but then her brows furrowed and she shrugged.

"I'll keep the window rolled down, just in case. Okay?"

"Okay," she whispered.

He lifted her up and into the seat, and she twisted her legs around so she was facing forward. Drew buckled her seat belt then jogged around to the driver's side.

The ride back to town was quiet, but he couldn't stop

himself from looking over at Caryn every few seconds. He didn't know how much she'd had to drink tonight, but she was way more out of it than after the girls' night with her friends. For a moment, he wondered if he should call Doc Snow, but then decided against it. He'd keep watch over her and if anything happened, then he'd call the doctor.

Drew's mind spun with the things he needed to do...make sure Art knew his granddaughter was safe, talk to Simon about the shit Paul Downs and his buddies had pulled. Call Bristol and tell her he wasn't going to make their meeting today. And Ethan, so he didn't expect him at the barn.

And thank Oscar for calling him.

That last one chapped his ass, as Oscar had gone to The Cellar knowing full well what Paul had planned for Caryn. But he *had* called him when his conscience finally caught up with him. It didn't absolve him of being a total asshole, but Drew was still thankful he'd had the balls to let him know where the other men had taken her.

He pulled up in front of his small rental house and cut the engine. Caryn's eyes were closed and it looked like she'd either passed out or fallen asleep. He hurried over to her side of the vehicle and unlatched the seat belt.

"Caryn?" he said, putting his hand on her cheek.

"Mmmmm?"

"I need you to stay awake for just a little longer."

"Feel awful," she murmured.

"I know. Come on, I'll help you walk."

She wasn't exactly steady, but thankfully she did manage to put one stumbling foot in front of the other. Drew hadn't taken the time to lock his door when he'd left earlier, so all he had to do was turn the knob to get inside. He steered Caryn down the hall to his bedroom and set her on the side of the mattress. She swayed a bit but didn't fall over.

Drew didn't even think about what he was doing. All he

had in mind was making her as comfortable as possible. He undid a few buttons on her blouse then said, "Arms up," as he took hold of the hem of the pretty black shirt she had on.

She did as he asked without complaint or comment, raising her arms over her head. Drew peeled the shirt off and dropped it on the floor. He removed the shirt he'd thrown on when Oscar called and pulled it over Caryn's head. Her hair was mussed, and if he wasn't so worried about her, he would've found it sexy.

He reached under the shirt and unclipped her bra at her back. It took him a bit of maneuvering, but he eventually figured out how to remove it without taking the shirt off again. She sat there, silent, practically falling asleep sitting up as he reached for the button of her jeans.

"Lie back, honey," he said.

She did, flopping backward onto his mattress. He would've chuckled at that, but he didn't have it in him at the moment. Drew pulled off her sneakers and socks, then her jeans. He pulled her back up into a sitting position. "I'm going to go to the kitchen for a second and get you a glass of water. Did you drink any tonight?"

She frowned and shook her head. "No."

Anger threatened to overwhelm Drew again, but he tamped it down. Caryn needed his care right now, not his ire. "All right, I'll be back. Try to stay upright so you can drink the water when I return."

"'Kay."

Drew was back at her side in less than a minute. She was still sitting right where he'd left her. His T-shirt actually fit her pretty well. He handed her the glass of water and said, "Drink as much as you can, hon."

She did as he asked and chugged most of the water.

"Easy," he warned. But it was too late. She went pale and started gagging. Luckily, Drew had grabbed an oversized bowl from the kitchen when he was getting the water...just in case. He thrust it under her just as she puked up most of the water she'd drank, hopefully along with some of the alcohol that was still in her stomach.

Caryn moaned and Drew rubbed her back with one hand while he held the bowl in the other.

"I'm sorry! God, I'm so sorry," she said in a small voice.

"I know you are. It's okay," Drew said. "You done for now?"

She nodded.

"All right, I'm just going to go empty this and get you more water."

"No more water," she moaned.

"You need it, sweetheart," he said firmly. "But this time, maybe you should sip it instead of chugging it down."

"Okay," she said docilely.

Drew made quick work of emptying the bowl into the toilet, rinsing it out, and refilling the glass of water.

This time when he reentered his room, Caryn was lying on her side, one of his pillows clutched to her chest. She looked so...small. This woman never looked small. She seemed to take up all the space in a room wherever she went. Her laugh was big. Her smile was bigger. To see her curled up with her knees tucked to her chest and her head buried in his pillow was somehow just wrong.

Drew sat on the edge of the mattress next to her. "Can you sit up and drink some of this for me?" he asked gently.

Caryn sighed but did as he asked. Drew helped her sit up just enough to drink. This time she was more cautious, taking a few sips rather than gulping the whole thing down.

"Okay?" he asked.

She nodded and lowered herself back down to the mattress.

Deciding he'd pushed her enough for now, Drew placed

the glass next to her side of the bed. She was going to be hurting tomorrow morning...well, later *this* morning...for sure. He stood, unfastened and took off his cargo pants, then walked around the bed to the other side. He didn't even consider leaving her alone. No way in hell was he leaving when she was this inebriated.

He got under the sheet and scooted over until he was at Caryn's back. She was curled into a small ball again, and he didn't hesitate to wrap himself around her from behind. One arm pushed under the pillow she was using and the other went around her waist.

To his satisfaction, she sighed and snuggled closer. Her ass was nestled against his dick, but he was far from aroused. Tonight had been too close. So many things could've gone differently...and not in a good way. She was actually fortunate Paul and his cronies were merely assholes and not rapists.

Drew kissed the back of Caryn's head. Her hair smelled like cigarette smoke from the bar, but he could also smell the scent of some sort of flower. Probably from her shampoo.

"You're gonna be okay, sweetheart," he said.

Caryn didn't reply verbally, but she grabbed hold of his forearm where it rested over her belly. Her fingers tightened for a moment, before they went slack.

Drew knew he wouldn't sleep a wink. He was too focused on the feel of her chest moving up and down against him. Of listening to the sound of her breaths entering and leaving her body. If she woke up sick again, he'd be there to hold the bowl and make sure she didn't choke on her own vomit. If she stopped breathing, he'd be there to breathe life back into her. And when she woke, he'd be there to nurse her through the hellacious hangover she was sure to have.

If he wasn't sure this woman was his before, he was now.

He couldn't help but feel as if he'd somehow let her down tonight. Which was crazy, since he'd had no idea of her plans.

But he couldn't shake the idea that if he'd done something different, maybe she would've trusted him enough to confide in him where she was going. He might not have liked that she wanted to meet Paul and the others at The Cellar, but he could've gone with her and sat at the bar while she hung out with the firefighters. Could've had her back.

Because that was what partners did...they had each other's backs no matter what.

He was disappointed in himself, in her, in the entire episode tonight, but it made him more determined to show this woman that she was no longer alone. That she could trust him. Could share her deepest fears and desires with him...just as he wanted to do with her.

They were at a turning point, and he knew it. Tomorrow would either make or break their relationship. Drew was scared to death that Caryn would use this to pull away from him. That she'd decide moving to Fallport wasn't what she wanted after all. It would shred him, but ultimately it was her decision. All he could do was give her a reason to stay.

Tightening his arm around her, Drew took a deep breath. He wasn't tired in the least. So he lay there silently...and prayed Caryn wouldn't push him away in the morning.

* * *

Caryn was dying.

That was the only sensible reason for feeling as awful as she did at the moment.

Keeping her eyes closed, she took stock. Her head was throbbing. Her mouth tasted as if something had crawled in there and died. And it was dry. Dry as the desert. Every muscle in her body was sore as well. She tried to remember what she'd done in her last workout that would make her so sore, but couldn't think of anything.

She heard a noise from the other room and her thoughts turned immediately to Art. What time was it? Was he up already? Did he need her to fix him something to eat?

The thought of food immediately made nausea rise within Caryn and it was all she could do not to throw up. When she had herself under control, she cracked her eyes open to slits. The first thing she spotted was a glass of water sitting next to the bed.

She reached out from under the covers for the glass. The urge to drink the liquid as fast as she could was strong, but something in the back of her mind warned her that wouldn't be smart. So she did her best to take her time. When she'd finished three-fourths of the water, she actually felt a little better. Her head was still throbbing, but she could think a little clearer now.

Lifting herself slightly, Caryn froze.

She wasn't in her bed at Art's house, that was clear. But she had no idea where she was or how she'd gotten there.

Slowly, memories of the night before began to slip back into her consciousness.

The Cellar. Paul goading her into matching him and his friends shot for shot. Stumbling out of the bar to Dennis's car. Being forced out of the car and shoved to the ground. Something about Bigfoot. That was where things got fuzzy.

Tensing, Caryn rolled to her back—and was enormously relieved when she didn't feel any pain between her legs. Frowning, she stared up at the ceiling. The room was dim, the curtains pulled tightly shut. But she could hear birds singing outside and sunshine was peeking through a crack in the curtains. Looking at even the thin beam of light hurt her head, so she looked away to examine the room.

She might not remember how she'd gotten here, but now that she was becoming more and more aware, she had a feeling she knew exactly where she was. The scent in her nostrils was a huge giveaway.

Drew.

She was surrounded by his woodsy scent. She'd recognize it anywhere.

As if her thoughts had conjured the man, the door creaked quietly as it opened, and Caryn looked over to see Drew peering into the room.

"You're awake," he said softly, which Caryn appreciated.

"Yeah," she croaked, then cleared her throat.

His gaze went to the glass of water by the bed, then back to her. Approval shone in his eyes. "You want some more water?"

"No, I'm good for now," she told him.

"How hungover are you?" he asked.

"On a scale of one to ten...about a two hundred and twenty-four."

His lips twitched. "Not surprised. You want to get up? Or hang out in here for a while?"

"What time is it?" she asked.

"A little after twelve."

Caryn frowned as her brain tried to absorb what he'd just told her. "At night?" she asked, despite all evidence to the contrary.

He chuckled at that. "No, sweetheart. In the afternoon."

She stared at him in confusion. Then said, "What day?"

"Saturday. What do you remember about last night?" he asked.

Caryn closed her eyes and turned back onto her side. She was too embarrassed to look at Drew. She didn't know what happened, but it was obvious he'd found her and brought her back to his house. She was deeply mortified. "I went out with Paul and the guys. Got drunk. Left. That's about it."

"You met them there to get to know them better. To try

to bond with people you would be going into very extreme situations with. And they abused your trust. They were doing shots of water while you were downing vodka. Then they drove you out to Eagle Rock Trail and left you there. Staggering drunk. By yourself. In the dark. When they knew your phone wouldn't work."

Yup. Caryn was more than embarrassed. She was disgusted with herself. She knew wanting to be accepted was her greatest flaw. She'd worked her entire life to try to fit in with different fire stations and groups of people, and failed. Apparently living in Fallport wasn't going to be any different.

"Oscar called me," Drew said.

He hadn't come closer. Was still standing in the doorway, leaning against the doorjamb. As if he couldn't stand to be near her...and Caryn supposed she couldn't blame him. She could smell the alcohol on her own breath still.

"He told me what happened. Felt bad about it all. Not that his regret absolves him of anything, but at least he ultimately did the right thing and let me know where the others were taking you."

Caryn nodded.

"They're lucky they weren't there when I arrived," Drew said in a deep voice.

She looked up at him then, and blinked at the anger shining from his eyes.

"I would've hurt them. Bad," he said. "I want to fucking kill them. The only reason I haven't gone on a rampage is because you're all right."

"You're mad," she said inanely. It was a stupid thing to say because his anger was like a living, breathing thing right now. Every muscle in his body was tense. She had no idea what was holding him back, but he reminded her of a kettle full of steaming, red-hot water, on the verge of boiling over.

Before she could control herself, a tear escaped and rolled

down her cheek. "I'll get out of your hair," she said as she sat up and swung her legs over the side of the mattress. The movement made the nausea rise within her once more, and it took her a few seconds of measured breaths to control it. She'd be damned if she was going to puke all over Drew's floor.

Before she could stand, Drew was there. Pushing her back gently so she was once more lying on the bed. He sat by her hip and leaned over her, hands on either side of her chest, caging her in. But instead of feeling nervous, Caryn wanted to throw herself into his arms.

"I'm *furious*," he told her.

Caryn winced. She'd fucked everything up with her stupidity. Another tear joined the first, running down her temple this time instead of her face since she was lying on her back.

Drew lifted a hand and wiped the tear away, but another followed.

"But mostly I'm relieved that you're all right. Nothing else is as important."

She couldn't believe he wasn't bitching her out. Telling her she was an idiot. "Why aren't you yelling at me?" she blurted.

"Would it change anything? Would it make either of us feel better? The answer is no to both of those questions. The bottom line is that those assholes took advantage of your desire to be part of a team."

"No one forced me to drink," she felt compelled to say.

"I realize that, but that doesn't mean they had the right to trick you that way either. There's a reason hazing is illegal."

"What now?" she whispered.

"You lie here until you feel better. I'll bring you some dry toast and we'll see if you can keep that down. I've got some sports drink as well, so we can get you rehydrated. When you feel up to it, you can shower. I put a toothbrush on the bathroom counter for you, and I've already washed your clothes from last night. When you're ready, maybe we can go on a short walk. The fresh air will probably make you feel better than anything else."

Caryn blinked in surprise. He was being so...nice. And it confused her.

"I called Art. He knows you're here, but not exactly why. I just told him you had a bit too much to drink last night and I brought you here. When you're up for it, he'd probably like to hear from you."

"Wait...we were supposed to go over to Bristol and Rocky's house today."

"Yup. But we aren't."

"You had an appointment."

"Which we rescheduled," Drew said without seeming too upset that she'd disrupted his life. "And I should be asking *you* what now," he said after a moment. He hadn't moved away from her, was still hovering. "What are your plans now?"

"Plans?" she asked. Her head was killing her and the throbbing made it hard to think.

"Yeah. On staying here in Fallport."

"Oh, *those* plans." Caryn hadn't even begun to think about what happened now.

Drew was as still as a statue above her. His gaze unwavering.

She took a deep breath in through her nose. "Well, I'm not all that fired up to work at the FFD anymore."

His lips twitched. "Don't blame you."

"And that leaves me without a job once again," she mused.

"What about that gig you told me about with Thomas Robertson? Where he offered to pass your contact info to his author buddies?"

For the first time, Caryn considered the suggestion seriously. She'd always kind of blown Thomas off when he'd brought up the fact that his friends begged him to talk to her about helping them. She'd assumed he was exaggerating, or just being nice. She was also a firefighter, not an editor, or whatever it was that she did for Thomas.

Now she had no desire whatsoever to work with Paul or any of his friends, but she still wanted to stay in Fallport. She wondered if she really could beta read for a living.

"I don't know," she told Drew honestly.

"Right. So...I'm gonna be blunt here, then give you some room to think," he said.

Caryn braced.

"You scared the shit out of me last night. When I got that call, all I could think of was possibly finding you battered and broken. I was truly ready to kill Paul and the others if they'd laid one finger on you. I was mad. At them. At you. But now that I've had time to think, I realize that my anger at you stemmed from my *worry* for you. I hate that you didn't feel as if you could confide in me. Tell me what you were doing last night. I might not have agreed with it, but I never would've stood in your way.

"Sweetheart, you're trying so hard to fit in, you don't realize that you already do. This is your town. You were brought up here, even if you were only here in the summers. Most people think extremely highly of you. But for some reason, you can't see it. If the fire service is too stupid to recognize how skilled you are, what a huge asset you'd be, then it's *their* loss, not yours. Not everyone is going to like you...but so what?

"I learned through my time in law enforcement that all I can do is be the best person possible, and always do what I can to help others, even if they don't want my assistance. I don't need to be best friends with everyone I meet or work with. I actually don't want to. I'm content with my inner circle. Ethan, Zeke, Rocky, Brock, Tal, and Raid. And my circle is slowly expanding to include Lilly, Elsie, and Bristol. And now you. Their opinions matter to me, no one else's...no one else's but *yours*.

"I want you to stay. See where this connection takes us. But if you can't see what's right in front of you—true friends who would bend over backward to help you, laugh with you when you're happy, cry with you when you're sad—I'm not sure we'll work out." He paused, taking a deep breath before continuing.

"*Fuck* Paul. Fuck anyone who doesn't see your value. They aren't worth your time or energy, Caryn. I have no doubt you'll find something to do here that you'll excel at. But you have to let go of this need to be accepted by every single person you meet. It'll eat you up inside until you're a shell of the incredible woman I know."

Then he leaned over, kissed her forehead gently, and sat up. He grabbed her almost empty glass on his way out, gave her a gentle smile, and quietly shut the door behind him.

Caryn had to pee, and she badly wanted to brush her teeth or at least swish some mouthwash, but all she could do at the moment was lie there and stare at the ceiling.

Drew was right. She knew he was. And she cried again because that beautiful man could see her worth, even when she didn't.

All her life, she'd been an unwilling loner. In school, here in Fallport in the summers, in college, even at the fire academy. She'd always dreamed of making solid connections with others. Laughing and joking with co-workers. Being invited to hang out with them at backyard barbeques or at happy hour.

It never happened. And instead of living her own life, finding her own tribe of people to hang out with, people who accepted her as she was, she'd tried even harder to fit in...with no success.

Last night, she'd hoped *this* time things would be different. Only to find herself the butt of a few assholes' jokes. Rejected worse than ever before.

Yes. Drew was right about everything. It was high time she stopped acting like a twelve-year-old, hoping to be a popular kid in school. She was never going to be that person, and it was way past time she came to terms with it. She had more than enough to offer, and new people in her life who seemed to like her just as she was.

Last night could've ended so differently. She knew it. Drew knew it. Hell, even Paul and his friends knew it. She'd been totally at their mercy, and while they weren't nice men, at least they hadn't taken advantage of her in the worst way possible.

Suddenly, instead of feeling as if her life had gone to shit because the fire department job was no longer an option, Caryn felt...free.

She'd been a firefighter for so long, she wasn't sure she knew how to be anything else, but she could use her skills elsewhere. With Drew and his friends on the search and rescue team. Her medical skills would also come in handy as well.

She smiled for the first time that morning when she thought about how Thomas would react upon learning she was ready to branch out and start reading for some of his friends. He'd be over-the-moon excited for her.

It wasn't going to be easy to change her mindset when it came to wanting to be liked, but she'd do it.

Once upon a time, one of her instructors at the fire academy told her she'd never make it. That she was too weak, too emotional, that women couldn't do as good a job as men in the heat of a blaze. He was wrong, she'd proven it. Now she'd prove to herself, and Drew, that she could turn over a new leaf when it came to how she thought about herself.

Sitting up, Caryn waited for the room to stop spinning

before standing. She still felt like shit, but she was ready to get up and stop feeling sorry for herself. She had a damn good life. She got to spend time with her grandfather, she had new friends, a boyfriend who was more than forgiving, and she was a world-famous author's right-hand woman.

Fuck Paul and his friends—and anyone else who didn't like her for any reason.

CHAPTER FIFTEEN

Drew stood in his kitchen with his hands braced on the counter, his head down, and he prayed he hadn't messed things up between him and Caryn. She was such an amazing woman, and it slayed him that she couldn't see it. Hated that she craved acceptance from people who didn't even deserve to share the same air as her.

He had no idea how long he'd been standing there when he heard something behind him. Turning, Drew saw Caryn standing in the entryway to the small living area. She'd obviously showered, and she wore the same jeans and blouse she had on the night before. He'd placed them inside his room earlier, after cleaning them. Shortly after, he'd called Art and Rocky, letting them know what was up with Caryn. The basic details, not exactly what had gone down.

Drew was exhausted after having stayed awake for the rest of the night, watching over her, making sure she was safe. But he still felt wired. Now, he held his breath, praying she wasn't going to tell him she was done. That she was moving back to New York.

She didn't speak, just padded across the room until she

was in front of him. Just as she'd done last night at the trail-head, she wrapped her arms around him and hugged him tight.

"You're right. About all of it...thank you so much for saying what I needed to hear. I'm staying, Drew. I'm going to call Thomas next week and tell him I'm interested in working with other authors. And maybe...we can organize some sort of local volunteer search group? I'll have time on my hands, and it's crazy that the Eagle Point Search and Rescue team goes out on searches strictly by themselves. Wouldn't it help if you had more boots on the ground, so to speak?"

Drew was so relieved, it took him a full minute before he was composed enough to speak. "It *would* help, but the last thing we need is untrained people tromping around in the woods getting lost themselves."

"Right. So we need to train them."

He and the others had thought about doing just what she was suggesting, but for one reason or another had never followed through. Mostly because they all worked full-time jobs. Putting Caryn in charge of organizing and training a volunteer group would be the perfect solution, and with her people skills, he knew she could do it better than anyone else on the team.

He pulled back so he could see her eyes. "You're really staying?"

She nodded.

"Thank fuck," he growled, before lowering his head.

He kissed her hard. It was passionate and intense, and Drew did his best to show her without words how relieved he was that she was all right, that she was staying, that she wasn't upset with him for saying all the things he had. All of it.

She kissed him back just as passionately.

When they both had to take a break to breathe, they stared at each other.

"Thank you for coming to get me last night," she told him.

"I'll always come for you," Drew said without hesitation.

"Um...as much as I wouldn't mind continuing this," she gestured between them shyly, "I'm still a little queasy. I thought maybe I could try that toast you mentioned, then if it's not too late, maybe we could still go over to Bristol's? I'm not going to be any help with the barn, but being outside sounds nice. As long as I have sunglasses to wear, I think I'll be okay."

"You sure?" Drew asked.

Caryn nodded.

"Okay. But I'll tell them we aren't staying too long. You're still dehydrated. And to be honest, I'm exhausted."

She frowned in concern. "Did you get any sleep last night?"

"No."

"No? Like, not at all? Or not much?"

"I wasn't going to sleep when you were that drunk, sweetheart. I stayed awake to make sure you were all right."

"Well, shit. Now I feel bad again," she muttered, dropping her eyes.

Drew put a finger under her chin and lifted it so she was looking at him once more. "Even though I was worried about you, and pissed about what those jackasses did, last night was one of the most memorable nights of my life. Holding you in bed for the first time? Having you snuggle back against me and groan in complaint when I got up? Best feeling ever."

Caryn blushed. "I'm sure if I was awake, and not drunk or hungover, and not puking in a bowl—which I now remember, and am mortified about, and we need to never speak of it again as long as we live—it would've been mine too."

Drew laughed. "This is gonna work out," he vowed.

"I hope so."

"It is," he insisted. "Have a seat and I'll get you some toast. Maybe a Sprite too? Think you can hold that down?"

"Yes. And, Drew?"

"Yeah?"

"This time, I mean it when I say I'm never drinking like that again. Not to excess. I might have a glass of wine or a beer, but nothing more. If anyone gives me shit about not drinking, I don't care. I've learned my lesson."

Drew was extremely proud of her. He didn't care if she occasionally got drunk or not, but he hoped there would never be another incident like last night, where she didn't remember what happened. She'd been way too vulnerable. She'd been lucky. They'd *both* been lucky.

"Okay, sweetheart. Go sit. I'll be right there with your lunch."

* * *

Later that afternoon, Drew couldn't keep his gaze from roaming over to where Caryn sat with Bristol, Lilly, and Elsie on the front porch of the house. She was a little pale, and hadn't taken off the sunglasses she'd put on when they'd left his house earlier, but she seemed to be in a good mood, laughing and smiling with the other women.

"You okay?" Zeke asked, making Drew turn to him.

By the time he'd arrived, the rest of the guys had measured and cut large beams of wood and finished securing the loft. Now Rocky was going over blueprints for the side of the barn he was turning into a stained-glass workshop for Bristol, discussing them with Ethan, who would be installing all the electrical components. The other guys—Brock, Tal, and Raiden—were taking a break, joking around with Tony and teaching him the joys of a rope swing. They'd attached it to a large tree just outside the barn earlier, and the sound of the boy's laughter ringing through the now empty structure made everyone smile.

"I'm good," Drew told his friend.

"Glad to hear it. Caryn looks a little rough this afternoon."

Drew nodded and gave his friend a quick synopsis of what happened the night before.

A muscle in Zeke's jaw ticked repeatedly. "How are you standing here and not in Paul's face, beating the shit out of that fucker?"

"I wanted to," Drew admitted. "I want to teach him a lesson he'll never forget. But I know Caryn wouldn't want that. She blames *herself* for what happened. And while yes, on the surface, it can be argued that she met them there of her own free will and could've said no to the drinks, the bottom line was that they used her desire to be accepted. Paul was in a position of power over her, because he's in charge of the hiring committee for that firefighter job. She knew it. He knew it. And he took advantage."

"So? What are we doing about it?" Zeke asked.

Drew smiled. He loved that his friends had his back, always. This was what he'd searched his entire career for. It was ironic that he'd found it after quitting. This kind of loyalty was also what he wanted for Caryn. To realize that she already had it, whether or not they ended up together. "Nothing," he said belatedly.

"Nothing?" Zeke asked, clearly outraged. "You've got to be kidding!"

"Nope. Caryn's decided not to apply for the job after all."

"She's leaving?" Zeke asked.

"No. She's staying. And she wants to organize and train a group of volunteers to help with searches when we need them."

Zeke's eyes widened at that. "Seriously?"

"Yup. The bottom line is that fucking with Paul could ultimately come back to Caryn, and I don't want to do anything that would make her uncomfortable."

"But?" Zeke asked, knowing Drew well enough to know there was no way he was going to just let what happened go without some sort of retaliation.

"I had a long talk with Art this morning, when I called to let him know Caryn was all right. Told him some of the details, but not how bad off Caryn was. I kind of hinted that if he wanted to tell people who came to the post office about what happened, and what Paul and his friends did...and even embellish a bit...I wouldn't object."

Zeke grinned. "Genius."

"What's genius?" Raid asked as he walked up to them.

After Zeke explained, Raiden laughed. "The gossip network will do its thing and he'll definitely be feeling the heat for a while. People in Fallport have long memories."

An hour later, after more work in the barn, Rocky approached Drew and slapped him on the back. "You're dead on your feet. Go home," he ordered.

Drew didn't bother to protest. His friend wasn't wrong. After the stress of last night, staying up watching over Caryn, and the physical exertion this afternoon, he was more than ready to call it a day. "Thanks. I think I'll take that suggestion."

"One thing..." Rocky said.

Drew glanced at him with a raised eyebrow.

"Don't do that shit again," his friend said sternly.

"Do what?"

"Not call one of us when shit hits the fan."

Drew sighed. He'd had a feeling this was going to come up sooner or later. "Everything happened so fast. I got the call after one-thirty and was literally in my Jeep headed to the trail at one thirty-five."

"Don't care. You could've called us on the way. Or when you got home. One of us would've come over and helped look after her while you got some sleep. We could've gone to talk to Art this morning. Brought you breakfast. *Something.* I know you're trying to build a relationship with her, but that doesn't mean you shut out your friends when you need them the most."

Drew nodded. "Point made."

"Good."

And just like that, any animosity Rocky might've had was gone. "She okay? You need anything?"

"She's all right. I think today was good for her. I had planned to just hang out at my house with her, but after seeing her with the other women...this was the right choice."

"See? Friends make everything better," Rocky said with a smirk.

Drew rolled his eyes. "Don't get all sappy on me."

"Can't help it. The love of a good woman does that," Rocky said without an ounce of embarrassment. "Thanks for your help today. I think we might just be ready in time for Ethan and Lilly's wedding."

"I know you will. Thank Bristol again for me, for being understanding about changing our meeting."

"Sure. But you know she's not worried. She knows you've got her back when it comes to that shit."

He did, but Drew appreciated her not being upset with him anyway. After saying goodbye to his other friends, he made his way toward the porch where the women were sitting. The three other women each had a glass of wine in their hands, but Caryn was holding a bottle of water.

As he walked toward them, she stood. "Done?" she asked.

"I am, yes," Drew said. Then he turned to the others. "You all good?"

"Why does everyone always ask that?" Lilly said with a

223

small laugh. "You guys have been watching us all afternoon. We aren't bleeding, haven't let out even one scream at the bugs that have landed on us, and we're sitting here calmly and comfortably. Why would you think we *aren't* good?"

"Just checking," Drew said with a smile.

"It's nice," Bristol replied.

"Very much so," Elsie echoed.

"Thanks for the water and conversation," Caryn said. "And thanks for not telling me what an idiot I was for last night."

Drew wasn't sure she'd tell them about last night, but he was glad she did.

"You weren't an idiot, *they* were," Lilly said fiercely.

"Right? What total assholes. If they think I'm donating any money to their new equipment fund, they're smoking crack," Bristol added with a scowl.

"And if they think I'm serving any of them if they dare step foot inside On the Rocks, they're dreaming."

Caryn smiled. "Thanks for the support, guys."

"Anytime."

"Of course."

"See you later?"

The last was asked by Lilly.

"Yup. Tomorrow at Sweet Tooth at ten, right?" Caryn asked.

"Uh-huh," Lilly said. Then she stood and hugged Caryn. The other two women followed suit.

After a few more minutes of small talk, Drew just took Caryn's hand in his and waved at the women. "Okay, we're going. Thanks, all. See you later."

Everyone laughed as he towed Caryn toward his Jeep.

"That was kind of rude," she scolded when they were seated and on their way.

"Caryn, you guys would've stood there for another ten

minutes saying goodbye. I just sped up the process a bit."

She giggled. "Okay, you're probably right."

"No probably about it," Drew told her. Then he reached for her hand, feeling good when she immediately curled her fingers around his. "You feel all right? How's your head?"

"It's okay. Not nearly as bad as it was this morning."

"Good. Hungry yet?"

She grinned. "Starved."

Once more, Drew was relieved. "I thought we'd go back to Art's and we could eat one of the four hundred casseroles he's got in his freezer. He's probably worried about you after last night and would no doubt like to see for himself that you're okay."

"Sounds perfect. I was going to ask if you could bring me home anyway."

Drew nodded.

"You need to sleep."

He nodded again. "Yup. But I'm alright."

"Maybe you could take a nap while I talk with my grandfather and heat up the casserole. It'll take a bit for it to be ready to eat," she suggested.

"Sounds good. If you wouldn't mind."

"Drew, you went out of your way last night. I don't know what would've happened if you hadn't come for me. So, no, I wouldn't mind you getting some sleep when you didn't get any last night because you were looking after me."

"I'd do it again, every night if necessary."

Caryn smiled over at him. "I hope you know that I'd do the same for you."

"I do. We're a good team, sweetheart." He was beginning to think that maybe, just maybe, she was finally seeing that for herself.

"We are," she agreed. "But so far I feel as if I've done more taking than having your back."

"It's not a contest," he said easily with a shrug. "I'm sure there will come a time when you save my ass."

The rest of the drive to Art's house was done in companionable silence. They walked to the front door hand in hand.

The second Caryn was inside, and Art saw her from his chair in the living room, he growled, "It's about time you got home, young lady. Get your butt over here. We need to talk."

"Shit," Caryn muttered.

Drew couldn't help but chuckle. He knew Art had spent the morning in front of the post office with Silas and Otto, and had probably already spread rumors about Paul and his cronies far and wide. But now he was home, clearly worried about his granddaughter and anxious to see for himself that she was in one piece.

"Keep your pants on," she told him. "I need to get a casserole out and in the oven. Then I need to change, because I'm sick of seeing this shirt and want to put on some fat pants. Oh, and Drew's gonna stay and nap while dinner's warming and we talk. Is that okay?"

"Of course it is. As far as I'm concerned, after what he did for you, your young man can move in if he wants to. But hurry it up and get your stuff done so we can chat."

Caryn turned to Drew. "Did Art just give you the okay to move in with us?"

Drew chuckled. "Sounds like he did. For the record, I'm more than okay with living together, although I'm thinking it might be a bit too early for that. But I wouldn't be opposed to some sleepovers." He winked at her. "And please tell me I can nap in your bed."

He loved the blush that spread across her cheeks. "It's only fair, considering I slept in yours last night."

"Best night ever," he reminded her. Then leaned into her, kissed her forehead, and gave Art a chin lift as he headed down the hall toward her bedroom as if he did it every day.

CHAPTER SIXTEEN

After watching Drew disappear down the hall, Caryn took a deep breath. Her head was still throbbing a bit, but she figured as soon as she ate, she'd feel a lot better. She grabbed a casserole from the freezer and preheated the oven. Then she headed for the living room, where her grandfather was waiting.

She'd sensed his gaze on her while she'd puttered around in the kitchen. He wasn't going to be happy after hearing the entire story. But she wouldn't keep anything from him. She'd always shared everything with Art, and even though she was embarrassed by her actions, she wouldn't sugarcoat them.

"Sit, girl," he told her gently, patting the cushion on the couch next to him.

Caryn took a deep breath and sat.

"So...The Cellar?" Art asked.

"I was stupid," she said.

"No," Art said sternly. "My granddaughter is *not* stupid. I don't want to hear you say something like that again."

Caryn couldn't help but smile. Art had always been her

staunchest defender. "Remember that one summer when you almost got into a fight with that guy at the park?" she asked.

Art chuckled. "He would've pounded my ass into the ground," he mused.

"If you knew that, why'd you stand up to him like you did?" Caryn asked.

"Because it was the right thing to do. Look, his kid was an ass. He had no right to push you off that caboose, then say you weren't allowed back on. He was a bully, and his dad wasn't doing a damn thing about it."

"It wasn't a big deal," Caryn said.

"It was. If you'd been mean to him, or if you'd been bossy yourself, I would've let it go. But you literally didn't do anything to that boy. He just decided that he was better than you and he was king of the castle. If *you'd* done that, I would've hauled your butt home and given you a stern lecture about how you aren't better than the next person. When his father smirked and gave his son a thumbs up, I kind of lost it."

"Do you really think that man, or the kid, learned anything from you acting like an overprotective grandfather?" Caryn asked.

"Nope. But you did."

Caryn stilled as she stared at Art.

"Didn't you?" he asked with a raised brow.

Slowly, Caryn nodded. "Yeah. We had a talk when we got home about how the boy was in the wrong and the caboose is public property and no one has the right to prevent someone else from doing something they want to do...as long as no one gets hurt."

"Exactly," Art said with a smug look on his face. "Would'a been worth getting my ass kicked."

Caryn loved this man so much. She didn't know what she was going to do without him. Of course, she hoped he had many more years to live, but she wasn't unrealistic. And his brush with death had scared her. Art was her only family left. Without him, she'd be alone.

Shaking her head slightly and refusing to think about that, she grabbed his hand and squeezed it. "I went to The Cellar because Paul and his buddies invited me. I thought they wanted to get to know me. I thought it would help my chances of getting that open position at the fire department," she told her grandfather.

"Understandable," he said. "That's what people do...feel each other out, see if they click. I imagine that's even more important when you work in a job where you're putting your life on the line to help others."

"Yeah. Anyway, at first it was okay. The Cellar isn't as bad as everyone makes it out to be, a few macho jerks aside. But then a tray of shots was brought out and everyone grabbed one. I kind of felt like I didn't have a choice. Throughout my career, I've always been left out of social gatherings with the crew. Especially as a female in a male-dominated field. If I hadn't taken that shot, I wouldn't have had a chance in hell of getting that job, and we all knew it. So I did it. And the next. And the next. I had no idea they were drinking water while giving me vodka."

"I guess the question is...why did you keep going?" Art asked.

Caryn sighed and looked down at her lap. Art still had her hand in his, and even though it sucked to talk about what she'd done, she also knew her grandfather wouldn't make her feel worse about it. "I guess it was a matter of finishing what I'd started," she said lamely.

Art made a noise in the back of his throat, and she looked over at him.

The disappointment on his face just about killed her. The

last person she ever wanted to disappoint in this world was Art.

"I know, I know. It was a bad decision."

"Understatement," Art said under his breath. Then he reached up and palmed her cheek. "Here's the thing—you messed up. But I'm guessing you also probably saved yourself a lot of time."

Caryn frowned. "I don't understand."

"What would've happened if you'd gone there and they laughed and joked with you, played pool, maybe you all had a beer or two, and then you went on your way?"

Caryn bit her lip as Art dropped his hand. "I guess I would've applied for the job."

"Right. And let's say you got it. Then what?"

"I don't know," she said gruffly.

Art merely lifted a brow at her. She let out a long breath, her cheeks puffing out as she did. "Fine. I would've accepted, started working with them, and eventually found out that they were a bunch of asses. I saw the station, Grandpa. It's a mess. They're all slobs. And lazy. Trash everywhere, the trucks dirty, the crew napping in the middle of the day...it was kind of pathetic."

"Right. So the way I see it, it's a good thing you found out what jerks they are before you wasted your time and energy on them."

He wasn't wrong. "True," she said.

"So...I'm assuming working for the FFD is out. What now?" he asked.

"Yeah. Paul made it clear I wouldn't get the job even if I *did* apply," she mused.

"You're still going to stay though, right?" Art asked.

She could hear the trepidation in his tone. She squeezed the hand she still held. "I'm staying," she said. "I might have to bunk with you for longer than I expected though."

"Girl, you can stay here for as long as you want, you know that. I'll just have to go over to my girlfriends' houses instead of bringing them here."

Caryn laughed. Art was so full of shit. He'd been completely and utterly devoted to his wife. When she'd passed away when Caryn was young, he'd been devastated. There hadn't been anyone else since.

"Right," she said with a smile. "I thought I'd send Thomas an email and let him know I'm open to talking to some of his author friends about beta reading."

Art beamed. "That'a girl."

"And I'm still training with Drew for the SAR team. There's a lot more to it than just walking around the forest looking for people."

"And *finally* we get around to him," Art said with a sparkle in his eye. "He's nice."

Caryn chuckled. "Yeah, he is."

"You like him."

She didn't deny it.

"And he wasn't happy with what happened last night."

Caryn frowned. "No," she said quietly. "He was really upset."

"With you?"

She thought about that for a moment, then shook her head. "No. Well, kind of. He said he was worried about me."

"Caryn, he got a call in the middle of the night that you were drunk and had just left The Cellar—where he didn't know you were even going in the first place—with four men. Of *course* he was worried. What happened when he found you?"

"I don't remember," Caryn admitted, feeling awful all over again. "But when I woke up this morning, I was wearing his shirt, tucked into his bed. He stayed up all night, watching over me to make sure I didn't die. He called you, canceled a meeting he had today, told his friends he couldn't meet with them to help work on the barn on Rocky's property, washed my clothes, and didn't yell at me for being a bonehead when we both knew what I'd done was extremely dangerous."

Art had a huge smile on his face.

"What are you smiling about?" Caryn asked. "I just admitted that I was so drunk, I blacked out."

"And you also told me everything I need to know about the man currently sleeping in your bed."

When he didn't continue speaking, Caryn said quietly, "And what's that?"

"That he likes you too," her grandfather said. "That he'll bend over backward to keep you safe. That he's a good man. Have I told you lately that I love you, and I'm so very proud of all you've accomplished?"

A lump formed in Caryn's throat. She shook her head.

"Well, I am. You didn't choose the easy road for your life. There were times I wished you'd picked a safer occupation... like maybe an accountant, like your man."

Caryn didn't protest the "your man" comment. She kind of liked how that sounded. "I'm terrible at math," she reminded her grandfather. "I would no sooner be an accountant than you would've been a cross-dressing performer at the circus."

He burst out laughing at that. When he had himself under control again, he continued. "All I'm saying is that you're right where you're supposed to be in your life. All the crap you've put up with, all the lives you've saved, all the different stations you've worked at...they've all led you here."

"I'm kind of struggling with the fact that I've spent my entire adult life honing my skills as a firefighter and paramedic, and now I'm turning my back on the job so easily," Caryn admitted.

"You never know what will happen," Art said. "I truly

believe everything we do in life is for a reason. Maybe you'll never step foot in a fire station again. But life has a way of surprising us."

"I could do with fewer surprises," Caryn mumbled. Then louder, she asked, "Do I want to know what rumors you started about Paul and his friends today?"

Art grinned. "I don't know what you're talking about. I don't spread rumors."

"Riiiight," Caryn said.

"I communicate with people," Art told her. "Honestly, I'm sick of talking about me. Everyone asking how I'm doing. Wanting to know if I'm going to keel over soon. So it was kind of nice to talk about something else."

"Like?" Caryn prodded.

"Like how I heard our esteemed fire captain came home with more than good memories from his recent vacation to Florida."

Caryn frowned. "I don't get it."

Art cackled. "I may or may not have insinuated that crabs weren't just something you order at a seafood restaurant."

Caryn did her best to keep her composure, but she couldn't stop the bark of laughter that escaped. "You didn't!" she scolded.

Art shrugged. "I also might've let it slip that Lou's been getting a lot of mail from debt-collection agencies, Dennis has overextended his credit at Grogan's General Store, and George's wife filed a protective order against him with Simon before she left town."

Caryn stared at him, wide-eyed. "Holy crap, Art. You can't do that! You'll get sued for slander or something."

"Not if it's true," he said with another unconcerned shrug.

"Holy crap, how do you *know* all that?"

Art shook his head at her. "Girl, you've been away too

long. I know everything that goes on in this town. Always have, always will."

"You're scary. What else do you know?"

He grinned. "That I'm doubting you'll need to bunk with me for long. Not when your man has a perfectly good house and bed of his own."

Caryn felt herself blushing. "I...we aren't...he... Shoot."

Her grandfather chuckled and patted her knee. "I'm ninety-one. Don't you think it's about time you got on with making me a great-grandfather?"

She was mid-swallow when his meaning sank in, and Caryn choked on her spit. All she could do was stare at Art.

"What?" he asked, trying to sound innocent—and failing. "You want me to sit here and act like I don't know you're a beautiful woman in your prime? I'm assuming you aren't a virgin, considering you were married, and it's kind of late for me to be worrying about your sex life. Drew Koopman is a catch. He's good-looking, full of integrity, he's smart as a whip, and he obviously cares a lot about you. I hope you're already doing the no-pants-dance with the guy, but if you aren't, you should get on that. Neither of us is getting any younger, and if you wait too much longer, it'll be harder for you to get pregnant."

"Granddad!" she protested.

"What?" he asked.

"I can't believe you just called it the no-pants-dance," she said. "Besides, we haven't known each other that long."

"I knew your grandmother for two weeks before I asked her to marry me. She led me on a merry dance for another month before she finally agreed. But by that time, I'd already shown her my prowess in bed and she couldn't resist me anymore."

Caryn lifted her hands and put them over her ears. "No more! I can't talk about sex with you!" she complained.

Art cackled. "All I'm saying is that when you find the person meant to be yours, you know. Time's a-tickin', and I want to see you happy and settled before I die. And I wouldn't mind getting to know my great-grandchild either."

"Can we please not talk about you dying? You're going to live to be one hundred and forty-seven. Period." The tender look on her grandfather's face nearly did Caryn in.

"I love you, girl," Art said. "You'll never know how much."

"I love you too."

"This is a turning point in your life. Firefighting might be out, but I still see great things in your future."

"I hope so."

"I know so," he returned. "Now, why don't you put that casserole in, then go snuggle with your man for a while. Make sure he knows how appreciative you are for all he's done for you lately. I'll get the casserole out when it's done."

"I'm not sure I like that my grandfather is pushing me to have sex with my boyfriend," Caryn muttered.

"I might be old, but I remember how awesome sex was," Art said with a grin.

"Right. I'm going. I can't stomach you talking about sex anymore," Caryn said. She stood, but Art grabbed her hand before she could leave.

"I'm glad you're all right," he said quietly. "Without you, I'd have nothing."

It was all Caryn could do not to burst into tears. Because she felt the same way. And the truth was, Art would be leaving her way before she was ready. "Love you. Thank you for spreading those rumors—sorry. For *communicating* those things about the assholes from last night."

"You're welcome."

They shared one more tender look, before she finally turned and headed into the kitchen. When she made it to her room a few minutes later, she cautiously opened her door and saw Drew fast asleep on top of the covers. His mouth was open just slightly, his hair mussed, his expression soft...and she swore she'd never seen anything as sexy as this man in her entire life. There was something about watching him when he was completely vulnerable that made her feel even closer to him. Because Drew Koopman was never vulnerable. He was always watchful, eyeing everyone and everything around him. Always on duty, so to speak.

She tiptoed to the edge of the mattress and slowly sat on the bed. Drew woke up right away, of course.

"Dinner ready?" he mumbled, his eyes still closed.

"Not yet. Mind if I join you for a while?" she asked.

Instead of responding verbally, Drew grabbed her around the waist and pulled her against him, spooning her from behind.

Laughing, and not really surprised he could get her settled against him without even opening his eyes, she snuggled close.

"Thank you for everything," she whispered after a moment.

"Would do anything for you," Drew murmured.

She had no idea if he was asleep or not, but his words settled deep inside her. All her life, all she'd wanted was to be accepted. And he'd been right earlier when he'd told her that she didn't need to try so hard, that she'd already been accepted into his group of friends with open arms.

For the first time possibly ever, contentment settled in her soul. She didn't need to be liked by every single person she met...as long as she had a few good friends, she could be content.

Caryn wasn't really tired, she'd slept way longer than usual last night, thanks to the alcohol in her veins. Drew had kept watch over her, and it was her turn now. She tightened her hold on his arm and smiled when he mumbled something under his breath and nuzzled her hair.

This man was her future. Like her grandfather had said, when you know, you know. It still scared her to death, the possibility of things not working out was high, but she was done playing it safe. She was falling for this man, and for whatever reason, he seemed to be falling for her too.

She was going to go after what she wanted—and what she wanted was Drew. Under her. Over her. Behind her. She'd learned a very clear lesson last night, and before that, with her grandfather's attack. Life wasn't guaranteed. She needed to live for the moment.

Which for her meant emailing Thomas tomorrow about her desire to beta read for others, spending more time with her new friends, eating more cinnamon rolls, loosening up a bit more, continuing to learn all she could about search and rescue...and making love with Drew.

Smiling at that last one, she intertwined her fingers with his on her belly. He tightened his hold briefly, then relaxed once more.

Caryn had no idea what her new life in Fallport had in store for her, but she knew without a doubt that whatever time she had with Drew would be life-changing. She wouldn't regret being in a relationship with him if things didn't work out. For once in her life, she was doing what *she* wanted, without worrying about the opinions of others. And it felt awesome.

* * *

Paul sat in his dark bedroom, fuming. He'd had more people texting, emailing, and calling him about the rumor that he'd come back from Florida with a sexually transmitted disease than he wanted to think about.

So what if he had a rash on his balls? It was totally worth it. The whore he'd hooked up with had been hot as hell. He'd never had a fuck like that before. So good, he'd paid her to stay the whole damn night, and he couldn't even remember how many times he'd come. She'd been worth every single dollar. The bitches here in Fallport couldn't compare to the pussy he got down in Miami. Not even close.

He had zero doubt it was that old bastard who'd spread the rumor. He had no idea how Art knew about his rash, but he blamed *Caryn* for the fact it was now common knowledge.

But his anger wasn't just about his trip to Florida. Last night was a just a fucking *joke*. Something he and all his friends did to each other—and no one ever took the pranks they played on each other personally. But of course, the bitch *had* to open her mouth and tell everyone what happened. Or at least her damn grandfather, who was a gossiping asshole.

And now Paul was paying the price.

The police chief had already been to the station to interrogate him. And he learned others patrons at the bar had also been contacted. The last thing he needed was an investigation. The fact that *anyone* might take Caryn's word for what happened, against Paul's own word and those of his friends, people who had saved more lives in this fucking town than she ever would, stuck in his craw.

Paul couldn't lose his job. He'd worked damn hard to get where he was. He was captain of the FFD, and he wasn't going down without a fight.

That bitch was the bane of his existence. Always had been. He *hated* her. Last night was about putting Caryn Buckner in her place and letting her know she'd never be one of them. The only reason he'd ever hire a woman would be to shut up those assholes on the city council concerned about diversification. Not a single member of his crew wanted a chick on their squad. No way.

He could've fucked her up good if he really wanted to. Dennis had said something about fucking her, but Paul refused. Really, she should be *thanking* him, not trying to ruin his goddamn reputation!

All they'd done was left her at a trailhead. They could've done so many worse things. It wasn't their fault she couldn't handle her liquor. No one held a gun to her head and forced her to drink. She'd done that of her own free will. The fact that the citizens of Fallport—people he and his friends had helped on countless occasions—were actually turning on them in favor of that bitch was infuriating!

He hoped she *did* apply for the open position at the FFD. He'd take great joy in rejecting her. He'd bring her in for an interview, just to shut the council up, and then choose someone else.

Thinking about hitting Caryn where it hurt most, how upset she'd be when she didn't get the job, made Paul smile.

He hated this goddamn town. He only stuck around because he made decent money as captain. The job was ridiculously easy. They rarely had any fires, there weren't a lot of serious car crashes. He spent most of his time on duty sleeping, earning an easy paycheck. In his down time, he watched porn at home or hung out at The Cellar. He was perfectly content to live in his parents' house, without a mortgage or paying for shit like Internet, TV, electric... He was free to spend his salary on trips to Miami and on his favorite webcam girls. Life was good.

He could *not* lose this job. If the investigation continued, that was a definite possibility. No way did he want to apply elsewhere and start all over. From everything he'd heard about bigger cities and departments, there were a ton rules and regulations the firefighters had to follow.

He needed to come up with a way to stop all the rumors about him and his friends...and put Caryn in her place once and for all. She'd never be a Fallportian, no matter how much she wanted to be.

Paul grinned to himself. He'd just made that word up, but he liked it. He was born and raised here, and had lived in Fallport his entire life. She was a fucking interloper. A non-Fallportian. There had to be some way to chase her out of town... he just had to figure out how.

CHAPTER SEVENTEEN

Something was different with Caryn but Drew couldn't put his finger on what it was. She seemed more...relaxed. That wasn't quite the right word, but it would do. After he'd woken up in her bed at her grandfather's house a few days ago, she wasn't antsy or buzzing with excess energy, like usual.

He'd gone home that night and slept for eight hours straight. When he'd woken up, he had a text from Caryn that said she'd emailed Thomas and already had two phone calls set up with a couple of authors, to see if they could work out the details of her beta reading for them.

They'd worked out each morning, she'd gone over to Bristol's to hang out, attended one of Tony's soccer games, sitting with Elsie and Zeke, and had even gone to a photo shoot with Lilly. She'd spent a morning at the bakery with Finley, and finally made her way into the library to get to know Khloe.

It was as if what had happened at The Cellar had fundamentally changed Caryn in some way. It worried Drew a little, but he was also thrilled for her. She'd taken a shitty situation and used it to her advantage. Putting all her effort into making deeper connections with the people she enjoyed being with most.

And she seemed to have more self-confidence. Which was a major turn-on. At his house, not only did they keep busy doing everyday things couples did—cooking, watching TV, talking—but their physical relationship had progressed. Every night, they ended up horizontal on his couch, making out. Caryn was sexy and sensual, and it was all he could do to stop each night before stripping her completely naked and fucking her until she screamed his name.

Something had definitely changed with her. With *them*. For the better.

Drew wanted more. He wanted to wake up with her every morning and be the last person she saw before going to sleep. He wanted to laugh over coffee and breakfast, wanted the right to go home with her after working out and pull her into his shower. Caryn had snuck under his skin in a big way, and he never wanted her to leave.

Which wasn't normal for him. Usually after dating a woman for a short while, Drew would begin to nitpick her personality and habits and eventually end things. But the more time he spent with Caryn, the more he wanted to be around her.

Tonight, as with the last few nights, they were sitting on his couch after dinner. They'd warmed up another casserole with Art earlier, and then he'd shooed them both out of his house, saying he was having a poker night with Otto, Silas, and, surprisingly, Dorothea and Cora. Having that many gossips in one house was downright daunting, and he and Caryn were more than happy to leave them to it.

"What do you think they're talking about?" Caryn asked.

Drew mock shuddered. "I don't even want to think about it," he said, knowing she was talking about her grandfather and the others.

"Right? After the rumors...sorry...*information* he spread about Paul and his friends, I've decided he's kind of scary."

"Honestly, he reminds me of a guy I know. His name is Tex, and he lives up in Pennsylvania. He's a former SEAL and is basically the eyes and ears for a ton of military, former military, law enforcement...probably even the mob, for all I know. He knows everything about everyone."

"He sounds like a man who'd be good to have on your side," Caryn said with a smile.

"Agreed. Just like Art."

She sobered. "I just don't want anything I do to blow back on him. I worry that Paul will retaliate somehow."

"Your grandfather is a beloved member of this community. It would be career suicide for him to do anything that would hurt Art. Or his friends. Or you. Besides, from what I've heard, he's already treading on thin ice after what he did to you."

"I don't care about myself, I just worry about someone hurting Art again."

Drew stared at her for a long moment.

"What?"

"You don't care what he might say about you? He could spread rumors about *you* too."

Caryn nodded. "I know. But I've spent a lot of time thinking about what you said the other night, and about my entire career. I've always done the right thing, or what I thought was right. I'm a damn good firefighter and haven't ever given any of the guys I work with *or* my supervisors a reason to distrust me, and they did anyway. So I'm making a very determined effort to be done with that.

"Worrying about what others think of me is unbelievably exhausting. I didn't even realize exactly how much until you pointed out that I already had a group of people who genuinely liked me, yet I was still more concerned about what

Paul and his cronies thought. I've decided that they can hate me all they want. It doesn't change anything about who I am as a person or my other relationships."

"Good for you," Drew said, inordinately proud of her.

"Thank you for calling me out on everything. Not just dumping me, or patting me on the head and blowing smoke up my ass."

"That's not who I am."

"I know. I have a feeling I can even count on you to tell me the truth if I ever ask whether or not my pants make my ass look big."

"Your ass isn't big. And even if it was, that just means there's more for me to love."

Caryn smiled at him, then shifted, sitting up to straddle his lap. She scooted forward until his cock pressed against her. She writhed a bit, and Drew could feel himself growing hard. "You're so different from other men, Drew."

"I am," he agreed.

"You're warier. More cynical."

His stomach clenched. He wasn't sure where she was going with that. She was throwing out mixed signals, pressing against him even while pointing out his faults.

"I'll be honest, those things irritated me about the officers I crossed paths with in New York. They frequently made me feel stupid or naïve for thinking the best about people. For not being upset or outraged because we were called out to the same area of town for one overdose after another. All I cared about was saving a life."

"That's not stupid. That's called being compassionate. But, to be fair, your job is very different from theirs. In their case, they'd probably arrested certain people for dealing, only to see them bailed out and back on the streets the next day, doing the same thing...and causing some of those overdoses. It can be exhausting."

"I realize that. But you aren't like that. You've still got a cynical streak, but you don't act as if everyone around you is a walking disaster. And you may be uber watchful, but in your case it's...reassuring for some reason. At least for me."

"Because you know I've got your back," Drew said with a shrug.

"Yeah. It's not something I've really experienced before. Is it weird that we've gotten so close, so quickly?"

"No," Drew said without any hesitation whatsoever.

"That's what my grandfather said too. By the way, he called sex the no-pants-dance," she informed him.

Drew snorted.

"He also told me to get on that," she said—then giggled. "And I'm just *now* getting the sexual inuendo in those words."

Drew wasn't sure where she was going with this conversation, but he couldn't stop his fingers from tightening on her hips.

"I want you," she said bluntly. "It might be too soon, people might think we're rushing this, but I don't care. I just want you to know where I stand so when you think you might be ready, you can feel free to make a move instead of trying to be noble."

Without a word, Drew pressed a hand against the small of her back, yanking her closer, and the other snaked up to her nape. He held her still as he leaned forward. Her head was a bit higher than his because she was on his lap, but he just pulled her down to meet him. The second his lips were on hers, he pressed forward with his tongue.

She opened for him immediately, moaning deep in her throat. Her fingernails dug into his chest as they kissed. They'd made out before, on this very couch, but this felt different. They both had an ending in mind...and it wasn't stopping after they were both so turned on they could barely think.

Without lifting his lips from hers, Drew scooted forward on the couch, then stood with Caryn in his arms. Her legs tightened around his hips and she wrapped her arms around his shoulders. She felt light as a feather as he stalked down the hall to his bedroom.

Ever since she'd last been in his bed, Drew had thought about this moment.

Still kissing her, he leaned over and placed her on his mattress, crawling onto the bed to hover over her. He finally lifted his head, not ashamed in the least at how heavy his breathing had become. Licking his lips, he tasted her there. The lemonade they'd had earlier seemed even sweeter on her lips.

"I'm guessing you don't think this is too soon?" she asked with a grin.

"No," he said. "This is going to sound corny as hell, but I don't give a shit—from the moment I met you in that hospital in Roanoke, I knew you were going to turn my life upside down. And it scared me. I think that's why I was an asshole."

"You weren't," she insisted. "But I definitely wasn't at *my* best."

"And when you stepped in and gave that man the Heimlich at Sunny Side Up...I already knew I was a goner."

"Drew," she whispered.

"Do what you want, when you want," he told her sternly. "No matter what anyone else thinks. Fuck 'em. You're amazing, Caryn. And I want you. I want to bury myself so deep inside your body that I can't tell where I end and you begin. I want to protect you, stand by your side when you're happy, and behind you when you're kicking ass. You don't need me, not even close...but I hope you *want* me."

"I do. God, Drew, I so do. You make me want to be a better woman, if only to earn the right to stand by *your* side."

Fuck, he wanted this woman. Now. "You don't have to earn that right, you've already got it," he managed to get out. Then, "How fast can you get naked?"

She grinned. "Faster than you," she said, her competitive streak coming out.

Without a word, Drew went up on his knees and whipped his shirt over his head.

After that, they were a tangle of arms and legs as they did their best to remove all their clothing before the other. Drew won, but only because he didn't have as much to take off.

When she was naked as the day she was born and laughing her head off, Drew looked down at her in awe. He couldn't believe she was here. With him. The used-up cop, the nerdy accountant. He was aware he wasn't hard on the eyes, but he'd never cared about that sort of thing. Looking down at the woman under him, he finally knew what *true* beauty was—inside and out. Underneath the tough outer shell that she'd built for self-preservation, Caryn was sweet and sensitive and thoughtful.

As for her outside...wow. Her gorgeous full breasts were topped with nipples that were currently hard and calling out to him. Her legs were long and toned, her thighs muscular and thick. And her neatly trimmed pubic hair made his mouth water.

Her laughter stopped as he ran his hands down her body. From her chest, over her stomach, to her thighs. Then he ran them back up, reveling in the feel of her satiny skin under his calloused palms.

She wasn't lying docilely under him though. As he worshipped her with his gaze and hands, she ran her own palms up and down his chest, her short nails scratching lightly. When she flicked one of his nipples, it was as if a bolt of lightning went from his pec straight to his cock.

He was throbbing, precome dripping from the tip of his

swollen dick, ready to bury himself inside her. While Drew could smell her arousal, he wasn't willing to rush into what they both wanted. He wanted to take his time, learn every inch of her body. Worship her. Prove that she was the most beautiful woman in the world and anyone who felt differently could fuck off.

By the time he was done with her, she'd know without a doubt that he wanted her exactly how she was.

Leaning down, he kissed her once more, but this time slowly. Sensually. Erotically. He showed her with his tongue what he was going to do to her pussy. At the same time, he palmed one of her breasts and kneaded. She arched her back under him as she pushed into his touch. One of her knees bent up then fell outward, making room for him as he lowered himself fully. He instantly felt her rubbing her pussy against him.

His belly clenched, and he felt another spurt of precome leave the tip of his cock. He was so close to exploding, but he needed to be inside her when he finally came. He leaned up suddenly, looking down their bodies. Her inner thigh was shiny with his juices, and it was sexy as hell.

He moved down her body, and Caryn eagerly parted her legs wider to give him room. Drew literally was speechless at the sight of all that beautiful pink. He wanted to tell her how much this moment meant to him. How much he admired her. Swear he'd never hurt her. But words wouldn't come. All he could do was bury his face between her gorgeous legs.

He inhaled deeply before licking through her soaking-wet folds.

He'd never been with a woman who was so ready for him, so quickly, and it was the biggest turn-on ever. "Mmmmm," he hummed as he nuzzled her clit.

"More," Caryn ordered, reaching down and grabbing his head with both hands.

Smiling, Drew had no problem following orders. He placed his hands on her thighs and pushed them even farther apart. She was spread wide open now, her slick pussy lips calling to him. He couldn't wait to get his hard cock in there, but first he wanted to make sure she orgasmed.

This wasn't something he'd done a lot. His past lovers were satisfied with his hands and cock, and the allure of eating a woman's pussy escaped him. But with Caryn, he couldn't get enough. Her taste. Her smell. Her deep gasps, and the way her muscles contracted every time he licked her clit. He may have shied away from this kind of intimacy in the past, but now he was ravenous. He could literally spend hours between this woman's legs.

He concentrated his attention on her clit, licking, sucking, keeping a steady pace of stimulation on the sensitive bundle of nerves. When she began to thrust against him, his dick got almost painfully hard, and it was all he could do to hold on and keep his mouth connected to her. When her thighs began to shake, he let go of one of her legs and eased a finger inside her tight sheath.

"Oh my God, yes!" she moaned. "More! I need you inside me. Now!"

He needed that too. More than she'd ever know. But before he took his pleasure, he was determined to get her off.

He added another finger to the first and marveled at how wet and tight and hot she was. She was going to strangle his cock when he got in there—and he couldn't fucking wait.

Thrusting his fingers in and out of her body, curling them just slightly, he sucked hard on her clit.

"Oh shit... Yes, right there. I'm coming!" she shouted.

She didn't need to tell him. He felt her pussy squeeze his fingers as her muscles quaked under his mouth. She jerked upward once more, then froze in place as she gushed all over his fingers.

It was the most erotic thing Drew had ever experienced. Caryn was so sensual and secure in her sexuality, it turned him on to the point he thought he'd come before he even got inside her. Lifting his head, he watched her juices leak out as his fingers continued to thrust gently inside her body.

She was quivering now, and when he brushed against her clit with his thumb, she jerked.

"Sensitive," she moaned.

Drew wanted to lower his head and make her come again, but he needed to be inside her more. He knew plenty of men got off on forcing their women to orgasm, but he'd never been the type, preferring mutual satisfaction. Now, he understood. The power he felt as he watched Caryn shatter was addictive. He wanted to see her explode again and again and again, under his mouth and fingers. Wanted to drive her completely crazy with lust. Wanted her so wrung out she could barely string two words together...just enough to ask for more.

But that would have to wait for another day. Right now, if he didn't get inside this woman, he literally didn't think he would survive.

Drew moved up her body and reached for a condom in his nightstand. He quickly rolled it down his throbbing cock and grabbed the base, trying not to explode right then and there.

Caryn lay under him, a light sheen of sweat covering her brow. Her blonde hair was sticking to her forehead and her upper chest was flushed. She smiled at him and stretched her long, stunning body, her arms reaching over her head and her back arching. She reminded him of a contented cat.

When he paused, taking a moment to enjoy the sight of his woman under him, she said, "What are you waiting for? I need you, Drew. Now."

How could he resist that invitation? He couldn't.

He scooted forward on his knees, spreading her legs wider

in the process. As if his cock knew exactly where it wanted to be, the mushroomed head slid between her wet folds.

They both moaned. Caryn gripped his biceps tightly as he braced himself over her.

"Ready?" he asked, wanting to make sure they were both on the same page when it came to making love.

"Yes," she said firmly, looking him in the eye. "Fuck me, Drew. Please."

Shivering with need, Drew's hips were moving before he'd consciously thought about it. He slid inside her on one long push, not stopping until he was in as far as he could get.

* * *

Caryn inhaled sharply as Drew entered her. He was thick. Bigger than anyone she'd been with before. For a moment, a slight pinch of pain made her tense, but once Drew was all the way inside, he paused, giving her time to acclimate to his size.

"Fuck," he muttered, dropping his head as if it weighed too much for him to hold up anymore.

Caryn could feel her inner muscles fluttering still from the orgasm he'd given her. She came harder than she did when she took care of business herself. She usually backed off when she got close, to prolong the anticipation, but that clearly wasn't Drew's style. When her legs began to shake, he'd sucked even harder on her clit, making her explode. She was soaking wet now, could feel her own excitement on her thighs and under her ass. But all she could *think* about was how right Drew felt inside her.

His head lifted, but instead of meeting her gaze, his seemed fixed on where they were joined. He shimmied closer, drawing his knees up and out, spreading her legs even wider as he put a hand beneath her ass and lifted. Amazingly, he seemed to go even deeper.

"Drew!" she whispered, not even sure what she wanted. For him to stop? To move?

"God, that's the most beautiful thing I've ever seen," he said reverently. "My cock buried so deep inside you, your legs spread apart, taking everything I've got."

Caryn lifted her head and looked down their bodies. His dark hair was a stark contrast against her blonde, and he wasn't wrong. It *was* beautiful. She clenched around him, and he groaned.

"Shit, Caryn, I can't...I want..."

Hearing him at a loss for words gave her the most delicious feeling of power. He might be on top, but she loved knowing she could make him lose control. She squeezed him again, and as if a switch had been thrown, he started to move.

He pulled out and slammed back inside her—*hard*—then stilled when she moaned.

"Caryn?" he asked.

"Yes, more! Please...*harder*."

With her permission, Drew began to fuck her like it was his job. She was so wet, his cock slid in and out of her easily. He braced himself on his hands. A look of near pain slid across his face as he worked his hips, giving them both a type of intense pleasure some people never experienced.

Caryn did what she could to help, lifting her hips into each of his thrusts and squeezing him when he bottomed out. He was grunting now, his breaths harsh, but Caryn barely heard him; she was moaning too loudly. He felt unbelievable. She tingled all over, and every time his flesh slapped against hers, his pubic bone rubbed her clit.

A second orgasm hovered just out of reach as he fucked her harder, faster, his thrusts going on and on, driving her out of her mind with bliss.

When she didn't think she could take one more second of pleasure, his pace increased even more, his thrusts turning short and sharp. "I'm gonna come," he gasped.

As soon as the words left his mouth, he slammed inside her and held still. Caryn could feel his dick twitch as he started to come. He was so beautiful—and he was all hers.

In a flash, her hand flew down between them. He was still coming, but he sucked in a breath, giving her just enough room to reach her clit. She began to rub it, hard, wanting to join him in his pleasure.

"God, yes, get yourself off, sweetheart. Now. Do it!"

She had no idea if it was his command, or if she was just that primed—probably a mixture of both—but she immediately began to come.

"Fuck yeah!" he grunted as she squeezed his cock hard and flew over the edge.

It felt different to orgasm with him inside her. She was so full, and even though she squeezed him like a vise, he rocked his hips, forcing his cock to move through the tightness, prolonging their pleasure.

"Holy crap," she breathed as she began to come down from her orgasm.

She'd been with men who'd pulled out immediately after they came, men who complained about having to deal with a condom, who fell on top of her after sex and made her feel suffocated. One or two who'd held her awkwardly, thinking it was expected.

Drew did none of those things. He rolled, pulling her with him. It surprised Caryn, and she let out a small squeak. She ended up plastered against his sweaty chest. He was still inside her, and he kept her right where she was with a hand on the small of her back and the other at her nape. She loved when he held her like that.

As they lay there, trying to catch their breaths, his cock

slowly slid out of her. Caryn wrinkled her nose at the sensation.

Drew must've felt her reaction against his bare skin, because he chuckled. "I feel the same," he said softly.

When he didn't move to get up, and didn't let her go, Caryn said cautiously, "Shouldn't you take care of that?"

"I will. In a second. I'm enjoying this moment too much to move."

"It's gonna leak," she felt compelled to say.

He chuckled again, and the sound reverberated through her body. "Don't fucking care."

"You might have to sleep in a wet spot," she said with a laugh of her own.

"I don't give the smallest shit about that," he said.

Caryn smiled against him.

A few minutes went by in silence, but it didn't feel uncomfortable in the least. Then the hand that had been at her nape moved to cradle her cheek in his large palm.

Caryn lifted her head so she could look him in the eye.

"That was...beautiful," he told her. "And I know I'm a guy and we aren't supposed to be all mushy and stuff, but seriously, I've never felt like that before in my life."

His words sank into her soul, and Caryn felt like crying.

"I'm gonna do whatever I can to make this work between us," he said softly. "I don't have a good track record when it comes to girlfriends, but I *want* this to work. I want it more than I've ever wanted anything in my life. If I fuck up, call me on it. Don't be afraid to tell me if I'm working too much. If I smother you, let me know that too. I can't promise that I'll never screw up, but I swear that I'll do my best to fix whatever I might do to upset you."

The tears Caryn had been trying to hold back came forth with a vengeance. "I don't expect you to be perfect," she told him as a tear dripped off her cheek and fell onto his chest. "I just need you."

"You've got me," he reassured her. "I never understood Rocky, Ethan, and Zeke's instant obsessions with their women. I do now."

"Okay, you need to stop being so nice," Caryn complained, closing her eyes.

"Never," he whispered.

She felt his lips on her cheek, kissing away her tears. "Now, stop crying and sit up."

Surprised at the order, Caryn took a deep breath and did as he asked.

She straddled him and braced herself on his chest.

"Fuck, woman. You're so damn beautiful," he said reverently as his gaze ran up and down her body.

For the first time in ages, maybe ever, Caryn *felt* beautiful.

Drew palmed one of her breasts. She felt her nipple harden at his touch at the same time she felt his dick twitch beneath her.

"There's no way you're ready again," she said in surprise.

He shrugged. "I'm not in my twenties anymore, but you're definitely an incentive. Lift up," he ordered, squeezing her hip.

She rose to her knees. His hands went to his cock and she watched as he removed the used condom, his dick shiny with his come. He tied off the condom and wrapped it in a tissue, then reached over to the table next to his bed and grabbed another, slid it down his erection, then smiled lazily up at her. "It's your turn to take *me*," he said.

Caryn grinned. She'd never had sex again so soon after the first time, but she was game to try if he was. And she couldn't deny that being on top had its appeal.

She reached down and took his cock in her hand, loving the moan that escaped his throat at her touch. She scooted back a little and notched him between her lips. She was still wet from her previous orgasms and had no problem taking him to the root in one long slide.

When he was all the way inside her again, she looked down, understanding why he'd loved looking at them this way earlier. "We *are* beautiful," she said softly.

"Move, Caryn," he ordered.

"I thought guys were supposed to be able to last longer the second time," she teased.

He reached down and began to stroke her clit with his thumb, and she let out a small squeal. She was sensitive—*very* sensitive.

"Fuck me," he ordered.

Caryn had no problem doing so. She rode him slowly at first, then faster and harder. Being with Drew was fun. Easy. Sexy. Exhilarating. Intimate. And she didn't feel self-conscious at all.

When her third orgasm of the night hit, she couldn't stop herself from calling out his name, just as he yelped hers when he reached the pinnacle once again.

This time, after they were both able to take a breath again, Drew fisted a hand in her hair and kissed her hard. It felt even more intimate after making love. More meaningful. As if it was a promise.

He eventually rolled her to the side, kissed her on the forehead, and climbed out of the bed. He went into the bathroom, and it was all Caryn could do to keep her eyes open. She jerked in surprise when the mattress dipped as he returned.

"Easy, hon. It's me," he said softly. Drew turned off all the lights and immediately pulled her into his side. They smelled like sex. The sheets, their skin, the air. And it was both a turn-on and soothing at the same time. Drew's hand brushed up and down her back as he held her against his chest. They hadn't slept this way before. He usually spooned her from behind. But she liked it. A lot.

"I meant what I said," he told her after a moment. "I'm going to do everything in my power not to screw this up. I want you in my life, Caryn. Hell, I *need* you in my life. I'm perfectly aware that you don't need me, but I'm going to do what I can to prove that you can trust me, rely on me, and I'll always be there for you."

She appreciated him trying to appease any worries she might have, but remarkably, she didn't have many. Drew was a good man. He didn't care about prestige, didn't care that she might know more than him when it came to firefighting and medical situations, wasn't a macho jerk. "You can trust me too," she said. "And I want this to work just as much."

"Then it will," he said simply. "Sweet dreams."

"I need to let Art know I won't be home tonight," she murmured, feeling the lure of sleep trying to pull her under.

"I'll call him in a bit," he told her.

She felt a touch guilty that he'd have to get up and do something she should do for herself, but she was too warm, too comfortable, and too sated to resist. "Thanks."

She felt his lips against her temple, and then she was out.

CHAPTER EIGHTEEN

The next week was one of the best of Caryn's life. Her grandfather was getting stronger every day, and was pretty much back to his ornery old self. She'd practically moved in with Drew, sleeping at his place most nights, and had to admit that he was incredibly easy to be with.

He gave her space to do her own thing, and in return she did the same, understanding that he needed a few hours every afternoon to check on his clients' investments. She hadn't run into Paul or his friends, which was fine with Caryn. If she never had to see them again, and remember what a fool she'd been, it would be all right with her.

She spent a lot of time with Bristol, Elsie, and Lilly. Sometimes they met at Finley's bakery, or they'd switch it up and get a coffee from Grinders. One afternoon, Caryn helped Bristol and Rocky set up her workshop in the barn. Seeing everything that went into making stained glass was a real eye-opener.

School had started the week before, and Caryn offered to pick up Tony each day this week and bring him to the library, or just hang out with him if he preferred. They'd played for hours at Caboose Park one day, and on another, when he'd begged her to show him some of the stuff she did as a firefighter, she'd brought him to Brock's shop and ran him through the obstacle course...minus carrying bodies at the end. But she did find a large sack and filled it with dirt for him to haul around.

All in all, Caryn was happier than she'd ever been. She still needed to go back to New York at some point and move out of her apartment, but she wasn't in any real hurry to get that done. She'd paid her rent for six months before she'd left because she hadn't known how long she'd need to be with Art as he recovered.

Her fire chief back in New York didn't sound all that upset when she'd called to tell him she was quitting. It stung for a moment, that she would be so easy to replace, but she did her best to shrug it off. She was moving on with her life.

Every morning, she and Drew continued to work out. More often than not, he took her into the woods to teach her more about search and rescue, and Caryn soaked in every morsel of knowledge he shared.

And nights were the icing on the cake that was her life right now. She loved sleeping in Drew's arms after they made love. He could be either tender or demanding, and not knowing which man she'd get each night was exciting. His obvious enjoyment of sex, and his affection toward her, made any inhibitions or hang-ups she might have fly out the window. With him, she could do or say anything in bed without worrying what he'd think of her.

A part of Caryn was waiting for the other shoe to fall. For something to happen to put a dent in her happy little world. Nothing could be this perfect for long. But she tried not to let those negative thoughts take up too much space in her head.

She was supposed to meet with Lilly this afternoon for a

late lunch. Her friend was meeting with a new client at her house, to take pictures of the woman's dog. Caryn had teased Lilly for taking the job, but she'd just laughed and said money was money. Then added that sometimes dogs were easier subjects than people.

Caryn first went to Art's house to make him lunch. He'd begun taking breaks from sitting outside the post office long enough to come home for lunch and a short nap, before meeting his friends back at their usual place in the afternoons. He'd finished his sandwich, and had just gone back to his room for an hour's rest when Caryn's phone rang.

She'd left Drew at his house working and was pleased when she saw his name on the screen.

"Hi. Miss me already?" she teased.

"There's a fire," Drew said without preamble.

And just like that, Caryn tensed. "What? Where?"

"The Conleys' house."

She froze. That was the surname of the woman who'd hired Lilly to take pictures of her Yorkie that morning. "*What?*"

"I'm headed over now. Rocky called, he and Ethan are on their way too. We're worried about Lilly."

Caryn was moving before he'd finished talking. "I'll meet you there."

"Be safe." Then he hung up.

Caryn didn't waste any time. She didn't wake her grandfather to tell him what was going on. He would be pissed at her —this was prime gossip—but she needed to get to Lilly. Needed to see for herself that she was all right.

She knew where the Conleys' house was because Drew had pointed it out one day when they were on their way back from a hike. It was on a couple acres outside of town, down a long gravel driveway. She drove way too fast, and saw the smoke rising in the air above the treetops long before she got to the home.

Her stomach clenching in concern, she took the turn onto the driveway too sharply and her tires spun as gravel spewed from behind her.

The second she pulled up and saw smoke and flames pouring out of a window on level two, on the Alpha/Delta sides of the house, her mind immediately switched to firefighter mode as she sized-up the scene.

She threw her car into park after making sure it was well out of the way of any other emergency vehicles that might arrive and ran toward the front lawn. Frowning at the chaos around her, it took her a moment to understand what was happening.

The Fallport Fire Department was in complete disarray. Two members were yelling at Ethan to stand down, as Rocky, Tal, and Drew did their best to hold him back from running into the house. A woman stood off to the side with a Yorkie in her arms, crying hysterically, and there was a cluster of onlookers yelling at the firefighters.

Paul was standing off to the side like a king watching over his subjects. Every now and then, he'd lift a radio to his lips and say something. Caryn could only assume he was acting as the incident commander. But it seemed as if the firefighters had just arrived, which was odd, considering they had to have been notified before Drew.

Three men were struggling to pull on their bunker gear, and no one had even deployed an attack line yet. And that would take a little bit because it had to be flaked out so it wouldn't kink once it was charged. One of the firefighters yelled to no one in particular, asking where the fire hydrant was.

It was pandemonium—and the firefighter within Caryn cringed in horror. They were doing everything wrong. It was a disaster and a disgrace. The men were acting as if this was their first fire ever and they had no idea what they should be doing first. No one seemed to be in charge, and no one was directing anyone. In all the fires she'd worked, Caryn had known exactly what her role was, and she did it without question or hesitation.

She took her attention from the incompetence of the firefighters when some of the people standing around began to yell even louder. She turned to look at the house and realized what they were yelling about.

Lilly.

She was still inside.

Every muscle in Caryn's body tensed. No! Not Lilly!

She looked from Ethan and his friends back to the firetrucks, then to the house. Everything she'd learned about fire and the science behind it ran through her mind as she examined the structure. From what she understood from the bystanders yelling and pointing, Lilly was on the second floor, on the Beta/Charley corner—away from where the flames were shooting out of the window on the opposite side of the house. It wouldn't be an easy rescue, but there was still time if the firefighters moved right now.

She headed for Oscar, who was doing his best to single-handedly pull the heavy hose off the top of the truck and get it ready. She was about to urge him to get his ass in gear when she heard Paul yelling at one of the people getting in his face that it was too late. That they couldn't go inside the house. That old houses burned much faster than newer ones.

She blinked in shock. Then her shock morphed into anger in a heartbeat.

It wasn't too late. Not even close. Not if they moved their goddamn asses.

A roar erupted from Ethan, who'd clearly heard Paul's decision, and Raiden and Zeke had to quickly add their strength to hold him back. All of his friends had him on the ground now, and the sounds coming from him would haunt Caryn's nightmares. The pain and anguish was easy to hear and worked their way deep inside her.

She changed course and headed for the nearest firetruck instead of going toward Oscar. No one was paying any attention to her as she grabbed an air pack from the truck. She could only pray it was full. She wouldn't put it past this inept fire department to be hauling around empty air tanks. She didn't hesitate to shrug the tank onto her back and strap on the face mask. She'd done it thousands of times. It felt as natural as breathing.

Not even bothering to be stealthy, and knowing she probably looked strange with her jeans and T-shirt and wearing the SCBA, but not giving a damn, she headed toward the left side of the house. The Beta/Charley corner, back left, where bystanders had seen Lilly.

This was dangerous, but she had absolute confidence in her abilities as a firefighter. Others might not agree, but she didn't care. She was going to do what she knew she could do, and deal with the consequences later.

No one stopped her as she raced around the house. There had to be a back door. A calm settled over Caryn as she neared the burning structure. She thought she heard her name being called, but all her attention was on the task at hand.

She shouldn't be entering the structure by herself. That was one of the first things that had been drilled into her head in the academy, but she wasn't waiting around to argue with a fire captain who'd already given up. She had to get to Lilly.

Caryn pushed open the back door and stepped into a kitchen. The lower level was just starting to fill with black smoke, and she cringed thinking about what the air upstairs must be like. Pushing the thought out of her head, she went into firefighter mode. Caryn headed into what she hoped was the main part of the house, where the stairs might be. She didn't need to crawl yet, but it wouldn't be long until it was too hot and smoky to do anything but get on her hands and knees.

She found the stairwell, but it took just one look to know it wasn't viable. Flames were licking at the top of the staircase. Then something she'd seen when she'd walked through the house niggled at the back of her mind. Turning, she headed for the hallway off the kitchen.

Yes! There was a back staircase. Many old houses had them, thank God. She moved with purpose, not running, and counting the stairs as she climbed upward. The temperature up here was much hotter, and Caryn could feel the hair on her arms burning. She immediately dropped to her hands and knees. She'd always had an excellent sense of direction, and she unerringly headed for the back left corner of the house where Lilly was supposed to be.

The doors in the hallway were all open except for one.

Praying harder than she'd ever done in any emergency situation before, Caryn pushed open the door. The air wasn't as smoky in the room, and she immediately slammed the door behind her once she was inside.

She zeroed in on a shape sitting under the window, facing the wall. Getting to her feet, Caryn rushed over and saw that it was indeed Lilly. She was unconscious, a scarf tied around her face, her hand still holding the windowsill. She'd done everything right, had stayed put, near where a rescue should've been imminent, kept the window closed, and had covered her nose and mouth.

Anger threatened to overcome Caryn at the thought of Paul calmly telling people there was nothing they could do to save her. Thankful for her strength—and for the fact that her former co-workers had always given her the heaviest dummies to haul around during training—Caryn took a deep breath and reached for Lilly.

Instinct told her that taking even a few extra seconds to check for injuries or try to wake Lilly could be deadly for them both. Her adrenaline surged. She easily lifted her friend up and over her shoulder in a fireman's carry. She immediately turned and headed for the door. She could've opened the window and cried out for help, but she had no idea how long it would take to be rescued—or if Paul would even try. And Lilly needed oxygen. Now.

She opened the door and the heat made her immediately fall to her knees once more.

It was too hot. She was too late.

Anger and frustration surged through Caryn. No. No fucking way. She wasn't going to die here, and neither was Lilly.

With the sound of Ethan's anguish echoing in her head, Caryn crawled on her knees as fast as she could toward the back staircase.

She got on her ass and scooted down the first few steps. It took four exactly before the heat almost miraculously decreased. Caryn got to her feet and practically flew down the remaining stairs. Lilly didn't move on her shoulder, which worried her. The kitchen was a very welcome sight, and she could feel the temperature drop when she stepped outside into the fresh air.

It was almost surreal that no one was standing at the back of the house. She heard more yelling coming from the Alpha side, but she ignored it. She remembered an ambulance pulling onto the scene just as she'd put on the air pack, and that was her destination.

The second she appeared around the corner of the house, Ethan spotted her.

"Let go of me! She's got Lilly!"

Every single set of eyes in the yard swung to her, but Caryn didn't change her trajectory.

Ethan raced over, and for a second, she thought he was going to pull Lilly out of her arms. She shoved the face mask off and said, "Ambulance!" Her voice was strong, even as her limbs began to shake from delayed reaction.

Ethan nodded, his lips pressed together in a grim line, and he walked quickly beside her, one hand on his fiancée's back.

"Hey! We've got her!" Tal called out to the paramedics.

"Get the oxygen!" Brock added.

Then another voice sounded nearby...

"What the fuck? *Stop!* Where are you going? You can't just steal our goddamn packs!"

Paul. Figured he was bitching about her doing what he'd *refused* to do.

As if they'd planned it, six very pissed-off SAR men suddenly closed ranks around Caryn, Lilly, and Ethan. They formed a tight circle and kept Paul—and anyone else who might dare try to stop them—from getting close.

Caryn could still hear the fire captain bitching, but all her attention was on the back of the ambulance. "Put her down here," someone said, but Caryn ignored them. She wasn't putting Lilly down anywhere but in the back of the ambulance.

She felt a hand on her elbow, then two at her waist as she stepped up into the back of the truck. With Ethan's help, she lowered Lilly onto the gurney, then grabbed his arm and pulled him to the end of the gurney as the paramedics began to look her over.

"She's okay," she said, trying to reassure Ethan as much as herself.

"Fuck!" Ethan said, his gaze glued to the disheveled woman on the gurney. Lilly had black marks around her mouth and nose when one of the medics removed the scarf around her face.

"That's normal," she told Ethan. She heard shouts behind her, and turned to see Zeke, Rocky, Brock, Tal, and Raid forming a barrier between them and some sort of commotion. She didn't see Drew, but thought she heard his voice. Turning her attention back to Lilly, she reached for Ethan's hand.

It was probably only thirty seconds or so that they all stood there, holding their breaths, but finally, *finally*, Lilly coughed.

Caryn sighed in relief. Her friend was going to be all right. She knew it.

Lilly continued to cough even as a mask with oxygen was put over her face. Ethan couldn't stand it any longer, and he went to his knees at Lilly's feet. He put a hand on her bare leg and told her that he was there. That she was all right. To just breathe nice and slow. He kept up a constant litany of quiet reassurances, and when Lilly opened her eyes and saw him, she seemed to relax.

"If you can please step back," one of the paramedics asked Caryn, gesturing to the open doors of the ambulance.

She nodded and stepped back. It looked like they weren't about to ask Ethan to leave, which was a smart move on their part. There was no way he was leaving Lilly's side. Not after almost losing her.

Caryn knew it had been close. If she'd been any later, the outcome might not have been so positive. She was still furious at Paul and his refusal to even *try* to rescue Lilly, but suddenly, exhaustion seemed to overwhelm her.

She felt hands helping her step down from the ambulance, then she was turned into a familiar embrace. Caryn's hands gripped the front of Drew's shirt as if she was never going to let go. Someone grabbed the oxygen tank on her back, and she had to let go of Drew long enough for them to shrug it off, but once it was gone, she was clutching him once again.

"Arrest her!" Paul yelled from somewhere behind Drew.

"If you don't shut the hell up and get control of yourself, I'm going to arrest *you*!" She recognized the chief of police's voice. "Why don't you get back to your goddamn job—which is to put out that fire—and leave her to me," Simon growled.

"She stole that air pack! She had no right! She put everyone in danger!"

That was it. Caryn had heard enough. But before she could say a word, Simon was in the other man's face.

"From where I'm standing, she's a hero. She saved Lilly when *you* refused to even try."

"It was too dangerous!" Paul yelled.

It was unbelievable that he was having this yelling match *now*, when there was literally a house burning down behind him.

"You have two seconds to turn around and try to save what's left of the Conleys' house before I slap handcuffs on you and haul you down to the station," Simon threatened.

"This isn't over!" Paul said, pointing his finger at Caryn.

She rolled her eyes, but otherwise couldn't muster up the energy to care.

The fire captain turned and stalked back to where his squad was just now charging the hoses and getting water on the house.

Caryn buried her face in Drew's neck.

"Is she hurt?"

"I've got some water."

"Here's a towel."

"Get her out of here."

Caryn was almost overwhelmed at the concern she heard in their friends' voices.

Drew still hadn't said anything, but he turned her away

from the fire and toward a line of vehicles parked along the gravel driveway.

Caryn wanted to protest, wanted to stay and check on Lilly, but she felt as limp as a noodle. She'd saved plenty of people from fires and other disasters, but this was the first time she'd personally known the victim. The first time she'd had to rescue a friend. It was overwhelming, and she was just so relieved she'd been able to find her so quickly.

"I'll drive," Brock said from next to them.

Drew helped her into the back seat of his Jeep, then climbed in beside her. He never let her go, and Caryn was all right with that. She leaned into him as Brock hopped into the front seat.

It wasn't until they were inside Drew's house, and she'd reassured Brock that she was fine and thanked him for the ride, that Drew spoke. He hadn't said a word the entire trip back, merely giving his friend a chin lift as he left.

"*Fuck*," he swore as he pulled Caryn back into his arms.

She couldn't help but chuckle. "That about sums up that shitshow," she said quietly.

"When I saw you going around the corner of that house, air pack on, determination in every step, my heart stopped." Drew pulled back and put his hands on either side of her head and held her tightly as he stared into her eyes. "I've never been so scared, or proud, in my entire life."

Caryn closed her eyes at the emotion she saw swimming in his gaze. It was too...intense. Too big.

"I knew you could do it," he whispered. "I knew you'd find Lilly and get her out of there."

His confidence in her ability felt good. *Really* damn good. Caryn opened her eyes and met his gaze. Had anyone ever believed in her like that? Not really. Even her fellow fire-fighters had doubts about her abilities to carry them out of a burning building in an emergency.

"You went in there in jeans and a fucking T-shirt," he said with an incredulous shake of his head.

"I didn't have time to grab bunker gear. Besides, if it didn't fit, that would've been even more dangerous than going in without it," she explained.

Drew nodded. "I've never seen Ethan like that. When he heard Paul say there was nothing they could do, I swear I thought he was going to completely die from anguish on the spot."

"I know. I heard him. I wouldn't have gone in myself if I truly thought it was too late," she felt compelled to tell him. "Even though Lilly's my friend, I wouldn't go on a suicide mission."

Drew nodded. "I'm so fucking proud of you," he told her, resting his forehead against hers. "But that scared me so damn bad. I don't think I breathed while you were in there. Every second you were gone was the longest of my life. I've never felt such relief as I did when you came around that corner with Lilly over your shoulder."

"I'm okay," Caryn soothed. "Lilly's okay."

"Yeah," he agreed. Then he took a deep breath and ran a hand over her head. "Shower," he declared.

"What?" Caryn said, having a hard time following his line of thinking.

"You smell like smoke. I can see the singed hairs on your arms. You need a shower. To cool off. To get clean."

She *did* need a shower, but she didn't want to let go of Drew yet.

He took the decision out of her hands, and since it seemed as if he didn't want to let go of her either, Caryn was all right with him taking charge.

He led them both through the master bedroom to the bathroom and shut the door behind them. He turned on the water, stripped them both, then took her into his arms once they were under the spray. For the longest time, they stood like that, rejoicing in the beauty of life. Then he soaped up his hands and cleaned her from head to toe. He washed her hair, twice, then dried her off when they got out.

Afterward, they ended up on his couch, Caryn on his lap, both content to soak in the other's presence.

"We should check on Lilly," Caryn said after a while.

Drew nodded, but didn't make a move to get up.

"And I probably need to call Bristol and Elsie. And Finley."

"Yeah," Drew agreed.

"And I'm sure my grandfather has heard about the fire and is worrying about me."

"Uh-huh."

Amazingly, the longer Drew held her, the more like her old self she felt. "Or maybe we could just sit here for a bit."

"Yes."

And they did just that, for a good long while.

Eventually, they forced themselves to get up. Much like the incident at The Cellar, she knew today had changed them both yet again. Caryn felt closer than ever to Drew and to the people she called friends. She was glad to know that when push came to shove, her training and skills hadn't failed her. It didn't matter if she got in trouble for what she did. She'd never regret it. Lilly was alive. That was worth any repercussions she might face.

* * *

Later that night—much later—Paul paced back and forth in agitation.

How *dare* that fucking bitch show him up! He'd made the determination that the house was too dangerous to enter, and yet she'd gone in anyway. Made him look stupid. Incompetent. The citizens on scene had looked at him with pure disgust.

And the second he got back to the station, he'd had a call from the mayor stating that he and the city council wanted a meeting.

The fire department was too small for a chief, and he was the captain. Basically, that meant the FFD was *his*, and Paul instinctively knew he was about to lose everything he'd worked so hard for.

He was already on thin ice because of the investigation that Simon had started over an innocent hazing incident. But now?

He was fucked.

All because that whore had to play hero.

She wasn't going to get away with that shit! No fucking way in hell.

He'd attend his meeting with the mayor and city council. Explain how fires worked and how unpredictable they were. He'd make sure they knew how dangerous it was to enter burning structures—and that the bitch wasn't certified to do what she did in Virginia. She'd put them all at risk and broke the law. It was a stupid move on her part.

And just like that, he was lost to his fury once more, pacing his living room like a caged animal.

He might lose his job. His reputation. Would be forced to move in disgrace. All because of a dumb slut who shouldn't even be here in the first place! This was *his* town. He'd grown up here. She hadn't.

Caryn Buckner was going to pay for making him look bad. She was *nothing* in Fallport. She'd regret ever sticking her haughty fucking nose into his business. No bitch was going to get away with upstaging him.

Paul's brain churned with plans. He wanted to humiliate her. Was determined to make damn sure she regretted what she'd done today. Regretted ever stepping foot back in Fallport. It would've been better if she'd just burned in that goddamn fire.

Pausing on that thought, he nodded...a malicious grin spreading on his face.

Fuck yes. She needed to *burn*. It would be a fitting end to a wannabe firefighter.

He'd have to cover his tracks carefully. And he already knew where to take her. He just had to work out the when.

Paul rubbed his hands together in anticipation. Caryn Buckner would never get the better of him. She'd burn in hell...and he'd laugh as she screamed in pain.

CHAPTER NINETEEN

Drew was having a hard time letting Caryn out of his sights. When he saw her running toward a house that was half consumed by fire, his blood had run cold. He'd been busy stopping Ethan from charging into the house to rescue Lilly himself, and hadn't been able to do anything but yell Caryn's name when she'd run by.

She either hadn't heard him, or was so intent on helping Lilly that she couldn't spare even a second to acknowledge his shout. Either way...

He loved her.

Drew knew that down to his bones. The few minutes she'd been inside that house, when he hadn't known if she'd ever come back out, were excruciating. He'd gotten an entirely new perspective on what Ethan was feeling in that moment. If Caryn had died, he knew without a doubt his life would never be the same. That he would've lost the most precious gift he'd ever been given.

Now, it was literally impossible for him not to trail her nearly everywhere. She was being cool about it, but it wouldn't be long before she got tired of his constant presence. His need to have eyes on her, to touch her.

Seemed like this morning, the day after the fire, she'd already had enough.

"Drew, I *know* you have work to do today. You don't have to come with me."

"I'm coming," he said, barely letting her finish her sentence.

They were sitting next to each other at his table, eating breakfast. He had a hand on her thigh as he ate, the touch comforting him.

"Look at me," she said gently.

Taking a deep breath, Drew turned to her.

"I'm okay. I knew what I was doing. I would never have gone into that building if I didn't."

"I know."

She tilted her head, then asked, "Do you?"

He didn't respond right away.

"If we were standing outside a bank and someone was inside, holding the place up...would you stand around and do nothing? If a woman was being assaulted in the parking lot behind On the Rocks, would you wait around for Simon or one of his deputies to show up? If someone was being robbed in the square, would you just watch while calling 9-1-1? If—"

"All right, point made," Drew said with a sigh as he interrupted her.

"You wouldn't," she said without a shred of doubt in her tone. "You'd be right there, doing what you could to mitigate the situation and save lives, because you've trained for that stuff. You know what you're doing, and you'd have a better chance than the average person of defusing the situation or kicking the bad guy's butt. You wouldn't stand around watching everything go down until an officer could get there.

"When I drove up to that scene, I knew immediately that

while the fire was serious, there was still time to rescue anyone who might be trapped inside. And when I heard Paul say there was no chance of going in, I knew—because of my training and experience—that he was wrong. And knowing it was *Lilly* inside? Yeah, there was zero chance of me standing around and watching her die when I was one hundred percent sure I could save her. I'm sorry I scared you," she said softly, taking his hand in hers. "I *hate* that...but there was no time to reassure you, or anyone else, that I would get Lilly out."

Drew swallowed and nodded. "I just found you, Caryn. I can't lose you."

"You aren't and you won't."

Turning in his chair, Drew gave up on trying to eat. Everything kind of tasted like sawdust anyway. Without prompting, Caryn got up and sat across his lap. They didn't make love last night, but Drew had held her almost desperately close as they slept. "I love you," he said softly. "And I've never felt this way before, so you're going to have to cut me some slack."

She put a hand on his face and gazed into his eyes. "I love you too. So much, it scares me."

"Then we'll be scared together," he told her. "And for the record? I'm so proud of you I could burst. You saved Lilly's life. That's big, honey. Huge."

She opened her mouth, and Drew said before she could respond, "If you say you were just doing your job, I'm gonna sic Ethan on you."

Caryn chuckled. "I'm sure if the roles were reversed, if a robbery or something was happening, you'd say the same thing."

"Probably, but this feels different. More personal. Both because it was *your* life that was in danger, and because it was *Lilly* who you saved," Drew said. "I may have only met Lilly this year, but she's important to Ethan, and he's one of my best friends. What affects him, affects the rest of us. You'll never know how proud I was when you came around the corner of that house with Lilly over your shoulder."

In response, Caryn leaned into him and turned her face into the crook of his shoulder.

"So...you gonna let me go with you today?"

She had a meeting with Jonathan Coleman, the mayor of Fallport, and the city council. Drew was sure they'd all gotten many calls about what had happened, and they needed firsthand information about the true facts of what went down at the fire. Because Fallport was so small, they were essentially Paul's bosses, in charge of the first responders in town.

"Yes," she said with a small nod. "Thank you."

"You don't have to thank me for having your back, sweetheart," Drew said, kissing her temple. "Now, finish your breakfast so we can get going. I'm guessing Jonathan won't be happy if you're late."

Caryn sat up and went back to her own chair at the table, but Drew immediately placed his hand back on her thigh when she was settled.

"I'm sure he's not as bad as you've made him out to be," she told him after she'd taken a bite of the potato hash he'd made them for breakfast.

Drew grinned and shook his head. "You'll see," he told her.

* * *

Almost two hours later, Caryn had to agree with Drew. The mayor was kind of a jerk. But then again, he had to deal with a lot of political shit that was probably a pain in his ass all the time. She'd met with him and the five-person city council for well over an hour. They'd wanted to know about her work history, her credentials...and why she'd felt it was okay to steal an air pack and go inside a burning house when she wasn't a member of the FFD.

Caryn had calmly informed them of her state and national certifications, of her almost twenty years of experience as a firefighter at various stations in the city; how she'd been to conferences every year to stay abreast of the latest safety and training techniques; and finally, exactly how she'd located and transferred Lilly out of the house safely. She also let them know Lilly was recovering from smoke inhalation at home... instead of lying in a body bag at the morgue.

They also wanted to know why she'd gone into the house herself. Why she hadn't worked with the Fallport Fire Department.

She'd explained that newer houses burned much faster than older ones because the materials used to build them were more combustible. Older houses were typically built with heavier wood or cinderblocks, which took longer to burn than modern materials. And that was how she'd known she had time to find Lilly. But that she *didn't* have time to argue with Paul about it, especially when he'd already declared that there was nothing he could do, and he wouldn't allow his firefighters into the home.

That had led to a long and frank conversation about everything Caryn had observed at the scene—and when she'd visited the fire station. She was brutally honest, saying that from everything she'd observed, the firefighters were woefully undertrained at best and negligent at worst. She told them that the station was a filthy disgrace, and the trucks and gear were disorganized, which directly resulted in the chaos at the scene and the delay in saving the Conleys' home.

Lastly, she informed them that if she was Lilly's relative, and if Lilly had passed away in that blaze, she would've sued the hell out of the town—and won.

That had startled them, to say the least, and they'd begun

asking more specific questions. About what should've happened and exactly where the firefighters had gone wrong.

She'd even been asked to briefly describe the hazing incident at The Cellar, which was more difficult to talk about than her harrowing experience at the fire, but she did it anyway. She'd come to realize that while she had some culpability in what happened, Paul and his friends were way out of line.

By the time she'd been dismissed, Caryn was exhausted. She hated being the one to call out Paul and his fellow firefighters, but they were little better than some of the rural volunteer departments she'd visited who had no training whatsoever. If they were allowed to continue as-is, she had no doubt someone's death would eventually be on their hands.

When she'd exited the meeting, Drew was right where she'd left him. Sitting in the uncomfortable metal folding chair outside the door. She was well aware he was having a hard time dealing with what she'd done, but since his concern stemmed from love, she was completely all right with that.

Love. It was almost crazy how fast things had moved between them, but she couldn't say she was sorry. Drew was... simply amazing. She'd kind of thought once they started spending more time together, she'd find things to be annoyed about, but that hadn't happened. He was a good roommate, a great boyfriend, and the fact that he loved her as much as she loved him was practically a miracle.

All her life, she'd wanted to find a partner, and here, she'd found him without even trying. As far as she was concerned, Fallport was magical. She'd always liked visiting her grandfather in the small town, but now she loved it.

"How'd it go?" Drew asked when they were on the way to Art's house. Her grandfather wanted to know all about the meeting and had even stayed home that morning instead of going out to meet Otto and Silas in front of the post office.

"It was tough," she said honestly. "I feel awful about calling out all the guys at the FFD, but seriously, it was embarrassing to watch them at that fire. They weren't working together. Not at all. And no one seemed to know what their job was. Paul wasn't helping, standing around as if he was a lord overseer or something." She shook her head. "But someone needed to bring everything to light. There might not be that many house fires here in Fallport, but I would hate for someone to die next time because the people who were supposed to help them had no idea how to do that...or were scared to actually enter the house."

"You think that was it?"

"Partly. I saw the look on some of those guys' faces. They hadn't seen a fire that big before. But it was also incompetence on simple things, like laying out the hose. You have to get it off the truck and make sure it doesn't kink when the water fills it so it works properly—but to do so quickly and easily, the hose has to be stored properly to begin with. And they should've known where the fire hydrant was. Hell, we had a long list of them back in New York, and we were tested on it all the time. We had to be able to recite where all the hydrants were in a two-block radius of a random address we were given. Water is life to a firefighter, and those guys had no clue where it was. That's completely unacceptable."

"You're not in trouble, right?" Drew asked, then went on before she could respond. "Because if they think of reprimanding you for even one second, they're gonna have a riot on their hands. Everyone in this town will call and write letters. Hell, there might even be a legit riot. You saved Lilly, that's indisputable."

"It's fine," she said, rubbing his arm as he drove. "They thanked me for helping and sent me on my way."

Drew frowned. "That's it?"

Caryn shrugged. "It's not like I expected to be named

Hero of the Year or anything. From what I understand, Tony already owns that title for this year," she joked.

Drew didn't even break a smile.

Caryn mentally sighed. She hated seeing him so worked up and anxious.

"This whole thing is embarrassing for them," she said quietly. "That's not what I was trying to do, embarrass anyone, but even so, that's kind of what happened. There's been a complete lapse of any supervision for the fire department. They have a meeting with Paul today, and then they'll make a decision about what happens next."

She bit her lip and paused for a second. "They *did* kind of ask me if I'd be willing to work with them and the FFD in a consultant capacity."

Drew pulled into Art's driveway, shut off the engine, and turned to her. "Seriously?"

Caryn nodded. "Yeah. They warned me that it wasn't an official offer yet. They have to verify my credentials and call some of my former fire chiefs, but I guess I surprised them with all the things I noticed that could be improved, and they figured I was a good person to help get the ball rolling on that."

"That's great...but is it something you'd want to do?" Drew asked.

Caryn inhaled deeply. "Honestly? I'm not sure. A part of me has been excited about moving on from something that frustrated me for so long. But another part was jumping up and down in joy when they asked. I could still have a connection to firefighting, without many of the most annoying parts. And knowing I could help train people to be better able to help others? That appeals to me a lot."

"That's great, hon," Drew said.

"Yeah. The salary they mentioned is ridiculously low, so I'd have to negotiate that a bit more, but I'm cautiously excited about it. I can do my beta-reading stuff, and still keep my certifications up-to-date."

"The best of both worlds," Drew said softly.

"In theory." Caryn frowned. "But Paul isn't going to be happy. Neither are his friends."

"Screw them," Drew said immediately.

Caryn smiled. "I love you," she told him.

His face gentled. "And I love you. I'm sure you'll make the decision that's best for you," Drew told her.

"For us," she said somewhat shyly. "What I do could affect you too, and I want to do what's best for us both."

"Fuck," Drew muttered.

Caryn had to admit she loved flustering this man. He was so *unflustered* usually, so seeing him trying to get his emotions under control was kind of a rush. Knowing she could affect him so much.

"You said it though. Paul is gonna be pissed at the mayor —but especially at you."

Caryn nodded. "I figured it would be best to avoid him at all costs for a while."

Drew pressed his lips together. "I'll have a talk with Simon too."

"Okay."

"You worried about him?" Drew asked.

Caryn couldn't lie. "A little."

"Me too," he agreed. "Right. So we'll just be a little more careful for a while, yeah?"

Caryn gave him the side eye. "What does 'a little more careful' mean for you? You aren't going to insist I not go anywhere alone, stay at home, and not see my friends, are you?"

He chuckled. "Would you agree if I *did* say that?"

"No," she told him firmly.

"Uh-huh, which is why I wasn't going to say it," he said

with a grin. "But I'm thinking making sure someone knows where you are and who you're meeting for a while wouldn't be a bad thing."

Caryn nodded. She could do that. "That's no problem. I try to do that anyway."

Drew reached out and put his hand at her nape and pulled her close. The position was awkward with the console between them, but Caryn didn't care. He put his forehead on hers. "Love you, sweetheart. So much."

"Love you too."

He pulled back and met her gaze. "How about we go inside, tell Art all the gossip so he can have something to share with his buddies that they don't know, then we go home and I show you exactly how proud I am. How relieved I am that you're safe and healthy."

And just like that, Caryn was turned on. She squirmed a little in her seat. "We could go now, and I could *call* Art."

As if he could sense that they'd thought for even one second of leaving, Art appeared at his front door. "Are you young'uns gonna neck out there all day, or are you gonna come in here and tell me what the hell happened at the meeting?"

Both Drew and Caryn laughed, hard.

"Right, so I guess we're going in," Caryn said. "But yes on the other when we're done."

"I never thought I could be like this," Drew said.

"Like what?"

"Laughing so soon after a crisis. I've been amped up after everything that happened. I'd normally go over it again and again in my head for days, analyzing what went down, wondering what I could have done to help, etcetera. But here I am, felling less paranoid already."

"Is that good? Because I don't mind your analytical mind, and a little paranoia never hurt anyone. I like you exactly how you are, Drew. Your experiences have made you the man you are today, and that man is pretty darn awesome in my eyes."

"It's good," he said. "And thank you."

"You've accepted me how *I* am. How could I do anything less?"

"Still waiting!" Art called from his front steps.

Drew grinned, kissed her hard, then turned to his door.

Caryn followed suit and as soon as she'd walked around the Jeep, he grabbed her hand.

"Keep your pants on, Granddad," Caryn said. "Sheesh."

"You can knock boots later, I wanna know what was said by the council and if I need to go crack some skulls!"

Caryn burst out laughing again. She dropped Drew's hand and wrapped an arm around Art's shoulders as he turned to go back into the house. "No cracking skulls necessary," she said. "Come on, have you eaten? Drew can make us some lunch and I'll tell you all about it." She winked back at Drew as she said it, relieved he didn't look upset about being relegated to the kitchen.

* * *

Paul was so furious, he couldn't even see straight. He had no idea how he'd made it back to his parents' house without wrecking his car. The last two hours had been the most humiliating in his entire life. Everything he'd ever done as a firefighter had been questioned by the city council assholes and the mayor.

They'd wanted to know the reasons for every single one of his actions at the fire the day before—and even had a recording of the radio transmissions he'd had with dispatch. They'd nitpicked every tiny detail. How *dare* they question his decision not to go into the burning house! He'd defend that decision to anyone. Nothing they said would change his mind.

And to know that the *bitch* had the nerve to talk shit about him and his department? To say that everything they'd done at the fire was wrong, and they'd put everyone in danger, and the station and gear and trucks were a goddamn wreck?!

Un-fucking-acceptable.

The icing on the shit cake they'd forced down his throat was when they'd informed him that he was being demoted as captain while they continued with their investigation and interviewed others on the scene...

And they were planning on hiring *Miss Buckner* as a training consultant for the department.

Over his dead body would he take orders from a fucking woman! Someone who thought her shit didn't stink, that she was better than all of them because she'd worked in New York fucking City.

The *only* reason she'd gone into that house yesterday was to show off. To prove that she was better than Paul and his men. In reality, she was desperate for recognition. For someone to pat her on the head and tell her what a good girl she was.

Well, fuck that. Paul would *never* kowtow to her. His fire department had been running just fine without interference from anyone. But it was clear the city council was determined to look good in the eyes of the townspeople. They were going to hire the bitch and nothing he said would sway them.

Unless she wasn't around to be hired.

Paul had to get rid of her. *Now*. Before she could fill the council members' heads with more lies about him and the FFD. Bottom line—there was no way he was handing *his* department over to some condescending wench who thought she knew what it meant to be a firefighter.

He needed to act quickly, before she could spread more

nasty rumors about his incompetence. He just needed to get her alone.

She thought she was a hotshot firefighter? Fine. He'd give her an up-close-and-personal look at the power of fire.

Afterward, she'd be in no condition to tell him—or anyone else—how to do their jobs.

Rage continued to course through Paul. She'd regret the day she decided to stay in Fallport. She didn't belong here, and he'd do whatever it took to send her back to where she came from.

If she didn't survive her unfortunate accident...so be it.

CHAPTER TWENTY

A week had passed since the house fire, and with every day that went by, Caryn fell more in love with Drew. It had taken him three days to be able to let her out of his sight, but instead of his clinginess annoying her, it felt...good.

She'd had close calls in the past, but hadn't had anyone who really gave a damn. Other firefighters had simply shrugged and said it was the price of doing the job. She'd slept like shit for weeks after each time, finding herself being way more cautious on the job as a result. But here in Fallport, in Drew's arms, she'd slept like a baby.

She'd broken down twice. The first time, Drew had been there to hold her. She'd admitted how scared she'd been. Not of the fire, but scared that she wouldn't be able to find Lilly, that she'd already be dead. That they'd get trapped upstairs. All the things any human would feel in a similar situation.

Drew had listened without interruption, had let her feel the way she felt, and then told her again how proud he was. How amazing she was as a firefighter. How lucky they all were to have her as a friend.

Then she'd gone to visit Lilly, and they'd *both* cried. Lilly hadn't remembered any of her rescue, since she'd been unconscious, but of course one of the people at the scene had recorded Caryn coming out of the house with Lilly over her shoulder. Practically everyone in town had seen it—including Lilly.

Mrs. Conley had gone downstairs to let her Yorkie outside to pee, and the fire had erupted while she'd been gone. Busy checking the shots on her camera, Lilly hadn't even realized what was happening until it was too late to try to get down the stairs, opening the bedroom door to a wave of smoke. She'd stuffed a blanket at the base of the door and had stayed by the window, waiting for rescue. A rescue that never would have come if Caryn hadn't been there.

Apparently, the electrical wiring in the house was old and needed replacing. A simple short in a wire and a quick spark had started the blaze in a bedroom. It was almost ironic, considering Ethan was an electrician. He was currently buried under requests from Fallport citizens, wanting their own electrical systems inspected and/or replaced.

Caryn, Bristol, Elsie, Finley, and even Khloe had descended on Lilly's house one evening for a much-needed sleepover, and stayed up late into the night talking, laughing, crying, and reaffirming their friendship. It had been way too close of a call, for everyone, and the next morning, they'd all felt a little lighter.

Today, Caryn had a meeting with the city council in the afternoon to discuss their offer for her to be a training consultant. She had some fairly large ideas about starting a junior firefighter program, recruiting men and women from the high school to learn the ropes, and maybe even a citizens' fire academy, to teach the townspeople what it was their fire department did and some techniques that could help save them in life-or-death situations.

She also had the idea to maybe use some of the cars in the

back of Brock's lot to practice using the jaws of life and extricating people from wrecked vehicles.

This morning, she'd woken up in Drew's arms and showed him how much she loved him up by sliding down his body and giving him a wake-up blow job. He'd been so appreciative, it had taken them an extra thirty minutes to get out of bed.

Caryn had stopped by The Sweet Tooth to get some cinnamon rolls before heading to Bristol's house. Doc Snow had approved her for a walking cast, and she was itching to get into the barn and start work on the special window she was making for the diner.

The second part of the two-part paranormal show had been shown just the other day, although there had been no watch party this time. Lilly had given in and watched it, if for no other reason than to put her mind to rest about how her co-worker's death was treated. She'd admitted that even though she detested the producer and everything he stood for, he did a damn good job on the episodes...if "damn good" meant capitalizing off of a crew member's death and the drama surrounding it. She had no plans to ever watch the shows again.

Caryn crossed the street and walked past On the Rocks. When she reached the parking lot behind it, Paul Downs suddenly appeared.

She immediately stopped and considered turning around and heading back to the bakery, but she straightened her spine and stood her ground. If she was going to stay in Fallport—and she *was* staying—the two of them needed to learn how to get along. Or at least be civil, regardless of what he'd done to her. She could be the bigger person, especially since she could've said no to that first shot of alcohol in The Cellar...and hadn't.

"Can we talk?" Paul asked without any preamble.

Her first reaction was to say no, but at the moment, the man in front of her wasn't scowling. Wasn't shooting daggers at her from his eyes.

"I need to apologize. I haven't given you a fair shot since you've gotten back to town."

Caryn nodded. "All right."

Paul looked around and shrugged. "Not here. Will you come to my car?"

Immediately, danger vibes shot through Caryn. She shook her head. "Are you kidding? After what happened the last time I got in a car with you? No, I'm not going anywhere with you, Paul. We can talk here."

And just like that, it was as if a switch was flipped. The hatred Caryn had expected to see transformed his face. His lip curled into a snarl. But she didn't care. She was done trying to make this man like her.

Quickly glancing around, Caryn saw the area was deserted. Any locals milling about this morning would be on the busy square, entering or exiting the bakery or the diner or the library. She and Paul were the only ones in the parking lot behind On the Rocks.

Wanting to get the hell away from him as fast as possible, Caryn gave Paul a wide berth, hurrying to get into her Sonata.

Without warning, she was slammed into the car—hard. Her head bounced off the steel and her vision blacked out for a moment.

That was all the time Paul needed to get the upper hand. He grabbed her arm, yanking her close. Caryn was a strong woman, but she was no match for him at the moment with her head throbbing and her vision just now clearing. He stood so close, it would look like an intimate embrace to anyone who came along.

Caryn instantly felt something sharp pierce her skin. She couldn't stop the small yelp that left her mouth. Then she froze when she saw the knife in Paul's hand, not wanting the blade to sink deeper into her flesh.

"I wanted to do this the easy way," he told her in a low growl, as if everything happening was somehow her own fault. "But no, of course you had to fuck that up too. Just like you've fucked up *everything* in my life. Come on, bitch. We're going for a drive."

Caryn tried to reach for her cell phone without Paul seeing.

"Don't even think about it," he snarled, pushing the tip of the knife farther into her side.

The pain was so intense, it was all Caryn could do to stay upright. If she pissed him off too much, she had no doubt that he'd stab her without thinking twice. At that moment, her best option—her *only* option—was to go along with whatever he said...and pray for a chance to escape.

He pulled her away from her car and toward another parked a couple spaces away. He shoved her into the driver's side. "Scoot over," he ordered, shoving that damn knife in her face.

Caryn realized she still held the cinnamon rolls. She should've dropped the bag in the parking lot. Maybe seeing it on the ground would've made someone wonder what it was doing there...enough to talk to Finley about it. The alarm would've been raised.

It was a long shot—and it was too late now. She was already in Paul's car, and he'd slammed the door and was peeling out of the parking lot behind the square.

"Paul, can we—"

"*Shut up*, bitch!" he shouted. "I don't want to hear a fucking thing you have to say. I'm not going to let you ruin my life any more than you already have!"

Deciding listening to the man was her best bet—Paul was already extremely agitated—Caryn bit her lip and pressed a hand to her side. Looking down, she saw she was bleeding. She had no idea how bad, but since there was literally nothing she could do about it at the moment, she turned her mind toward escape.

She could throw herself out of the car, but chances were, Paul would try to run her over if she did. And if she hurt herself bad enough in the process that she couldn't run, or defend herself if he came back to get her, that would make the situation worse.

She sat quietly, her body tense, waiting to see where he was taking her. And hoping she'd have a clear course of action when they got there.

To her surprise, Paul pulled into the Fallport Creek Trail. It was only about a mile from the town itself, and was always fairly busy. Especially now that amateur Bigfoot hunters were already coming to town. It was an odd choice to bring someone you'd just kidnapped, but then again, Paul wasn't exactly thinking straight. He was too furious.

"Get out," he ordered, aiming the knife in her direction. "This way, toward me. And don't try anything or I swear to God, I'll gut you like a fucking fish."

Caryn carefully scooted back across the front seat and as soon as she was close enough, Paul grabbed her arm and hauled her out. The tip of the knife went right back into her side, slicing her once more, and it was all she could do not to jerk away. She blanked her mind, doing her best to forget about the pain the knife was causing.

As Paul dragged her into the forest, she thought about her grandfather. Art had been stabbed, and it seemed incredibly ironic that she was about to share that same experience. Caryn had no doubt that at some point, Paul would sink the blade into her flesh. It was obvious he didn't care if he hurt her, that he wanted to make her feel pain.

He started down the trail, but didn't go far before he

turned and began to bushwhack into the woods, away from anyone who might be on the trail this morning. Caryn had hoped she'd be able to somehow signal someone that she was in trouble, but Paul wasn't giving her that option.

It was slow-going, trying to get through the brambles and downed trees, but Paul somehow managed to not only keep hold of her arm, he kept that damn knife at her side. Every now and then it would prick her flesh again, since they weren't exactly walking along a pristine sidewalk, and small spots of blood dotted her shirt at the waist. With every step they took through the woods, Caryn's chances of escape diminished.

She didn't try to talk to Paul again. It was obvious whatever she said would only set him off even worse. The longer they walked, the more Caryn realized she was going to have to make a move. She couldn't wait for him to get to wherever he was taking her. Whatever he had planned, it wouldn't be good.

Kicking herself for not doing something when they were in town or still on the trail, even if it might've been reckless, Caryn took a deep breath and prepared for the fight of her life. She wasn't ready to die. She and Drew were as close as ever, her grandfather was finally back to his old self, and she'd just heard back from an author friend of Thomas's. They were negotiating her price—and she was shocked to learn that the woman was willing to pay *double* what Thomas did to read her first draft and offer suggestions.

Caryn had a lot to live for—and she refused to go down without a fight.

She'd just taken a deep breath, preparing to spin and run, when a small, dilapidated wooden cabin appeared. It was obvious Paul had scoped out this spot ahead of time, because there was no way he'd just stumbled upon this place.

Seeing the structure made ice freeze in Caryn's veins. If

he thought he was going to force himself on her in there, he was so damn wrong. She wasn't going to let anyone sexually assault her. No fucking way.

But that wasn't what Paul had in mind.

Without a word, he spun and punched her in the face.

The move surprised Caryn so much, and the pain was so intense, she fell to the forest floor with a grunt.

Then his foot swung forward and he kicked her. *Hard.*

He didn't stop. She struggled to her knees, trying to fight back, but with every blow Caryn was able to block, Paul succeeded with another. A kick to the side, a fist to her shoulder. An elbow to the face.

He was beating the crap out of her—all without saying a single word.

It was eerie. Terrifying. Except for the occasional grunt, Paul methodically pummeled her over and over.

Caryn eventually rolled into a ball on the ground, doing her best to protect her head and sides and praying he'd get tired of hitting her sooner rather than later.

The only small consolation was that he was using his fists and feet, and not the knife.

Caryn briefly opened her eyes, trying to locate the blade, thinking maybe she could grab it and protect herself, but it was no use. It took all her concentration to try to protect herself from the blows Paul was raining down on her.

She could feel her strength fading. It was getting harder to even hold her arms over her face. As pain blossomed throughout her body, Caryn's eyes closed and her last thought was how she'd let herself down by not being stronger, smarter, or able to find a way out of this.

* * *

Clyde Thomas was a loner. He knew it. Didn't care. He'd never met a woman he wanted to spend his days with or who understood his love of moonshine. He'd spent his life living on the outskirts of Fallport. All in all, it wasn't a bad town. There were good people who lived there, just as there were bad people. And as long as they all left him alone, Clyde was content.

He wasn't happy that his sanctuary had been disturbed, however. First, it had been that TV show guy who'd camped way too close to his house. When the police had come and found the asshole's tent and the other remnants of his campsite in Clyde's trash, they'd had the audacity to believe for a while that *he'd* killed the guy.

He snorted just thinking about it. If he'd offed the man, he wouldn't have been dumb enough to throw his shit in his own trash. No, if Clyde wanted to get rid of someone, he'd do so without a fucking trace.

He knew there were some people in town who still thought he had something to do with everything that happened, even if the real killer had already been found. But whatever, he didn't care. As long as he was left alone, that was the important thing.

But that damn show meant there were more people in *his* forest. They frequently got too close to the shacks he'd set up to make his hooch. He'd had to move some of his operations farther into the forest, which was a huge pain in his ass.

He supposed people would be surprised to know just how much money he made from his moonshine. So much, he'd never be able to spend all his money in the bank—or the cash he'd stashed in various places around the forest. Just in case.

Some of that money he'd used to put up trail cameras around his stills. The best money could buy. He had to make sure no one messed with his shit. Yessir, he had quite an impressive electronic footprint in the forest now. He knew if a squirrel farted too close to his cabins.

So when he received an alert on his fancy new watch that one of his cameras had captured something moving near his closest cabin, Clyde frowned. He hoped whatever had triggered the camera was an animal. It was a bit early in the day for hikers to have wandered off the trail already. Especially all the way to where the cabin was located.

Picking up his tablet, Clyde clicked on the app that would show him all the live feeds from his cameras. It took a moment to find the correct camera that had sent the alert.

When the replay of the video clip began, at first Clyde had a hard time understanding what he was looking at.

He knew Caryn Buckner. He'd met her when she was a little girl, and for some reason she'd never been scared of him like a lot of kids were. He'd found her wandering lost in the woods, had gotten her back to the trail. After that, she always smiled at him when their paths crossed, and had no problem coming straight up to him to ask how he was doing...and a thousand other questions. As an adult, every time she came back to town, she made it a point to visit, and say hello when they ran into each other.

Just a couple weeks ago, he'd been in town delivering a batch of his apple pie moonshine, one of his bestsellers, and she'd given him a huge hug and let him know that she was probably going to move to the area permanently. Then she'd bought four mason jars of his hooch and told him she'd be back for more soon.

Clyde liked her.

But seeing her in his forest, being dragged along by the arm by Paul fucking Downs, was strange. He'd heard the rumors about the man and what he'd done to Caryn. And he wasn't happy about them. He definitely didn't think Caryn would voluntarily go into the forest with the man. They'd walked by one of his cameras, heading in the direction of his cabin, resulting in the notification being sent to his watch.

Clyde switched to a live view from a different camera, one hidden on the cabin itself, and frowned as he leaned closer to the tablet.

What he saw made his blood run cold.

He was a hard son-of-a-bitch, and nothing much fazed him, but seeing Paul hauling his leg back and kicking at Caryn when she was already on the ground, using her arms to protect herself, was just plain *wrong*.

After that kick, Paul stood there, staring down at Caryn, who was obviously unconscious from the vicious blow. Even on the video, Clyde could see all the dark splotches on Caryn's skin.

Blood. The bastard had beaten her to a bloody pulp.

As he watched, Paul leaned over and grabbed Caryn's ankles, dragging her toward the cabin. Her shirt rucked up as he pulled her through the brush until the material was around her neck, her bra exposed.

A red haze settled over Clyde's vision. No fucking way was this prick going to rape someone on his property! And definitely not Caryn. She'd always been kind to him. To everyone. And he'd heard through the Fallport grapevine that she'd recently braved a fire to save Lilly, the chick who'd found herself in the middle of the shit that went down with that damn missing TV star.

It suddenly clicked in Clyde's head. Paul was probably pissed that someone had taken away his glory. He was the kind of man who lived to be in the spotlight. Wanted to be worshiped. But that kind of reverence was earned, and Paul definitely hadn't done a damn thing over the years to earn respect from anyone.

Clyde reached for his phone. Cell service sucked at his place, and in the forest where his stills were, so he'd bought one of those fancy satellite phones a couple years ago. He hadn't had to use it much, but he was damn thankful for it now.

He didn't call the Fallport police. No. There was only one person who immediately needed to know what was happening.

When the person on the other end of the line picked up, Clyde didn't mince words. "Paul Downs has your woman. He's hurt her. Bad."

"Where?"

That one word communicated both fear and fury at the same time.

Clyde told the man where he could find Caryn, then added, "I'm going there now. I'll do what I can." Then he hung up without another word.

He needed to get to that cabin. Do what he could until the cavalry arrived.

CHAPTER TWENTY-ONE

Drew hadn't been worried when he'd seen the blocked number appear on the screen of his phone. But when he'd heard Clyde's voice say, "Paul Downs has your woman," his blood immediately ran cold.

He was on the move even as Clyde spoke. Caryn had left his bed not even two hours ago, sated and happy. It was almost impossible to wrap his brain around how fast circumstances had changed.

It shouldn't have been. He knew better than most how a simple traffic stop could turn deadly. Or how fast a domestic incident could change on a dime.

Drew was already in his Jeep as Clyde told him exactly where Paul had taken Caryn. The cabin Clyde described was actually familiar to Drew. He and his fellow search and rescue team had used it as a landmark more than once while searching for people who'd gone off the Fallport Creek Trail and gotten turned around.

"I'm going there now. I'll do what I can," Clyde said before severing the connection.

Drew immediately clicked on the first name in his contact list.

"Yo, kind of early to be calling, especially when you've got Caryn to snuggle up to," Brock joked as he answered.

"I need you," Drew told him tightly. "Paul's kidnapped Caryn. Taken her to Clyde's cabin near Fallport Creek Trail. The one that has the biggest setup for his hooch."

"*Fuck*," Brock swore. "I'm on my way. Don't wait for me."

Drew didn't need to tell his friend that he wouldn't. Brock knew it already.

"I'll call the others."

"Hurry," Drew told him. He was breathing hard, almost as if he'd been running a marathon. Adrenaline was coursing through his veins and he felt shaky. He'd never felt like this before. Ever. Even when he'd faced off with a mob of crazed and drunken men and women who were hyped up on the joy of their team winning a national championship. Even when startled by someone who'd pulled a weapon on him.

But this was *Caryn*. He could picture her just as she'd been that morning. He'd woken up with her mouth around his cock, and she'd smiled lazily from between his legs, so satisfied with herself. He'd never been with someone so giving and open, and the thought of that light being snuffed out was unbearable.

As Drew flew into the parking lot at the trailhead, he realized that Brock had disconnected the line with him at some point. He didn't remember the drive to the trail, couldn't recall anything Brock might have told him. All he could think about was Caryn's beautiful face.

Determination rose within him. She wasn't dead. No way could someone with as good a soul as her be dead. But Paul Downs sure as hell would be if Drew got his hands on him.

As he ran into the woods, Drew realized how badly he'd fucked up. He'd missed any signs that Paul was going to make a move. He should've known. With all his training, with how observant he considered himself...even with how angry Paul had been at the Conley fire, Drew still missed the fact that the man was fucking crazy.

He and Caryn had talked about him, about how upset Paul was going to be when he was reprimanded by the mayor and the city council, how it was likely he was furious that he'd been demoted, and how he'd hate the fact that Caryn would most likely be hired to whip the FFD into shape. They'd even talked to Simon about it, and his advice had been to avoid the man and let him know if Paul did anything remotely threatening. But neither of them had *ever* thought he'd do something like this.

Like kidnapping Caryn and bringing her into the woods to do who knew what.

A branch slapping across his face brought Drew back to the present. He needed to get out of his head and concentrate. He was willing and able to do whatever it took to protect Caryn from Paul. He just prayed he wasn't too late.

It took way too long to reach the cabin, and as he neared it, a new horror Drew hadn't even thought about made itself clear.

He smelled smoke.

He put on a burst of speed and crashed into the area around the cabin—and looked on in horror as flames licked up the right side of the structure, while Clyde did his best to reach the door behind...boards?

"Kick it in!" Drew yelled as he approached.

"I tried," Clyde grunted as he clawed at, yes, one of several wooden boards nailed across the door.

"This place looks like it could fall down at any second," Drew said frantically. "It's gotta come down if we both hit it at the same time."

"Might look dilapidated, but that's what I *want* people to

think. I've reinforced this thing with enough boards that it's not gonna come down easily," Clyde said.

"Fuck!" Drew swore. "You're sure she's inside?"

"Yes," Clyde said shortly.

"Where's Paul?"

"Saw him running through the woods just before I noticed the smoke. Asshole used the boards and nails I kept inside for repairs."

Drew studied the cabin in front of him, trying to be rational and calm instead of panicked. Caryn was inside, probably unconscious, otherwise she'd be doing her best to get out.

"More bad news," Clyde said as he finally managed to rip one of the boards off the door with his bare hands. Blood stained his fingers, but he didn't seem to notice. "There's a fresh batch of moonshine inside. I'd just finished it the other day. If the fire gets to that alcohol..."

His voice trailed off, and Drew understood what he was saying.

They needed to get Caryn out *now*.

They worked together to get the rest of the boards off the door. "I forgot the damn key," the gruff older man said as the last board came free. "Fucking stupid! Was too anxious to get out here."

Drew couldn't blame him for that. He couldn't remember where he'd put the keys to his Jeep at the moment. They might be in his pocket, on the ground by his vehicle, or even still in the ignition.

Both men went to work attempting to break the deceptively weak-looking door. They were able to break through two of the vertical boards, but the lock refused to give.

"I'll keep trying to get the damn thing open. You go in and drag Caryn over here and we'll pull her out," Clyde ordered.

Drew nodded and stuck his head and shoulders through the hole they'd made in the door. As he squeezed through, he saw Caryn for the first time. She was lying on the dirt, motionless. Her arms were handcuffed behind her back, bruises already forming on her face and arms.

Pure hatred for Paul threatened to render Drew motionless, but he forced the emotion away. He had to get Caryn out of there. Already he could feel the heat from the fire gaining in strength and intensity on the nearby wall.

He forced the rest of his body through the door and swerved around the main components of the moonshine still. The gas burner was sitting idle under a large copper pot probably filled with mash...powdered malt and water, which was heated to make an alcoholic vapor. It wasn't the first or second barrel that captured his attention—it was the large barrel of moonshine connected to the condenser. If it got knocked over, and the fire reached it, this place would go up in a millisecond.

Caryn moaned then, and her legs straightened, barely missing the large barrel of freshly brewed moonshine.

"Don't move," he ordered as he rushed to her side.

Her eyes fluttered, and she looked up at him in confusion.

Drew grabbed her under her armpits and began to drag her away from the fire and toward the door. When she cried out in pain, he stopped.

"What? What's wrong?" he asked.

Amazingly, she stared up at him and seemed perfectly aware of what was going on around her. "Handcuff key," she croaked.

Shit. He'd forgotten all about the conversation they'd had the other day. They'd been exchanging good-natured ribbing about each other's professions, and she'd demanded he pull out his wallet and show her the handcuff key she just *knew* he kept inside. He'd tried to convince her that he didn't have one

—though, of course he did—but she'd managed to get his wallet out of his pants and triumphantly pulled the little metal key from between the few bills he had in there.

"I knew it!" she'd crowed. Drew had been somewhat embarrassed for a beat—until she'd admitted she carried a key everywhere she went too. That she'd learned to be paranoid from the police officers she ran across in New York. She'd showed him the little pockets she'd sewn into the back waistband of all her pants.

They'd ended up having fast, rough sex right there on the floor of his living room, the handcuff key from his wallet forgotten on the floor as she knelt on her hands as knees and he took her from behind.

His own wallet was still at home somewhere. He hadn't grabbed it on his way out the door, too desperate to get to Caryn. And in that moment, he had to admit that while Caryn sewing little pockets into her pants made her even more paranoid than he was, it also made her a lot smarter.

She sat up, coughing as the smoke thickened, and Drew fumbled at the small of her back to find the key. It seemed to take way too long, but finally he had it in his hands. It took him two tries to fit the key into the slot of the handcuffs, something he'd done a thousand times in his life, but never under these kind of conditions. Never with the life of the woman he loved in his hands.

As soon as one of the cuffs dropped to the ground, without prompting, Caryn turned onto her hands and knees and headed for the light coming from the wide gap in the door. Drew was right on her ass, doing his best to shield her from the heat and fire crackling behind them. He didn't know how badly she was hurt. Their first priority was getting out of this death trap. He was impressed that Clyde had managed to make a reinforced and secure building look so shitty, but he would've preferred the place be a house of sticks right about now.

"Clyde!" he yelled as they neared the door. A large bloody hand reached inside and Caryn took it without hesitation. The second her legs disappeared, Drew thrust his head and shoulders through the gap. Clyde was helping Caryn away from the cabin as he exited.

Drew made a beeline for her—and almost threw up at what he saw. Her hair was full of dirt, she had bruises on her face—especially around one of her eyes—and every visible inch of skin. Her shirt was torn, there were several blood-stains on the material, and she was even missing a shoe.

His woman had been beaten to within an inch of her life, and yet here she was. Alive. Relief swam through his veins, battling with the red-hot fury he felt toward Paul. He was even more determined than before to see that asshole go down for what he'd done.

"The cabin..." she whispered in horror.

Turning, Drew saw the fire had grown in size and strength.

"We need to get that fire out!" she exclaimed.

Drew started to tell her not to fucking worry about that right now. He had to get her to Doc Snow. But she was moving before he could even blink. She hobbled as fast as she could toward the fire, when most people would've been running in the opposite direction.

"You've got water piped in, right, Clyde?" she asked.

"There's a black hose piped into the roof that's connected to the stream. It's got a shut-off valve about forty yards away."

"If I pull on it, will it come out?"

"It's connected to the condenser but it should pop out," Clyde said quickly.

"I'll grab it, you go turn the valve. We need to get some

water on this thing before the alcohol catches. The last thing we need is the entire forest going up in flames!"

Drew was momentarily stunned. Caryn was injured, obviously hurting, and yet she was still determined to do what she'd trained to do for years...fight fire.

He wanted to protest. To scream. Tell her to forget saving the goddamn forest; she needed to save *herself*.

Instead, he put his trust in his woman and followed.

When she winced as she stretched to grab the hose sticking out of the top of the shack, he gently pushed her aside. "I got it. Just tell me what to do."

Grateful, she stepped aside without complaint. Drew yanked on the hose. He felt it pop out of whatever was holding it to the condenser inside the building, well aware that time was running out. If Clyde was worried about what would happen when the flames hit the moonshine inside, he was doubly so.

A surprisingly strong stream of water whooshed out of the end of the hose as Drew and Caryn ran around the side of the cabin, toward the flames. When he got close, Drew instinctively aimed the water at the top of the structure.

"No, aim at the base of the fire," Caryn instructed. "That's it. Sweep it side to side. Good."

With Caryn at his back, Drew did his best to put out the flames. The heat was uncomfortable, his hands quickly went numb from the freezing-cold water of the stream passing through the hose in his grip, and his lungs burned from inhaling the smoke pouring off the burning shack. He was shaking with adrenaline and stress, but through it all, Caryn stayed at his back, giving him tips and pointers as he struggled to extinguish the blaze.

He was concentrating so hard on what he was doing, he didn't see or hear Paul until the man was practically on top of them. He raced toward them, a thick wooden branch in his hands, and he swung it as hard as he could.

Even as Drew was stumbling to the right from the extremely hard shove Caryn gave him, he had the absurd thought that it was *completely insane* of Paul to stick around somewhere, close enough to watch Caryn die in the fire. On the heels of that, he wondered why the man hadn't tried to stop him or Clyde from rescuing her. Maybe he didn't want to take on two men. Maybe he was conceited enough to think they wouldn't save her, and only when he realized they'd succeeded did he act.

All of that flew through Drew's mind in the split-second before he landed on the ground, water spraying everywhere and his elbow slammed into the dirt. Caryn had pushed him out of the way of Paul's strike—and now she was struggling with the man, wrestling over the branch.

In a flash, Drew was on his feet. With Paul's hands occupied, it wasn't hard to punch him in the face. He grunted and let go of the branch.

Drew hit him again. Then again. Over and over.

He didn't stop when the man fell to the ground, just straddled him and kept punching, his knuckles raw, his only thought to subdue the fucker so he could never hurt Caryn again.

"He's down!" Caryn yelled.

Drew barely heard her. He had to make Paul pay for what he'd done.

"I got him," he heard vaguely.

Then Clyde was pulling Drew back with a strong hand on his arm. And just like that, he came back to the present. Caryn was staring at him, her expression one of concern.

He backed away from Paul, who was sprawled on the ground moaning in pain. Spitting in the dirt next to the man, Drew growled, "How's it feel, asshole?"

"Drew, the fire," Caryn urged. "It's spreading to the grass!"

Clyde dragged Paul away from the cabin, and after that, things were a blur.

Brock arrived. It would've been nice if he'd gotten there in time to prevent Paul from attacking, but Drew was still grateful for his help now. And less than a minute after he ran onto the scene, the rest of the Eagle Point Search and Rescue team arrived too. At Caryn's direction, they worked together to put out the fire. She and Raiden threw dirt on the grass around the cabin. Zeke kept an eye on the still-moaning Paul. Rocky, Tal, Ethan, and Clyde finished breaking down the door—and risked a hell of a lot to go inside and pull out not only the barrel of moonshine, but the propane bottle sitting against the wall opposite the fire, which Drew hadn't even noticed. They also dragged out the copper pot with the remnants of the mash used in the last batch Clyde had brewed, then the doubler and the condenser.

It was dangerous work, and Clyde literally looked like he was going to cry with gratitude for their help when the last piece of his still was dragged to safety. The materials weren't cheap, and it obviously meant a lot to him that the team had done what they could to save everything.

Raiden took the hose from Drew, leaving him free to finally join Caryn.

She was standing off to the side, her gaze glued to the fire that had mostly been extinguished. She swayed on her feet, and Drew didn't hesitate to pull her into his arms. She went willingly, and Drew swiftly picked her up.

"What are you doing?" she asked.

He ignored the question, carrying her over to a log well away from the shack and settling her on his lap. He buried his nose into her neck and held her as firmly as he dared, his own body trembling with adrenaline. He felt her arm go around his back and the other clasped his biceps tightly.

"I'm okay," she reassured him.

"You aren't," he countered, lifting his head. "You have bruises forming on your beautiful face. And you're bleeding. And he fucking *handcuffed* you."

"To be fair, I don't remember that part," she admitted.

"Is that supposed to make me feel better?" Drew asked. "I have no idea what the fuck he was thinking. I mean, if he wanted to make it seem like an accident, handcuffing you was the most idiotic thing he could've done." He shook his head. "Then again, he didn't leave the area. Maybe he just wanted to make sure you couldn't escape, and when the fire was out, he would've gone back and taken them off." The utter heartlessness of that idea made Drew physically sick. "But did he really think that no one would report a fucking fire, or that it wouldn't spread?" He knew he was asking questions that he'd likely never get answers to, but he couldn't help but verbalize them.

"I don't know what he was thinking either," Caryn said quietly.

Drew took a deep breath and did his best to turn his mind away from that asshole. "You had my back."

Her brows furrowed. "What?"

"I didn't even see him coming. You didn't hesitate to have my back and push me out of the way."

"Of course I did. Did you think I was going to let him hit you?" she asked.

"Remember that conversation we had about wanting a true partner?"

She nodded.

"You're mine, Caryn. My true partner. In every sense of the word. When Clyde called and said Paul had you, I couldn't think. Even with all my training, I felt as if I was moving through molasses to get to you. All I knew was that I wasn't going to let anything happen to you, not if I could help it."

She took a deep breath. "I've never known what it's like to have a true partner until you," she said.

"If you guys wanna do a spit-shake or something to seal the deal, great, but I'm thinking we need to get Caryn out of here and over to Doc Snow. I'm not liking those bloodstains on her shirt."

Drew was startled by Brock's voice, and he immediately looked down at Caryn's waist, frowning anew at the blood. He'd noticed it earlier, but with everything else going on, it hadn't truly registered. "What the fuck?" he asked, reaching for the hem of her T-shirt.

"I'm okay," she reassured him, but didn't stop him from looking at her injuries.

Seeing the obvious knife cuts on her skin made his mind go utterly blank for a split-second...then he stood slowly. He placed Caryn on her feet, made sure she was steady, and turned to where Paul was still lying on the ground.

He didn't get two steps before Caryn's hand on his arm stopped him. "You can't be my partner if you're behind bars," she said softly.

Drew stopped, but he didn't take his gaze from Paul.

Caryn stepped in front of him and put a hand on his cheek. "I'm okay. He didn't win."

It took everything inside Drew to douse his desire to kill Paul Downs. The man had hurt the most important person in his life. Without Caryn, Drew would still be the paranoid hermit he'd been before. She'd brought love and joy to his life, and he'd be damned if he'd let anyone take that away—including himself. And getting arrested for murder would definitely hurt Caryn.

He focused on her instead of the man on the ground. "Damn straight, he didn't win," Drew said.

She sighed in relief when she realized he wasn't going to go after Paul. "How'd you know where I was?" she asked.

"Like I said, Clyde called me. I have no idea how *he* knew," Drew added.

"Game cameras," Clyde said from his spot standing over Paul, making sure the man wasn't getting up anytime soon. "Expensive ones."

"Tell me you've got recordings," Rocky pleaded.

"Hell yes, I do," Clyde said.

"Think you can get those SD cards to Simon?" Tal asked.

"How about I just email him the videos?" Clyde asked.

"You've got email?" Zeke said, clearly surprised by the idea.

Clyde looked at him as if he was completely stupid. "Of course I do. And I've got a satellite phone. How else do you think I called Drew? And a website for my moonshine...and a degree in computer technology I earned online."

"Holy shit." Ethan laughed under his breath.

"I know everyone thinks I'm some backwater hick, but I don't give a damn. I had to learn how to earn a living, and I've done just fine for myself."

"I'll say," Tal agreed.

"You probably don't need it, and that wouldn't surprise me at this point, but if you ever want help from an accountant or investment manager, my services are all yours, free of charge. Forever," Drew told the older man, respect and gratitude in his voice.

Clyde nodded once.

"Right, so...Drew, you need to get Caryn to Doc Snow. We'll call and let him know you're on the way," Ethan said.

"I'll go with him," Brock volunteered. "I can drive while you sit with Caryn."

"What about the fire?" Caryn asked, looking at the still-smoldering cabin. "You can't leave it, it's likely to rekindle."

"We'll stay and keep an eye on it," Zeke reassured her.

"We need to stay until Simon or one of his deputies gets here, anyway. Someone's gonna have to help carry the garbage out of the woods," Tal said, looking pointedly at Paul.

"And once the fire's out, we need to help Clyde get his still put back together," Raid added.

Drew had never been as thankful to have such good men in his life as he was right that moment. He could concentrate on Caryn and not worry about anything else.

Caryn walked toward Clyde. Drew was about to pull her back, not wanting her anywhere near Paul, in case he managed to find the strength to get up, but he shouldn't have worried. Zeke and Ethan stepped between her and Paul, even as Clyde moved forward.

"Thank you," Caryn said as she hugged the large man. He had on his signature jean overalls and white T-shirt. His large belly almost prevented her from getting her arms around him, but she managed. His fairly mangy black beard, peppered liberally with gray, contrasted starkly against her blonde hair as he held her.

But it was obvious the two now had a bond that would never be severed. Caryn had already thought highly of the recluse, and he had a feeling between her and her grandfather, the entire town of Fallport would see him in a new light. Clyde might not be thrilled with the fact he was about to become a hero in many people's eyes, but he'd just have to deal.

Drew came up behind Caryn and put a hand on the small of her back. He hated seeing the bloodstains on her shirt. They made him more anxious to get her out of there.

"You have my thanks too," Drew said, holding out his hand. "I appreciate you calling me."

Clyde shook it and nodded at him before taking a step

back. "As her man, I knew you'd get here faster than the cops."

It seemed as if Clyde, despite being a recluse, was still dialed into the goings-on in Fallport. It shouldn't have surprised Drew, given the man's other revelations, but it still kind of did.

"If you need someone to upgrade your IT system—you know, to make sure it's secure with all those monetary transactions you do for people—let me know," Clyde said.

Drew chuckled. "I just might take you up on that," he told the older man. Then he looked at Caryn. "You ready to get out of here?"

"More than," she said.

"I can carry you, if you're in too much pain to walk," Drew said, his brows lowering in concern as he saw her wince when she turned.

"Don't even think about it," she said with a glare.

Drew heard chuckles around him, but he ignored them. "All I care about is you not being more hurt than you already are."

"I'm tough," Caryn informed him.

"Damn straight, you are," Drew said immediately.

Tal approached with Caryn's missing shoe. "If she's gonna walk out of here, she's gonna need this."

Drew immediately knelt at Caryn's feet and helped her get it on, tying it so she wouldn't have to bend over and aggravate the small wounds on her sides.

They started walking back through the woods, toward the trail, Drew and Brock asking questions about her abduction. What she told them made Drew's fury at Paul flare yet again.

Then, after a brief silence, Caryn sighed. "I don't know what happened to my cinnamon rolls," she said in a tone that implied she was sad about the loss of the sweet treat.

For a moment, Drew thought he'd misheard. She'd matter-of-factly told him and Brock everything that happened, how Paul had gotten her into the woods, without breaking down. She seemed to be handling the entire situation amazingly well, actually. So well, Drew assumed she must be in shock.

Now, to hear her complain about cinnamon rolls, of all things, made him realize she truly *was* all right.

"We'll get you more," he reassured her.

"I was supposed to bring one to Bristol too," she added.

"I'll go see Finley and explain what happened, and get both you and Bristol fresh ones," Brock offered.

Drew looked at Caryn as they walked...and he saw a small smile spread across her lips. He resisted the urge to roll his eyes. He knew all about Caryn's opinion that Brock liked Finley, and how the baker was too shy to do anything about it. He wouldn't be surprised if she and the other women had a plan in the works to get the two together. She was obviously delighted by Brock's offer.

"Awesome, thanks," she told him. "Please make sure Finley doesn't freak out when she hears what happened. She's pretty sensitive, and I don't want her to worry."

"I'll handle her with care," Brock promised.

Drew mentally shook his head. Brock was a goner. He just didn't know it yet.

EPILOGUE

Two weeks had passed since the incident in the forest, and Caryn was feeling good. The first few days afterward had been tough. Every muscle in her body hurt and there were bruises everywhere...her face, arms, legs, back, torso... Every time Drew saw them, his teeth would clench and a muscle in his jaw would start ticking.

He was still angry. Absolutely furious. But there was no one to take his anger out on except himself, which wasn't acceptable to Caryn. They'd had their first fight because of it.

Caryn had confronted him the night she'd taken a bath to try to loosen up her muscles, and had needed help getting out of the tub. He was scowling hard, and she'd asked him what was wrong. He broke. Apologizing for letting her down. For letting Paul get his hands on her. For not seeing the signs.

But Caryn wasn't going to let him go on thinking anything that happened was his fault. They'd both yelled—a lot. But in the end, he'd agreed that she was a grown-ass adult, and neither of them could've ever known that Paul was so completely unhinged.

Caryn wasn't one hundred percent sure Drew wasn't

315

holding onto some sort of residual blame, but he seemed more relaxed—or resigned, maybe?—to what happened. It helped that the bruises on her face were almost gone, now just a pale yellow, and Caryn herself was moving on.

Paul had been fired from the Fallport Fire Department, along with Dennis, George, and Lou. Apparently, Paul had told them some of what he'd planned to do—kidnap her, beat her, and leave her in the forest. They claimed not to know about the fire, but since none of them had tried to stop Paul, or called the police and let them know what their friend was planning, they were deemed just as guilty.

Paul was currently in the county jail, having been arrested for kidnapping, arson, attempted murder, and a few other charges. He was being held without bail, which Caryn was more than grateful for. She didn't want to have to worry about him coming after her again to finish what he'd started.

Surprisingly, Oscar had been promoted to captain at the fire department. Drew and his search and rescue friends had been livid about that, but Caryn thought he was a good choice. Yes, he'd been at The Cellar, but in the end, he'd made the right decision to call Drew that night. He also seemed to genuinely care about the station.

Caryn was officially hired by the city to oversee the training for the department, and had already met with Oscar about the next steps. They'd made some preliminary plans and Caryn was pleased with his eagerness, as well as the obvious cooperation of the rest of the firefighters. There were now five open positions to be filled, and Caryn encouraged the city council to advertise a lot more robustly to find appropriate and diverse candidates.

All in all, things were going extremely well in Caryn's life. She'd even received the first manuscript from one of Thomas's friends, her second-ever beta reading client. She sometimes had to pinch herself that she was responsible for the first read through of such famous authors' works. She'd warned the woman that she didn't pull any punches when she critiqued a manuscript, but she'd reassured Caryn that was perfectly all right.

Caryn hoped she meant it.

Ethan and Lilly were in the final stages of planning their wedding at Rocky and Bristol's barn on Halloween. It was going to be a laid-back event, and Lilly had said if anyone showed up in a suit and tie or a fancy gown, she was kicking them out. It was going to be a jeans-and-T-shirt kind of affair —or a costume, if someone wanted to wear one—and Caryn was very much looking forward to it.

The sun was just beginning to inch over the horizon, and Caryn felt extremely lazy. She'd slept in every day for the last two weeks, with Drew's encouragement. She'd insisted on working out, ignoring his protests, but they'd waited until later in the morning to venture outside and stuck mostly to easy hiking. The early mornings were for relaxing, reflecting on everything that had happened, and being thankful for how things had turned out.

"Morning," Drew said softly as he rolled over and pinned her to the mattress with an arm around her belly and a leg thrown over one of her thighs.

"Morning," she returned.

"You sleep okay?" he asked.

"Like a log."

It was interesting that even though she'd been the one beaten up and left in that cabin to burn to death, it was *Drew* who'd had nightmares, and not her. Caryn guessed that was because she was unconscious and had no idea what Paul had planned. Yeah, getting beaten wasn't fun, but she'd hoped once he had his fill, he'd leave her there to find her own way home, much like he'd done before. Murder hadn't entered her mind...though perhaps it should have.

"What about you?" she asked Drew. "Any nightmares?"

"No."

"Good. What's on the agenda today?" She knew exactly what they had planned, but wanted to get his mind off what had happened to her.

Drew rested on an elbow and ran the fingers of his other hand over a particularly nasty bruise on her side. The one that was taking the longest to heal. "What are your thoughts on marriage?"

Caryn's breath froze, then her heart started hammering in her chest. She stared at him for a long beat before asking, "In general?"

Drew shrugged. "Yeah."

"Um, well...I approve."

"And specifically? You opposed to getting married again?"

Caryn had no idea where this was going. Was this his way of asking her to marry him? Or was he trying to break it to her gently that he never wanted to tie the knot? Taking a deep breath, she decided to be honest.

"No. I mean, I was kind of bitter after my first marriage ended. I figured a second one just wasn't in the cards for me. That I was somehow too messed up to have a successful partnership with anyone, even if I desperately wanted one. My mom was awful, and she wasn't a good role model when it came to relationships, but I think that made me want the loving parents other kids had even more. And then there was the relationship between my granddad and grandma. Art loved his wife so much, he was devastated when she passed away. I was really too young to remember much about her, but I've heard a lot of stories."

Drew nodded. "I've never felt a great desire to be married," he told her. "I saw too many marriages not only fail, but fail spectacularly over the years. I figured there was no way I could make a relationship work. I was too focused on my job. Too selfish. I wanted to do what I wanted, when I wanted, even if most of the time that was just sitting at home or helping my fellow officers with their taxes."

Caryn swallowed hard. Was he trying to tell her that there was no chance they'd get married? That he didn't mind dating but that was all this would ever be?

"But with you...I've found that my thinking has done a complete one-eighty. I want the right to call you mine, Caryn, legally and officially. I want you to wear my ring so everyone knows you're off limits. And I want to show the world how proud I am that I'm yours too. Not that anyone's banging down my door to be with me, but I want to be able to prove that I'm completely off the market and taken."

The muscles in Caryn's body that had tensed with his previous words, suddenly loosened. "You are definitely off the market," she reassured him. "And I want to be yours officially as much as I want you to be mine."

"I *am* yours," he said without hesitation. "But..." His voice trailed off.

"But what?" Caryn urged.

"Getting married also scares the crap out of me. I've seen perfectly happy couples turn on each other as soon as those rings go on their fingers. I don't want anyone else. Ever. The only person I want to wake up to and go to bed with is you."

"But you aren't ready to actually get married," Caryn finished for him.

"Does that change how you feel about me?" Drew asked.

"No way!" Caryn said firmly. "To be honest, I'm not ready to get married yet either. Everything with us has been fast—not that I mind that, but I think I want to settle into our relationship before we go down that wedding road."

Drew sighed in relief. "When we're both ready, I'm totally going to marry you," he said.

"Awesome," she said, with a smile. She was kind of

relieved the pressure of wondering if and when he was going to pop the question was off the table for now. Changing the subject, she said, "It's been two weeks."

Drew was totally on the same page, because he didn't even ask what she was talking about. "It's too soon. You've still got bruises, and don't think I haven't noticed how careful you've been moving on our walks."

Their workouts hadn't been strenuous in the least, but every day they'd gotten out of the house and walked or hiked.

"I'm *fine*," she insisted. "I'm not going to break if you make love to me," she said.

"If I hurt you..." Drew closed his eyes as he took a deep breath.

"You'd never hurt me," Caryn said, putting a hand on his cheek. Then she pushed on his chest until Drew was on his back. She straddled him and reached for the hem of the tank top she'd worn to bed. She pulled it over her head and braced herself on his pecs as she smiled down at him.

"Damn," he breathed, his hands coming up to gently grasp her sides. His thumbs caressed the skin right under her boobs, and his pupils dilated as he stared up at her.

"I need you," Caryn said as she moved backward until his erection was between her legs.

"You set the pace," Drew said firmly. "And you'll be on top the entire time. I'm not going to risk doing anything that might put pressure on those bruises."

Caryn was completely all right with that. She felt fine—better than fine—and it wasn't a hardship to have Drew under her. Not at all.

In response, she climbed off him and quickly got rid of her pajama shorts. As she was doing that, Drew kicked off his boxers. Kneeling between his legs, she took hold of his cock and stroked him from the tip down to his balls, then back up, glorying in the groan that escaped his lips.

"Fuck, I'm not going to last long," he muttered, more to himself than to her.

Caryn simply smiled.

Their lovemaking was fast and furious, and even though Drew tried to hold back, to be gentle, Caryn wasn't having it. She gave him a very enthusiastic blow job, and just when she was sure he was going to blow, he pulled her up and over him until she was straddling his face. He ate her out until she *did* explode in orgasm, then he pushed her back down and she took hold of his rock-hard cock and slowly impaled herself.

Things after that were a blur, but at some point, Drew held her still over him and fucked her hard from below. Then he yanked her down so he was buried inside her to the hilt and came. Even as he did, his thumb rubbed her clit, so her own orgasm wasn't too far behind.

Caryn's aches and pains from her ordeal were aggravated a little bit from their lovemaking, but she'd rather die than admit that to Drew. What he didn't know wouldn't hurt him. And she wasn't a shrinking violet. Wasn't one to milk any injuries. Never had, never would.

"Holy shit, woman," Drew said when he'd recovered. His cock was still lodged inside her. "That got out of hand."

She giggled. "It's your fault. You shouldn't have waited so long."

He looked her in the eye and said, "Wrong. I'd rather cut off my own arm than do anything to hurt you. I'll always do what's best for you, even if neither of us likes it."

"I love you," Caryn said.

"And I love you too. Now...what's on the agenda today?" he asked.

Caryn couldn't help but giggle when he mimicked her earlier question, and to her regret, the movement caused his softening cock to slip out of her body. "Well, shoot," she complained.

Drew chuckled. "I suppose it's too late to have the safety talk?"

It wasn't until right then that she realized they hadn't used a condom. "We talked about marriage...but how do you feel about babies?" she asked.

Drew looked mildly alarmed. "Shit. How do *you* feel about them?"

She should've been upset that he'd turned the tables and wanted her answer first. "I'm forty-one," she told him. "If I got pregnant today, that would mean I'd be forty-two before any baby was born. Doing the math, that means I'd be sixty before the kid graduated from high school. I'm not sure I want to be the granny mom."

"I'd be sixty-three," Drew said. "And you'd be the hottest granny mom out there."

"So...kids?" she asked.

"I'm not opposed to having you to myself for the next sixty years."

Yeah, she liked that thought a lot herself. "But...*if* it happens, I wouldn't mind having a son who looks exactly like you," Caryn told Drew with a gentle smile. She wasn't sure kids were in the cards for them, but having this man at her side, as a partner, was already a dream come true. She could always spoil her new friends' kids.

"I agree. Do we have to worry about what just went down here?" Drew asked, stroking her back with a calloused palm.

Caryn shook her head. "I'm on the pill. Have been for years."

Drew nodded, then urged her to lie down fully on top of him. After a while, he said, "If you wanted kids, I would bend over backward to give them to you. But I'm okay with staying childless. Besides, I'm sure our friends will have more than their fair share, and we can be the annoying aunt and uncle who stuff them full of sugar then send them home."

Caryn wasn't surprised they were on the same page. She liked the thought of them having sleepovers and parties with their friends' kids. "Sounds perfect. Think Elsie would let us borrow Tony every now and then and share him with Art? He was talking to me a few weeks ago about giving him great-grandkids."

"Absolutely. In fact, I think if we aren't careful, we'll end up babysitting way more often than we'd like."

"I'm okay with that."

"Me too. So...this means we can ditch the condoms, right?"

Caryn chuckled. "Right. I'm clean, you're clean, I'm protected...we're good."

"Thank God. Because the thought of going back to using them after being inside you bare," he mock shuddered under her, "isn't a good one."

Caryn rolled her eyes. "So dramatic."

"Yup."

"So...back to our plans for the day?" she asked, somewhat amused that they kept getting sidetracked.

"I think lying here in bed sounds like the perfect plan," Drew said lazily.

Caryn propped herself up and shook her head. "We need to go see Clyde. He wants me to try the new batch of caramel apple moonshine he's making for Ethan and Lilly's wedding. Since it's around Halloween and all. Then I have that video meeting with the prosecutors for Paul's case. Oscar and I are meeting with Brock to discuss how we can use some of the wrecked cars in his lot to help train the firefighters, and then Finley is having all us girls over for a cake-tasting party. She was thrilled to be asked to make Lilly's wedding cake, but now she's stressing about it and we need to reassure her that whatever she does is going to be awesome.

"And *you* need to do some work, and then we have dinner

with my grandfather tonight. By the way, I'm not telling him I'm going to be living in sin with you for a while...that's gonna be up to you to divulge."

Drew chuckled, and the sound reverberated through Caryn's body. "I'll take care of Art...and why are we even asking what our plans are for the day if they've already been solidified?"

Caryn smiled and shrugged. "I don't know. You finish sewing those handcuff keys into your pants yet?" The day after they'd arrived home from the forest, Drew had ordered two dozen of the little suckers online and had been determined to get them sewn into every pair of his pants—just in case.

"You aren't going to ever *not* give me shit about that, are you?" he asked with a small smile.

"Nope. You're the big bad cop, and I was the one who had that key in *my* pants."

"For the record, I'm okay with you making fun of me, because you were so right."

They smiled at each other. "I love you, Drew. I had no idea coming home to Fallport to look after Art would result in finding my soul mate."

He closed his eyes for a moment, then opened them and nodded. "I'd never, *ever* say I'm thankful that your grandfather got hurt, because that would make me a dick, but I'm grateful that things worked out the way they did."

"Same," she agreed. "I'm guessing we need to shower before we go for our walk."

"Yup," he said with a nod. "And after. Then maybe before we go to bed too."

Caryn rolled her eyes. "You're such a weirdo."

"Nope. I just love having you in my shower with me."

She loved that too, so she couldn't really complain about

it. Leaning down, Caryn kissed him softly. Of course, that softness lasted only a few seconds before the kiss deepened.

Their walk was cut short because they didn't get in the shower until much later than they'd planned. But Caryn didn't care. She was alive, healthy, and happier than she'd ever been in her life.

* * *

Brock took a deep breath as he paused outside The Sweet Tooth. He'd really thought he'd made some headway with Finley, breaking through the wall of shyness she always seemed to have around him, but lately she was falling back to her old habits.

When he'd stopped by the bakery to let her know what happened with Caryn, and to reassure her that her friend was all right, he'd seen a side of Finley that he hadn't even known was there. She'd immediately forgotten all about being shy. Demanded he tell her every single thing he knew about what happened, then practically dragged him by the arm out of the shop, locking the door behind her and insisting they go to Caryn immediately.

Now she was back to not looking him in the eye, finding any excuse to shoo him out the door, and generally not talking to him more than necessary.

But Brock had seen the real woman behind the shield she erected to keep out most of the world. The loyal, feisty, and demanding woman hidden deep inside. And he liked that woman—a lot. Even more than he'd liked her already.

And she definitely wasn't hard on the eyes.

All his life, Brock had been attracted to women with a little more meat on their bones. He wanted someone who was the complete opposite of himself. He was rough around the edges, always had been. Never afraid to get his hands dirty. As a Customs and Border Patrol agent, he'd spent a lot of time in the field, tracking people who were trying to cross into the United States illegally. Both in the deserts of the southwest and the forests on the northern border.

That meant he worked out a lot to stay in shape, and still did. Making his body honed and hard. Despite that, he'd never been attracted to the more athletic women who came on to him at the gym.

No...he liked curves. Lots of them. And Finley Norris had them in spades. When she'd grabbed hold of him and tugged him out of the shop two weeks ago, his skin damn near sizzled from the soft touch. And when she turned to lock the door, her backside brushed against him, and that was all it took for Brock's dick to sit up and take notice.

She smelled like flour, vanilla, and cinnamon, and she was so soft...all over.

He wanted her more than ever.

But if he couldn't coax her to even look at him, he was never going to convince her to go on a date. Brock had no idea where he'd even take her in Fallport, but he'd figure out something...if he could get her to relax around him long enough.

So that was his goal. Spend as much time as he could around Finley so she'd realize he was a good guy. That he liked her exactly how she was. Of course, he had a feeling that was going to be easier said than done. She'd been in town for a while, and it wasn't as if they were strangers, especially now that she was hanging out with Lilly, Elsie, Bristol, and Caryn on a regular basis. The five women got together all the time, and that meant she saw him and the other guys on the Eagle Point Search and Rescue team more often too.

Lilly and Ethan's wedding was approaching, and Brock wanted Finley to be his date. She'd be there anyway, as would he, but he wanted the right to sit by her side. To chat with her while they ate. To dance with her. But if that was going to happen, he needed to step up his campaign to get under her skin.

Grabbing hold of the doorknob to The Sweet Tooth, Brock decided he was going to treat this like one of his missions. He was a stubborn man, never quitting until he accomplished his goals. In the past, that was tracking and finding people crossing the border illegally, or searching for a part for a vintage car.

Today, it was getting Finley to trust him, and eventually agree to go out with him.

Smiling, he entered the bakery—and immediately caught Finley's gaze. A blush bloomed across her cheeks and she looked away, breaking eye contact.

Yeah, the woman wasn't immune to him, and that gave Brock all the reassurance he needed. He had no idea what the future held for them as a couple, but he had a feeling it would be full of ups and downs. His Finley had more passion buried inside her than she realized...and he wanted to be the one to coax it out.

I have a feeling Finley doesn't know what's coming for her... and how stubborn Brock can be when it comes to something he wants...and he wants Finley. Check out the next book in the series: *Searching for Finley*

Want to talk to other Susan Stoker fans? Join my reader group, Susan Stoker's Stalkers, on Facebook!

Also by Susan Stoker

Eagle Point Search & Rescue
Searching for Lilly
Searching for Elsie
Searching for Bristol
Searching for Caryn
Searching for Finley (Sept 2023)
Searching for Heather (Jan 2024)
Searching for Khloe (TBA)

The Refuge Series
Deserving Alaska
Deserving Henley
Deserving Reese (May 2023)
Deserving Cora (Nov 2023)
Deserving Lara (TBA)
Deserving Maisy (TBA)
Deserving Ryleigh (TBA)

Game of Chance Series
The Protector
The Royal (Aug 2023)
The Hero (TBA)
The Lumberjack (TBA)

SEAL Team Hawaii Series
Finding Elodie
Finding Lexie
Finding Kenna
Finding Monica
Finding Carly
Finding Ashlyn

Finding Jodelle (July 2023)

SEAL of Protection: Legacy Series
Securing Caite
Securing Brenae (novella)
Securing Sidney
Securing Piper
Securing Zoey
Securing Avery
Securing Kalee
Securing Jane

Delta Force Heroes Series
Rescuing Rayne
Rescuing Aimee (novella)
Rescuing Emily
Rescuing Harley
Marrying Emily (novella)
Rescuing Kassie
Rescuing Bryn
Rescuing Casey
Rescuing Sadie (novella)
Rescuing Wendy
Rescuing Mary
Rescuing Macie (novella)
Rescuing Annie

Delta Team Two Series
Shielding Gillian
Shielding Kinley
Shielding Aspen
Shielding Jayme (novella)
Shielding Riley
Shielding Devyn

Ace Security Series

Claiming Grace
Claiming Alexis
Claiming Bailey
Claiming Felicity
Claiming Sarah

Mountain Mercenaries Series

Defending Allye
Defending Chloe
Defending Morgan
Defending Harlow
Defending Everly
Defending Zara
Defending Raven

Silverstone Series

Trusting Skylar
Trusting Taylor
Trusting Molly
Trusting Cassidy

Stand Alone

Falling for the Delta
The Guardian Mist
Nature's Rift
A Princess for Cale
A Moment in Time- A Collection of Short Stories
Another Moment in Time- A Collection of Short Stories
A Third Moment in Time- A Collection of Short Stories
Lambert's Lady

Special Operations Fan Fiction

http://www.AcesPress.com

Beyond Reality Series

Outback Hearts

Flaming Hearts

Frozen Hearts

Writing as Annie George:

Stepbrother Virgin (erotic novella)

ABOUT THE AUTHOR

New York Times, *USA Today* and *Wall Street Journal* Bestselling Author Susan Stoker has a heart as big as the state of Tennessee where she lives, but this all American girl has also spent the last fourteen years living in Missouri, California, Colorado, Indiana, and Texas. She's married to a retired Army man who now gets to follow *her* around the country.

She debuted her first series in 2014 and quickly followed that up with the SEAL of Protection Series, which solidified her love of writing and creating stories readers can get lost in.

If you enjoyed this book, or any book, please consider leaving a review. It's appreciated by authors more than you'll know.

www.stokeraces.com
www.AcesPress.com
susan@stokeraces.com

facebook.com/authorsusanstoker
twitter.com/Susan_Stoker
instagram.com/authorsusanstoker
goodreads.com/SusanStoker
bookbub.com/authors/susan-stoker
amazon.com/author/susanstoker

Ingram Content Group UK Ltd.
Milton Keynes UK
UKHW022027290323
419383UK00015B/95

9 781644 993330